Meg,
        Thank you so m
me   with this book, along with everything
else I've done. I hope you enjoy the thing
book! Lots of love ♡

                    - maddie

(P.S. sorry the cover's so fuckin creepy)

A Mirror of Many Reflections

JOSEPH A. FORAN
HIGH SCHOOL PUBLICATION

ISBN: 978-1-4834-8491-4 (sc)
ISBN: 978-1-4834-8490-7 (e)

Lulu Publishing Services rev. date: 4/27/2018

Contents

✳✳✳

Photograph by Jordan Lang

About the Book

During the 2015-2016 school year, students from Joseph A. Foran High School were awarded a grant to publish a book and took part in the pilot class, Advanced Creative Writing. Through the vision of student authors and visual art students that year, Foran's first anthology, <u>Foreign Visions</u>, was published. Through the marketing and sales of that book, and the subsequent success found by last year's authors in writing <u>Through Different Eyes</u>, this year's students were able to publish <u>A Mirror of Many Reflections.</u>

Throughout the course of the 2017-2018 school year, students worked on various types of writing, spanning a plethora of genres, all sharing the common goal of becoming better writers. In Foran High School's third anthology, 20 young authors have come together, along with students from advanced art and photography classes, to create the third installment of Foran anthologies.

Susie

usie came into my life in July. I was scooping ice cream for a regular customer- two scoops of black raspberry with chocolate sprinkles in a sugar cone turned upside down. I turned away from the window and wiped the dripping purple ice cream off my forearm.

"Here you go, it's going to be $4.79." The line had finally stopped trailing out of the parking lot and down the street, so it was a perfect time to check my phone. A text from my father popped up that read, *Going to meet her after you get out of work!* I felt my heart jump in my chest as I smiled down at my phone, practically skipping over to the next family in line, barely able to hide my excitement. That shift went by so slow I could hardly focus on counting change or dripping cones.

The summer was the beginning, the summer was easy. She was like my best friend. I could sit with her for hours listening to music, talking about boys, or screaming in anger about customers at work. She would never judge me for what I said, and I knew it wouldn't be repeated so I never held back. Our friendship came easily and I quickly grew attached to having her around whenever I needed her. There was one day, sitting next to her on the sand, with a few other friends for the first time- little did we know this would become our go-to plan. Almost every night I would take Susie down to the beach after work and meet up with the rest of the group. The sun didn't set until eight that deep into July and would fade set so slowly. We would all talk about college and our future plans or lack there off. Some of us knew what we wanted, I myself had

1

been planning on becoming a writer for as long as I could remember. Most of my group however, were just going through the motions with no idea where they wanted to end up.

"Hey guys, do you think well be okay in college? I know I can get into a few schools but what then?" We all paused, my friend's question was going through my head as well. I tried to be optimistic, "I mean… no one really knows what they're doing in college. You just sort of have to figure it out like we did our freshman year." I paused and forced a smile before adding, "We'll be okay." I didn't even believe myself.

The sand was starting to cool, but the air was warm- the perfect weather. We sat there until dark, eating the cookies someone brought, along with take-out pizza from my friend working at the Italian place downtown. It was a detox to sit listening to country music, laughing with each other or just sitting listening to the waves and enjoying each other's company. Hours would pass by, feeling like mere minutes, until it was dark in the sky and the only sound we could hear was our music competing over the sound of crashing waves. We made that beach our home until curfew, and then Susie and I would head back the next morning. Those were the days I wished could last forever.

Slowly the seven o'clock beach meetup began to get darker and darker. The bugs began to ruin the atmosphere, and sweatshirts and blankets became a necessity for the wind. Susie and I began to spend less time loitering under the sun, and more time starting a new babysitting job to get some more money before summer ended. The drive was a half hour, and it became a peaceful part of the day. Driving down the back roads to get to the house with Susie, and throughout August, the trees lining the streets began to change color. My windows spent more time rolled up than ever before, and my sunroof hadn't been cracked open in weeks. The work assigned to students during the summer began to saturate the hours of daylight, and I had less and less time to spend with Susie

Early sunsets brought other activities for me and Susie, ocean drives and beach days became pumpkin picking and apple orchards. Susie and I, along with my other friends, painted our names on the rock at our school, a senior tradition that always took place the night before our first day. With the strongest attempt we could muster to hold onto our last hours of freedom, Susie and I began our last summer adventure. With windows down and the music on, we traveled across town to watch the moon climb into the sky. Sitting on the side of the road, staring at the sky, I sighed heavily, hoping this wouldn't have to change but knowing the stark reality that it had to.

Our last stop that night was to the craft store to pick out the shiniest and cheapest rhinestones I could find to later bedazzle my senior shirt for the next morning. Pulling into the driveway three minutes before curfew, I embarked on this late night craft. Hot gluing the gems on the lettering on the shirt until well past midnight, I sat on my carpet half-heartedly humming the country songs from my summer playlist.

I was pulled out of my crafting daze to hear a small knock at the door. Turning my music down, my mother's voice became clear.

"Turn that music down, it's almost one in the morning!" She swung open the door to see me sitting crisscrossed in the center of my room surrounded by glitter and glue sticks.

"Sorry mom I forgot to do this earlier, I keep forgetting that tomorrow is a school day." She walked in and kissed the top of my head then took a deep breath, "I know honey, but get some sleep it's a big day tomorrow and you have to be up early to get Susie all ready to go."

Once I walked into the building for my first class, I knew everything was different, it was my last first day of high school. My last first class. My last first. Everything felt so different. The small desks felt too small for my big dreams. Trying to imagine myself in five years, sitting in an apartment typing away on a manuscript or editing novels, became harder each time I was scolded for pulling my phone out to check the time. The coming weeks went by the fastest. Before I had a second to stop and taste the sprinkles, Susie and I went home from my last shift at the ice cream shop, as it closed until the following spring. We spent hours cleaning the place and tossing the extra ice cream, and making the sweetest, most sickening sundaes to take home.

After locking up the shop, my fellow scoopers and I joined Susie outside. Laughing about the constant grief from our customers over the size of kiddie cones and the price of the slushies, we reminisced on all the crazy stories from the summer. Exhausted, I threw my hair up into a bun before examining my uniform for hot fudge.

My coworker turned her head around to me, "Hey! Where did this scratch come from?"

My eyes scanned from myself to Susie, and they fell upon a small scratch I hadn't ever noticed before. "I don't know."

She looked at me quizzically, "Well was it here this morning? Maybe it happened when you were working."

"Yeah maybe." My heart sunk as I reached towards the scratch.

The fall was new. Halloween was spent writing a college essay and eating the candy that was meant for the neighborhood trick-or-treaters until my hand hit the bottom of the bowl. Standing up, I shook off the plastic wrappers that gathered at my lap and I grabbed my keys to take Susie to go buy some more.

Speeding down the street I sang along to the music playing until the melody died down, replaced by the ringtone of a call coming through the speaker.

"Hey girl! Are you around?" I immediately recognized my cousin Jess's voice- except more slurred than usual.

"Yeah I'm around what's up?" She giggled and I heard her drop her phone.

"Oh shoot! Wow who knew phones could be so slippery. Anyway, can you come pick me up? My ride is…" She paused and hiccuped on the other end. "She's gone I think. I saw her like an hour ago but I think she left with this guy and, I don't know. Can you come get me?"

I turned around, ditching my route to get candy and sighed "I'm on my way."

Jess was a freshman this year and decided she was too old to trick or treat, so this was her first high school party. She went as a vampire-very unique. Jess pretty much tried to be the opposite of unique these days; I couldn't really blame her, since I wasn't the most outgoing at her age, anyway.

Stumbling up to Susie and I with a huge grin on her face, Jess exposed her plastic fangs before joining us. Susie played our favorite songs as I watched Jessica sing along at the top of her lungs, each word more slurred than the last. Not wanting to take her home yet, I turned into our favorite drive thru place to her some food and put something else into her stomach.

"You know, that really wasn't *that* fun. It was way too crowded in there and my teeth kept falling out!" Jess sipped her shake and I reached for a fry as I looked through the pictures she took at the party, helping her pick which she would post.

Jess hiccupped loudly as I took a sharp turn and reached out to grab my arm. She mumbled something to me that I couldn't quite hear. "Do you have a bag?"

"What?" I tried to understand her words as she burped again.

"A bag!" She screamed as she lurched forward spilling her guts all over Susie. Her head bobbed up and down and I started to gag at the noise of her retching.

Swerving to the side of the road, I stopped before forcing my door open and ran over to her, holding her hair while she finished emptying her belly of the food we had just eaten.

"Sorry," She stared up at me with puppy dog eyes and I sighed. "It's okay" I muttered. "I just have to clean Susie before my parents get home."

Three hours and two rolls of paper towels later, Susie was finally clean, and Jess was fast asleep in my bed after handing me her phone to text her parents that she is staying that night.

The next time I saw Jess was at my house for Thanksgiving. My mom's tradition of buying seven mini chocolate Santas for us kids still made its way into Thursday's itinerary, but only as a snack eaten through the topic of genderless bathrooms and under aged drinking. By four in the afternoon it was pitch black and I grew tired of watching football next to my sleeping uncle. The stuffy air and smell of the apple cider candle my mother was burning made me queasy. I looked over to Jessica and leaned down to quietly ask, "Want to go take Susie to go get milkshakes again?" But before we made it out the door I noticed she was missing.

"Mom! Where's Susie?" I poked my head into the kitchen to see my mother doing some dishes and humming to herself. She smiled up at me.

"Oh I let your brother take her to go grab some more whipped cream, why?"

My shoulders dropped in frustration as I mumbled to myself, *when is he going back to college again?* I looked back at my cousin and shrugged in annoyance before sinking back down into my couch.

So many of my snowy Sundays were spent wondering if Susie had given up completely. It was clear she was fair-weather. It would take her longer and longer to warm up to me. I combatted this with ignorant hope she would be okay. Even in the bitter chill, Susie and I went with friends to a drive- through Christmas light show, watching the decorations on houses dance to the music she played.

The week before Christmas, an early present arrived, a college acceptance letter. It was the definitive sign that things were no longer hypothetical, I was going to college. My dreams of writing for a newspaper or drafting my own stories finally seemed within reach. I pushed back the thoughts of what would happen to those closest to me. I began to grow closer with some classmates that I had never even spoken to. We quickly became a group, hanging out all weekend long, hopping from house to house until our parents kicked us out. It was a cruel joke finding such great people just as it was time to leave them behind.

Susie wouldn't go to college, she was planning on staying home. Every time I ran to the mailbox and pulled out a thick envelope or folder, I'd grow excited only to become deflated, remembering how I wouldn't be able to bring everything I'd grown to love with me to school. And then Susie would pop race into my mind, another example of something I'd have to leave behind.

The next months were a daze. Christmas break and the New Year were spent hanging at friends' houses until curfew, waking up, and doing it all over again. My classmates were now family, and I seldom went a day without being with Susie and my group of companions.

School, the one place I used to call my home seemed insignificant. Walking into the building was putting on a pair of shoes that I once loved. A pair of shoes I adored, and made my own, wearing them in with each step. But they don't fit anymore; high school didn't fit anymore.

My Instagram was filled with pictures of smiling seniors, slapping on university sweatshirts, ready to move on. My thumbs grew weak and my heart grew heavy scrolling through my feed whenever I thought of Susie.

But for now at least, I still had Susie with me. On my eighteenth birthday, she joined me at the beach, except this time without my peanut gallery of friends. I sat there, writing in a journal I had been given after blowing out my candles that morning. The pages felt soft on my skin as I turned them within my hand. Susie played soft music so I could still hear the waves crashing and the wind that began racing around us. In what felt like a second the sky had shifted to a deep blue and the clouds rolled above us. The sound of my pen hitting the journal was now drowned out by a heavy downpour- the classic April shower. It was a wakeup call that I could now buy cigarettes, be fully charged for crimes, and most importantly be called an adult. This was a loose term of course for a girl completely financially dependent on her parents, but a milestone none the less.

Susie joined me on my final adventures during senior privilege, the hour of the day seniors were allowed to leave, while underclassmen were forced to stay. She was at my senior picnic, my graduation, and every college road trip. I sang throwback songs unapologetically loud to her and pretending it wasn't the end of our hours spent together, but it was.

The summer was the end, but also the start. I spent the months soaking up the sun and every moment with my friends and Susie. Every hangout was filled with laughter and ease, and the screaming silence of our refusal to talk about when we would all say goodbye.

I put the final bag into the trunk of my dad's car and shut it. My dog and cat stood in the doorway watching me through the glass, wagging their tails waiting for me to come inside. My heart jumped into my throat realizing they have no idea I'm not coming back inside. My pets and I had a daily ritual, every day around two p.m. they knew I would be home, and stared out the door until I got back, just to shower me with kisses. This tradition would be changing.

I ran into the car and threw my seatbelt on, I had to keep moving. Seconds before pulling out my eyes fell to Susie. I told myself I would be back for her Thanksgiving break, that's no time at all. All the memories of her flashed through my head, she was one of the best things that ever happened to me, regardless of the work or time she needed. After all the hours at the beach, aimless trips around my town, and adventures during my senior year, I knew I would never forget Susie, my first car.

Rocky Waters

The waves were crashing in the distance as my feet walked along the water, toes finding sand with every step. The beach was my second home; most kids would learn how to ride their bikes without training wheels, while I learned how to manipulate the sails of a boat to steer it in the right direction. My father encouraged me to join him to sail all over Long Island Sound.

Sailing was much more than a sport to me, quite honestly; it was my childhood. I never would have thought that the activity that put me at ease would make me feel the exact opposite. Mom and dad would fight every time I tried to escape the house to go to the beach; my mom believed if I spent any more time at the beach I would turn into a fish, my dad never thought that was a bad thing.

Dad was always defending me, whether it was about wanting ice cream before dinner or sailing when a storm was on the way. He was my best friend as a kid.

***

"Car, help your father out a bit today." Mom says walking into the living room as I lazily hung off the couch. Rolling my eyes, I climbed the stairs to my room to accompany my dad as he painted the walls.

Classic rock music escaped the crack in my door as I peeked into the room. My dad was all covered in paint, even his face. A little giggle escaped my mouth, seeing my dad dance all goofy.

Opening the door a little more, I gaped at the walls painted with waves that trail all across the room. He painted carefully with a determined expression.

"Dad, would you like some help," I finally spoke up, causing him to whip around to me.

"Of course, honey! Your help would be greatly appreciated, but you must do one thing first." He smiled wildly, the sun making his teeth look brighter than usual.

"Okay! What do you need," I asked in confusion and curiosity.

Before I know it, my dad's running towards me. Scooping me up in his arms, he swirls the paintbrush all over my face.

"Ahhhh! Stop Dad, stop!" My yelling was replaced by laughing as he finally lets me out of his grasp.

His loud laugh bellowed deep throughout the room as he goes back to painting. Picking up a paintbrush of my own, we stood side by side, painting the place we love the most. The ocean.

***

My favorite days on the water were spent in torrential downpours when the waves would almost cause the boat to tip. Some emotion bordering excitement and fear overcame me when I sailed. Most people would pass up the opportunity to sail during a storm, but I would jump at every opportunity there was. The rough waters allowed me to appreciate the calm ocean that sparkled under the sun.

***

Ice cream quickly races down my cone and onto my hand as my dad and I walk from the ice cream parlor to the busy, public beach down the road. The radiant afternoon sun beams brightly down on my already tan face. Squinting down at the sidewalk in an effort to shield my blue eyes, we make our way toward the sand. People pass us on their banana seat bikes, or strolling with their families; conversation surrounded us although we remained silent.

"How was work today?" I ask my dad, trying to make small talk, something that used to come easily to the both of us. We walk on the sandy beach right to the edge of the shore.

"Good," was all he said, keeping it short and blunt. The lack of conversation frightened me. My dad could talk about why the sky was blue for days, and when it came to speaking about himself, he could talk for years. Looking for a topic as I stare at the water, nothing comes to mind to talk about. A mixture of sadness and anger radiates off of him as we get closer to the beach.

He's definitely still upset about sailing, I think to myself.

"So…" he says expectantly, waiting for me to spark up more chatter. Finishing his cup of ice cream, he throws it in the overflowing beach garbage can, where seagulls circle hoping for a quick meal.

"So…" I repeat looking at my half eaten ice cream cone. My nerves get the best of me and I stop eating the cone in my hand, opting to throw it out.

"Are you ready for this upcoming sailing season, Car?" My dad asks, his voice filled with disinterest. For a few more seconds than it should, his question bounces around in my mind.

"I mean, um, yeah. Uh, yeah, I am," I reluctantly answer while lightly kicking my feet around in the sand.

"Why the long pause, sweetie?" My dad senses the tension I felt when he mentioned sailing. The beach cabanas taking residence closer to the main road by the hotel they belong to catch my attention, their curtains being whisked away by the breeze.

***

The sun shone through the curtains in my bedroom, casting a calming glow around the room. I lazily turned to my bedside table to check the time. The clock read 12:23. *Oh no,* I thought to myself, *I'm late.* Jolting out of bed, I clambered down the stairs, not even bothering to change out of my mismatched pajamas. My feet kept a fast pace as I grabbed an apple for breakfast, maneuvering around my mom. Eyes glued to the television that broadcasted the weather for the afternoon, she stood by the coffee maker waiting for the stream of caffeine to pour into her mug.

"Carley Ann, you better be back at this house before that tropical storm rolls around. I don't want you to get hurt. I'm thinking about your safety, honey," my mom called after me as I sprinted out of the door.

"Okay sounds good!" I answered, barely listening to what she was saying to me. All I could think about was getting to the marina.

Yelling a quick "goodbye" to my dad as he bent down to pick up the morning paper, I sprinted out the door. Jumping into his pickup truck, I pushed down on the horn causing my dad to jump up as he gives me an annoyed look.

I pulled up with no time to spare as I ran down the dock towards Jake's boat. His head was peeking out of an opening to the small room inside the boat. Clouds ominously hung from the sky in the distance, yet the sunshine beamed down on the water.

Calling to get his attention, I yelled out, "Jake!"

Hit head hit the door as he popped up from where he was sitting. Not even trying to contain it, laughter escapes my mouth. "Huh, who's the clumsy one now," I said mockingly once my laughter died down.

"Whatever, Car, you and I both know you're the clumsiest person on this planet," he said, acting as if he was insulted.

"That is so not true and you know it!" I yelled at him playfully hitting his arm out of fake anger.

"Yeah right, remember that time we were helping out with the youth sailing club and you turned around to tell me something but in the process you tripped over a kid tying his shoes," Jake ruffled my hair as he walked past me, down into the small room again. I placed my hands on my red cheeks as they became hot from embarrassment.

The steps creaked underneath Jake's feet as he climbed up the stairs carrying a box of photo albums. Trying to grab one out of curiosity, Jake dodged my hand.

"Fine, we can look at them together," I said in defeat, plopping down on a comfy chair on the deck. Jake sat down next to me with the box placed between his feet as he grabbed a photo album labeled "Summer of '03." Flipping through the pages together, we reminisced about the first time we met each other and began to sail. I began sailing at 5 when Jake had started at age 4. He was always more skilled than me when it came to sailing, but I was connected to the sea.

One picture that stood out to me showed Jake and I smiling so wide that our eyes looked like they were shut. Behind us were our fathers, looking as if they were laughing about something. Jake and I stood on one paddle board together, our dads held the board to keep us from floating away.

"Remember how scared I was to stand up on the paddleboard because I didn't want a wave to knock me over," I said slightly smiling down at my younger self in the picture.

"How could I forget? You were using me as your support to get up. I was almost knocked down in the process," Jake chuckled. Glancing at him for a moment, I noticed how his green eyes are bright from the reflection of the water and how the breeze tousled his brown hair. His positivity practically radiated off of him, something I admired the most about him. I admired his positivity I could practically see it radiating off of him.

"Hey, how about we go for a little sail?" Jake closed the photo album and placed it back in the box. I stood up from the chair looking Jake up and down.

"Do you know who I am?" I asked sarcastically, placing a hand on my hip. "If anyone on this planet wants to go for a, 'little sail,' as you call it, then it's me." Jake stared at me unamused by my small rant, continuing to remove the boat's rope from the dock.

"Okay Car let's go for a *big* sail," he countered, sounding annoyed. I shook my head and laughed while adjusting the sails to venture off into the ocean.

***

"Car?" My dad's voice snaps me back to reality, as well as his hands that lightly squeeze my arms. Something he started doing recently, as he catches me in a daydream.

"You okay, sweetie?" I turn to look at him and I'm met with his piercing blue eyes that hold concern.

"Yeah dad, I'm alright," I answer distantly, looking away from his worried face. The guilt I felt when he looked at me made my heart ache.

"So, why don't you seem excited about this summer? Sailing will be so much fun this year, you could meet new friends." The mention of friends made my heart drop to my sand covered toes.

"Dad, I'm so sorry. I really can't go back to sailing, not yet." My voice shakes from the thought of going back to sailing after what happened. Sailing reminds me too much of *him*.

"Carley Ann, it's been months since then. It's time to go back to sailing. I can help you, we can take baby steps," he tries to convince me as I cross my arms in discontent.

"No. I can't do it. Please don't make me." Now I'm pleading with him. He doesn't understand how I feel and he's making me feel worse. Remembering the memories Jake and I had brings me so much pain. can't imagine going back to the place that reminds me the most of Jake and the memories we had made together.

"Don't be ridiculous, your mother and I have spent thousands of dollars on you so that you could sail, but you'd rather throw it all away." As he speaks, his words become progressively louder. My voice gets lost in my throat as I turn to walk away from him. My feet stop walking. Reaching a line of rocks jutting out into the water, I continue moving until I'm at the water's edge and take a seat on the large rock. Looking off into the horizon, I note how many boats rock calmly in the distance.

***

"Carley grab the tiller at the stern," Jake called to me, causing me to tear my eyes away from the other sail boats blowing past us. I hop up from sitting to grab the long wooden stick that steers the boat. The boat began leaning on the left side towards the water, bringing me so much joy. My body tensed with fear, yet excitement, and I let out a holler as Jake gave me a bemused look.

"Don't make that face at me, don't you ever feel like you're so happy that you could scream?" I shouted over the sound of the water pushing against the rocking boat. Glancing up, shading my eyes from the sun, I watched the sail ripple from the bellowing wind. Jake just responded with a laugh and a shake of his head.

"Do you see those clouds on the horizon?" Jake asked me while pointing at the menacing looking sky. I was alarmed at how fast the clouds managed to creep closer to us. Instinctively, I put my life jacket on and prepare for the rough waters ahead.

"Let's go towards it, you know, experience the water rocking the boat," I shouted over the wild wind. Shielding my eyes from the rain as it began to pour, I grinned to myself preparing to go further into the storm.

"Don't be stupid Carley. We have to make our way home. We could die if we stay out here," he yelled back to me causing my hands to let go of the ropes. The grin on my face slowly melted off, lips formed into a pout.

"Jake, please if we're careful then we won't get hurt, please just trust me." I hadn't been in a storm in months. Craving for the adventure and exhilaration, I continue to move the sail to make us move further into the dark gray horizon.

"We're about three miles away from land so we have to manipulate the sail as best we can to get us back." Jake informed me, ignoring my comments about going away from shore. He takes control of the tiller to turn us toward the beach. The storm came sooner than we thought and the wind caused the rain to whip at our faces. Ramming against the boat, the waves rocked us wildly back and forth. We were thrusted left and right. The wet floor of the boat didn't make it any easier as we tried to balance ourselves. Rumbling sounds of thunder entered my ears.

We began arguing over the sound of the waves crashing from every which way. Our voices became louder than the storm around us. Too distracted by our argument, we stopped trying to move the boat closer to shore.

"Let's just wait it out- that would be safer." I tried to compromise with him.

"No it wouldn't Carley. We're going back to the docks," Jake growled angrily at me. He ignored my advice, the wind lurched the boat from side to side. We would have been better off just taking down the sails and staying still in the water.

A gust of wind forced the boat so far to the left that it knocked me off of my feet. A scream escaped my mouth before I was flung off the boat and the sea swallowed me up. My voice was muffled by the salt water crashing into my open mouth. I thrashed in the water trying my best to get to the surface so oxygen could fill my lungs. The sound of the ocean being stirred up all around me fills my ears. My clothes, soaked from the rainwater and seawater, weighed me down, rendering my life jacket useless. An object plunged through the ocean, managing to hit me in the head and knocking me out from its weight. My vision went black as my body was thrown around in the water.

My eyes reopened to see Jake kneeling beside me on the boat's deck. He held his head in his hands, I couldn't tell if I saw tears fall from his eyes or if water dripped from his soaking hair. The sky was more clear and blue than ever before, the waves of the marina lightly rocked the boat.

I guess this is the calm after the storm, I jokingly thought to myself.

Water traveled up my throat and I let out a raspy cough causing Jake to look my way. The look he had on his face held a mixture of hope and relief. Staring at me, he waited for me to talk as if he couldn't believe I was alive.

"Hi," I whispered, my raspy voice strained from the salt water. Jake came over to me and scooped me up in his arms, capturing me in a cold, sopping hug. Nuzzling my head into his shoulder, he tightened his grip.

"Oh thank God you're alive! I actually thought you were dead. I'm not kidding. I was just thinking about what I'd write for your eulogy," he darkly jokes, his mood changing to his normal goofy self.

"How'd I get knocked out?" I asked looking up at his face as it changed once again. He became somber for some reason.

"Um, it was nothing," he said looking away from me, sadness apparent in his eyes.

"What was it? Why aren't you telling me?" My words held confusion and frustration because of his hesitation.

"It was my family photo album," my heart dropped to my toes, "I'm more scared than angry because my mom loved those photos. They're memories she never wanted to forget."

"Oh my gosh Jake, I am so sorry." I reached up to his face and turned it toward me to show him how I feel apologetic.

"It's alright Car, it was my fault anyway. You don't need to say sorry."

Sheepishly I smile and hide my face in his hand as he places it on my cheek. His eyes studied mine for what feels like forever, they quickly darted to my mouth. I noticed him lick his lips, eyes closing, slightly leaning in-

"Jake! Carley!" Jake's dad shouted from the grill at the marina picnic area, "Time to eat!"

We jumped out of each other's arms when we heard our names being called. Feeling awkward, we walked towards the benches to have dinner.

***

"Car, could you pass me the corn?" My mother's voice snaps me out of my thoughts. I look at her, unsure of what she said to me.

"What was that," I ask monotonously.

"I asked for the corn, dear." Knowing I've been having trouble focusing lately, she gives me a concerned look.

"Yeah, here," I hand her the bowl just like she asked. The sound front door swinging open, and shutting soon after, travels into the kitchen causing us to look towards the kitchen entrance.

"Honey? Are you going to join us at the dinner table?" My mother calls to my father who, I assume, just got back from taking the sailboat out.

"Of course." He walks into the kitchen, pulls out a chair, and begins to dig into the mound of food on his plate, not even acknowledging me. I left him at the beach after sitting on the rocks, I got home without even thinking about where I was going, too distracted by my thoughts.

"So how was your day, guys?" My mom tries to reduce the obvious tension in the room.

"Fine," both my dad and I say at the same time, causing the tension in the room to increase. Excusing myself from the table, I rinse my dish in the sink. Dad's presence brings me guilt and makes me uncomfortable. Mom understands that I need space and lets me go to my room.

My room is my safe place now. It used to be the beach, but that only brings back memories that's accompanied by pain and sadness. The walls are covered in wave patterns that dad and I painted together many years ago. Staring at them from my bed, I imagine that I'm on a boat rocking back and forth. Beginning to feel sick, my feet carry me

outside of my room and to the bathroom door. Arguing can be heard from downstairs. Moving quietly, I tip-toe towards the stairs and sit down on the top step to listen into my parents conversation.

"Katherine, it's been long enough. She needs to sail again. You and I both know how much time, energy, and money sailing has cost us over the years. She can't just throw it all away."

"You cannot put a time limit on how long someone is allowed to mourn for, Fred. You know how much Jake meant to her. He was taken from our lives too soon, I know you feel just as distraught as Carley does, but that does not mean you can take it out on her." My mother's stern, yet loving, voice carries throughout the house and to my ears. *At least she understands me*, I think to myself.

"I worry for Linda and Sam, their only son has passed away. I don't want anything bad to happen to our daughter, but I also want her to live her life by doing things she loves. I know she will regret not going back to sailing one day if she stops forever." His voice is filled with sorrow. A tear rolls down my cheek and onto my knee. I can't hear them talk about this, it hurts too much. Just as quietly as I sat down, I got up and went back to my room.

***

Two days passed since I eavesdropped on my mom and dad's conversation. I know my dad's an emotional guy and he's quite passionate about the activities I take part in. This was evident the night he spoke to mom, but he should be able to understand why it's so hard for me to sail so soon.

Lying down on the couch in the living room, I practice my rolling hitch knot even although it won't be put to use without sailing. The sound of a car pulling into the driveway makes me sit up and look through the huge bay window to find my dad climbing out of his car.

I better talk to him before he brushes me off and goes to the marina, I think to myself, already moving toward the front door.

Opening it before he does, I'm met with his face which holds a look of surprise that instantly changes into disappointment.

"Dad, can we please talk," I ask quietly looking down at the floor.

"About what, Carley?" He pushes past me and walks into the kitchen as I follow closely behind him.

"Well, I wanted to explain to you why it's hard for me to go back to sailing." He stops in front of the kitchen island and turns to me expectantly. "Oh, well, I want to be able to get back to sailing eventually, but for the time being I need to distance myself from it," I say. We stand in silence for a few moments before my dad opens his mouth. His eyes move look around uncomfortably before they change into a forgiving look.

"Sweetie, I want to apologize for how I have been acting. I should have taken your feelings into account before I yelled at you. The past few days I spent thinking about what you've been through, and your mother has spoken to me too," he pauses giving me a small smile, "I want you to get back to sailing so bad because I remember doing it as a kid and how many lessons I've learned from it. But now I see you've matured and the ocean doesn't have any more lessons to teach you. I don't want you to stop sailing and regret it later in life. I will help you get back to it, like I said, baby steps."

I smile at him, finally feeling at peace now that my dad has accepted that I can't sail in the near future.

"Thank you, dad. That means a lot to me. It will be bittersweet getting back to sailing, but I know he'll be watching over me while I do what we both love," I say mournfully as I walk over to hug my dad.

✳✳✳

A cool, salty breeze hits my face. Waves lightly crash against the shore, water reaches my toes. Slowly, I walk towards the ocean, feeling the grains of sand stick to my wet feet. The sun is tucked behind the horizon, painting hues of pink and orange across the sky.

Not knowing I was holding my breath, I exhale, walking until the water reaches my knees. Peace overcomes me, and I know that in this moment I'm supposed to be here. The ocean is my place and I can finally go to the beach without feeling a knot in my throat and tears in my eyes.

He'd be proud of me right now.

A Ruff Life

Oh god, time for the worst part of the day. I reluctantly rise from the floor, walking over to the child. She rocks back and forth, bubbling with energy. I can never quite understand how she is so excited all the time. Even though I'd rather go lay in my bed, I wag my tail back and forth and give a quick shake.

"Mom, I'm going to walk Jet!" The girl calls behind her shoulder.

"Okay, Carrie! Don't be too long, Alice's birthday party starts at five!" A muffled voice returns from the bathroom.

"Okay!"

Carrie raises her arm, revealing the black, rope material. She brings it down towards my neck, pulling back on the metal clasp. I squeeze my eyes shut, wincing when she rotates my collar. The sound of the clasp returning to its resting position pierces through my ears, but I stay calm. I've been put on the leash before.

The girl slides open the backdoor, and waves me on to go. "Go ahead, Jet," she says, raising her voice an octave, "we're going for a walk."

As if I didn't already know. Whenever the leash gets clipped to my neck, one of two things happen: we go for a walk, or we go for a longer walk. Today, I know that it'll be a short walk, since Carrie has a party to go to.

Carrie walks with a skip in her step as we move down the street. The sun is warm, and has melted just about all of the snow by now. A sudden movement catches my attention, and I immediately turn my head to it.

My eyes focus in on a red-tailed squirrel, digging in the earth near the base of a large oak. Without realizing what I'm doing, my body tenses, and I slowly start to creep towards the tree. An excitement builds inside me. This is what I was born to do. The squirrel doesn't see me; if I keep my path around his backside, I could probably get within striking distance, and then I'll…

"Hey, Jet, come on, buddy! This way."

Carrie tugs on the leash, pulling my neck and head away from the squirrel. After giving one last longing glance, I am forced to move on. In my head, I picture myself running, free from the leash, chasing the animal all throughout the neighborhood. When I capture it, instead of killing it, I imagine myself letting it go. As the squirrel runs away, I count to ten, then begin my chase all over again.

A loud, blaring horn interrupts my state of imagination.

"I'm sorry!" Carrie shouts innocently at a black truck, billowing smoke rising out of two exhaust pipes. The man driving waves and nods his head, waiting for us to finish crossing the intersection at the end of the street.

Okay, time to get back on task. I make a list of priorities in my head: first, make sure that Carrie is safe. Look out for any other dogs, people, cars, etc. Second, go get the ball when Carrie throws it. Third, bring the ball back.

My paws tread against an uneven sidewalk, and I start to pant slightly. The TV said that this is one of the warmest first weeks of spring we have had in a long time. Judging by my body heat right now, I agree.

The park that we walk to nearly every day now comes into view. It's a big open field, surrounded by trails leading through the woods. I've only been on a few of the trails; Carrie's mom doesn't like her going through them alone. Usually, we just "play" fetch in the field. And by "play," I mean that I run twenty feet, pick up a ball, bring it back, and repeat. I don't understand why other dogs seem to find this action so fun. I would much rather be able to run where I wish. To make the time more enjoyable, I usually try to picture the ball as a chipmunk, scurrying across the beat down grass, and it is my goal to catch it. If the ball stops rolling by the time I reach it, then the chipmunk escaped. If the ball is still rolling when my teeth bite into the rubber, then I consider the animal caught.

I lead the way through a metal chain link fence, stepping onto the grass. My paws sink a bit, feeling wet with mud. Ugh, great, I get to cover my legs in mud today, too. Carrie hops over to me, finally taking the leash off of my neck. I shake my head back and forth, enjoying the freedom. My ears flop around as a result, and Carrie giggles.

"Okay, ready?" She asks me, enthused. She winds her arm back, the dirty tennis ball ready to fly. As soon as her arm begins to move forward, I start my sprint. The ball bounces about ten yards in front of me, and it immediately turns into a little chipmunk. Its legs propel it forward, trying to outrun me. Digging my claws into the soft earth, the chase intensifies. Very quickly, I come up behind the chipmunk, and snatch it in between my jaw. I almost bark with joy; the ball was nowhere near stopped. My chest fills with pride, knowing that I could chase down a chipmunk if I had the chance.

Trotting back to Carrie, the wind shifts, blowing her curly hair in front of her face. Using her hand not holding the leash, she pushes it back, laughing the whole time. I have never met another human so full of life. It both amazes me and makes me wonder about humans in general. If one could be happy, why couldn't the others? Does age make humans less happy? Carrie's mother always seems to be in a hurry, rushing around. The only time I see her smile is at night, when she's not in front of a stack of papers.

I drop the ball in front of her feet and lick her hand.

"Hey! Stop that, Jet. You're gonna get me all gross and slobbery," she playfully scolds me. Carrie picks up the ball again, this time holding it with the tips of her fingers to avoid my "slobber." The ball soars into the air, and again I'm off, in pursuit of a non-existent chipmunk.

After throwing the ball about ten more times, she clips the leash back onto my collar. I plant my backside on the ground, wanting to stay a little longer.

"Come on, Jet. I'm gonna be late!" She whines.

Internally, I sigh and stand up. My hind legs are covered in dirt, changing my usual golden appearance to a murky brown; definitely in need of a wash. The sun feels ten times hotter now after all the running, my tongue hanging loosely out of my mouth, my body heaving in and out. Trotting along the sidewalk, I pick up my speed, in need of a cool place to lay and a full bowl of water. Carrie jogs to keep up with me, her pink shoes slapping the concrete behind me.

As we reach the intersection, a ball comes rolling out in front of me. Confused, I stop, and watch it roll out into the street. A flash of movement follows from my left, and Carrie comes into my eyesight, running out to get the ball, her head down tracking it. From my right side, another object comes into view, moving much faster than Carrie. The object takes the shape of a car, moving way too fast for this street. She tunnels her vision in on the ball, unaware of the car speeding closer and closer. A quick glance shows the driver looking down into his lap, his eyes diverted from the yellow lines and the young girl he is on path to hit.

Instinctively, I leap forward, biting the back of Carrie's jacket. Using the strength of my jaw, I pull her backwards. She turns around to face me, confused, while the ball keeps rolling. It gets squished under the car's tire, and the driver of the vehicle looks up from his lap only for a moment. My heart races in my chest as I consider all of the possible outcomes that could have happened.

"Hey, I told you we can't play anymore or else I'll be late," Carrie states, oblivious that her life was just in danger. She skips over to the tennis ball and scoops it up. "Let's go."

Rather than be treated like a hero, I am greeted by Carrie's mother with a very stern tone. "No biting! No! Bad!" She growls at me.

Apparently, my teeth put a couple holes in the back of her new jacket. If she could understand my reasoning, I bet she wouldn't be so upset. Sauntering to my bed, I lay down, feeling ashamed of myself when I know I shouldn't be.

I glance over to my water bowl; it still hasn't been filled. Carrie and her mother both leave the house before Carrie dashes back in, quickly filling up my bowl with lukewarm water. Briskly walking over to me, she cradles my face in her hand and kisses me on the top of the head.

"By the way, I'm not mad at you," she tells me before dashing back outside to the car.

Waiting for Carrie to return proves very boring, as always. For a while, I try to sleep, but my imagination runs too wild. So instead, I sit down by the back sliding door and observe.

After just thirty minutes, I count ten birds, five squirrels, a really big bird, and a rabbit. I long to go outside, but all of my attempts to open the door fail. Sitting with my bottom on the cool tile, I picture myself chasing the rabbit this time. He's faster than the chipmunks and squirrels, able to change direction much more quickly. In my head, whenever I get near him, he hops in a different direction, leaving me to chase him for hours.

My trance is broken by a loud noise coming from the front of the house. When my vision comes back into view, it's much darker outside. Rushing to the front of the house, the door swings open just in time for me to greet Carrie and her mother.

I wag my tail and patiently wait for attention. Carrie scratches behind my ears, and pats me with her free hand. The other is holding a small bag filled with candy.

After saying hello, I return to my bed, feeling tired. I wait until Carrie and her mother enter their bedrooms, and then fall asleep.

Waking up, I stretch and try to recall my dream. I know it had something to do with the rabbit, but can't quite figure it out. The clock reads 7:00. Usually at 8:00, on the days where Carrie doesn't go to school, we go for a walk.

Changing my rest position to the kitchen floor, I wait for Carrie to get up. Time passes and my energy starts to really build up. Finally, a door opens, and I scratch my way over to the hallway.

Carrie's mom walks out of her daughter's room with a thermometer in her hand and a washcloth. She removes her cell phone from her pocket and begins to have a conversation.

"Yes… Carrie is sick with a fever, I need you to watch her, I can't take off today… Yes, I'll drop her off… Thank you, Max, I really appreciate it."

Carrie's mom goes into her bedroom and shortly returns wearing her work clothes. She makes eye contact with me and puts her hand on her forehead.

"Oh, jeez, come here, Jet, come outside." Her hand whips open the slider door, then she hustles back to Carrie's room. Feeling upset,

I walk outside to do my business. The sound of the car starting echoes over the roof of the house. Now feeling anxious, I dash around the side to see Carrie being placed in the backseat. Her mother then gets in the driver's seat, as the car pulls out of the driveway.

Did she forget about me? Walking back to the backyard, it hits me: I'm finally free. First, I walk back inside to check if everyone really left. A quick trot through the house proves what I had suspected; they are gone. They are gone, and the door is open. There's no leash around my neck, there's no glass preventing me from being outside. Nothing.

My body shakes with excitement. This is it! I can finally chase animals, run through the woods, and be the dog I am supposed to be. These eager thoughts are soon shoved out of my brain when I see the rabbit. It hops near the fence, slowly moving closer to the garden. The excitement courses in my body. This is what I always imagined.

As I hunch down into my stalking stance, the sound of a baby crying from inside the neighbor's house pierces my eardrums. The rabbit doesn't seem to mind; it continues to nibble at leaves, coming closer. The sound, though, reminds me of Carrie when she was a small child. She used to cry when she was upset. Boy, she cried a lot.

I push the thought out of my head and take a step forward. The rabbit moves, too, searching for new leaves to pick at. My paw presses down into the yard and I take another step.

The loud whining once again floods into my ears. The sight of Carrie, crying as a child, forms in my brain. The memory of me comforting her through her early years is one I cannot get out. I pause, aggravated at myself. All of these years I've wanted to be outside, with no leash, like I am right now. But something isn't right.

The baby cries once more, and this time, I imagine Carrie right now, sick and laying in bed. What good am I if I can't fulfil my duty of keeping her happy and safe?

Slowly, I return from my stance. I don't need wild animals. There's a human that needs me. The rabbit now sees me, dashing away. I let it run.

Returning inside, I lay down by the backdoor, making sure nothing comes inside. I remain here for hours, waiting for Carrie.

Just as the sun starts to set, the sound of the car's engine returns to the driveway. Carrie comes inside the house first, walking herself this time, but still clearly sick.

"Hey, Jet. Sorry we didn't go for a walk today," she says sadly.

I lick her hand and she smiles.

"Gross," she giggles.

A loud gasp comes from Carrie's mother as she notices the back door wide open. "Oh my goodness! I left the door wide open! Good boy, Jet! Good boy."

I wag my tail in response.

As the day turns to night, I climb into Carrie's bed and lay next to her. She wraps her arms around me in a very uncomfortable way, but I don't mind. Carrie unbuckles my collar and scratches my neck. Pressing my nose under her arm, I close my arms and fall asleep.

Playing With Fire

"Hey Derrick, how's the wife and kid?" Alex asked.

"Good, good. How's yours?" Derrick replied.

"They're fine. My stepson finally called me "Dad" the other day, instead of just "Alex." We're making progress." He said with a sarcastic smile.

Derrick was at the fire station with all of his co-workers, relaxing until they got the dreaded call of a fire happening nearby. It was a beautiful Monday morning, the sun was shining, barely a cloud in the sky. The rest of the guys were laughing together, telling horror stories about their wives or restating highlights of last night's football game.

Suddenly, the alarm started blaring.

In unison, the men all jumped out of their seats and pulled on their gear. As soon as all the men had loaded into the fire truck, the radio's static caught their attention and their destination was revealed.

"There's a fire on 36 Oakland Drive, a woman named Ariel Matthews and her infant are in their kitchen trapped in between the flames. The fire is in the first floor of their home, and it is approximately 9 minutes away from the fire station." stated the dispatcher

"Hello? There's a fire on 36 Oakland Drive! I live here, my kitchen is on fire please hurry-" a woman was yelling on the other end, her sentence cut short by her coughing.

"Okay ma'am, we're on our way. Stay low to the ground and away from the fire, paramedics are on their way." Jeremy said calmly. Hanging up, he turned and said, "Alright, boys let's go!"

Sirens blaring through the streets, the truck and paramedics sped to the house. As the truck turned the corner, the men saw there was fire erupting from the ground floor windows. Waves of heat engulfed the men before they even jumped off. Running towards the flames, Derrick could hear faint wailing within the house. Men were spraying water into the windows with their hoses, and Matt kicked the door down as large clouds of smoke filled the air around them. A woman cradling her baby in her arms came into focus from inside the house, leaning against what looked like the kitchen wall. Pulling their oxygen masks over their face, Derrick and Matt sprung into action.

Derrick settled the woman and her child on the curb as the paramedics came with a stretcher. Pausing to look at them for a moment, he felt a faint sense of familiarity about her. Disregarding this, he turned his attention back to the dire circumstances. However, he did not think much of it, and brushed it off due to the dire circumstances.

"Hello, Miss?" Derrick exclaimed. Gently pressing his thumbs on her eyelids, Derrick raised them; her dark grey eyes had just rolled to the back of her head. Her breath was ragged as her body shut down from the shock of today's events. Screaming and sobbing, her baby boy thrashed in her arms, still holding him tight to her chest. They took the mother and the child into the ambulance and drove off in what felt like a second. Everything was moving fast. The smell of charcoal filled the air, as the men inside the house had finally contained the fire. The interior of their home was stained with grey and black burns, almost like a black and white abstract painting. Everything was destroyed, the cupboards were now charred and scattered pieces of wood along the wall and floor, the plates were shattered and the furniture was all completely scorched. Black marks made by the fire lined the staircase and walls like scars. Gaping holes that once were the windows allowed for the smoke to filter out of the house, and for dim light to trickle in.

"We will will call her husband, or next to kin. Thank you for all your help." said a paramedic.

"Damn," Derrick muttered. "It must suck to be him right now."

✳✳✳

Driving home, the thought of the mother Derrick had saved earlier came into his mind. Typically, victims didn't have such an impact on Derrick; he'd been doing the job for so long that, while he wasn't numb to someone's tragedy, it was no longer something he took home with him at the end of his shift. But this one was different for some reason. The image of the child crying, his mother lying unconscious, simply wouldn't leave his head. Pulling into his driveway, he turned off the car as he ran his hands through his dark hair. Opening the front door, he let out a long sigh and forced a smile on his face.

"Hey sweetie how was work?" his wife asked, once he was inside. It was already 7pm, and the wonderful aroma of fried chicken and mashed potatoes filled the air.

A smile crept onto Derrick's face as he walked into the room, seeing his wife making dinner with her hair pinned into a bun was one of the best things to come home to. The other was running down the stairs.

"Hi Daddy!" Mary exclaimed, with a beaming smile on her face.

"Hey, it's my two favorite girls. Work was alright, same as usual. How are you sweetheart?" He asked, referring to his daughter.

"Good, I did my homework."

"Homework? You're seven; you should be playing with your dollies or something." He said with a chuckle.

Giggling, Mary embraced her father and both of them walked over to his wife.

Samantha smiled at the sight. "She *was* playing with her dollies, I told her to finish her homework before you got home."

"That's my girl." Derrick replied and kissed Mary on the forehead, then his wife on the cheek.

"What's for dinner?" as if he hadn't already smelled it.

"Fried chicken, mashed potatoes and green beans, which I just finished. The last of the chicken is almost ready, and for dessert I made your favorite. Chocolate covered strawberries."

A squeal came from Mary as a smile spread across her face. "I love those Mommy!"

"I know sweetheart." She said with a soft smile.

Sitting together for dinner, it was the perfect family moment. Filled with good food and feeling content with his life, Derrick got ready for bed soon after.

"Goodnight sweetie." He heard his wife say next to him.

"Goodnight love." He replied, closing his eyes and drifting into a deep sleep.

Gasping for air, Derrick shot up from his sleep in a cold sweat. Breathing heavy, he clutched at the sheets surrounding him as he tried to calm himself down. He had had the worst nightmare imaginable- he had remembered the woman from the fire.

Her face shown so clearly in his memory, from the fire and from that night. Her blonde hair, grey eyes, even her red lipstick that was slightly smeared at her cupid's bow.

That night, that he had tried so hard to forget about for months. The night he had managed to put out his mind, until now.

It was almost 2 years ago, May of 2014, Derrick and his friends were out at a bar. It was a guy's night out, so what better thing to do than go out with your friends and watch sports. Derrick was with his wife at this time, as were most of his friends, while a few still lingered in the single realm. Drink after drink, all of the men were having the time of their life. Seated in a round booth, there were eight of them all together and Derrick was sitting at the end of the booth.

He was drinking beer after beer, still heated about an argument he had with his wife earlier. She had wanted to have another child, but he had said that right now was not a good time. He had said that they didn't have the financial means in order to have a second child, and Samantha disagreed. She said that Mary was now six, and that the timing was perfect to try for another. It did not end well, and Derrick stormed out of the house to go meet his friends while Samantha angrily went to go pick up her daughter from her friends house.

All the men talking to one another, laughing at, or with, each other, it was like their college years all over again. After one shot too many, a pretty blonde girl stumbled onto Derrick's shoulder.

"Oh my gosh! I'm *so* sorry!" She mumbled as she stood up straight and laughed.

"It's okay, don't worry about it, Miss." Derrick replied, shrugging it off.

"Hey, you're cute." She started, her friends giggling behind her like school girls.

"Why thank you, you're mighty fine as well." Derrick replied with a sly smile.

"Can I sit?" Biting her lip, she gestured to the empty seat next to him.

Her grey eyes looked endearingly into his as he almost hypnotically nodded for her to sit.

She seated herself down, and even though there was enough room for her to sit comfortably, her side was brushing against his. The subtle contact caught his attention and instinctively began to put his arm around her. The alcohol was getting into his mind, but he didn't care; he was having a good time. One of his friends next to him realized what was going on and nudged Derrick.

"What are you doing?" he whispered.

"What do you mean?" Derrick asked with a lazy grin on his face.

"Uh, your arm is around her. You have a wife, remember?"

Derrick's expression dropped and slowly took his arm back, running his hand through his hair to play it off. "Right, sorry. Thanks." He replied apologetically. His friend gave him a half smile in return and turned his attention to one of their friends that was leaving.

"Alright guys, I think I'm gonna head out for the night. The wife wants me back." Said one of the guys. Everyone in unison mumbled their goodbye's and exchanged slaps on the back as a farewell. Shortly after, a few more of the friends left. It was already 11pm, and most of them had church or work in the morning. Derrick on the other hand, had the day off.

"Hey, what are you doing later tonight?" Asked the blonde girl. Her friends had already stumbled into a taxi or were attempting to pick up another cutie at the bar.

"Probably heading home, you?" answered Derrick. He hoped that by the time he got back, his wife wasn't still hung up on the argument. The argument was over and he didn't want to dwell on it, he just wanted a good night. Pushing his annoyance to the side, he focused on the girl.

"Aww c'mon, that's boring. Let's go do something *fun*." She cooed, lightly touching his arm.

Flinching a little, he leaned back away from her contact. Derrick asked, "Like what? I don't even know your name."

"I'm Ariel. Ariel Matthews, what's yours?" She was getting friskier flirtier and flirtier with every passing minute. He was beginning to enjoy it.

"Derrick Thompson."

"Oo. Derrick. I like that name." She smirked.

Laughing, Derrick asked, "So what are your plans for the night? Got someone waiting for you?" She looked about his age, mid 30's, still trying to make the most of life while still young.

"Nope, I'm all by myself. I was thinking of heading home too, actually. It's getting kind of late. Walk me there?" She asked, batting her fake lashes in the most innocent way. It wasn't innocent at all. Derrick didn't seem to catch that.

"Sure, hun. How far?" Derrick said with a grin on his face. She was cute. And he had too much to drink. "Just around the corner. It's late, I don't want to walk alone at night."

"Yeah, I understand."

They excused themselves from the table and walked out the door together. Derrick held the door open for Ariel, and she gave him a wink as a thank you. They walked the block together, talking and laughing, stumbling around and acting like high schoolers.

"What's your favorite food? Every time I go to that bar I get hot wings. I absolutely love hot wings!" She explained, dragging out "love" when she said it.

"My favorite food is steak. Specifically sirloin, made rare. Nothing beats that."

"Typical," she snorted.

"Typical? Typical how?" He said with a smile on his face.

"You're such a *guy*. Have you ever tried risotto? Or tofu? There's more to life than just sirloin steak."

"Well my taste buds are clearly not as advanced as yours, but I'd never eat tofu. That's like eating cotton balls. There is no taste, a weird texture, and it's not even filling."

"Tofu is good if it's made right. But anyways, tell me about yourself. What do you do?" She said, looking at him intently.

"Alright, well I'm a firefighter, I have been since right out of college. What about you?" He failed to mention that he met his wife in college, but the alcohol in his system made everything in his mind fuzzy.

"Right now I'm a waitress at the pizzeria called Pizza Magnifique down the street from my house, we should pass it soon. But what I really love doing is painting, so I make a few paintings here and there as a side thing and make a couple bucks from some buyers." This girl was a talker, even if she was half drunk and mumbling half the things she said.

"That's pretty cool. I'd love to see one sometime." Derrick grinned. Mary loved art. It was her favorite class in school. Before he could fully comprehend that he still had a wife and child, Ariel excitedly pointed out the pizzeria she worked at.

"This is the place!" she exclaimed. "The bane of my existence! But I need the money so I deal with it."

Laughing together, they reached her house around the corner. She lived in a small house that had a ledge outside of each ground window containing plants and succulents. There was a pathway leading up to her front door and they stopped at the front steps of the house. Smiling, Derrick looked at her and she looked back at him. She was about four inches shorter than him; being 6ft most people were shorter than him. She was staring up at him and began to lean in. It was 11:30 pm, too late to think straight, too late to care about anything else going on. They were living in the moment, whatever that meant. Ignoring everything else around them, their lips brushed up against each other's, and they kissed. It was a drunk, sloppy kiss, but a kiss nonetheless. Reaching her hand out behind her, she opened her front door and they stumbled in, lips still locked and hands intertwined. They passed the kitchen and made their way, quite disruptively, to her room. They kicked off their shoes and landed on her bed, laughing while on top of each other. Breathless and dazed, Derrick stood up off from the bed, well- he tried too. Ariel grabbed his hand to pull him back down on her, and his wedding ring slipped off of his finger in the process. The sound of the ring dropping was barely audible over the sound of them together. The night took an unexpected turn, but for a brief moment both of them were happy.

Derrick slowly opened his eyes as sunlight seeped in through the cracks of the blinds, creating a stripped pattern on the floor beneath him. With a throbbing headache, Derrick stood up groaning as nausea bubbled in his stomach. A glistening gold object caught his attention as he averted his eyes to the bottom of the couch. Running his hand through his hair, he reached over to find that it was his wedding ring. His heart sank as he finally realized what he had just done. A sense of guilt and regret fell over Derrick during what felt like years it took to walk back to his car. It was still parked at the bar, his family must be worried sick.

His family.

Fumbling for his phone in his pocket, he turned it on to receive a flood of messages and missed calls. Hands beginning to shake, he called his wife back immediately. After three rings, she picked up.

"Derrick where were you? Where are you? I was worried sick! I thought something had happened to you- why didn't you call? What is going on, I had to tell Mary you were just running late, having fun with your friends! What happened?!" Screamed his wife from the other end.

"Babe, I'm so sorry. I was drunk last night and crashed at a friends house. I'm so sorry, it's my fault, I shouldn't have drank so much. I'm on my way home right now." Lying to his wife felt like a knife to his heart. He did not know whether to come clean, or to never let her know. He never wanted to hurt her. He didn't even know he was capable of something like this, even after having an argument with her earlier the day before.

"Okay, okay. I'll see you at home, I'll have your omelette ready for you when you get back."

"Alright, thanks." He hung up the phone. Almost immediately the tears welled up in his eyes and he began to cry. Reaching his car, he put his arm against the side door and leaned his head on it, letting the tears stream down his face in regret. He could barely stand the sight of his own reflection. Taking a deep breath, he willed himself to stop crying and drive home. Anxiety and fear rose in his chest, but he pushed it down in order to act nonchalant in front of his family. No one could know about this. No one could find out.

All of this had rushed back to the surface of his memory, and feelings of anxiety and guilt consumed him once more. No. Derrick decided to visit her in the hospital. Why? To check if she was okay. To see if she remembered him. Or maybe he just wanted to see her. Derrick was a mess of mixed emotions, and because of that he wasn't thinking clearly. He didn't really know what he was doing. He was being impulsive and stupid, once again.

Wait.

The baby.

Whose was it?

Not his. It couldn't be his. Pushing that thought out of his brain, he got out of bed and went downstairs to eat breakfast.

"Daddy, why aren't you smiling?" His daughter Mary asked him.

"Sweetheart I'm fine, Daddy's just a little tired." He replied with a soft smile.

"What's wrong, hun?" His wife said as she dug into her scrambled eggs.

"Nothing, nothing. Just had a weird dream last night."

"Oh, what was it about?" Samantha inquired.

"I don't really remember," He lied. "It just made me have a weird feeling."

"Oh, alright. Well hope that weird feeling goes away." She said with a warm smile. She was so caring, she didn't deserve what he had done.

"Thanks darling."

With a sick feeling in his stomach, Derrick ran his hand through his hair and headed out the door to start his day. It was a Tuesday, which meant he had a day off. He usually took Tuesday's to do errands for his family, when his wife went off to work as a hostess at a local restaurant, after she dropped off Mary at school. Today, Derrick did not do errands. He drove straight to the hospital, with thoughts popping up every second in his mind, and anxiety filling his body. Parking, he felt his heart rate escalate as he made his way to the lobby. The typical hospital smell filled his nostrils, leaving him with a sense of uneasiness. He stepped up to the secretary, her gaze unmoving from the computer screen in front of her.

"Can I help you?" she said, nonchalantly.

"Uh, y-yes." He stammered. "I'm here to visit, uhm, Ariel."

"Last name?"

Digging back through his memory, he remembered her last name. "Um, Matthews. She was a fire victim, her son is here as well, I was the one who saved them from the fire. I just want to check up on them to see how they are holding up."

"The Ariel Matthews you're looking for is in room 302. You're the firefighter that saved her, you say?" She looked at him suspiciously.

"Yeah, I just wanted to check up on her and her baby. Thanks." Shrugging off the secretary's questioning glare, Derrick scanned the halls as he made his way to the elevator. The ride to the second floor felt like an eternity, having a sense of dread fall over him. The elevator door opened, shaking him out from his daze as he noticed a plaque that read 302 as he looked to the right. He stepped towards the room and upon arrival, Derrick felt the blood rush to his cheeks as his nerves were getting the best of him. He stared at the light blue curtain that covered the view to inside the room. It was slightly opened, so he could just see the corner of the bed. Should he have brought flowers? He thought to himself. No, that would be weird. He shouldn't even be here. What was he doing here? Conflicted thoughts began to fill his brain as he stood there, contemplating his next move. He could turn around, forget about her completely again, go grocery shopping as he was supposed to, and return home to his beautiful wife and daughter. Why couldn't he bring himself to turn around?

Because he was guilty. He was guilty that he left her the morning after, no note, no text message explaining why he left, he didn't even tell her who he was or about his family. And now he had just saved her life. He had just saved hers and her child's life. And he was going to disappear from her completely again? What kind of a person would he be, to impact a human beings life in such a way, and then pretend like they don't exist. He had to do this, for closure. Closure for the both of them.

Grabbing the curtain with his hand, he took a deep breath and walked in. Seated in her hospital bed, her head was turned to look out the window by her side, gazing at the scenery below her. There were cars driving down on the street, looking like kids toys. The trees swayed in the wind, and people were walking to and from buildings.

Her blonde hair was in a loose ponytail, cascading down her shoulder and reached just above her elbow. Feeling the presence of someone else in the room, she turned around, her eyes instantly widening as she realized who it was.

"You." She said in a voice so small, it was as if she was afraid that if she said it too loud he would disappear. Her facial expression went from surprise, to confusion, then back to a poker face.

"Hi, uh. How are you." Derrick started off, cursing himself in his thoughts for being so awkward.

"I'm fine. What are you doing here?" She asked, her voice more cautious than interrogative.

Derrick stood there, trying to form a response in his mind. What *was* he doing there?

"I wanted to come and check up on you, to see if you were okay. And when I realized who you were, I wanted to come back and apologize, for um. Leaving without saying anything. So, I'm sorry. But it was a mistake." Rubbing the back of his neck, he looked at the ground in embarrassment as he felt her eyes study him and his intentions.

Speechless, she sat there processing what he had just told her. She first stared at him, then down at her blanket, then down at her hands. For a few brief moments, there was a silence that pierced Derrick's heart with every passing second. Did he say something wrong? Did he come on too strong? Whatever, he said what he came to say.

"Are you serious?"

Taken aback by this, Derrick looked up at her abruptly and furrowed his brow. "What?"

"Are you serious right now? You invite yourself to my hospital room to tell me *that*? I'm fine. Thanks for saving me. But no thanks for disappearing from my life entirely. A simple 'goodbye' would have sufficed. Guess your mother didn't teach you class. Get out." Her voice was rising as her anger did, his spontaneous appearance seemed both ridiculous and rude to her.

"Whoa, I tried to be nice! I know what I did was messed up, and I'm sorry! I have a wife and kid at home, I just had to get this off my chest and leave." His cheeks flushed, not expecting her to be this angry.

Her eyes widened at the words, 'wife and kid.' She looked down at his clenched fist, and saw the golden wedding band on his ring finger.

That complicated everything. "I'm sorry is not good enough. You have a wife and kid?" Anxiety rose in her chest.

"I do. And I love them very much. I never want to hurt them and I just came here for closure, alright? Sorry for bothering you." He began to walk out the door, but something Ariel said made him stop in his tracks.

"Derrick- goddamnit." Her voice broke as she was trying not to cry. He turned around and stood looking at her from the doorway. "I- the baby. The baby is yours." Quickly her hands covered her face, she couldn't hold her tears back any longer.

His jaw dropped and he began to breathe heavily as he processed what she had just said to him. Leaning against the door post, his gaze shifted from her to the ground, almost hyperventilating. His thoughts were running wild, his pulse was rising, what could he possibly do now?

Everything had just changed for him. Life, as he knew it, was no longer the same. For an entire two years of his life, he had been unaware of a human being that was partially his, growing up each day and he was living life as though that specific night had never happened. What was he going to tell his wife, what was he going to tell his daughter, what was he going to tell Ariel, and most importantly, what was he going to do about the baby?

"Are you okay?" her timid voice broke his thought process. He blinked and looked up at her.

"I don't know." Derrick hated when people asked him that. The answer was never good. Being a firefighter, he was exposed to flames, tragedies, deaths, and life all at once. How was he supposed to say anything was okay when he has a job like that? How was he supposed to say anything was okay when he lived a life like this?

The hopelessness Derrick felt within mixed with the shock of this news made him want to hurl. "Oh my God." he breathed. He stared at the floor breathing heavily as he gathered his thoughts. "You're telling me, that the baby I saved with you, from that fire, is mine?" Derrick trailed off and turned around, this was not how he pictured this visit going. Leaning on the door frame, he pressed his eyes shut, panic bubbling in his chest.

"Yes." her voice was monotone, she didn't know how to feel.

Silence filled the room for what felt like an eternity. Derrick was consumed in his own thoughts. What would he have to do? This was serious, this was reality. This isn't something someone can just sweep under the rug and deal with later. This was life. The weight he felt on his shoulders tripled; there was a human being added to it. Opening his eyes, he said, "Where is the baby?" Sounding more like a statement than a question of concern.

"Down the hall, take a left." Ariel said in a quiet voice, almost inaudible. Before her child, she was saving up for her painting supplies, paying rent for her house and paying off her college loans as well. She had everything planned out for her life, all her money saved, she knew what she was doing. Until she found out she was pregnant. Nine months later, a little baby boy came and her life changed. Her life now revolved around him- her money now revolved around him.

"I'll go see him, I'll think this over tonight." Derrick responded, still not facing her.

"I get discharged tomorrow with the baby, so I won't be here, I'll be home." She stuttered. "Incase you want to talk about all of this, it's understandable if you don't- um. Just an offer.""

"I'll come by in a few days. I have to tell my wife about this. We'll see what happens." He said, walking out of the room.

Derrick was at a loss for words. He silently walked down the hall, subconsciously taking a left. He no longer felt like he was in his own body, none of this could possibly be real. He looked into the window pane where he saw the room where a baby was being cared for. The baby was in a blue cap and white pajamas, and there was a nurse feeding him with a bottle, gently cradling his head with her hand. The baby had her same grey eyes. Emotions filled Derrick's heart, emotions like confusion, love, anger, and helplessness. That was *his* baby he was staring at. That was part of *his* flesh and blood. He wasn't the kind of man to have the mentality to abandon flesh and blood.

Taking a deep breath, he walked out of the hospital without another word.

The rest of his day consisted of doing groceries, putting them away as soon as he got home, doing the finances, and contemplating what to do with another child in his life. It all felt like a blur to him, the hours bled into each other and before he knew it, the time approached to when his wife and daughter would come home. Dreading their return, he knew what he had to do.

It would be the hardest thing he had ever had to do in his entire life, and he's a firefighter.

***

"Honey, I'm home!" he heard his wife say from the front door. She had just pulled in, and Mary was following close behind her. Derrick's heart sunk.

"Hey."

Noticing his tone of voice, Samantha asked, "Is there something wrong?" with a concerned look on her face.

Derrick let out a heavy sigh and closed his eyes. His attention diverting to his daughter, "Sweetie, go upstairs and start your homework, okay? Dinner will be ready in a few."

"Okay, daddy." Mary said, skipping up the stairs.

"What's wrong?" Samantha's brows were furrowed and she was playing with the hem of her shirt.

Not making eye contact, Derrick took a deep breath and told her to sit down on the couch.

"Derrick you're scaring me, what's going on?"

Derrick ran his hands through his hair, and then dropped them to his knees. Looking up at his wife, he began to tell her the story.

"I'm so sorry baby," he told her. "I made a mistake."

"Spit it out Derrick." She looked at him pleadingly, a hand gripping the couch cushion.

Taking a deep breath, Derrick squeezed his eyes shut. "I-" He stammered. "I met someone- a while ago. I made a mistake and- Samantha I'm sorry. I have another kid."

She didn't move, and neither did he. Even through the frozen silence, he saw her heart break. He saw it in her eyes. After a pause, he continued his confession.

"It happened around two years ago, that day when I didn't come home from the bar. I was drunk-" Derrick was beginning to choke up.

Swallowing hard, he tried again. "I was drunk that night, and some blonde girl asked me to walk her home, so I did. I walked her home. I didn't think anything would happen. I didn't-"

"Yeah." Samantha's shaky voice broke his dialogue. "You didn't think." Tears streamed down her face as Derrick looked at her, this was killing him. Emotional pain coursed through her body with every broken heartbeat, her worst nightmare was coming true.

"I didn't think." Derrick repeated. He looked down at the floor. "I walked her home and then it happened, I didn't mean for it to happen, I was stupid. I didn't know she had a kid until I saw her at the hospital-"

"You saw her at the hospital? When was this?" His wife interrogated him, her voice rising. "Where you just planning on not telling me all of this? The only reason you did is because you have a kid! You got caught! What the hell is wrong with you?!" She was now screaming at him, crying and screaming as Derrick pressed his eyes shut and breathed heavy. Tears now escaping his eyes as well.

"She was a fire victim! I saved her from a house fire! I saved her son too- I had to know if I knew her. She looked familiar and curiosity got the best of me, I don't know why I did it! I don't think! I'm sorry!"

"I'm sorry doesn't fix anything. I'm sorry doesn't make anything better, I'm sorry doesn't change what you did."

"Mommy, what's going on?" Mary peeped her head from behind the rails of the staircase. Her eyes were wide with fear and worry.

"Don't worry about it honey, we'll talk later. Daddy and I are just having a little argument." Samantha paused to sniffle and wipe her eyes. "Go back upstairs, dinner's almost done."

Mary nodded and glanced at her father for a brief moment. He looked back at her, his heart breaking even more as she walked back up the stairs.

"She told me at the hospital. I haven't spoken to her or seen her since that night at the bar. I promise you. Honey, I'm so sorry, I never meant for any of this to happen."

I don't want to hear it. I never thought this would happen. All these years, 12 years! I've been nothing but good to you, and this is what happens. What are we supposed to do with this baby now? What does that woman think we're going to do with it?"

He looked up from his hands. Her eyes were glossy and filled with anger as she sat there, her hands slightly trembling.

"I'm sorry. I don't know. I don't want to just pretend he doesn't exist..." he trailed off.

"Yeah, like you pretended that woman didn't exist when you visited her at the hospital? Like you pretended what you did never happened, when you lied to me about having sex with another woman!" Samantha stood up from the couch, breathing heavy, her teeth clenched. "I need time to think." She stormed past him and began to prepare Mary's dinner.

Derrick was left alone, sitting in silence.

***

Samantha woke up alone the next day. A feeling of dread consumed her body, as everything from last night had set in. After she had went upstairs, Derrick stayed downstairs and slept there. Mary had asked her what was wrong for the second time, but all Samantha said was that she was not feeling too well that night.

It was 6:30 am now, Samantha had to make breakfast for the family. Except she only made breakfast for Mary and herself. Derrick was the least of her worries this morning. Today was Wednesday, which meant Derrick had to go back to work and Mary had dance practice after school. Samantha knew he was planning to talk to her today about the baby. She didn't know how she felt about that. In a way, she understood. She understood that the other woman had a child, and that if it was her, she would want the father to know, and want her child to grow up with a father. On the other hand, she was heartbroken at how he could possibly do this to her, and do this to another woman as well. How was he going to juggle two kids now? They had talked about having another kid together one day. Now who knew if that was ever going to happen.

Derrick assisted in two fires that day, and he was hungry and upset. Waking up this morning on that uncomfortable couch had made his neck sore for the entire day, so it hurt whenever he had to turn his head. Samantha barely looked at him, leaving quite suddenly to take Mary to school. Neither of them knew how they were going to tell Mary about this. Neither of them wanted to tell her.

Samantha was the only thing on Derrick's mind the entire day. The only escape he had from his mind was working, throwing himself into flames to save other peoples' lives. The adrenaline rush was his favorite part, holding a human life in his arms and knowing that he saved them was a rush every single time. But right now, reality stayed there, weighing him down. He was the one trapped in the flames, and he could barely save himself.

Mary was the only thing keeping Samantha from breaking down. She had to stay strong for her daughter, the most precious thing in the world to her. Thinking about her husband made her heart ache, and she was at a loss when it came to what should happen next. Should she talk to him? Should she never talk to him again? It was all too soon. Feeling sick to her stomach, she pushed her pain away and continued on with work. Her day was a complete blur, nothing felt real anymore. Nothing felt right.

**

A few days passed with the same routine, Derrick on the couch with no breakfast, Samantha taking Mary to school, and both Derrick and Samantha telling Mary that everything was fine, just a little bump in the road was all.

"Then why can't you get over the bump?" Mary asked Samantha, innocently. It was Saturday, three days of awkward silences and unresolved tension.

Samantha stopped to think for a moment. "Well sweetie because this is one of those bigger bumps in the road, that are harder to get over."

"Then why doesn't Daddy help you get over it? My teacher at school always says two heads are better than one."

Tears welling up in Samantha's eyes, she remembered the first time her and Derrick had a little 'bump-in-the-road.' They were still dating at this time, and she had gotten mad at him for forgetting a family dinner her parents had planned. They had prepared the food, but Derrick cancelled last minute, saying that he had forgotten it was this weekend and that he was out in New York watching a Red Sox game with his brother. She was so mad, she had reminded him the day before but of course he was too busy playing video games to be listening to her. He came back from New York on a Sunday, and barely spoke to Samantha the entire day. Which made her all the more furious. Little did she know, he had prepared an entire dinner himself, at his place, and called her parents to come at 7pm on the dot. When Samantha arrived with her family, she was so surprised, and so overwhelmed. He apologized to all of them individually, and when he apologized to her, he kissed her hand and gave her a single rose. That was the moment she knew he was the one.

"Yeah, your father and I can get over this bump together. Thank you, hun." She smiled.

"Welcome Mommy!"

***

Once work had ended that day, Derrick came home. He saw his wife had just arrived as well, and decided he would approach her. "Samantha?"

"Yes Derrick?"

"Will you come with me tonight, to talk to her. It feels wrong if you aren't there too. You should be there."

There was a drawn out silence as Derrick worried about her response.

"Sure. Mary has a playdate after school anyways."

Derrick let out a sigh of relief, "Okay, thank you." They ate dinner together, sitting on opposite sides of the table. Not speaking to each other, they finished their food and got ready to go to Ariel's.

It wasn't a far drive, Derrick remembered each turn the fire truck had made the first time he went there for the fire. Once he got there, it was around 8pm. His wife knew what he was about to say. In a way, he felt better that he didn't have to continue lying to her, but he felt like the worst person on the planet for everything that was going on. He was the worst person on the planet.

Taking a deep breath and running his hands through his messy hair, he stepped out of the car and walked to the front door. The window's had just gotten redone, and the new paint smell was still lingering in the air. Knocking twice, he stepped back and waited with his wife, who still wasn't saying anything. It was only a few moments before he heard shuffling within the house and Ariel opened the door. An expression of astonishment fell over Ariel's face and she gasped quietly. Astonishment quickly turned to fear and guilt.

"Come in." She said quietly, looking down at the floor. She was holding her baby by her shoulder, gently burping him and bobbing him up and down to keep him calm.

Derrick gave a small smile and walked into the house with his wife. The kitchen was still not in shape, but better than it looked before. There were new cabinets lining the walls, and the walls were no longer stained with burns. It was remotely empty, since she now needed to replace everything that was lost, but it was slowly returning to normal.

The three of them made their way to the living room, and Derrick was watching the baby's little face resting on her shoulder the entire time. His eyes were closed, and his chubby cheeks were squished against her shirt. His mouth was slightly agape, but it was the most adorable thing he would see that night.

Seating themselves apart, Ariel was sitting on the chair next to the coffee table and Derrick was sitting with Samantha on the couch.

"Hi, uh. I'm Ariel." She said, introducing herself to Derrick's wife.

"Hi." Samantha said, not meeting her eyes.

Taking note of the tension building, Derrick decided to start the conversation. "So this is my wife, Samantha. She knows everything that happened." Before Ariel could say anything, Derrick continued, "and I would like to be a part of the baby's life- *We* would like to be a part of the baby's life. I wouldn't want it to grow up without a father, and I am assuming you wouldn't want that either." He stopped.

Ariel didn't speak. She was looking from Derrick, to Samantha, then to her baby, and finally to the ground. Embarrassment shown all over her face as she carefully stood up to put the baby in the crib. Sighing heavily as she sat back down, she put her face in her hands as if she wanted to hide herself from the situation. This was definitely not easy for her either.

"Are you okay?" asked Derrick, confused as to what she was feeling.

"No, I'm not okay. That's a stupid question." She looked up from her hands. "I'm not going to ask you to be a part in my baby's life if you have a family of your own, I can only imagine the pain you've caused her!" Ariel exclaimed, gesturing towards Samantha. "That wouldn't be fair to her, and it wouldn't be fair to Jacob either. His name is Jacob. I don't want him to grow up confused, having two moms and one dad and one half sister. This was all a mistake…" She trailed off and began to cry. Soft whimpers escaped her lips as she put her face back into her hands.

Derrick, taking all of this in, sat there and felt pain rise in his chest. Each heartbeat hurt. This all hurt. The circumstances were awful and his mistake was awful.

"It's something we all have to live with." Samantha finally broke the silence. "I understand it is important for a child to grow up with a father figure. We can iron out the kinks as time goes on." She said, eyes locked on the carpet below her, not daring to look up at anyone.

"This is all extremely difficult, I know that. But we have to settle this now, instead of later. Waiting isn't going to fix anything. This happened, and we have to deal with the consequences. If you want, I can give you time to figure out what you want. Whether you or the baby ever want me - or us - in your lives." Derrick added, including his wife.

Ariel sniffled and looked up at them, wiping her eyes. "If it's okay with her, I'd like Jacob to know you. It's hard taking care of him on my own, and now having to pay the hospital bills is another thing on my plate. I'm not asking for money, that would be selfish, but if you could be a part in his life, and see him maybe once a week that would be enough for us. If that's okay."

Samantha took a deep breath and closed her eyes. "Yes, that's fine." She hated every second of this, but her mother had taught her to always be the bigger person and to turn the other cheek. Those are the same morals she had raised Mary with.

"Thank you, that sounds great." Derrick said. He took his wife's hand in his and looked at her. "I'll see him on Tuesdays, and take care of him as much as I can manage. Like she said, we can iron out the kinks as time goes on." Still looking at his wife, he kissed her hand and she looked up at him. He was blessed with an amazing and understanding wife, and he will never take her for granted again. He couldn't even fathom what she was going through, but her strength was admirable.

Samantha only stared back at him, hoping that someday this pain will fade back into the love she remembered she had for him.

Wrapping up their conversation, they thanked each other and left the house. Before Samantha could leave, Ariel lightly tapped her shoulder.

"I am so sorry, I'm so sorry. I would never do this to you, I am not this kind of person. I'm so sorry and I hope you can forgive me one day." Through her eyes, Samantha saw that Ariel meant every word. Her brows were furrowed and her pain was evident in her deep grey eyes, this was a lot for any person for handle. Tears welled up in Samantha's eyes and she turned around. "I know, I forgive you and I don't hate you. I just hate what happened."

At that, Derrick and Samantha left with Ariel standing by the front door, watching them drive off.

Mary came home from her friend's house at 9, which was perfect timing; Derrick and Samantha reached at the same time. Since it was still Saturday, they decided they would tell Mary about everything tomorrow, when all of them had time together.

Derrick read Mary a bedtime story, and Samantha tucked her in. Once Mary fell asleep, the both of them went to bed themselves. For the first time in a while, they slept in the same bed.

"Samantha?" Derrick whispered in the dark.

"Yes, Derrick?"

"I love you."

There was a long pause.

"I love you too." Samantha finally replied, sounding a little choked up.

Derrick closed his eyes feeling a little bit of relief. He hadn't lost everything.

The next day, they tried their hardest to explain to Mary what had happened in the most child friendly way. They sat her down on the couch after breakfast, and told her that she has a little brother. Confused, she asked where they got him. Derrick and Samantha said that it was a complicated story for when she was older, but she would be able to see him Tuesday after school. He was an addition to the family, and she would also meet his Mommy. Mary went with it, the excitement of having a sibling taking over her emotions. She did not ask any further questions, besides why her new brother wasn't living with them. Her parents shifted uncomfortably in their seats, but came up with telling her that he had to be with his Mommy and could visit every once and awhile, but things were complicated for him to be living with them. She nodded her head in somewhat understanding, then went outside to go play soccer with the neighbors.

***

That coming Tuesday, Derrick went to go visit Jacob, since it was his day off. His wife would be meeting him here later after work with Mary. He greeted Ariel at the door before speeding off to work. Walking into the house, he saw Jacob playing with his binky in his crib, as happy as a baby can be. He was beautiful. In every way. And he was a part of Derrick.

The two spent the day together, Derrick feeding him, burping him, playing with him and reading him books as the time passed. Derrick even took the baby car seat with him into ShopRite as he did groceries for his family. Occasionally, he would ask the baby what kind of food he should get, choosing between Captain Crunch Cereal and Frosted Flakes. Laughing after Jacob made a spitting noise towards Captain Crunch, Derrick chose the other.

That evening, Ariel arrived to the house to witness Derrick playing peek-a-boo with the baby. It was definitely a sight to see. Both of them had drool stains on their shirts, and Derrick looked exhausted while Jacob looked like the world's happiest baby. Ariel was smiling and said, "Looks like the two of you are having fun." Grabbing Derrick's attention, he looked up at her with a startled expression.

"Yeah, this little guy really likes me. It's been a long but good day."

"I'm so glad. I can take him now, I'll give him a bath before your wife gets here."

Ariel stepped closer as Derrick picked up the baby and placed him in her arms. She took him to the sink and began to give him a bath, smoothing out his wet hair and using soap that smells like peaches. Derrick stretched his body, sore from carrying a baby the entire day. Yawning, he received a text.

It was from Samantha, saying:

On my way with Mary. See you there.

"My wife and daughter are on their way," Derrick told her. "Where's your bathroom so I can wash my hands and face."

"Down the hall, your first right."

Derrick walked down the hall and into the bathroom. Looking into the mirror, he finally noticed the drool stains on his shoulder and how tired his eyes had become. Washing his hands and running them through his hair, he silently hoped that this would work out. That Samantha would be okay, that they could feel like a family again and that Jacob was going to be a blessing instead of a curse.

The sound of knocking on the front door distracted him from his thoughts, he immediately shut off the running water from the bathroom sink and walked over to the front door. Opening it, he saw Samantha's beautiful face, and he kissed her as a welcome.

"Hey! What about me!" Mary's cute voice called to him. He kissed her cheek and allowed them into the house.

"I just gave Jacob a bath so he won't smell so bad, hello how are you?" Ariel said directing the question to Derrick's wife. She greeted her with an inviting, but awkward smile, and Samantha returned it.

"Mary, isn't he so cute?" Samantha said.

"Baby brother!" Mary squealed. She skipped past her father to greet the baby, and both Ariel and Samantha laughed.

This was definitely something they all had to get used to. All three of them were still greatly hurt and affected by this experience, although the two happy children made things a little bit easier.

"Yeah, I had a good day with the little guy. He likes Frosted Flakes, just like me." Derrick chuckled.

Ariel was making small talk with Mary as she excitedly stuck her finger out so the baby's little hand would grab it, and Derrick smiled at the sight. Soon after, Samantha gently touched his arm. Turning to her, Derrick saw the seriousness in her eyes and his smile faded.

"Derrick, this hurts. This hurts a lot."

His heart fell with those words. As soon as he opened his mouth to reply Samantha interrupted him.

"But I want this to work. That is a beautiful child, and he's a part of you, which means I love him too. This hurts a lot, but from now on I need full honesty from you. We need each other to get over this bump. I need your help to be okay with all of this."

Taken aback, he looked at her for a moment. Cupping her cheek with his hand, he said, "I promise you, I will never lie to you. Words can't describe how sorry I am, but I will do everything to make things alright again. You have my word."

She gently placed her hand on his and moved it off from her cheek, giving him a sad smile. "Thank you." she whispered. Derrick watched as she walked over to her daughter with Ariel. Taking a deep breath, he followed after her.

Derrick hoped that it would not take long to gain his wife's trust, and for life to return back to normal. He knew that when his son grew up, he would teach him good morals and values, and use this situation as a lesson to learn from.

After all, when you play with fire, you get burned.

* * *

The Watchmaker

Luty (February) 1955

huddering, I lift the quilted blanket off myself and hand it to my sister, Kazia. She takes it and hurries over to the kitchen, long braid swinging with her steps. On the way out of the room, her foot presses against the creaky floorboard. I cringe, willing the universe to block that from our grandparents' hearing.

The cold air hangs over my head. The twins, Stanisław and Sylwester, are next to one another on their bed, already fast asleep. I watch as their thin shoulders rise and fall shakily in the dark. We call them Stasiek and Sylon for short; two peas in a pod. My little sisters sleep on the bed near the door. And despite our protests, Kazia and I had to take the bed near the window. Three beds in total occupy the bedroom-- ever since Konstanty, our oldest brother, moved away to work. The minutes pass with our joint breaths in the frigid room, my own teeth chattering as I wait for my sister to return with the blanket. I reach to rub my frozen feet in hopes of keeping them warm, but my hands are just as cold.

My six siblings and I share one bedroom out of the three in this house. We only keep the fireplace going during the day. Warming up our blankets over the kitchen stove is our joy every night-- but by now everyone was too cold to stay awake but me. We have the smallest home in all of Żabina; it doesn't help that the walls are made of stone. Icicles have been forming in the hallway for a few days now. They hang in small spikes, coming from the ceiling and cracks between the stone. Sometimes our father, Tata, will stand on a chair to scrape them off the wall, but he worked late today.

The sudden crash of a metal pan jolts me from the bed and I tumble towards the floor. "Kazimiera!" I hear my grandma scold her from the kitchen. Groaning, I reach to comfort my aching backside from the sudden fall. But the shuffling of feet comes from the hallway and I quickly scramble back to my spot. Stasiek lets out a tired sigh. With the footsteps coming closer, I desperately pretend to be asleep. Another whispered scold is met with Kazia's apology-- "Sorry, *Babcia*." The footsteps stop, yet I still hold my breath. Before I know it, a warmth envelops my body. I turn around and face my sister, immediately hugging the soft blanket.

"She let you take the blankets?" I stare at her.

"*Tak*, now go to sleep. She nearly yelled at me for being clumsy." She says to me. Without another word, we make room for one another under the blanket and fall asleep.

✱✱✱

"Filip, wake up! Wake up, wake up!" I stir to consciousness from my little brother Sylon's squeaky voice. His tiny hands grip my arms and pull the blanket off of me.

"Sylwester, stop it. I'm getting up," I say with a tired yawn. Letting me go, he hops down from the bed. Stasiek must have already been up; those two have minds like clockwork. In time they'll realize that mornings become dreadful when you get older. Shrugging on a long-sleeved shirt, I get up from the bed. The space around me is doused in a shade of dampened blue. Looking out the window I see that the sun is barely beginning to rise.

I turn to my brother once more, watching as he rushes excitedly to the hallway in anticipation of my following. "Do you know what Mama wants us to do today?"

"She wants you to take Stasiek to the market," he replies. "I think you're selling the eggs." Sylon glances behind himself before meeting my eyes. "And one day you'll have to get up extra early," he whispers. "Tata is planning for another firewood trip!"

I groan, rolling my eyes at his giggles. This happens every few months now. For the longest time, the village church had given a sturdy supply of wood to the community. There was no need to go out into the forest and find able trees-- but that has changed.

I tell Sylon to leave a basket for me in the kitchen and I put on my boots. They are made of tough blackened leather, long worn from my various adventures. They're the same boots that take me to school, the same ones I use to clean the horse pen, and the same ones I've worn to chop down trees. But not from the forest. Instead they are from government property. Usually it was Konstanty and I that make the trip; he's the second oldest child and I'm the third. Our father made the mistake of bringing Sylon one time. Now he begs us to go, as if there's something fun about it. I, for one, have no idea what he sees in it.

✱✱✱

Stanisław and I longingly stare through the window of Łucia's Bakery, our hands pressed against the glass. Every time we come to the market, we're drawn straight here. The fresh bread is displayed right in front of us, barely a foot from the window. Squinting my eyes, I can see the steam rising from each loaf, still hot from the oven. To the left are plates of *paczki* powdered like snow.

A man steps out from the bakery door into the street, a box held between both hands. It's a very square box, made of thin cardboard the color of printing paper. A fold runs down the middle, held together by a brown string. When he stops to open it momentarily, there's no doubt about it-- he's just bought a box full of *paczki*. I spot the neatly divided doughnuts and stare, fixated, at the dab of jam on the sides. Too soon, the man closes the box and begins to walk away.

Not wanting to let my yearning stay conscious, a familiar bench to the side catches my attention. Every other time I'm around, an abandoned stack of newspapers is placed cleverly on the bench for free. Sure enough a pile is there. Small and fluttering, the newspapers sit in the open all alone. Scattered among the words on the paper are sayings of the government, of socialists. Above the headline in bold is a graphic of our country's flag. It stands proudly, white and red. Knowing my parents always enjoy reading the newspaper, I reach over with my hand and take one-- don't mind if I do.

Feeling something pull on my sleeve, I turn around. It's my brother, Stasiek. He tugs on my shirt again and points to the storefront next door. I give him a concerned look, yet comply. Following his lead, I walk over and approach the store. Something stands out to me; the window is swollen and cracked like it survived an attempt at being smashed.

"Stasiek, *hej*, wait right out here for me. Okay?" He lets out a huff in protest but nods anyway. I timidly grasp the door handle and twist it.

The bells on the door jingle as I step into the shop. Immediately I am hit with the thick, dusty air and the smell of wood. Clutching onto the basket of eggs, I take a hesitant step forward, as if I'm expecting the floorboards to creak underneath my feet. On the wall toward the back, I see Cuckoo clocks hanging, each one silent and without a tick. I'm struck by the sight, wondering for a moment if the owner may be German. It's not really as strange as it seems, however. My grandparents tell me that many German people are becoming citizens here, especially settling toward the Northwest. I turn to observe the rest of the store's interior. To my dismay, there are few modern wristwatches. At home, my grandfather still owns the same one he wore during the war; the big circular watch resting tightly on a toughened, brown leather strap. Then I see the broken pocket watches under the shattered glass of a smashed case. Each of the scattered pieces lay untouched. Enthralled to figure out why the place is in such a wreck, I muster up the courage to ask the shopkeeper. But no one is behind the counter, leaving me in confusion. They must be around here somewhere. Patiently waiting at the counter, I speak up.

"Hello--" A cold hand on my shoulder stops me in my tracks. Whipping around, I come face to face with a large old woman. Her hair is sheltered with a floral head wrap.

"We are closing. Out of business." Her stoic face examines my own, which is stricken with surprise. I can't tell if she's implying that I should leave or not. I'm drawn to ask about the broken glass, but I stop myself. She taps her foot impatiently on the solid wooden floor.

Sucking in a breath, I improvise. *"Przepraszam,* but I have fresh eggs. I'll give them all for the broken watches you have. They'll be off your hands, I swear." I give her a hopeful look. The woman studies my proposal with a calculating gaze. Suddenly I'm wishing for one of those clocks to work; to accompany our silence with reliable ticks of its gears.

Then she grasps the basket of eggs from my outstretched arms. I don't protest. The old woman picks a single egg from the pile, returning the basket to the counter. Observing as she cracks it open, part of me feels disgusted. She wastes no time to eat it raw and I feel a compelling to do the same. Tata eats eggs like this all the time. They're all from our chickens on the farm. I can do this. The smooth brown surface feels flat against my fingers as it's removed from the basket. A silent deal passes between us, a sacred exchange. Puncturing the center, I swiftly bring the loose shell to my mouth. Quivering, I force myself to swallow the yolk and be done with it. With my thoughts contained and the empty shell crushed, I return to the woman.

"You can have your clocks, child. Keep your eggs." She frisks her hand through the air leisurely. I know the dismissive motion well enough and nod furiously. My heart is beating, and my eyes are wide open. Before I can ask about the shattered glass, the woman turns and walks through the back door. I figure that's where she walked in from before.

The eggs. They're on the counter still. I grab the woven basket, clutching it against my chest. Below the counter are the pocket watches, as they were when I walked in. Excitement bubbles in my chest; they're all mine for the taking. Working as fast as possible, my hands paw through the fat disks and their silver chains, shoving them into my pockets. When my pockets are full I fit the rest into the basket quickly. With no time to lose, my grip stays tight on the basket and my legs push to make a run for the exit. As I swing open the door, I'm greeted with an exasperated Stasiek.

"One hour! It's been like, one full hour, Filip!" He runs over to me, shouting. I sigh and close the door behind me before joining him on our way to sell the eggs. And it wasn't an hour wasted in that shop. It most definitely was only fifteen minutes well spent.

***

"Let me see!" Joanna's bright voice perks up from behind Ludwiga, both my sisters craning their necks. It's a few minutes before sunset and we've taken care of all our chores early. The chickens are inside their coop and fed, the horses and cows in the barn, and the floors spotless. Now, the six of us are crowded in a circle on our bedroom floor.

"Hey, there's enough for everyone. Sylon," I grab my brother's flailing arm, "let your sister see." I say with a lopsided grin. Sylon leans back and waits with everyone else. Stasiek whispers something to him, their heads bumping together.

In the middle of us lies the pile of pocket watches. Reaching in, I take one by the tail and hold it up for my siblings to see. The chain is a fine deep grey, a smoky color. It holds onto a beautifully engraved watch, roman numerals and a tiny set of hands underneath the lid. Even Kazia looks surprised as we stare at the suspended object. In the center, a small group of letters spell out 'Zielony.' I carefully pass it to Ludwiga who readily shows Joanna. Pulling another tail-like chain from the pile, I pass it to Kazia. I do the same for Sylon and Stasiek.

"Filip, you have to tell us where you found these!" Ludwiga pipes up. She looks up at me through her brown bangs, blue eyes blinking expectantly. Instantly my mind flashes back to the old woman. Feeling slightly ashamed, I wonder if there was any way to thank her.

"You know Łucia's Bakery, no?" I ask. The others immediately burst into laughs.

"Someone drags us there every time we're in the market," Kazia smirks. I hush the others and continue.

"Well, right next door, Stasiek and I found a secret shop. Now it's out of business, but there was an old lady who gave these to me." I say.

"Are we going to sell them?"

"Please let me have this one, Fillip,"

My head rushes with the constant things asked of me. Selling the watches could make our family some money, but I doubt anyone in our village could afford them. My school friends might try to trade for them, but I have a better idea.

"I'll tell you what," I begin, hushing their questions. "After I do my best to fix the watches, we can decide what to do with them."

"Aww, alright." Their disappointment is unmistakable, but I can't make a decision on the spot like this; not just yet.

"You have to keep at least one, though! For me!" My sister pouts.

"Me too, me too!" Joanna grabs onto her arm.

A laugh is sparked inside me. I grin so hard it almost starts to hurt.

"Maybe I will," I say.

The last time I've felt something like this, like nothing can pull our bond apart- our togetherness- was the winter that the barn got piled in snow. It stands out to the back of our property, red and worn with work. But the barn still shelters our animals and it's been there forever. That winter, there was so much snow that we could climb to the roof. Our parents were inside cooking dinner, and our grandparents let us play. We laughed for hours, stomping on the pile of snow and running over the hill. It was perfect; peaceful and happy.

"Dzieci! Chodź na obiad!" The call from Mama sends us scrambling.

My brothers and sisters race to the kitchen to help Mama with dinner-- except Stasiek, who stays behind. He taps on the shell of a pocket watch. Dull and singular, the piece had been stripped from its center.

"Do you have the other parts for this scrap?" Stasiek asks me, dark blue eyes shining. He stands still, quieter than normal. His blonde hair-- golden in the light, set over his head like a halo-- barely moves as he holds out the shell to me. I frown and take it.

"No, doesn't look like it," I tell my brother. He swipes the metal back from my palm and looks back up at me.

"I can make them. The pieces." He says. "I'll ask Tata for help."

"Okay," I smile. Stasiek grins back and scurries off with the piece in hand. So there I am, the last one left in the room. The window distills the sunset and casts its muted hues over me. Almost giddy, I begin to wonder what it would be like to make watches as I stare at the remaining pile, still on the floor. They glint in the dim orange light. I wonder who made these and how long ago. Thoughts of a wise, master *zegarmistrz* flood my mind. The precision and calculation of the work strike me with beauty. I've never reflected upon it before.

"Filip, we could use more help in the kitchen," Kazia's voice comes from the doorway. The sound pulls me out of my solitude, and I slide the watches underneath my bed before joining her.

Not even two weeks later, Stasiek and I stand behind the house at work on the pocket watch. The sky is bloated with grey and we expect snow by the next morning. Miles off in the distance, bare trees surround the hills. A padlock rests in my hand as I watch my brother. Proficiency in locksmithing is desirable in the coming age of the workforce-- at least, that's what Tata tells us. I've practiced making various latches, positioning pivots and stops. Stasiek has been alongside me while our father teaches him metalwork. Below our feet lie dead, crunchy leaves, still surviving over the soggy grass. If I listen closely, above me is the faint sound of birds calling. I figure today proves to be an arbitrary day of late February where the cold hides away, giving us a taste of spring. Too bad it will be spoiled by tomorrow. Stepping closer to my brother, I let the mud dry on my boots.

"Kazia says that this morning, Dziadzia tried to get us steel pipes for the house. But no one would sell to him," Stasiek speaks steadily, eyes not straying from his work. He aims a wooden-handled screwdriver with care.

"Tata always said it was easier to buy from the Germans than the Polish during the war," I chuckle, but there's a twang of pain under my chest. The war's been over for almost a decade now. My younger brother pauses.

"I think we should find some pipes. We do need a working toilet, don't we?" His eyes bore into my own with a nervous determination. "Besides, Tata also said that Socialism means everything is ours. You need something, you steal it."

"And where would we steal pipes from?" I frown.

"Remember the factory in Koszelewy? Kostek took us there one time back when--"

"No, that could never work," I stop him. It's insane, we'd be so easily caught. Even though the factory is owned by a Polish company, the two of us could get in great trouble.

"Think about it," he pushes, "if we take a carriage out at night, they won't see us. And the tracks will be covered by snow in the morning." Sighing, I realize he does have a point.

"You're right about that, but that still doesn't mean we should do it," My arms cross as I speak to him.

"Come on, big brother! We could have a nice toilet like we talked about."

Yet again, he's right. Just thinking about the outhouse in the back of our property makes my nostrils flare in disgust. I long for the insurance of sanitary, proper plumbing.

"I wouldn't want the others to get in trouble," I say. "If we do go, it has to be just you and me." Some part of me, deep down in my gut, wants to do this.

"Deal," Stasiek nods. A bore of guilt has nestled its way into my stomach; a result of my intuition telling me not to steal. I suck in my breath and tell myself there's no other choice left.

After that, it is set. The both of us keep our plan underneath our tongues for the rest of the day, praying for nightfall to come quickly.

Before dinner, Tata asks us to bring firewood from outside. We step out into the fresh air and walk to the area where wood is stored. Stasiek, however, stays inside. My little sisters trail behind me, carrying smaller pieces inside that they share between their arms. I spot Sylon trying to carry a huge bundle of wood by himself but quickly stop him.

"See, Joanna and Ludwiga are smarter than you. They know not to take more than they can carry," Jokingly, I scold him.

"Yeah, but we need to bring big pieces too!" Sylon pipes. I quirk an eyebrow and take initiative on a new option. Hunching so that my knees are slightly bent, I stand at my little brother's height.

"Here," I say. I wrap my hands under half of the firewood and Sylon smiles as he clutches the other side. Our sisters giggle and remark how silly we look, but the two of us trudge forward.

As we eat, Kazia notes on how suspiciously quickly we finish our food. But Stasiek and I both know that not even our oldest sister can hear of our plans. When night comes, I'm dressed in my mother's black trench coat, and Stasiek in my father's black jacket. If this were any other situation, I'd complain at the thought of wearing my parent's clothes. However, we have to stay unseen, and there's no other dark clothing that's warm enough. The both of us creep down the hallway on our tiptoes, garbed in our heavy coats. As we sneak out of the house, our cheeks start flushing at the freezing night air. But there is no time to waste.

A sensation of loss tells me that this trip will be vastly different from the others. Distanced from the evenings my siblings and I spent picking up hens by the base of their wings, carrying them to the safety of their coops. We laugh the whole time, perching them inside and petting their feathers so they can fall asleep soundly.

It's different from the times our parents bring us to the city, too. Whispering jokes into each other's ears as we sit patiently in the back of a carriage. And from how we join each other on walks to school.

Now it's up to Stasiek and I to face this alone.

Lantern in hand, I hush our work horse and guide my brother through the dark. The other horse in the barn makes no move besides a distant snore.

"You grab the reins and lead him outside," I whisper. Stasiek takes hold of the horse's reins after I unlock the gate. We take the smallest wood carriage, the one our family uses to carry hay in. Guiding the horse over, Stasiek and I attach the carriage to his harness.

It's only when we reach the outside of our village that I begin to have second thoughts about our dangerous mission. The trip to Koszelewy might take us hours in the dark. We could get lost, or worse, sick. I turn to look at my brother, who's nearly dozed off. The bitter wind blows past us and I huddle toward our oil lantern, listening to the faint gruffs of our work horse. He trudges us along and I imagine that only God knows how much time has passed. To me, it seems like hours. Part of me as well feels empathy for the horse.

We named him Artur. I think back as long as I can remember, and he has been in our stables. I've snuck him carrots and radishes, brushed and cleaned him, cared for him for years. Our parents tell us that the horses lived here even before we were born, which is why we should be so respectful of them. I hold that belief to this day.

I shake my head, blinking, and pull back on the reins. Now we stop in the outskirts of the town. Stasiek hops down from the carriage and ties the horse to a fence post. I blow out the lantern, my senses heightened. The moon peeks down at us through the thick clouds of snow.

Large walls of corrugated metal loom there in the distance. My brother and I sneak down an alleyway, our boots washing through dirty puddles. The factory goes on for the length of a field, emptied window sills allowing moonlight and flurries of snow to the floor. Eventually we reach an entryway through the alley. We don't say a word to each other. With a quick glance to my brother, I pick the lock and push it open.

The door announces our presence with a wretched scruff of rust. After we hurry inside, the place stays still. Stone blocks are piled in a corner, and I catch the sight of plywood planks resting against the wall. Despite the amount of materials, it still feels empty and big and unexplored. A thought of "we shouldn't be here" echoes in my mind. But Stasiek's thoughts come first as he finds a section of steel pipes and waves me over.

The pipes are heavier than expected, but we've successfully loaded the end of the carriage with a small pile. My brother and I stay in silence as we carry out this task, both of us keeping the horse in the back of our minds. Lucky for us he stays quiet. Clouds shroud the moonlight once more as we head back home, shivering and aching from the lifting. Stasiek looks paler than usual-- the adrenaline, or possibly the more obvious cold-- but I pull off the long shirt underneath my coat and give it to him anyway. He's right, the snow drifting to the ground does a great job at covering the horse and carriage's tracks. Doing my best to keep my hand steady, I relight the lantern and we set off again. Flakes tickle at my nose and eyebrows as we push through the flurrying wind.

"Stay awake for me, Stasiek. It's nearly dawn. We're almost there," I promise him.

"Okay Filip," He whimpers, forcing himself to sit upright. I grab his hand in my own, both of us shaking and frozen, but victorious.

The sky ahead of us melds into greys, blues, and whites as we approach our farm. A rustled neigh comes from the barn and my gaze shoots over. That means only one thing, someone's waking up the other horse. Which means someone-- probably Tata, knows this one is missing from the stable.

"Listen, if that's father out there, I'll take the blame. Don't say anything," I tell my brother. In range of the barn, we unload the carriage and lead the horse back inside.

Behind the barn doors is a very tired, yet relieved, Mama.

"M-Mamo?" Stasiek says weakly.

"Filip, Stasiek! What are you doing out here this early?" She questions.

"It's a long story, Mamo," I begin. She breathes out and brings the horse back into its space to rest. Stasiek and I glance at each other, still shivering with faces white as snow.

"Kazia told me that you had snuck out during the night. I've started a fire in the fireplace. *O Jezu,* you two must be freezing. Go on!" The two of us run inside without another word, stumbling out of our shoes and collapsing in front of the fireplace.

I'm not even upset with Kazia for telling on us; things could have gone much worse. In fact, I'm thankful. Even with the snow falling more heavily now, and the wind gusting against the walls, I feel calm and safe. My little brother and I, still in our parents' coats, fall asleep next to the fire.

Marzec (March) 1955

Instinctively leaning forward to catch the sack my father throws, I take a sharp inhale of the fresh air. We're out by the back of a building, one of the Governor's many. The home stands tall, painted with white and accented with gold. It's a beauteous display of money that the people don't have. And it's abandoned over half the year, only used for whatever important days the government needs it. Thankfully this is not one of those days and the home rests empty.

My father and I haven't gone far; by the looks of it we're still within Gmina Rybno. I got up early this morning to get ready for the trip. Since then, we've taken a horse and carriage through the hills. My father is already making his way down to the small strip of trees on the southwest end of the property. I follow, an axe and sack in hand.

"Would be nice to do this for a living, yeah?" Unsure if he's referring to the tree-cutting or the grandeur house, I shrug and agree with him.

"Yeah. Hard work, but sure." I say. He swings his own axe, splitting a crack into the tree.

"You know, there is a nice blacksmith who lives in Rybno. Your cousin Ania's husband. He is offering to be your mentor," Tata says. My mentor. He wants me to study carpentry or ironwork, in hopes that one day I'll be successful and wealthy. Or at least make enough to get by. But that was never my dream. Sure, Kostek is working out in Koszelewy for carpentry, and young Stasiek wants to become a blacksmith, but not me.

I want to be a watchmaker.

Kwiecień (April) 1956

It's the day before I'm supposed to move into the blacksmith's home. His name is Mr. Janusz, the husband to my good cousin Ania, and he will be my new mentor. This is as according to my father's guidance. I'm somewhat uneasy, miles from home and unable to pinpoint the cause of my discomfort.

As the horse pulls the carriage along the dirt road, I hold tightly onto the reins. Looking in front of me, I can see the home through the trees. At least there is no problem finding lumber here. From my sight I notice a man standing outside the house as well, presumably Mr. Janusz.

Lightly running my hand down the horse's nose, I feed it a carrot before stepping away. Then I open the back section of the carriage and reach for my possessions. But on the seat I find something: a pocket watch. The one that Stasiek and I fixed together.

All the memories rush back to me-- the old woman, my brothers and sisters astonished as I show them my collection, my parents and my friends. Shaking, I take the watch into my cupped palms. Then I step out and approach the man.

"Cześć," He greets me with a smile. Warm; understanding. We strike up conversation for a minute before he invites me inside. I stop him, reaching a hand to his shoulder.

"Thank you, Mr. Janusz. I would love to study with you, but I know there is someone better for you to teach," I say. Confused, but knowing, the blacksmith takes another look at me.

"You won't study as my apprentice?" He asks me. I rub my thumb over the pocket watch, still in my palm.

"Unfortunately, I must decline." I say slowly. "How about a new offer instead?" To this, he quirks an eyebrow. I strike the man a smile.

"I will become a watchmaker. But a watchmaker is nothing without his metal," I begin. "See, my young brother learns ironwork from my father. He would make for an excellent apprentice of yours. We are family, Mr. Janusz. I say, I will start my own shop with my brother Stanisław." A twinkle crosses the man's eyes. At this point I know it is my time.

"Return home, Filip," he shouts. "Return home and tell your father we've got business to attend to!" He waves a handkerchief as he sends me back off, my heart thumping with determination like the time when my siblings and I climbed to the top of the snow-clad barn in our youth.

Accusations

Glenn Woo got off his cot, kicking over a bottle of Jack Daniels from the night before and walked to his mirror, peered at his chin and his five o'clock shadow. Picking up his razor, the boat made him catch his balance as he let out a deep sigh into his reflection.

"Another day, same bull-"

"Lieutenant! You need to see this!" a voice came through his wooden door. Woo threw on his tank top and exited to the deck, where he was met by four men.

All of the men stood shoulder to shoulder out in the humid Hawaiian weather, legs shaking and voices breaking from panic. None of them said a word, only stared at their Lieutenant in charge of them.

Sun blaring, Woo was forced to put on his aviator sunglasses. He didn't realize it until then, but an alarm was echoing through the whole level.

All throughout the ship, there was chaos. Surrounding the five men, were ear- piercing screeches of emergency alarms. Soldiers of all ranks were sprinting through the corridors, incomprehensible alerts were played over the loudspeakers, and still the men had their vision fixed on the skies.

"What the hell is that!?" Glenn yelled at one of his men.

"Sir, in the sky, Sir!" Private Jefferson responded back, his voice starting to shake as it filled with anxiety.

The sight of Japanese fighter planes flying over the deep Hawaiian horizon threw the Naval Lieutenant into shock. A fleet of eight planes erupted past the USS Tennessee, and dropped hell from their back. On the bottom of either wing, a red circle was displayed. Eyeing those marks, Woo's confusion quickly turned to rage, only to be replaced by fear. The planes moved in unison, not breaking from their formation as they circled around the harbor. Flying back towards the ship, the fear in the Lieutenant's eyes was matched by that of the men in his charge.

Breaking out throughout the entire harbor, fires were as far as the eye can see. Anything in the water was prone to fiery destruction, including the SS Tennessee, where Lieutenant Woo and his men were stationed. Still in shock at the sight, he snapped out as one of his men, Private Jefferson, addressed Woo.

"Sir, we need a plan of action here," he said looking confused, but more importantly, scared, "we're sitting ducks out here."

Woo clenched his fists, and broke his stare from the sky and glared at his naval men.

"Jefferson, man the guns! I need Roberts and Johnston on the bow, and Fishmen with me at the comms station!"

The men broke out of their blank stares and rushed to their positions on their BB-43 Battleship, ready for the fight of their lives.

"Keep up, Private!" Woo yelled back to the scared soldier running a few steps behind him, trying to keep his footing while the restless waves crashed along the vessel.

"Echo-1-2, do you copy? This is Lieutenant Glenn Woo of USS Tennessee stationed at Pearl Harbor! We are under heavy attack, requesting evac. immediately!" Woo roared into a radio, praying to hear a voice on the other end.

Man, this is really happening, he thought to himself, I can't believe this is actually happening.

"USS Tenn-, we hear ya', sending a team over ASAP," a southern man answered back, calmly.

Loud sounds rang out through the air, as shells hit the water and began pummeling the ship. As one of the last ones made contact with water, mere inches from the stern of the ship, Private Fisherman was forced to his knees, his hands breaking his fall to the deck. Sitting up, Fisherman folded his hands together.

"Our father who-"

His prayer was cut short as the sound of bullets began piercing through the air.

"We're gonna get out of this, son." Woo said to the kneeling man, hand on his shoulder.

Suddenly, the explosions stopped.

"Jefferson to the bridge, they're turning around, I repeat they are turning around!"

The two men looked at each other as Fishmen got to his feet and both start sprinting up to the main level.

"Jesus, look at this," the private says while observing the waters, "how the hell are we gonna get out of this?"

"Lieutenant? The captains approaching starboard side!" Roberts said, in utter disbelief.

"Ah, if it isn't Mr. Glenn Woo. I call you mister here because you are here-by stripped of any authority here, you good-for-nothing scum," Captain Hotch claimed, nostrils flaring and fists clenching, "Was this your plan all along, Jap? Gain our trust, then stab us in the back? You make me sick." Woo's expression took a turn for the worse, being examined by his hero. "Throw him in a cell, boys!"

Motioning at the platoon men, Hotch tells them to take away their Lieutenant.

"No, sir!" Jefferson said from behind the men, slowly making his way to the front to address the captain one-on-one, "Our Lieutenant is the best there is, and he had nothing to do with this attack, Sir!"

"What the hell is this? Lock Mister Jefferson up while you're at it too, boys!"

The men stood there, angry and confused, unsure of what was happening or what to do next.

"No, Sir!" they all said, one by one, to the captain.

Stomping progressively got closer. Indistinct chatter is heard by all of the men, when a soldier emerged from the stairwell.

"Evac team, in position!" one soldier exclaimed into a headset. Just then, four more men came into sight.

"Is everyone alright?"

"Yes but some of these men aren't," Woo pointed to the monstrosity before them, fire and debris were floating all around the harbor, "they need your help, soldiers."

"Don't listen to this man, he's one of them! He's responsible for all of this!"

"Now you listen here, Captain. I have given my life countless times for this country, and I was born in raised in the wonderful state of Georgia, which is where my family is right now. So if it all means the same to you, I'm going back, you bigot." Woo shouted back, throwing his jacket over his shoulder and walking to the lifeboat in the water.

"Fine, Woo, but if I hear you have anything to do with this, you'll be sorry."

***

Out of His Shadow

The silk sheets brushed up against Cuinn's legs. He felt the warm sun coming through the window of the high-rise apartment. Art surrounded the room, vibrant colors popping off of the canvas and filling the small space. He shuffled around in his bed trying to get up but the king-sized fortress seemed to trap him. There was no urgency to leave; he didn't have a job or family or any friends, well maybe one.

"Knock, Knock- Cuinn, open up," Luke shouted without knocking. Luke was close with Cuinn. Ever since his parents died, he had been like a son to Cuinn. Being his mentor, Cuinn taught Luke everything he knew. "Come on Luke, you know you don't have to knock."

Luke admired Cuinn; he wanted to be just like him and appreciated how much he had taught him over the years. Luke slowly cracked open the door to the art-filled apartment. Warmth and joy filled the air as the bright colors bounced around the room. The art that lined the hallway lead to Cuinn's bedroom, filled with bags of money, fake ids, and endless disguises and suits. Cuinn didn't live a normal life. Constantly pretending to be other people, and having to run away from all of the problems he caused took a toll on him.

The rough hat gently scratched Cuinn's forehead as he slowly slipped it on over his head. All the months of continuous preparation lead to this moment. Cuinn swiftly stepped out of the van, with a smirk on his face. It was an easy job, Cuinn thought to himself as he approached the back door of the Museum. Avoiding detection, he carefully swung open the door and crept towards the storage area. Cuinn knew the perfect time to go in, the employees who worked in the back where all on break. He had three minutes to get out with the painting. He was after a newly acquired Van Gogh, just purchased at an auction for three million dollars. With no worries, Cuinn walked into the small area and scoured the room for his target. Hanging from the back shelf, there was big wooden box marked with a tag that said *Van Gogh*. Cuinn darted towards the painting and quickly exited the building.

Never having any set obligations, Cuinn was always free to do whatever he wanted to do. Luke and Cuinn headed out on the streets. The streets of New York were always welcoming with the onslaught of people. It may seem intimidating but Cuinn was used to it. It was home to him, wandering the streets and exploring for as long as he could remember. Walking out of the room they headed towards their favorite coffee shop. The smell of fresh coffee filled the air and welcomed them into the small shop.

"Hey, Nancy how are you," Cuinn said as he slowly strided towards the counter.

"I'm doing better now that you're here sweetie," Nancy said, while reaching for the already made coffee.

"Thanks, I'll see you tomorrow morning Nancy," he said, gently placing a twenty on the counter

Cuinn had met Nancy when he first moved to the city a few years back. On the run after almost being caught in his last big heist, he had to leave everything he had grown to love behind. Starting out in a new place was never easy for him; with the low profile he had to maintain to keeping most people at an arm's distance, he was rarely ever able to connect to someone. But something was different about Nancy. Despite his disdain for their coffee, he'd grown quite fond of their quick, daily banter. Nothing quite livened up his day like his daily small talk with Nancy. Cuinn always looked forward to his quick cup of coffee every morning.

"Hey Cuinn" Luke said, putting his hands into his pocket.

"Yes, Luke, what do you want" Cuinn responded angrily, knowing what Luke was going to ask.

"Can we finally pull a bigger job I'm tired of all of these small street jobs."

"Not yet, Luke, some things take time and you're not ready yet." Cuinn responded sternly.

Luke was more focused on the big jobs, always wanting to put himself in harm's way. No matter how many cons they did Luke was never pleased.

"I'm never going to learn if you don't teach me," Luke said furiously, as he threw his hands into the air

Cuinn stayed silent, he knew he had a point but he wanted to make sure Luke was ready before they did something that big. Doing a first big job is a lot harder than it seems. After all of the constant preparation, things tend to go wrong. Without the experience and pure dedication to the job, accidents happen frequently. But Luke didn't understand that he was just looking out for him.

***

The dark sky created a sense of eeriness, but the streets were still very much alive. Street and office lights illuminated the quiet sidewalk. The constant rush of cars made the city always full of life and noise. Silence was something they learned to live without. Endless businessmen filled the sidewalks, keeping the hope of a con alive. Loudly echoing off of the buildings, the ending of their footsteps marked the end of their short walk. The red neon sign marked their destination as they confidently entered the bar. Each night they traveled to a new bar, hoping to pull off an easy con. As they entered, they were greeted with looks of confusion and disgust. But these didn't seem to have an impact on Cuinn, as he slowly approached the bar.

"What can I get you, two gentlemen," The bartender said sarcastically.

"I'll have a scotch on the rocks, and just a club soda for him" Cuinn responded, turning his chair towards the pool table.

Cuinn smirked at Luke as he watched him head towards the pool table. Luke approached the group of men crowded around the table.

"Can I get a game?" Luke said confidently.

"You must be joking suit" One of the men replied laughing

"No, why are you, afraid tough guy?" Luke fired, as he picked up the pool stick.

"Not at all suit why don't we put some money on it if you're so confident." The man blurted out, slowly spinning the chalk on the end of his cue.

Cuinn loved how easily Luke could get someone so riled up. It made his job a lot easier.

"Yeah why not, how about 500 dollars," Luke responded with carelessness.

"Alright high-spender, we got a deal, but you're asking for it." The man snapped back with a cocky smile.

As Luke watched the man rack the pool balls, his confidence grew. He knew there was no chance of him losing, which made the game more fun. Luke has been playing pool ever since he first met Cuinn, and frankly was even better than he was. From the first shot, the man knew he was in for a surprise.

"Alright Luke if you want to be like me you need to learn the art of pool" Cuinn said, as he started to rack the pool balls.

"What's so important about pool?" Luke responded, squinting his eyes.

"It's the easiest con you can pull off, all you need is a little practice" Cuinn stated, as he leaned against the table getting ready to take the first shot.

"Okay Cuinn, but I'm going to need a lot of practice." Luke said, as he clumsily picked up the pool stick.

After time Luke slowly got better and better at pool. The daily hustle at the bar got easier every day. Learning to be a better thief, Luke wondered if he needed Cuinn anymore. All Cuinn did was hold him back, and keep him from doing the jobs he really wanted to do.

Luke pompously marched towards the bar with his newly acquired rewards. He loved the thrill of a simple hustle. The surprising stares always filled him with joy, as he quickly scammed them out of their hard-earned money.

"Did you see that Cuinn, I'm the best pool player in all of New York!" Luke said as he threw his hands into the air.

"I think you forgot about me," Cuinn said as he began to smile

"I don't know about that old man, when was the last time you beat me"

"I mean I did teach you everything you know," Cuinn said, adjusting his coat as he prepared to leave.

"Just face it Cuinn, you know I'm better than you."

Scam after scam, Luke was slowly realizing he didn't need Cuinn anymore. He was tired of being treated like the kid he used to be after all of the things he has been through. Constant "lessons" and "training" felt more like an excuse to keep him from doing what he has always wanted. Maybe he could do a heist on his own, he thought. It's not like he needed Cuinn anymore.

As Luke approached the bar, Cuinn smiled to himself. Maybe Luke was finally ready, he thought. Luke reminded Cuinn of himself when he was young; he remembered how free he felt and the constant need for activity. Sympathizing with Luke, Cuinn thought it was finally time to surprise him with his dream heist.

✳✳✳

It was a normal day like any other. Peeking through the window, the sun blinded Cuinn, waking him up. He sat up and gazed at the endless paintings filling his small bedroom. The countless scenes hung on the wall all represented a special moment in his life, helping him remember all of the heists he had done. Luke always thought it was corny and wondered why he wouldn't just sell them. Maybe he was just old-fashioned and sentimental, all the younger generation seemed to care more about money than the memories you make throughout your life.

Luke and Cuinn headed down the narrow sidewalks of New York. Ready to complete their nightly routine they scoured the corner for a small bar. Luke was tired of just watching Cuinn, he was ready to finally do this on his own. Cuinn looked up towards the buildings and spotted the small bar. Pacing towards the entrance, Luke tried to contain his excitement towards his first hustle.

"Are you ready Luke?" Cuinn asked, fixing his suit.

"I've been ready," Luke responded with passion, as he hastily headed towards the bar.

The small green door swung open as Luke walked towards the pool table. His heart raced as he approached the men at the table. Cuinn watched from a far as Luke missed every shot. With a look of disappointment Luke walked over to Cuinn.

"It's alright Luke, we don't have to win every time" Cuinn said as he pat Luke's back.

Without a single word, Luke walked by Cuinn and headed back out on the streets.

Luke awoke from a quick sleep. His eyes felt glued shut after the late night preparing for his first real job. The thought of doing something on his own terrified him, but he knew he was ready. After five years of continuous training and preparation, Cuinn finally wasn't holding him back. Coffee stains filled the small wooden table, scattered blueprints and plans occupied the remaining space in the room. It was an easy job, or so he thought- break in, get the painting, and leave. His target was an auction, he was after a rare Degas painting estimated to be worth millions. The plan was simple, after the auction when everyone was distracted he would slip in the back to "deliver" it to the buyer's house. All he needed was a delivery van and a uniform, just real enough to fool the man who guards the storage area. Once he got in the man would lead him right to the painting and just hand it to him. It was a foolproof plan Luke thought to himself, after countless restless nights and days studying the plans he thought he was finally ready.

✳✳✳

The morning sun lit up the room as Cuinn slowly edged his way out of bed. Ready to start the morning, he headed towards the closet. Preparing for the long day ahead, Cuinn slipped on his suit and exited the small apartment. He hadn't heard routine knock at his door in almost a week. Thinking nothing of it Cuinn walked down the sidewalk, heading towards the small coffee shop. Luke just must be tired he thought to himself as he entered the small building.

Cuinn loved his daily routine, he didn't have many people in his life who he cared about. Ever since he met Luke he was happy to finally interact with someone like him. Coming from a dark past, Luke didn't have anyone else to care for him. He was just focused on becoming a better thief. Cuinn liked that, it reminded him of himself when he first started becoming a con-artist. Constantly burying himself in his work, he always lost track of time. Maybe Luke was just planning a job for them Cuinn thought, he knew he would be back. Luke always came back.

Cuinn began to worry, as time passed he wondered what had happened to Luke. He has never been gone for more than a day, let alone a whole week. Beginning to ask himself what was wrong, Cuinn felt as if everything was his fault. The apartment felt empty without the constant laughs and small talk filling the room. Cuinn knew Luke had left him, even after all he had done for him. He couldn't help but to feel angry, all of the training and late night cons were for nothing. Luke was gone and felt like he could do better on his own.

***

The warm breeze brushed up against Luke's skin. Heading around the corner with urgency, he was finally ready to prove himself. He was tired of just being Cuinn's shadow, his whole life he had been trying to live up to Cuinn's expectations. Everything had to go perfectly or else it was wrong. Luke enjoyed being free, even though he appreciated everything Cuinn had done for him it's better that he is on his own. The street seemed to go on forever as he continued towards his destination.

The large gold columns marked the end of his short walk. Well-dressed men and women plagued the stairs of the grand building. Luke was nervous as he slowly headed towards the back of the building. Luke glanced at the *DO NOT ENTER* printed on the door in red letters. If Cuinn taught him one thing it was to be confident. Casually walking into the building, he took of his coat exposing his delivery uniform. His confidence diminished as stares were darted into his direction.

"Hey, who are you" Shouted a man from a distance.

"I'm Fred, from the delivery service," Luke said confidently, pointing to the badge on his shirt.

"Oh, right this way! The auction just ended" The man said, as he slowly lead them to the storage area.

Luke followed closely his heart beating faster each step. When the painting was in sight he knew what he had to do.

"Thanks sir, But I can take it from here." Luke stated, clenching his fists

"What company did you say you were from again?" The man stated in confusion, as he squinted at Luke's uniform.

"I'm from Freddy's delivery service," Luke said nervously, feeling the sweat start to accumulate on his palms.

"Sorry for the hassle but I need to check with my supervisor, it will just take a minute," The man said as he lifted his walkie-talkie.

Luke didn't know what to do, he couldn't let him talk to the supervisor or else everything would be ruined. Not every heist has to go according to plan, he had to improvise or he could get caught. Thoughts raced through his mind as he thought *what would Cuinn do.*

"Alright buddy, all of this time is just gonna add to my paycheck I'm not saying don't call your supervisor but if you really like your job, you should just let me do mine" Luke followed up.

The man slowly lowered his walkie-talkie as his confidence diminished. Without speaking, he walked Luke over to the storage area. Luke was astonished, hundreds of paintings crowded the small room. The colors seemed to light up the tiny space, the grassy scenes seeming to come alive. Luke felt immersed in the scenery, as if he was in the painting. He had dreamed of this moment since he became who he was. Continuously obsessing over his first real heist and he finally did it. Luke thought back to all the training, hours practicing the little things needed to do a job this big. He hated to say it but he couldn't have done this without Cuinn. Without the training Cuinn gave him, he may have never been able to accomplish this.

"Alright Freddy, this one is Mrs. Skies," the man said, handing him the painting.

"Her address is on this sheet." The man stated as he pointed to a line on the paper.

"Thank you, have a great day," Luke said, trying to contain his excitement.

Luke casually walked out of the building with the painting in hand. The sound of screeching tires filled the air as Luke rushed towards his getaway. He raced into the passenger seat of the large, white delivery van. Luke was proud of what he finally accomplished but knew Cuinn was the reason he was able to pull it off.

***

Cuinn woke up to a sharp knocking at his door. The sound of his footsteps bounced off the wall as he darted out of bed and approached his door.

"Hey Cuinn, open up," Luke said from behind the door.

Racing towards the familiar voice, Cuinn grabbed the door handle and swung open the entrance to his apartment. After Opening the creaky door, Cuinn was met with a surprise. In Luke's hand was a canvas, filled with vibrant colors.

"I brought you a memory, of my first real heist."

Between the Ivies

Kicking her feet back and forth, Ophelia looked up, doe-eyed, at the adults looming over her. She wasn't sure what they were talking about but they sounded upset. Ophelia was too busy to pay attention, distracted by the pretty princess stickers on the wall in front of her. It served as a good diversion from her fear of how high up she was. When she'd looked down earlier to see how far down the ground was, Ophelia began shifting uneasily, crinkling the thin paper over the padded table. Looking down again, she noticed the plastic tipped ties on her paper gown. Playing with them, Ophelia pretended to be one of the princesses on the wall. She looked up again.

"What do you mean you there's nothing wrong with her? She hasn't said more than ten words after two years. We've tried everything you said, nothing has worked," Ophelia's mom yelled.

Mommy sounds angry, Ophelia thought, sensing the tension that engrossed the room.

"Well, there is a possibility she won't speak. There are children who actually don't speak. I have a pamphlet with information on it here. It's not as uncommon as you would think," the doctor responded, outstretching a folded paper to Ophelia's parents.

Ophelia spotted the paper in her dad's hand. On it was another kid who resembled her in age, looking up, his hand covering his mouth. Around him were speech bubbles coming from everywhere except the child's mouth.

Eyes shining, Ophelia made eye contact with her parents and the doctor, her parents worry written across their half-grins directed at her.

***

There was no manual on how to be a silent teenager, so Ophelia learned the ropes as she went along. Ophelia walked hallways alone, listening and observing. Listening to the conversations of her classmates, Ophelia crafted stories blossoming from her own imagination. Because of the pieces of dialogue she missed, she created the beginning and ends of stories. For Ophelia, she liked to dive into their thoughts and feelings the most.

As she continued her daily walk down the hall, Ophelia felt a bit snappy in her judgements. She saw the new girl walking down the corridor, a pair of almost identical girls next to her. Ophelia identified the two girls as Andrea and Charlotte, to her own dismay. Just the sight of them prompted a memory Ophelia longed to bury.

***

Ophelia bounded into the large, carpeted classroom as fast as her short legs could carry her. Radiating joy, she headed for the writing table. Ophelia practically launched herself into the plastic red chair in front of the worn wooden desk. Hopping up, she grabbed a fresh sheet of white paper and a blue crayon as she began practicing her letters, a skill she had almost mastered because of all the practice she had at home. Guiding the crayon carefully along the page, Ophelia squinted and stuck her tongue out at every curve. So enthralled in her writing, she didn't even notice the two heads of bouncing curls that had come to sit beside her. Feeling a poke on her shoulder, Ophelia lifted her head towards the source of disruption, shifting her attention from the paper in front of her.

"Hi, my name is Andrea. This is my bestest friend Charlotte. What's your name?" Charlotte asked.

Looking at them, Ophelia didn't respond. Ophelia only ever really talked to her parents and her stuffies. She didn't really understand why, but she just didn't.

Andrea poked Ophelia again, this time repetitively, brow furrowed slightly as Charlotte had a look of confusion plastered on her small, round face.

"Hellllooooo? I asked you what your name was. It's not nice to ignore someone," Andrea said matter-of-factly.

Once again remaining silent, Ophelia looked at the two girls and then put her back down towards the table with the whiteboard.

"You're a meanie," Andrea said, Charlotte nodding next to her. Getting up from their chairs, they stuck their tongues out at Ophelia and ran off to another group of girls. "That girl over there is a weird meanie head. She doesn't talk when you talk to her and my mommy says it's rude to not answer when someone talks to you." Andrea went around telling her friends.

Ophelia felt a hot and heavy sinking feeling in her stomach. A tight lump formed in her throat as she heard all the kids start to not-so-quietly whisper about her. That's when her teacher stepped in to help.

"Andrea, calling someone a weird meanie head is not a nice thing to say about someone. Saying that about anyone who might be different than you is very mean. You need to apologize to her," her teacher said gently.

"But I don't want to apologize. She was being a meanie and a weirdo," Andrea said back, a slight whine in her voice.

"If you don't apologize, I'll have to put you in time out," the teacher prompted.

Andrea responded by crossing her arms over her chest and huffing.

Still with her head down, Ophelia glanced over and saw Andrea being guided by their teacher to a chair in the corner.

The word 'different' rung in her head, bouncing around the walls of her mind. She wasn't sure what it meant exactly, but it didn't sound very nice. Stares from her classmates bore into her back, leaving Ophelia to experience something she hadn't before, a feeling of being exposed and an inability to fight it. Without true understanding, Ophelia had felt toxic vulnerability for the first time in her short years, and it definitely wouldn't be the last time.

Ophelia looked back down and diverted her attention to her writing, a few little droplets falling onto her paper as she made sure the curves of each letter were perfect.

Consumed in her inner ramblings, Ophelia headed to her locker, trying to push her nervousness aside to get to her books for the day. As she approached, she noticed the group of kids look at her and quickly turn their backs. With the desire to melt into her locker and become invisible, Ophelia entered the combination as fast as possible, her fingers practically tripped over the other in her attempt, actually delaying the time it took her to normally open her locker. Shaking as she spun the dial, Ophelia sensed Charlotte and Andrea getting closer, not helping the trembling at all.

"Here comes Helen Keller again. Wonder if she'll actually speak today," Charlotte whispered loudly.

Jaden reacted first, his soft giggles turning into cackles and chuckling. Andrea grinned too.

Ophelia felt the all too familiar lump forming in her throat. The years of torment had given her a thick skin, but it never got easier. Wiping the stray tear that had escaped her eye, Ophelia looked over in their direction and saw them still laughing, all except for one. Nelly looked away from the group, a look of distant revulsion on her face.

Why wasn't she laughing at me? Is this some kind of sick joke? They're already laughing at me, why not make the pain worse, Ophelia thought to herself, nauseated from the encounter.

After what felt like hours, Ophelia grabbed her books and tried to compose herself. The gang of kids walked away, still basking in the glory of their torment, when Nelly looked back at Ophelia. Ophelia, consumed by her own feelings, appeared confused, her face slightly contorted. She looked up to meet the gaze of Nelly's concerned face. Both quickly looked away and hurried off to their first period class.

Sitting in her English class, Nelly tapped her pen to her lips, not paying any attention to the assignment on the board or the book in front of her.

Why had that girl not said anything to her? And why did she look disgusted with her afterwards? She hadn't done anything to her, she didn't laugh or make fun of her. But was that the issue she had with her, she thought to herself, guilt beginning to pool in the pit of her stomach.

No, I didn't do anything wrong to her, Nelly thought, getting defensive with herself. She shook her head, as if to try to physically rattle the feeling away. Looking up at the clock, Nelly realized she had spent the entire period wrapped up in her mind instead of in the book she was supposed to be reading. She quickly jotted down the assignment in her planner just as the bell rang for her next period.

Ophelia pushed open the double doors, the cool fall air, painting a rosy blush on her face. She followed her classmates outside to the football field, feeling the weight of her bag pressing heavily into her shoulder. Ophelia didn't participate in gym class, and her teacher didn't argue it anymore. At first, she feigned a different injury each week, providing a forged doctor's note every time. In the beginning, they were believable, however after a while, her gym teacher caught on and didn't bother trying to persuade her participate. So Ophelia sat on the bleachers.

The bleachers were her favorite place to write. They appeared to be run down, rust in some areas, screws missing in other. It creaked and echoed every time someone walked up the uneven stairs. It was about thirty feet high, and it was semi-secluded as it was pushed back towards the wooded area of the school. But Ophelia's favorite part was the vines of the ivy leaves tangled intricately along the sides of the bleachers, their deep emerald contrasting the dark gray metal. Too many, they were in bad shape, in need of renovation, but to her, they were her favorite place, a safe place for her.

Opening her worn leather-bound journal, Ophelia skimmed the numerous pages of her life, scribed carefully and neatly. She ran her fingers over the bound sheets, the feeling of the small depressions from her pen a familiar comfort. The cover of the journal was carved in various leaf patterns, including the ivies from the bleachers, Ophelia had done herself. She moistened the leather and engraved delicate patterns to emulate the veins of the chosen leaf at the time, firmly grasping the cool metal of the swivel knife between her thumb and middle fingers. Ophelia did this with all of her journals, not necessarily always using leaves, but personalizing them, figuratively and literally leaving her own mark on it. Her bookshelf was her own personal art gallery that displayed her skill across all medias. Some had watercolor swirled on the covers while some had pencil sketches stemming from her own pure boredom and writers block

A sudden loud twang of metal echoed on the corroded seats,

startling Ophelia out of her own head and demanding her attention to the source of the sudden noise. She heard Nelly grumbling to herself, not noticing Ophelia at all.

"Why do so many people take gym so seriously? It's just a game that I don't even want to play," Nelly mumbled, sounding annoyed as she pulled her thick sweatpants over her gym shorts.

Ophelia had seen her before, in the cafeteria, making her rotations to the different tables in the attempts to find her niche. Knowing how slim the pickings were for transfer students, Ophelia watched Nelly struggle to find her place. It was a hunter gatherer society; people stayed close to their own and no one crossed into other groups' territories.

At the end of week two, Ophelia saw that Nelly landed at the table belonging to Andrea and Charlotte. Sitting at a table close to theirs, Ophelia strained to listen to their conversation.

"So Nelly, what do you think of Northeastern so far," Andrea questioned intently.

Nelly looked down, pushing the food around on her Styrofoam tray with her plastic fork. She was hesitant to answer because the first two weeks hadn't been the best. No one had given her a hard time, but had been so isolated, she almost wished they had.

"It's been alright. My classes are decent but,-" Nelly started but was soon interrupted by Andrea.

"Yeah that's cool. So listen, we all think you'd be a good fit with our group, you have a lot of potential with us here," Andrea said. Charlotte nodded while looking down a study guide. Jaden was completely oblivious to their conversation, talking to a group of underclassmen.

What the does she mean by 'potential', Nelly wondered to herself, questioning if that was a compliment or an insult.

"Thanks… anyway I just wanted to thank you guys for being so ni-," Nelly tried to say before getting interrupted once again by Charlotte. She was beginning to stand up, eyes glued to her phone. Andrea stood up almost reflexively and zombie like, Jaden slowly rising as well.

"Anyway, we have to go now, it's been really great hanging with you. We should hang again on Monday. See you later," Charlotte said, looking up for a second flashing a smile and returning her gaze back down to her phone. She walked away, Andrea and Jaden following close behind.

Wait, what just happened? Was she even listening, were any of them listening, Nelly questioned to herself silently, sitting there in shock after the conversation she just had. Was it even a conversation if they were interrupting her every sentence? Why did she even bother talking, she thought.

That was Nelly's first introduction to Northeastern High School and these were the people she decided to stick to, even though she didn't have much of a say in the matter. She hasn't been able to complete a sentence since she's been at the school.

Looking up, Nelly saw the girl she had bumped into in the hallway. She saw the girl look quickly back into her journal.

What's the point of trying, she didn't make a peep before, she thought defensively.

Then again, no one was really extending the olive branch to me, Nelly thought again. Clambering up the bleachers, Nelly approached the girl, her nose buried deep within the pages of her antique looking notebook. She sat down carefully, not sitting too close to her.

Damn it, what's her name? This is going to be really uncomfortable if I don't know her name, Nelly thought to herself, scanning the mystery girl's things to try and gather information on her. Looking down, she stopped when she spotted an English test sticking out of her backpack.

"Ophelia Johnson," she read carefully, making sure that was actually the girl's name before speaking.

"Hey, Ophelia."

Ophelia quickly looked back into her notebook after Nelly looked over at her. She was trying to figure out what Nelly's angle was. While it sounded like paranoia, it was really Ophelia's cautious nature. In her experience, everyone had an angle. She began to feel very uneasy as the girl sat down next to her, leaving a large space between them. Ophelia felt her heart begin to race, sweat beading on her forehead. Hear breath became more labored, feeling more and more lightheaded. Not moving her head, Ophelia saw Nelly looking her up and down in her peripheral. Feeling the anxiety bubbling in her stomach, Ophelia desperately wanted to avoid a second confrontation when she heard Nelly say, "Hi Ophelia."

Ophelia had become paralyzed with apprehension and for the first time in her life, her thoughts stopped. She began to shut down. She heard Nelly continue to speak to her, but couldn't understand what she was saying. It sounded like Nelly was underwater, but it was Ophelia who felt like she was drowning. She felt herself put down the journal, but it was like someone else was in control of her body and she was just along for this unpredictable ride. Internally, she screamed to pick the journal back up, but Ophelia's body refused to listen, too far into flight mode to come back. Ophelia heard Nelly's voice begin to raise when she felt herself stand up, grab her bag, and sprint down the bleachers, her mind blank and her body numb.

"Hey Ophelia."

Nelly had gotten no response from Ophelia, furthering her frustration. She decided to repeat herself.

"Hey Ophelia." No response.

Okay, now this is getting annoying. What is this girl's deal, Nelly questioned to herself.

Ignoring the silence, Nelly continued,

"Listen, I'm not very confrontational but I want to know why you gave me such a dirty look in the hallway at your locker. I didn't say anything to you and I didn't laugh at you, so what gives?" Nelly surprised herself with how forward she was being. She had been on edge since transferring to the school, but this was the first time she unleashed it.

Her response was again silence. Nelly's blood began to boil. Why wouldn't she answer her?

"Hey, I'm talking to you," Nelly snapped as she watched Ophelia put the journal down. Forget feeling guilty, this girl was downright rude, Nelly thought angrily.

"Say something, you freak," Nelly exclaimed, raising her voice louder.

Ok Nelly, that was too far, she thought, scolding herself.

It must have struck a chord with her because right after, Ophelia got up and ran off the bleachers, leaving her journal behind.

Nelly picked it up and stood up, about to call after her, wanting to apologize for the name calling, but realized she was too far away to hear her. Plopping back down still a little peeved about the lopsided altercation, Nelly realized she had been white knuckling the journal. She took a deep breath and eased her grip, watching her skin go back to its natural color. Taking note of the ink that spilled over the side of the paper, Nelly delicately brushed her fingertips across the pages. Curiosity overcoming her, Nelly opened the journal to a random page. Words exploded across every sheet, scrunched up and neat, as if trying to make sure she didn't run out of room to write in a journal with 500 pages easily. She continued to flip through and saw that it was nearly filled, each teeming with Ophelia's thoughts and writings. Nelly was absolutely floored.

"You know, for a girl that doesn't talk, she sure does say a lot," Nelly said out loud to herself. As she continued to flit through, she landed on a creased entry entitled, *Between the Ivies*. The page had clearly been opened to a lot, judging by the deterioration of the spine on that page. Nelly couldn't stop herself from reading, the previous feelings of anger now turned to interest.

Between the ivies is where I stay for peace of mind and balance. What a strange concept, finding solace in a place where so many people have filled my life with torment, but you can't control where you find inner peace, at least I can't. It's a place where I've reflected on my life's choices, on why I've continued this life of solitude and on why I've continued a life of silence. It's funny to me, because I'm the loudest and quietest person I know. No one has really accepted my "selective silence" and I wonder if maybe someday I'll speak outside the confines of my home, finally share my ideas with the world, see if they make any change in even just one person's life. That would be enough for me. But I can't imagine they will. I've already been branded the "weirdo" and the "freak". I've been carrying that badge for a while. Oh well, damned if you do, damned if you don't. For now, I'll stay entwined with my ivy leaves and remain being as loud as I am.

So enthralled in the writing, Nelly almost missed the bell ringing, signaling the end of class. She looked up and saw everyone heading inside. Snapping the journal shut, Nelly stuffed it into her bag and ran down the bleachers, heading back into the school.

Ophelia opened her front door, sending it almost off the hinges. Reaching her arm behind her, she slammed it so hard it practically shook the foundations of the house. Ophelia's mom emerged from the doorway leading to the kitchen, wiping her hands on a dish towel.

"Rough day, huh," she asked her daughter, her eyes sympathetic and caring.

Ophelia shot a look towards her mom and asked, "Is it that obvious?"

Her mom walked towards her, opening her arms to pull Ophelia into a hug. Usually, Ophelia wasn't one for affection, but today, she reciprocated it without hesitation. Burying her face into her mother's strong shoulder, Ophelia allowed a few tears to fall, before the true emotional exhaustion of the day wracked her body with soft sobs.

***

Ophelia and her parents had an interesting relationship. She was an only child and her mother stayed home, while her father worked as an engineer. Even though he worked in such a science heavy career, he was actually the one who introduced Ophelia to literature and the art of writing a letter. She remembers the lesson he gave her when she was in the third grade.

"Ophelia, I'm going to show you the ancient art of letter writing. It's starting to die out but it's people like you that can keep it alive," her dad told her, looking deep into her dark brown eyes. She nodded enthusiastically and watched her father intently as he scrawled across the page with a fountain tip pen. It was mesmerizing and earth altering for Ophelia. It opened a new world for her. Ophelia's father recognized this early on, watching her chicken scratch spread across loose leaf paper from her school notebook. On Ophelia's tenth birthday, he gifted her with a leather bound notebook and a set of pens and from that day on, that's how Ophelia communicated with the world. She wrote letters to her parents and they wrote back to her.

***

Sitting alone on her bed, Ophelia stared at the ceiling, the silence closing in on her. Usually, she appreciated this time of day, a time to collect her thoughts and maybe write them down, but she felt like she was missing a huge chunk of herself. She was forced to deal with her emotions inside rather than scribbling them out on pages and pages of her notebook.

How could I have been so stupid, Ophelia thought to herself, her stomach flip flopping as she thought about Nelly reading her countless entries.

What if she shows Andrea and Charlotte? Who am I kidding, she *is* going to show the rest of them. They're probably already laughing about it right now. Is it considered social suicide or manslaughter if I did it to myself, Ophelia questioned to herself dramatically. She reached over to her nightstand and pulled the chain, letting darkness flood the room. Ophelia knew she wouldn't be sleeping tonight, but she didn't want any light on at all.

Nelly hadn't left her room since she got home except for the occasional snack or bathroom break. She was absolutely captivated by Ophelia's journal. Her thoughts and feelings were written in a way that transcended writing and became their own genre of art. One entry read:

After years of being called various names behind my back, one that always hits me hard is being called Helen Keller. It still hurts, but hurts for so many reasons. One reason is that it presumes that I cannot see, which is the complete opposite actually. I see perfectly fine, I just see differently than other people. But what I think is the real shame is that so many people can see but have no perception, no understanding and they are so unwilling to open their eyes.

Nelly had never met someone like this, and she still technically hadn't. But she felt like she had, as she ran her fingers across the pages and down the spine. Reading these emotions and these ideas, she felt like she had known Ophelia for years.

This is a massive invasion of privacy, but I can't stop reading, Nelly thought, feeling a bit guilty. Reaching for her bedside table, Nelly pulled the chain on her lamp, illuminating a small area of her room, getting ready to settle in for a long night of reading.

Ophelia walked into school feeling naked. She had been so anxious and unnerved from the previous day's events to the point of nausea. She was ready to walk into school to be crucified by Andrea and Charlotte or even worse, Nelly, whose anger and annoyance with her was fresh. Ophelia walked to her locker, her head down, when she saw a pair of shoes standing by it. She looked up to see an all too familiar face, holding the object of Ophelia's anxiety and a white envelope with Ophelia's name scripted on it.

Well this is the end for me. I just hope it happens fast, Ophelia thought to herself, bracing for the worst torment she ever anticipated getting.

Nelly yawned as she walked to her locker, clutching her coffee in her hands, her lifeline for the day. She had spent the night, pouring over the pages of Ophelia's journal, trying to gain insight on her and her thoughts. It turns out, the guilt she felt in English class was rightful guilt. Nelly had been quick to frustration, but she wasn't really sure on how it could have gone differently. Ophelia didn't speak, so how was she supposed to break through to her, to understand her?

Nelly walked down the hall to Ophelia's locker. Her original plan was to return the journal to her, but that was before she spent hours on end reading it. Wanting Ophelia to understand her misjudgment, Nelly wrote her a letter to explain everything. Approaching the locker, Nelly began to slip the letter into one of the narrow openings, but before she could do so, she was stopped by the sound of approaching footsteps. Turning on her heels, Nelly met Ophelia's gaze. The air between the two was saturated with a mutual unsettling feeling. At this time yesterday, they had been strangers, only seeing each other in passing, but as they stood here, they were two people who had greatly misunderstood the other.

I guess I'm going to have to break the tension here, Nelly thought as she began to speak. She looked down at the journal and extended her arm out to Ophelia.

"I wanted to, uh, return this to you. You, um, forgot it yesterday on the bleachers."

Ophelia slowly reached out and grabbed it from Nelly, who wasn't done speaking.

"I think we got off on the wrong foot yesterday and both, uh, misread the situation, so I wrote you this to try and explain myself a little bit," Nelly stammered out, struggling to find the right words. She extended her arm again with the white envelope this time, the metaphorical olive branch she had wanted to extend the day previous. Ophelia grabbed the envelope and opened it slowly.

With no clue as to what she was enclose, Ophelia ripped open the envelope. Her mind was racing almost as much as her kick drum heart. With shaky hands, she pulled out the letter and began to read it.

Dear Ophelia,

I'm so sorry. I'm sorry for not sticking up for you, for blowing up at you, for invading your privacy (so not cool of me at all), but most of all for seeing but not understanding. After reading your journal, which I apologize for doing so again, the insight I gained goes way deeper than surface level. Your words reached deep inside my heart and traveled up into my brain at the same time. Your view on life is like no other and goes far beyond the pages of your journal. You have helped me start to view the world in a different light and I hope you can forgive me for my actions these past few days. I would like to get to know you outside of your journal.

I do feel a little conflicted though. While I regret the way I spoke to you yesterday, I stayed up late wondering how I could have done it differently and I couldn't figure out how. I could have kept talking to you until I was blue in the face and I'm not sure we would have ever communicated once. Without reading your journal, I wouldn't have ever known you were mute, or as you put it, "selectively silent". I hope you can understand where I'm coming from because I now understand where you're coming from. Maybe we can try this again?

-Nelly

Ophelia looked up from the letter and at Nelly who was waiting, patiently, picking at her fingernails.

"I'm hoping we can start over because I feel like there's a chance we could be friends but if not it's totally cool I get it, I completely underst-," Nelly stopped for a second and then said,

"I'll shut up now and get to my point, hi, I'm Nelly. You don't have to answer that." Nelly stretched her arm out again, inviting Ophelia to shake her hand, smiling softly. A few moments passed and time seemed to freeze. Ophelia's mind raced and went blank for the umpteenth time in the last few days. She felt the knot in her stomach begin to untie itself and felt the anxiety release its grip on her. Her brain didn't know what to do next, but her heart did. Her arm stretched out to meet Nelly's and what happened next was almost like an out of body experience.

"Hi, I'm Ophelia."

＊＊＊

According to the Law

"**B**y nature of a law enforcement job, one can conclude that there are many occasions when a police officer faces a moral dilemma. The question is *when* an officer will be faced with one. The process can be difficult but it will be worth it in the end when you get to have a part in helping others by making your community a better, safer place." said the chief. His eyes scanned the room of recruits, silently and with gratification for what was to come for these future officers. A satisfied, almost nostalgic, expression rested upon his face, as if he missed the years he worked as an officer. I could imagine Chief seeing us as a reflection of himself when he was in our shoes years ago. After a pause, his speech resumed, "No matter how hard it gets, a job as a police officer is, by far, one of the most rewarding occupations available. As hard as academy training was, the field training was even harder, and you guys have worked your butts off for the past four and a half months. Tomorrow will be the start of your new beginning, and with that, Brontell Police Academy wishes you all the best of luck at your new job."

Following the end of his speech came a round of applause from the other police officers in training. The replay button suddenly popped up on my screen, signaling that the video was over. The palms of my hands held up my head as I stared at the screen, reminiscing my time at the academy. This video would always be special to me because without it, I would have nothing to remember my time there, besides my graduation certificate and memories. I would be forever grateful for my best bud,

Herbert, who filmed this important moment. Unfortunately, Herbert got a job at a station two towns away, so I'll have to find someone else I would connect well with. Through the dark, my eyes settled on the glow of the digital clock. It was getting close to eleven and I needed as much energy as I could muster up for the following day, so I decided to get some sleep.

Waking up the next morning was rough. Dark circles definitely gave away my restlessness. Climbing into my uniform, my mind moved a million miles an hour. I was thinking of all the possible things that could go wrong. Like a child anticipating his first day of school, my fingers fidgeted nervously. Walking through the doors of the police station, I suddenly felt refreshed, my lack of sleep and anxiety had completely dissipated.

"New officer?" asked a woman at the front desk.

"Uh, yes ma'am."

"Name?"

"Dan Kozowski"

Crossing my name off the list, she instructed me, "Just follow the signs to the conference room, good luck!"

Shortly after I arrived at the room, an older man walked in and proceeded to the podium at the front. The chatter slowly came to a stop as people looked up, recognizing he was waiting on their silence.

"Hello fellow officers, I am Chief Derek Beckett. To get to know each other, I will be assigning partners who you will be on duty with every day and working with for every case that comes your way for the next two months. You'll get to know the rest of the bunch by passing one another here in this station. Brennan and Brown."

I watched as a heavyset officer walked to the front of the room followed by another, her blond ponytail flowing behind her. Chief continued reading off the pairs of officers, each time, both getting up, making their way to the door. The process lasted what seemed like forever until finally, he called my name.

"Kepner and Kozowski."

My feet seemed to move on their own, forcing me to walk up to the front. My eyes scanned the room to see who else was walking. I didn't know what to expect; maybe someone well-built and tough looking.

It landed on a male, brunette just like me, but about a couple inches shorter.

"Phil Kepner," he said with a friendly smile, his hand extended in front of me.

"Dan Kozowski," I said shaking his hand. He seemed nice, I think we'll get along fine.

Chief Beckett's voice could still be heard calling names. Ugh. This was going to be awhile, he was still on letter K, and the roster seemed to go on for miles.

"Okay, so it looks like today we're on highway duty. We have to park at the nearby restaurant and catch people speeding. It is important we are available in case of a car accident," I said. I offered to drive, feeling as if I wasn't going to get much more action than this.

"Can we grab some food before we head there, though? I know we both brought cold lunch from home, but in case I get extra hungry," questioned Kepner.

"Sure, the more food, the better."

As I was driving, Kepner turned on the radio to a pop rock station and started singing along, startling me. Noticing me flinch, he laughed and nudged my arm. He only became more confident throughout the car ride and I couldn't help but join in; I loved this song. The atmosphere between us was light and it reminded me of my days with Herbert. I could really see us being great partners and working well together. Maybe he'd turn out to be the friend I was looking for.

The sound of a siren could be heard intertwining with the words of the song. The sound was still pretty new to me, so I didn't realize that it wasn't part of the song until after cars started pulling to the side.

"Oh! Whoa, why did you turn on the siren?" I exclaimed.

"Because we have to get to our chicken nuggets. I'm starving."

"You can only turn the siren on for emergency purposes."

"This is an emergency, I'm starving and we need to get to our spot soon. The quicker we get our food, the quicker we get there."

That wasn't a logical reason. Yes, we were new to this whole police officer thing, but I still understood what we should and shouldn't be doing. Although I was reluctant, I didn't want to cause a rift between us, so I let it go until we got to the fast food place.

We ended up ordering much more food than we initially planned. Kepner gave half of it to a homeless man sitting outside, who we had passed when walking into the place.

"Huh, I'm surprised Kepner."

"What?," laughed Kepner.

"I don't know, you just seemed like the type of guy who would believe in the whole 'Nothing is handed to you, work hard and earn it' mentality."

"Well, everyone loves food right? Sharing is caring!"

Once outside the restaurant, we ate our food, watching cars cruise by. So far, no exhilarating car chases or wheel screeching. A couple miles here and there above the speed limit wasn't necessary to give out a ticket.

"Kepner?"

"Yeah, man?"

"You don't think we're being too lenient right? Letting everyone drive by?"

"Nah, don't worry about it. We all know that a 55 miles per hour limit is really a 60. Besides whenever I drive next to a police car, they've always accelerated faster past me."

"If you say so," I shrugged.

"Hey Dan, that car kind of looks hot boxed," said Kepner pointing at a beaten up black Camry that was pulled to a stop at the end of the parking lot.

"It does look foggy but I think it's because they're just taking a smoke."

"I'm going to question them just to be safe," said Kepner as he steps out of the car. My eye twitched; this didn't sit well with me. He was making me nervous and I was going to yell something out after him, but he was already a couple feet away from the teenager's car by the time I thought of what to say. I snapped out of it and quickly ran to Kepner's side.

"License and registration please," said Kepner to the driver.

"What? We haven't done anything wrong officer," said the passenger of the car, the driver too stunned to say anything.

"Then why does your friend over here," asks Kepner pointing to the driver, "look like a deer caught in headlights? Your car is a little foggy."

"Officer, I have no idea what you're talking about, we don't smoke weed and we don't have any on us," said the passenger, as his tone shifted and eyes narrowed, knowing what Kepner was implying.

"It doesn't even smell like weed in here," said the driver, finally finding his voice as he held up his cigarette.

"Oh yeah? Pop open the trunk," demanded Kepner.

"Kepner, a word," I said to him, stepping away from the car.

Annoyed, Kepner bumped into my shoulder, "What do you want Dan? They were just about to crack."

"You cannot search their trunk, it isn't right. They haven't done anything wrong, they don't have to obey," I said to Kepner.

"Well, they will, I'm a police officer."

"They have to obey if they're in the wrong but even then they don't have to if they know their rights."

"They're teens. They're stupid, they'll obey," replied Kepner as he walked away, ending our conversation.

At their car, the driver, most likely not wanting to cause any more trouble, handed over his paperwork and opened up the trunk. Inside there wasn't weed, but fireworks.

"Well kids, you might not have weed but you have fireworks and in this state, fireworks are illegal."

Turning to me he said, "Kozowski, I'm going to write this stuff down." Pulling out a notebook, Kepner headed back to our cop car.

***

After the incident with the teens, nothing else went on. Kepner played Candy Crush on his phone while I was on the lookout.

"Hey, Kepner?"

"Yeah, man?"

"Even though everything is and has been going smoothly, I think you should still be alert. And stop playing that game," I said as I pointed at his phone. It wasn't like he could see me anyways when his head was faced down.

"It drained me, I'm really tired out from it."

I rolled my eyes, nine o' clock seemed so far away, yet so close.

"Hey man, let's head back to the station now," said Kepner, looking at his brightly lit screen.

"It's not nine yet. Our shift ends at nine."

"It's eight-forty man, nothing has happened all day and nothing will happen in twenty minutes," said Kepner, agitated.

"The station is literally seven minutes away, we'll be back too early," I said back annoyed.

"Then we'll just drive to the gas station real quick, grab a late night snack. We've been sitting in this damn car for hours," said Kepner exasperated, getting angrier each time I talked back. Our argument continued on for a couple more minutes, as the time turned to 8:47, so I decided we could leave because we would only be back early by about five minutes.

Back to the station, Chief Beckett was stood behind the front desk, waiting for all the officers to come back from their shift.

"Kepner. Kozowski," said Chief Beckett nodding, acknowledging us.

"Hello sir," I said.

"How was the first day as a police officer?" he questioned.

"Good sir, it was very good," answered Kepner.

No. No, it was not a good first day, Kepner. You kept doing things that an ethical police officer wouldn't do, and I wasn't comfortable with that. I didn't agree with some of your actions but you kept reassuring me that it was okay, I thought to myself

"That's good to hear. Please return your body cams here," Chief Beckett said pointing at the bin on top of the front desk. Placing our body cameras into the bin, it was then that I realized our cameras had a green light on.

Beyond All Odds

"Good morning, children," Mrs. Heinsworth said in a saccharine sweet voice, looking over to Chloe and her brother, Joseph.

The children opened their eyes slowly and yawned as they huddled under their bedsheets.

"Don't wanna wake up," Joseph mumbled.

"Five more minutes," Chloe groaned.

"Nope, get breakfast while it's hot!" she ordered.

Mrs. Heinsworth grabbed them, a wrist in each hand, and dragged them out of bed. As the kids fell onto the carpet, they both woke up immediately.

"Ouch, okay, okay!" Chloe yelped, standing up and helping Joseph up as well.

They followed Mrs. Heinsworth down the hallway where her husband, Mr. Heinsworth stood before the stovetop, flipping burnt pancakes.

"Took you two long enough to get up," the man muttered.

The children sat down at the table, while Mr. Heinsworth dropped their plates in front of them with a clatter. They sat down, and nibbled on pancakes. Silence was a common trait of the Heinsworth household. It was very businesslike and formal. Mr. Heinsworth sipped his coffee while scrolling through the news on his iPhone, while his wife began cleaning up breakfast.

"Oh, honey, don't forget to remind the children," she suddenly spoke.

"About...? Oh! Yes. Children, there is couple coming to visit you today. They're thinking about adopting you." Mr. Heinsworth informed the siblings as he went through the mail.

Chloe and Joseph looked up from their plates and they both dropped their forks.

"*Really? What?! Today?* What time?" Chloe and Joseph asked excitedly.

"Calm down. People don't like noisy children," Mrs. Heinsworth snapped, while rolling her eyes, shooing the children away. "Grab your backpacks, the school bus will be here shortly,"

The school kids slipped on their bland grey tennis shoes.

"Chloe, I wish I had light up shoes," Joseph sighed and put his head down. "All of my friends have them. Why can't I?" Joseph complained.

"At least you have something to cover your feet and keep them from the hot pavement. Don't worry about what they have and what you don't have. The Heinsworth's won't be happy to hear about you complaining about what shoes you want," Chloe gladly explained to Joseph.

Chloe and Joseph raced out the door with the backpacks in hand. Dashing all the way to the corner where the yellow bus picked them up, the children began their day. While there were other kids who walked down to the bus stop with their parents every day, Chloe and Joseph played tag with one another until they could see the bus in the distance. Joseph tried to dodge Chloe's hand from tagging his arm. He was running on the curb when one of his sneakers slipped off, and then he was running in the road. Chloe took a big step and lunged toward Joseph. Grabbing his sleeve, she pulled him back on the sidewalk yelling at him. He ignored her and continuing the game of tag and running away from her.

As Chloe saw the bus making its way to the corner, she let out a sharp scream to her brother.

"Bus!"

Joseph's head spun backwards, as his body did a 180, turning to run towards his backpack. Picking them up, both brother and sister swung their backpacks over their heads in unison, landing on their backs with a loud *thud.* Pulling up, the bus made its way towards the kids, all anxiously waiting to get on. As was typical for any morning, as soon as the doors flew open, there was organized chaos as the other kids clambered with one another to get on first, so they could rush to the back to find their seat. But, just as was normal for these kids, Chloe did what her and Joseph did every morning-taking Joseph by the hand, she looked both ways across the street before leading him towards the open doors of the bus. Pushing Joseph ahead of her, Chloe followed, her old shoes clambering up the stairs.

"Bus!" yelled Chloe as she saw it coming around the corner. They ran over to the fence, where they had left their backpacks. In unison, they swung their backpacks over their heads and onto their backs. As the bus arrived, the two stood on the curb waiting for the flashing lights and the stop sign to swing out from the side. Chloe grabbed Joseph's hand looking both ways before leading him across the street. The door of the bus opened and Chloe pushed Joseph ahead to get on first, following him. Her shoes clambered up the old stairs.

"Good morning, Mr. Larry," Chloe greeted the bus driver.

"To you too, Miss Chloe," he kindly nodded to her as she took her seat, right next to Joseph, who favored the spot closest to the window.

They were one of the first stops to be picked up; they had a while before they arrived at school.

Joseph asked in a worried voice, "Chloe, do you think they will like us? The parents?"

"Of course they will. Why wouldn't they?"

"Because Mrs. and Mr. Heinsworth sure don't," Joseph mumbled while looking down at the ground. Chloe paused.

"Well, that's just because the Heinsworths are old and nasty and weird," Chloe whispered the last part.

The bus suddenly lurched to the side, as the rear tire bounced over the curb, turning into the school parking lot. Chloe held onto Joseph so he wouldn't slam into the window. The other children screamed in excitement as they bounced up in their seats.

"Is everybody okay?" Mr. Larry yelled back.

"Yeah," shouted the kids.

Mr. Larry brought the bus to a stop at the entrance of the school, and swung open the door. All the kids stood up at once and piled into the center aisle. Chloe stepped out into the isle and blocked the kids from walking past to let Joseph get out ahead of her.

"I forgot where my classroom is," Joseph informed her, embarrassed. They had been in several different elementary schools, and Joseph often mixed up all of his different classrooms.

"That's okay, I remember." Chloe assured her brother. She led him down to the first grade hallway, all the way to the last classroom, where Mrs. Garcia's class lined up.

"This is your class, right?" Chloe checked to make sure.

"Yeah, that's Ryan and George right over there! Bye, Chloe!" the younger sibling said, racing off to talk to his friends. Chloe smiled and turned around and began to walk to the third grade wing.

School went by slowly that day. Chloe's mind wandered as her attention focused on the couple who was coming to see them. Just as any other day, she couldn't wait until lunch because she was able to eat with her brother. She barely paid attention to the new math chapter about adding decimals.

In the chaotic clamor of the lunch room, she impatiently knelt on her seat at the lunch table waiting for Joseph. She watched as he made his way into the lunch line, picked up his food and waved to him as he picked up his head and looked for her. Today was their favorite meal, popcorn chicken and curly fries. Although school lunches weren't the best, they always looked forward to it.

"Joseph, we have to be on our best behavior tonight. It is really important that we show our manners because nobody wants kids who are rude."

"Okay Chloe." replied Joseph, munching happily on a bite of chicken. They mainly talked to one another since they always had new things to talk about. Each was the other's best friend, as they knew that they could only rely on each other.

Chloe and Joseph had gone back to their respective classrooms to finish the rest of their day at school. The bell ringing was like a beautiful melody to Chloe's ears. She packed up her pencil case and raced to the first grade wing to meet her little brother.

The siblings climbed up the stairs, while grabbing ahold on the railing to pull themselves up. They walked to the fourth seat behind the bus driver, looking back at the older kids in the back of the bus.

"Are you ready?" exclaimed Chloe, "I'm so excited to meet this couple coming tonight!"

"Me too, Chloe! I hope they have a dog!" At the stop before theirs, Chloe helped Joseph put his backpack on. At the last stop, the bus pulled to the side of the road and their bodies jolted forward as Larry pressed his foot on the brakes. Chloe stood in the isle, as Joseph followed and they walked down the stairs. The two raced back up the street to the front porch. They swung the door open, bashing it into the wall.

Mr. Heinsworth's voice echoed off throughout the house as he yelled, "What did I tell you about the door? Don't bash it into the wall!"

"Sorry, Mr. Heinswoth, we didn't mean it," Chloe apologized for the both of them. Not really caring about the door, they went into the bedroom that they shared.

Chloe sat down next to her bed and spread her homework across the floor.

"I can't believe I have to do all of this by tomorrow. I don't even know how to do half of these math problems! I need someone to help me," she said frustrated. Joseph sat on his bed playing with his pillows, pretending they were people as Chloe tried to start on the easier problems, but couldn't focus with Joseph's voice in the background. Chloe had always needed to work in silence. But with Joseph in the room, it was never quiet. There were different voices coming from across the room and banging when toys hit the floor.

"Joseph, you are so lucky that you don't have any homework, it's not fair. I don't want to do any of this." Joseph giggled in response to Chloe. She knew that she needed to get it done before the couple came because she wouldn't have time to do it when they left. The past times, the people stayed late and she was too exhausted from all of the excitement of the day.

After spending a few hours talking amongst themselves about what their life might change into if the meeting went well, and finishing homework, Mrs. Heinsworth called the kids to wash up and wear the formal clothes she had laid out on the bed for them.

"Wash your face, Joseph," Chloe told her brother, pushing him into the bathroom. She went back to their bedroom to change into the pink dress that had an elegant white collar and belt. Once she was done and had slipped on some white socks with a pink ruffle at the top, she went out to see how Joseph was doing. He was in the middle of brushing his teeth. He was leaning over the sink into the bowl when she walked into the bathroom. He looked up with his toothbrush still in his mouth.

"You look pretty," he smiled goofily with light blue toothpaste dripping down his chin.

"Hurry up, you gotta change." Chloe reminded him. Joseph spit out his toothpaste and rinsed his mouth, as he began to dry off his hands with the towel that was hung next to the sink. Chloe stopped him and lovingly wiped a smear of toothpaste off of his chin before he was able to run out of the bathroom and downstairs.

When Chloe was alone, she noticed how itchy and annoying this dress was to wear. But she continued to brush her teeth and wash her face. Hanging the towel back on the nob, she looked at herself in the mirror. Fixing the collar of her dress, she smiled at herself. She opened the door, as she turned the light off and saw Joseph was waiting for her. With his hands behind his back, chest pushed out, and his head held high, he gave such a big smile that his eyes squinted. They took a deep breath and walked down stairs into the living room where Mrs. and Mr. Heinsworth were watching a boring tennis match. Chloe and Joseph leaned on the armrest.

Bouncing questions off of one another, "What are they like?" Chloe asked.

"What are their names?" Joseph added tugging on Mrs. Heinsworth's pants.

She whipped her head away from the television and in a strict voice said, "Will you stop that! You will see them when they get here," she brought her eyes back to the TV and continued, "Now go over there and be quiet."

For the next couple of minutes, the only sound was cheering and announcements coming from the tennis game that they were watching. The doorbell rang and Joseph jumped off of the couch and ran over to the door. Chloe sat on the couch patiently waiting for them to come in. Mr. Heinsworth walked over to the door and shielded Joseph away, like he didn't want a dog getting out. Two women stepped through the door frame and into the house.

They introduced themselves, "Hello, I'm Rachel and this is my wife, Julia. The adoption agency told us we had a meeting with Chloe and Joseph."

Mr. Heinsworth quickly suppressed a look of disgust while looking them up and down and finally back at Mrs. Heinsworth.

"Oh. Okay," he said unsurely.

"You ladies can... follow me," as he led them to the kitchen. When the two women saw the children, Julia knelt down to Joseph's eye level.

"Hello, there!" she said cheerfully, looking into Joseph's big blue eyes.

"Hi! My name's Joseph and I'm six years old!" He said, only stopping to grab his sister and drag her over. Rachel joined Julia in kneeling.

"This is my sister Chloe. She's eight years old and she's so smart!"

The couple laughed softly, and Rachel extended her soft hand. "It's very nice to meet you, Joseph and Chloe. My name is Rachel, and this is my wife, Julia." The children looked confused, but Joseph still took her hand and shook it.

"You two are married?" Chloe asked, tilting her head to one side. "Like, you love each other like Mr. and Mrs. Heinsworth love each other?" Chloe inquired, slowly to understand.

"Yes, we do love each other just like that." Julia answered, smiling. Chloe grinned, shaking their hands and running with Joseph to take their seats, with the couple following behind.

Rachel pulled out a chair for Julia at the kitchen table, and Mr. Heinsworth pulled a chair for Rachel. Once the visitors and children were seated, Mrs. Heinsworth came into the kitchen with dinner. Dinner tonight was a large steak. Once all the food was set out, Mr. and Mrs. Heinsworth sat down at the opposite end of the table from the two wives, with Chloe and Joseph in the middle.

After everyone got their dinner, there was a soft silence for a few moments.

"So," Joseph smiled.

"Do you want to hear about what we learned in school today?" he

117

asked, not directing the question to any pair of couples, but to both. He didn't give enough time for anyone to answer. He continued, "I learned how to read a clock, see that one on the wall? It says that it is… six… th…irty five."

"That's great, dear," Mrs. Heinsworth responded.

Chloe started to add in, "I learned how to add decimals today. I thought that it would be so much harder than it actually was, but there is a trick to it. The better I get at counting by those numbers, the easier it will get."

"That's exciting, Chloe," Mr. Heinsworth said. The Heinsworth's excused themselves to watch TV, leaving Rachel, Julia, Chloe, and Joseph at the table.

Chloe and Joseph spoke more than the wives at the table, spewing information about themselves.

"I like reading. Have you ever heard of *Charlotte's Web*? I read the book and then Mrs. Heinsworth let me and Joseph watch the movie. It was such a sad movie!" Chloe told the two women.

"I like superheroes. You know Iron Man? He's so cool! And smart, and brave! I love that one comic where he teams up with Captain America and gets all the bad guys- Chloe reads me the comics when I can't get them, because Chloe is in a higher grade." Joseph explained, an excited grin tugging at his lips.

"What do you guys do for work?" Chloe asked, sitting up straighter.

"Oh, well I work in Parksborough Middle School, I'm the 7th grade science teacher there." Julia smiled.

"And I work at an office." Rachel offered.

"I think I want to be a doctor when I get older." Chloe smiled sheepishly.

"I wanna be a superhero, or a super scientist, like Iron Man," Joseph added on, causing everyone to laugh.

It was time for the kids to head upstairs and get ready for bed. The conversations at the table continued as they made their way up the stairs slowly, not wanting to leave Rachel and Julia. Sliding off of their chairs, they slowly walked over to the stairs and made their way up. Chloe walked with her head hanging over the railing to watch Rachel and Julia. Joseph wasn't tall enough, so he stuck his head through every other spindle on the railing to watch what was happening. At the top of the staircase, the two stopped and looked at each other for a moment, and suddenly burst into laughter. Worried that the Heinsworths would yell at them, they raced into their bedroom. They were in their matching monkey pajamas when Chloe called Joseph off of his bed, and onto hers so that they could talk over the excitement of the day. This was their favorite part of the entire day. They talked to one another about anything and everything.

"I like them Chloe, I can't wait until we get to go live with them. I really can't wait," Joseph exclaimed, leaning his head into Joseph.

"Me too Joseph, I'm really excited to finally have a real family." Chloe nodded.

"Nothing is for sure, though. Maybe they won't adopt us. Don't get all excited, this might not even work out." Chloe warned him. They whispered excitedly together about their hopes for the future for a half an hour after lights out, until Joseph fell asleep mid-sentence. Chloe fell asleep soon after.

***

Rachel and Julia were getting settled into bed. They sat up, lying next to each other.

"What did you think, Rachel?" Julia asked, breaking the silence.

"They were both so lovable and kind, Julia, but we can't afford two children right now, we agreed on getting one child," Rachel replied.

"I know, I want both of them too. I wish that we were able to adopt them, but we aren't. We have to decide on one. This is going to be such a hard decision, what are we going to do?"

"Honestly, I don't know what we are going to do. I'm not even sure what I am leaning towards. What are you thinking?" Julia asked again.

"Well, I think that we should decide on only adopting one of them. As hard as it is going to be since they are siblings, I think it's what we are going to have to do. We financially can't afford to care for both of them. I guess we can call the foster parents and get more familiar with the kids, besides meeting them and what's written on their profile. We can probably set up more meetings with whichever one we're more interested in." Rachel reasoned.

"Let's go to sleep, and we can call the Heinsworth's tomorrow."

"Deal," responded Julia, satisfied.

"Goodnight, love you." Rachel mumbled, getting comfy.

"Love you, too," Julia answered, closing her eyes.

Julia flipped the eggs off of the pan and on to two separate plates. She took the bacon out of the microwave and forked the sausages. Rachel brought over two full glasses of milk to the table and sat down. She was flipping through the paper when Julia brought over the breakfast. This morning was quieter than normal, Julia was grading papers while Rachel flicked through channels on the small TV in the kitchen. A commercial with a family on vacation came across the television, and Rachel and Julia looked at each other and knew that it was time to call the Heinsworths again.

"Hello, it's Rachel and Julia. Is this Mr. and Mrs. Heinsworth?" Rachel asked.

"Yes, what are you calling for?" Mr. Heinsworth's questioned in his grumbling morning tone.

"We just wanted to hear more of your personal experience from fostering Chloe and Joseph." Julia answered.

"Ah, well, Mrs. Heinsworth is certainly home more than I am, so I'll let her discuss the children with you." Some ruffling noises were heard on the younger couple's line, until Mrs. Heinsworth's voice picked up.

"You wanted to hear about Chloe and Joseph? Well, they just left for school, but I can tell you what I've learned about them while I have been fostering them."

"That'd be great, thanks."

"Chloe is very protective of Joseph, probably because of their experiences in foster care," Mrs. Heinsworth let out a long sigh before continuing. "She's sweet and intelligent. But she is a child, and she can get very annoying. She is definitely easy to handle and get along with. On the other hand, Joseph is a handful," she included with a sharp tone in her voice. "He takes medication every morning that gets refilled monthly. Oh, and he has an anxiety disorder, which he doesn't take medication for but he does see a therapist every Tuesday. If he gets worse, he'll need medication in the future. Otherwise, they're both fine kids. Are you two thinking about adopting them?" Mrs. Heinsworth asked.

"Well, I think that we are leaning more towards only adopting one of the siblings," Rachel informed Mrs. Heinsworth.

"Oh, that's a shame. I hate to see them be split up. Are you leaning towards Chloe or Joseph?" she asked the two women.

"We haven't decided." Julia said quickly. "But, I clicked with Chloe last night, so can we arrange to meet her again?" Rachel added.

"Yes, I liked Chloe too," Julia agreed.

"This Tuesday, in the hour that Joseph is at therapy, would probably work best if you'd like to meet with Chloe."

"That sounds good. We'll see you on Tuesday, then?"

"Yes, I'll text you the details."

After the couple hung up the phone, Julia turned to her wife.

"I don't want to separate these kids, Rachel. It doesn't seem fair."

"I know, Julia, but we both like Chloe a lot, and she doesn't have medication costs and therapy expenses. She's the best option. We haven't had luck like this with any of the other kids that we got to visit! We didn't click with them the same way, something is telling me that this is the right decision. Chloe is the one out of the seven other kids that we visited that has felt right."

"I guess, I just feel so terrible for little Joseph," Rachel sighed.

"Me too."

The following Tuesday, Rachel and Julia went back to the Heinsworth's house while Joseph was at therapy. Chloe was not aware they were coming.

They knocked on the door, just enough to open it. Rachel peaked her head in and Julia followed in. Chloe was sitting on her bed looking through one of her books she got at the school library. When she saw them in her room, she was surprised and said, "Hi, but what are you guys doing here because Joseph won't be home for at least another hour."

"We know, but we wanted to see you; to get to know you better," Julia explained.

"Okay, but you will still need to come another time to get to know Joseph better then. You guys would be so lucky to have him in your life."

"Okay, we'll try our best." Rachel budded in.

They went to the ice cream parlor in the center of town, which always had a long wait. When it was finally their turn, Chloe jumped up to the window trying to see over the counter where they were putting the ice creams together.

"Chloe what would you like?" Julia asked.

"Um, maybe just a small cone with plain vanilla ice cream," Chloe responded quietly.

"Are you sure? You can get whatever you want. Anything."

"Well… then can I get mint chocolate chip? That's my favorite!" Chloe said excitedly.

"Of course you can!" Julia smiled down to the eight year old. Chloe shuffled her feet excitedly as they waited in line for the ice cream.

The couple in front of them moved to the side, waiting for their ice cream to be made. Rachel stepped up to order, "Can I please have a chocolate, a strawberry, and a mint chocolate chip?" She asked, handing over the money. She handed the ice cream cones to the correct person.

"Let's go for a walk!" Chloe suggested.

They were walking in a nearby park, learning more about each other as they spoke. Mrs. Heinsworth was right- Chloe often jumped back to the topic of her brother and her memories with him.

"What about yourself? What do you like to do?" Julia asked, softly prompting the eight year old to talk about herself more.

"Well, I really, really, really, love singing! I like to sing on the bus, in the living room, in the shower, anywhere! I wish I could sing like the people I see on m TV, maybe I will one day! I also really like fish! I have three goldfish, they all look the same so honestly I can't tell them apart, but I named Greg, Frank, and Oswald. They're so fun to watch." She went on and on, until it was time for Julia and Rachel to take her home.

When they dropped her off, Chloe turned around and said, "Thank you so much for taking me out to get ice cream, I had a great time!" She said, holding out her hand for a shake from each of them before respectively returning into the house.

***

A little less than two weeks later, the phone started ringing. Mrs. Heinsworth answered the phone and it was from the adoption agency, they had approved the adoption of Chloe. That same day, as the siblings raced home from the bus stop, up the stairs, and into their room, Mrs. Heinsworth yelled up to their bedroom and called Chloe down. She slowly walked down the stairs because this was her time to play with Joseph. Normally the Heinsworths wouldn't bother them about anything while they were playing.

"Mrs. Heinsworth, I was playing with Joseph," Chloe complained.

"Chloe, Julia and Rachel want to adopt you. They want you to be their child." Mrs. Heinsworth explained.

"What about Joseph? He's coming too, right?"

"No honey, they are adopting you, not you and Joseph. You will move there about three months from now, maybe longer. It depends on how long everything takes to be sent through"

"What?" Chloe looked down and stared at the carpet, confused.

Mrs. Heinsworth did not give her an explanation but repeated, "This weekend." She went back into the kitchen to finish doing the dishes. Chloe slightly understood what was going to happen as she ran back upstairs. She didn't want to tell Joseph because she didn't know how to explain it and didn't want him to be upset. Chloe decided to continue playing with the toy cars on the town carpet that they had on the center of their bedroom floor.

The last two days of the week, Chloe had spent even more time with Joseph than she ever has before. She knew that Mrs. Heinsworth said *this weekend*. She walked him to his classroom each day even though he remembers where it is. She would rush through her homework so that she would have more time to play at night. Not telling Joseph what she knew was coming broke her heart. Part of her wanted to warn him, but the other part of her couldn't do it.

The day had finally come. Joseph woke up to banging noises coming from outside of the window. He opened his eyes and noticed Chloe's sheets off of her bed, the lamp on her nightstand gone, and empty draws open to her dresser. Joseph jumped out of his bed and ran down the stairs. Rachel was closing the full truck of the van and was walking back inside. Joseph didn't understand what was happening when he walked into the living room. He saw Chloe sitting on the couch with her hands in her lap and tears streaming down her face.

"Joseph, I'm moving… moving in with Rachel and Julia… they adopted me." Chloe tried to explain.

"What do you mean? What about me? I'm coming too right? Where's my stuff?" Joseph cried.

"Chloe, it's almost time to go. Make sure you have everything," Mrs. Heinsworth called out, interrupting their conversation. Joseph started crying, not understanding why his sister was being taken away from him. The only person that he looked up to and trusted was leaving him. Chloe started to cry even more and tackled Joseph on the couch, hugging him. Her tears dripped off of her cheeks and onto Joseph's forehead. She didn't know what she was going to do without her little brother. She wouldn't have someone to push along onto the school bus, play with, and talk to all night, or trust like they had both trusted each other with their lives. Who was going to be there for him? Stand up for him? Make sure he did what he needed to? Chloe felt like her world was being torn apart. Julia was standing behind the wall watching the two. She realized how broken they are going to be apart from each other, she knew that she was doing this to them, and she wanted it to stop. She wanted all of the pain that Chloe and Joseph were holding to be let go. It's just as easy as adopting Joseph, or not adopting Chloe at all. She knew that she couldn't do anything about it. Chloe did not want to let go because she knew that when she did, that was it. She held on tighter and tighter because she knew that soon he would be gone. Mr. Heinsworth basically had to tear the two apart from one another. He picked up Joseph as Rachel and Julia walked out of the door with Chloe.

The next day was Chloe's first morning of waking up without Joseph in the bed next to hers. Instead, it was Benny, the dog that Julia and Rachel owned. Chloe yawned, sitting up. It was the weekend, so it was pretty early for her to be up. It was eight o'clock in the morning, but she got herself out of bed. She was anxious as to how Joseph was doing. Was he awake yet? What was he doing today? What did Mrs. Heinsworth make him for breakfast? Chloe couldn't stop thinking about him as she walked out of her room. The apartment she had moved to was just big enough for the three of them to live, and it was easy to navigate. Chloe walked out of her room, down the hallway, and into the dining room.

Julia and Rachel were already sitting at the table. Julia was biting into a piece of toast, only looking up from her phone when she heard Chloe.

"Hey, Chloe! You're up early! How did you sleep?" Julia asked.

"Alright, can I call the Heinsworths later, so I can talk to Joseph?" Chloe asked shyly. She should have been grateful for being adopted, but she felt devastated that Joseph wasn't able to enjoy it with her.

Although she tried not to, she felt some resentment against Rachel and Julia for only adopting her, and not her brother. They were siblings, "joined at the hip," as Mrs. Heinsworth would say. But she really liked her new parents, still. They were kind, and caring, and they actually wanted to know what she learned at school. It just felt different without Joseph here. The house felt silent- almost boring- without her brother bouncing off the walls.

Chloe sat down at the table.

"Of course you can call your brother. I just don't think he's awake yet- how about around lunchtime you call him?"

"Yeah, that sounds good, thanks." Chloe said quietly.

"You okay?" Julia inquired, although she knew the answer. The young woman felt terrible for separating her and Joseph, but they simply could not financially take care of the boy, and their application for adoption of Joseph was denied.

"I just... miss Joseph." was all Chloe said, munching into the toast on her plate.

Rachel came into the kitchen, her hair twisted in a towel.

"Morning, you two!" She said cheerfully, finishing drying out her hair.

"What's the plan for today?"

"Nothing in particular, maybe we can just hang around the house today and relax, I think we all deserve it," said Julia.

"Yeah, I guess that's alright," Chloe sighed. Chloe sat there listening to the grown up conversation, which got boring after only a few minutes. Her eyes wandered around the new dining room and kitchen. She still was unsure where everything was, but sitting there got boring so she went back to her room. The couple cleaned up the mess that was left in the kitchen and dining room after they had eaten breakfast. Julia was walking to her room, and as she walked by Chloe's bedroom door, she saw her sitting there, looking at her fish tank, watching her fish swim in circles. The oddest thing was that she wasn't singing. She was almost always singing whenever and wherever. She was sitting in the wooden chair slumped as if it was a rainy day outside. The sun was shining and it was only the start of the day, hard to be upset about anything really. Julia seemed to be bothered by something as well. She kept to herself and rested on the couch.

"Rachel, I'm worried about Chloe. She seems like she doesn't like it here as much as I thought she would. By not having her brother with her, she isn't able to enjoy having a family because to her, he *is* her family. I want her to have the life she wants; when we first met her, she'd always be singing and playing and she was so full of life. Now she spends so much time sitting alone; I don't know what to do," Julia explained

"Yeah, I have noticed that too, but I don't know what we can do about it. I think that it is mostly because her brother isn't here with her." Later that night, they decide that they have to do something about it and they call Chloe down from her room and sit down at the dining room table to talk to her. They ask her why she hasn't been being herself recently, why she's been so quiet, and why she seems so sad. Chloe explained how she hadn't ever lived without her brother and over the past six years that he has been alive, she was always there to watch over him. She protected him, leads him, played with him, talked to him, they basically did everything together. Living without him felt terrible and she never wanted to have to experience it.

Julia and Rachel decided to surprise Chloe with a visit to go see her brother. She thought that they were going to a new grocery store that had recently opened. When they turned onto the street, Chloe's head straightened and her back came off of her seat. She recognized the area. Then she saw her old house.

"Joseph!" Chloe shouted, jumping up in her seat. "Do I get to see him?" she continued.

"Yes Chloe we wanted you to be able to see your brother since you seemed so down lately. Chloe ran to the door and rang the doorbell until the door was opened. She jumped up the stairs and pushed Joseph's door all the way open. Joseph turned to see who it is. He rushed off of the bed and fell, Chloe ran toward him and hugged him on the ground.

"Joseph, I missed you so much you wouldn't even believe it, I can't do this anymore, I need you to come with me. They are so cool. They actually care about what I learned at school and how my day went. They love me, Joseph, they really do."

Joseph and Chloe spent the rest of the day just as any other when they lived together; playing, talking, singing, and anything else they might've done. After dinner everyone was getting tired and it was time to head back to their house. Chloe did not want to leave Joseph again; they didn't want to let go of each other. They were hugging and crying, not knowing when the next time they were going to see each other would be. As they were saying their goodbyes, for the second time now, the young couple decided to talk to Mr. and Mrs. Heinsworth. The women knew that they can't keep only one of them, but they also knew that they don't have the money to have both of them. This broke their heart because they knew how reliant Chloe and Joseph were on each other.

As they started to drive away from the house, Chloe was still crying, leaning against the window. Rachel decided to pull over to one of the drug stores. She parked the car, leaving it on for Julia and Chloe, and ran into the store. She got in the line with a bag of skittles to make Chloe feel better.

She stepped up to the cash register, "Hello, how are you today 'mam?"

"Could be better, how are you," Rachel responded, handing over the skittles.

"Would you like a lo-," started the cashier.

"No thank you," Rachel responded before letting him finish.

"They still haven't found a winner for Powerball and there is always a good chance for the lottery," argued the cashier.

"You know what, what the hell, I'll take a lottery ticket," Rachel said as she gave in.

"Okay, your total comes to $3.75."

Rachel moved the skittles and her wallet to the side so the next person in line can cash out. She used the quarter she got back to scratch off the ticket. The first numbers she scratched off were the ones she needed, 67, 89,43, or 56. She had a total of nine chances to get at least one of the numbers right. She scratched of the first row, none of them matched. Then she scratched off the second row, and none of them matched. She scratched the last three numbers individually. The first one, didn't match. The second one, didn't match. She slowly scratched the first number away from the final number and it was a four. She crossed her fingers, hoping it would be a three. She scratched it, blew away the dust, to discover that it was a nine.

Rachel stood in silence, staring at the lottery ticket. She knew that luck couldn't help her. She knew that money was tight between her and Julia. But she realized what was most important. Chloe needed Joseph in her life, and Joseph needed Chloe. No one could make that happen but herself.

Heading back to the car, Rachel threw the ticket away. When she got in the car, Chloe's head was resting against the door and her eyes were shut.

"Julia, we need to change this. When I was in there I bought a lottery ticket… but not even one of my numbers matched what I needed. I know it's going to be so hard for us, but we need to pick up another job or two. Chloe needs Joseph," Rachel said in a slight whisper.

"Is that going to be enough though? I'm not sure that getting another job will fulfill supporting the family in addition to what Joseph's finances are for medication and sessions that he goes to," Julia said, looking up to Rachel.

"Well, then we are going to have to cut some things out. We have to make this work. I can't deal with the fact that we are the ones who are keeping Joseph and Chloe apart. When Chloe first came home with us, to the second time when we brought her to visit Joseph, tearing them apart was so painful and I can't even imagine how they feel."

"I think that we can do that, we can get another job and make things work. I can't stand to see them getting ripped apart from each other either. It's terrible," Julia agreed.

***

Chloe and Joseph woke up in beds beside each other. They got ready for school, and ran down the stairs to eat breakfast. With Rachel and Julia across from one another, Chloe and Joseph across from one another, the table was complete. Nothing was missing. After they finished their pancakes and bacon, they went to the bathroom to brush their teeth. Joseph stood on his stool and Chloe on the ground next to him. They looked at each other in the mirror and laughed at the toothpaste strolling down Joseph's face.

As the time came, the siblings raced to the bus stop, with Chloe's beautiful singing voice following them. They played tag as they did any other day at the bus stop and when it was time to get on the bus, Chloe pushed Joseph up the stairs. The school bus conversations didn't have any worries anymore, but all excitement. Chloe grinned as Joseph walked to his classroom without having to look back for help.

The Basement

As I walked into "Susan's Corner Store" I got the same friendly greeting from Susan as everyone else did.

"Good Morning Ronald, wonderful weather we're having isn't it?" Susan said smiling hoping to strike a conversation. Living in a small town, Susan knew everyone that went into her store. Everyone knew each other and always said hello to one another.

"It sure is… how is uh, the store?" I said, keeping myself from accidentally mentioning her husband who had divorced her a year ago.

"The store's still good, as long as I have you buying more window cleaner and floor cleaner, we both know that's why you come here every week."

I hated going to the store when other people were there, it felt as if they were watching me. Noticing how many people were staring at me, I looked down and quickly grabbed what I needed. As I went to retrieve my cleaning supplies and take them to the counter to pay for them, I gave Susan a smile.

"It's my way of thanking you." she said, typing in the regular discounts she gave me. I never knew what she meant, but I always thanked her and she'd always smile right back.

Walking out of the store, I began down the sidewalk that ran all through the town. Everyone always had a smile on their face.

"How's it going, Ron?" I turned my head to see who it was. To my pleasant surprise, it was Ms. Williams.

"I'm good mam, how are you?" I said, trying to not get stuck in the conversation that would usually occur.

"I'm good, just enjoying the outside to pass time." Ms. Williams never really stayed indoors if she could help it. If the sun was out, so was Ms. Williams. She just loved the outdoors and wanted to be surrounded by people in the few years she had left. Ms. Williams always wanted to find someone who enjoyed nature as much as she did.

"That's good, I hate to leave now but I have to go meet with Gary."

"No problem honey, tell him I say hello."

No one ever really tried to start a full conversation. It never bothered me to talk but I had to go meet with Gary; he hated waiting for me to start cleaning.

And with all the good also came the bad. As with any town, our town had our share of delinquents. Hanging out well past midnight, people could regularly find the group of teenagers doing something illegal or rotten. They were the ones who were constantly getting the cops called on them. The little delinquents that hung out in the park a block away from Reginald's house. Right as I realized I didn't take the way home that avoids the park, I heard them.

"There goes Ronald, the scaredy-cat," They would tease me every time. Another one heard the first comment and chimed in.

"Don't." It never made sense why they would pick on me. Gary always told me they were nothing but stupid kids and that their words meant nothing, but they did to me. I just hoped they'd grow up soon and not act like a bunch of little devils.

As I got to the house, another day of cleaning Reginald's house as we did had to everyday. It wasn't always much, but it still required us to drag ourselves there and clean up the house. We didn't mind for the most part since his Wife had died two months ago. Most of the time we would just rearrange things so it looks cleaner to him. Gary would clean the basement whenever possible as to keep me from having to clean it. Every time I went down there my stomach would churn and uneasiness would overtake my body. Sometimes it make me have to take a step outside and get fresh air. I'd always loved the military and debated serving from time to time but Gary always told me the military wouldn't need a person like me. My doctor would never take me off the pills even though he said for my age I'm in "perfect" shape.

Gary and I had been friends since I could remember. He'd told me we'd been friends since I was a child, but the memories he kept talking about were something that I couldn't seem to remember. The only thing that ever really stuck was that Gary was like a brother to me. Anytime I needed any help Gary was there for me and he always tried to make sure he could help even if I didn't need anything. We'd always spend the days with each other and he'd make living alone a little easier.

The worst part of cleaning Reginald's house was the mystery of it. In the basement he had one room in which Regi, as I always called him, said to never go in and clean. Gary always joked his dog would get locked in there while we cleaned but something about the room just rubbed me the wrong way. Certain things just made me uneasy but I never could quite tell why. But nothing gave me the chills quite like Regi's basement did. I hated when Gary made me clean it, I'd spend no more than 10 mins in there.

One day we were cleaning Regi's house, like we did every time he'd go on vacation or visit his friends. Gary tapped me on the shoulder.

"Why does he even want us to clean if there no one in there to dirty it up? Unless of course he's keeping a secret there." He laughed as we walked in the front door but I still felt a chill run down my spine as his words echoed in my head. I had a puzzled expression on my face as Gary looked at me and changed from a joking manner.

"Don't worry Ron I'm only joking there's nothing but dust and spiders in there." I laughed, to not let him know how skeptic I was. Looking back at him, I began.

"I know Gary what even would be in there." But I honestly felt scared to go into the house for some reason. The house smelled like old mildew and liquor. Regi always had a whiskey on the rocks after dinner. He always left the glass out and it'd be filled with the melted ice and old whiskey. The house was filled with random furniture as to make it feel more inviting. His back porch overlooked the lake. You could see the sun's rays sparkling in the water and the ripples of the rocks thrown in by the children. Taking in a deep breath, I smelt the warm inviting smell of his pine scented candle.

"If I don't have a house like this by the time I'm Regi's age than I don't wanna get any older." Gary said taking in a fresh breath of air. If you listened closely, you could hear the echoes of conversations across the lake and the splashing of water after the ducks land on it. It looked like a dream vacation spot with the orange and pink sky reflecting off the water.

As we got back to cleaning the house Gary kept eagerly checking his phone almost every five minutes as if he was waiting for something. I was going to ask him but I wanted to just clean so I could just go home and have dinner since it was supposed to rain later. We both finished the second and main floor of Regi's house. Walking down the stairs I heard Gary's phone ringing. I quickly went to the phone and tried to bring it to him. Noticing Gary walking down the stairs, I tossed him the phone.

"I've been waiting for this call all day." Gary said as he swiped the phone out of my hands before I could even reach out to give him it.

"I'll come right now to go get it, thank you so much. Have a nice day." Gary stated as he clicked his phone shut.

"What was the call for?" I asked trying to not be nosey.

"It's for my passport remember? I told you I needed it for my tr-."

"Of course I do, did you think I would forget?" I said, trying to make it seem like the whole conversation hadn't slipped my mind.

"Of course not Ron, but can you just finish up cleaning? I gotta go deal with this." I wanted to say no so he'd clean the basement quick with me but he seemed in a hurry.

"I guess so."

"Thanks man I'll do the whole house next time bro." Gary rushed out of the house and gave me a thumbs up as he left.

Here I was, all I had to clean was the basement but it was easier said than done. Opening the door, I felt a cold sensation trickle down my back. Stepping down the squeaky stairs one by one as my heart began to beat faster. Looking around, I saw there was basically no sign Regi was here... except one. The door that lead to the room he told us to not to go into was cracked open. My heart begin beating harder and I began to tense up. The room seemed to get smaller as if was a narrow hallway leading to the door. I wanted to go back upstairs and just leave it till tomorrow morning before Regi gets home. Before I could stop myself, my legs began walking towards the door. As I reached the door itself my stomach dropped like an amusement park ride. Reaching my now sweat-covered hands to the doorknob, things got worse. As the cold metal brushed against my clammy palms I felt my hairs stuck up like a wolf before it attacks. Grasping the doorknob, and slowly turned the door as my rapid pulse shot to my fingertips. The door swung open and my body went numb as I saw it. There it was in the corner of the room, a body. There was no blood just the body being covered up by blankets. Time stood still and I couldn't move. Trying to rationalize what I was seeing but nothing made sense. Did he leave her body here to rot? How long has she been in there? My feet felt glued to the floor and I couldn't help but just stand there in horror. The room began to spin before my eyes causing me to shake my head. Swinging the door shut, my legs propelled me up the stairs.

My stomach curled as if I'd drank spoiled milk. I ran home as fast as I could and saw all my neighbors look at me like I was insane. Once I came to the realization of what was going on, I stopped running and just looked around. Mrs. Terrance, who lived a few houses down from me, looked up.

"Ronald are you okay? You look like you've seen a ghost." I tried to make a rational response but could barely get a word out.

"I-I-I just need home right now." She gave me a weird look as I walked past her. Nothing in my mind made sense and I couldn't even form a sentence. Everywhere I looked, all that I could see is was Regi's wife. Time seemed to stand still and all anyone was focused on was me. All of their beating eyes staring at me like I was crazy only made my heart beat faster. I could hear the mumbles of conversations from other people saying.

"Here he goes again," Mumbled a girl to her boyfriend in disgust.

"Someone's gotta help him." I didn't understand why that's what they said but my feet just kept walking until I entered my house and fell on the couch. The body in the room was the only thing that I could think of. Then it hit me, the body was his wife. She's died a short time ago but I never remembered him having a funeral in town or anywhere.

I tried to think of explanations for what I'd seen but I just couldn't. I tried to sleep but the thought of Regi's wife being in that room made me sick to my stomach. I stayed up all night trying to explain what I'd seen but nothing made sense. I'd always thought he was the nicest guy but now he seems like a horrible monster and a murderer. Calming down, I began to lay my head against the pillow of my bed and take some much needed rest.

When I knew I had to get something to eat. I called up Gary and asked him if he wanted to grab "a bite to eat" and he said he'd go to the town diner with me. I had to tell him at the diner, he had to know about Regi.

When I got there I looked around eager to tell him what I saw. I looked around at all the people judging me. This one kid kept tapping his fingers on the table. It sounded like a gun and began making me increasingly nervous. Losing my patience, I got up and was about to go over and make him stop, but was interrupted by Gary opening the door. We sat down and I tried to act normal but after all the years of being friends he could tell something was wrong. I kept looking around the diner at all the people to see if one of them was Regi.

"You don't seem yourself, you sure everything's alright?"

"I think I may have seen Regis wife Gary" I said squirming as a chill went up my spine

"She's dead Ron what are you talking about? Is this some kinda messed up joke because it's not that funny." Gary said as he was trying to look around.

"Trust me it was in Regi's basement, in the room we aren't supposed to go in," I screamed back at him, not noticing the volume of my voice. Everyone was looking and Gary kept lowering his head as to not be seen with me. Even the kid who was tapping on the table was looking at me like I was weird. They looked at me like they were better than me and that made me even madder.

"Ron I've been in there before with Regi there was nothing in there."

Stopping myself from trying to reason with Gary since he didn't wanna believe me.

"You didn't see his wife"He said calmly as I stormed out of the restaurant. All he did was tell me that I should find something to do with my time.

Racing around my house trying to process why Gary wouldn't believe me. No one ever believed me. Gary didn't even give me a chance to explain what I saw. He treated me like I was insane and made me feel like a lunatic in the diner. The way the people looked at me stuck in my head. Especially the kid who had been tapping the whole time. He looked at me like I was the one who was making everyone else nervous and annoyed. Spitefully throwing the picture of Gary and me at graduation at the wall and watched the glass protector shatter, my thoughts began to drift off. The shining of the light off the glass reminded me of the dim lighting in the closet. The lighting that showed his wife, that had changed him and made everyone look at me like a monster in the diner. I was going to go to Gary's house and try to reason with him but I had gotten myself so worked up that my head began beating like a drum. As I did any time I felt this I went to my room put on calming sounds and tried not to think of the horrible things I've seen.

As I woke up the next day I received a text from Regi thanking Gary and me for the cleaning. I texted Gary separately to see if Regi was acting weird to him either but he never responded. I tried calling him but it went straight to voicemail. Texting him didn't get me a reply either. Something had to be wrong since he always texts me back if I need him. Beginning to get more nervous, drops of sweat began trickling down my head. I needed to go find someone that believes me but I couldn't let anyone know what I saw.

I went back to Susan's and asked her if she ever thought there was something strange about Regi. She seemed shocked by the question but still gave me an answer,

"Regi is about the sweetest old man in the world. Only strange thing about him is how he seems happy in the morning." Susan said laughing at her own joke. I tried asking other customers in the store but all the same, everyone thought Regi was a saint. They all gave me weird looks when I'd ask them, but something wasn't right with Regi.

I got home and decided to try and call Gary. The call went straight to voicemail yet again and began to think he may be in trouble. What if Gary confronted Regi and he killed him too. What if I'm next on his list? My heart began to beat faster than before and only seemed to get faster. Picking the phone I sat there for a second before dialing the numbers 9-1-1. The last time the phone was used was to call Gary and his words echoed through my head. What if he was right and I was making a big deal about nothing. Still, it didn't make sense when he said, "You didn't see a body" as if I'd been known to lie about things. My fingers tingle as the need to get answers was eating me alive. I waited for the ringing of the phone but still felt on edge.

"Reginald killed his wife and has the body." I spurted out as the lady answered.

The operator seemed to know exactly who I was. She told me that what I was doing was a big offense if I'm wrong and gave me a chance to hang up.

Telling her again, "Regi killed someone, and has her in the basement," I could hear her speaking to someone else, probably another operator, on the other end.

"He's doing it again- maybe we should send an ambulance," I heard someone in the background chimed in.

"There's no way Regi, of all people, would kill anyone."

The responses just increased my anger as the operator hung up. I couldn't let Regi hide the body and the truth. I tried calling Gary one last time but it went straight to voicemail. Thoughts of Gary being taken began to fill my head and before any other thought could cross my mind. I'd figured out where Gary had gone. Regi took Gary, and I had to get him back. I had a plan but needed sleep first.

The next day I made a plan to sneak into Regis house tonight while he went for his usual night time walk. I needed to make sure no one saw me go into the house though. Dressing in all black, the camera and knife were the only things left to put in the bag. I couldn't ask Gary for help anymore. Once I break into his house, turning back was no longer an option.

As the sun began to set I walked through the backyards and made it to Regis house. Sneaking through the open window, my eyes looked for any sign of Regi, while pulling out the knife from my bag. I walked around and felt my heart race. Walking closer towards the basement, my heart began beating faster and faster as if I had a car piston inside it. I thought I heard Regi upstairs so I hid in the top of the basement stairs. I walked down the stairs and walked closer to the door. Before I could open it Regi came down the stairs. He looked at me puzzled as if he knew. He tried to seem confused but I knew he wasn't the man he says he is.

"Ron I thought you were a burglar, I was gonna call the cops but -" Regi said calmly before I shouted over him,

"I know you killed your wife and put her body in the closet Reginald and I know you took Gary." Looking at him and raising the knife at him, he had a phone in his hand with a person talking through it.

"Come quick." Regi said into the phone in his hand before speaking again.

"Ron I don't know what you're talking about but you seem pretty bad maybe we should get you to the hospital."

"I'm not going anywhere Regi, you're gonna let Gary free though." I said, beginning to twirl the knife near him.

"Gary's on vacation Ron, he gets back tonight. What do you mean let him go? Why are you acting like this, you need help." Regi said trying to reason with me. I knew he was trying to avoid the truth.

"That's why you never wanted us in the closet isn't it? You were hiding your wife in it. You killed her didn't you monster." I said, screaming as loud as my voice would let me. He didn't think anyone would figure out his secret but I knew that he wasn't the nice man everyone thought he was. Regi began to keep backing up slowly. The monster wouldn't even admit to what he was did.

I began to hear sirens, and knew the police were here to stop this sick creep. Regi tried to walk away from me. Shouting at him again to stop him from escaping.

"Get back you old man! I know what you did, don't try run away." Regi tried making up excuses to distract me from the truth.

"Ron you're acting like a lunatic just calm down and I can help you."

Before I could speak police kicked down the basement door, and rushed down the stairs. The cops pointed tasers at me.

"Put the knife down Ron we don't wanna hurt you." The cop said firmly, trying to fool me of what was really going on. I couldn't believe they tried to pin this on me. My heart raced even harder than before. My body began shaking from being so nervous.

Finally it hit me. No one saw the situation like I did. They were all different than me. They couldn't see the things that I saw. The cops didn't even check the closet for the body. They treated me as if I was different. Maybe they were right. This must be why they don't believe me or why everyone tries to be calm near me. I began doubting myself and realized I was acting insane. Realizing what was going on, my fingers loosened my grip on the knife. Right as I went to throw it, I felt a stinging pain go all through my body. A thousand needles ran up my spine until my body felt as if it weighed as much as a rhino and crashed to the floor.

I began to regain consciousness and looked around. Everything around me looked like monitors and it soon came to me that it was an ambulance. I could see the horrified looks of the neighbors and police. My mind began to ponder as to why they were looking at me and not Regi. I saw a police officer and Regi talking. I could faintly hear their conversation.

"Any idea why he broke into the house and had the knife in his bag?" The cop questioned trying to make me seem like the bad guy.

"He thought I killed my wife and put her body in a closet. The only thing I had in my closet was a dummy for the shooting range, and a few guns I brought back from war. Plus I usually keep the dummy wrapped up in a blanket." He was lying straight to their face and I tried to tell them but couldn't find the energy to speak.

"Do you know of anything that would cause Ron to think this way sir?" They made it seem like that dirt bag was innocent but the officers face lit up when Regi spoke.

"If I had to bet it'd probably be his PTSD and schizophrenia from the accident in the war. He's never been able to deal with military things ever since he got back from the war. The painting and pictures in the basement probably made him delusional and caused him to act out the way he did. The guns in the closet probably played a factor in it as well."

"He's lying I know he is," muttering as loudly as I could. My plea begged to be heard but no one listened. The doors of the ambulance were slammed shut and my version of the truth was never heard. No one ever wanted to hear the crazy man's side of the story.

The Five Seasons of
Kevin Borkowski

The sun rose over the city of Boston, Massachusetts, opening up to a fresh, bitter morning. In most ways it was like this every day. Not a calm morning, not a pleasant morning, but a silent morning. Silent, besides the constant howl of cars that passed by outside Kevin Borkowski's house. And unpleasant in the way that it didn't involve a warm breakfast, but cheap toothpaste and shaving cream.

His dog, Goodie, laid over a blanket on the couch in the other room. The sweet retriever watched Kevin with sleepy eyes as he squeezed a portion of the cheap toothpaste on his brush. Lights flicked after being switched on, creating an artificial glow to match the morning light. He dutifully brushed his teeth and wiped his mouth. Like the rest of the house, Kevin's bathroom was quiet. Catching his eyes in the mirror, he grabbed a comb and sifted it through his dark hair. The cool brown irises looked hollow in the lighting. His hair, however, had stayed short and well-groomed since the haircut he had three weeks ago. It felt too early for this, but it always did, so Kevin had to make do. With his morning routine finished, the man slipped into his coat and stepped out of the bathroom to read the time. The clock pointed at 7:49 and the television was on.

"*...with a high of 46° and a low of 33°--*" Kevin picked up the remote from the counter and pressed a button. Crackling with static, the television screen soon shut off. The remote was placed back down as he brushed a hand over the surface of his coat, although it was already flat and clean. Kevin pet his dog's golden fur. Then, headed toward the front door, he glanced at the flattened tin bird nudged into the doorframe. The red metal reflected light from the nearby window. Sharp-edged feathers curled up over time; so much that Kevin barely had the memory of making it as a kid. Nonetheless, it was there for a reason-- a commemoration to his youth and a reminder that the holidays were around the corner. He turned the lock on the door and entered the brisk air with a deep breath, in hope that it would clear his head.

***

Kevin's job kept him busy and on-task; it gave him a sense of purpose. He remained in the office from 9:00 AM and left at 6:00 PM. On weekends, he typically stayed at home to enjoy his own company. There's nothing wrong with that, he thought.

"I'm still expecting that confirmation emailed to me by noon. Keep it up." Kevin nodded, acknowledging his manager. This routine had become redundant over the past few days. When he was mentioned, it was always 'oh, I know that guy. He's really smart; gets the job done.' It's not much to complain about, but behind the faux-respect there was the given that he was 'getting by.' Kevin came to realize that 'getting by' was not the same as 'getting through'-- the 'by' is meant to mean around, and rather than skimping around the sidelines, he worked hard and efficiently. That's how he saw it. With a push of his thoughts aside, he began a fresh e-mail to send out.

***

Not long after, the sky was a soft grey. Many around the city would call it rather fitting for Christmas Eve. Kevin enjoyed a hot mug of coffee and the company of Goodie, who was equally as happy to stay home. A cheesy recording of a fireplace glowed on his television screen. It was as peaceful as the snow drifted to the ground outside, collecting in fluffy mounds. Later he would attend church to finish the calm day. For now, the man and his dog sat and spent the well-earned time. Patience was all that they needed.

Kevin left around twenty minutes earlier at quarter to midnight. Entering the church had cleared his mind. As the door sealed, the wind and snow were cut short, fastening the warmth inside. Kevin took a moment to breathe, his ears compressed from the cold. He made his way down to the aisles and took a seat.

"May almighty God have mercy on us, forgive our sins," the Priest said, "and bring us to everlasting life." Kevin listened to the Priest. His words had less and less meaning as his gaze began to float around the room. Soft candlelight lit the church, emanating a golden atmosphere. The occasional murmur accompanied the man's speech. Kevin averted his eyes to the Priest, uttering an 'amen' and joining the congregation as they rose from the pews. He was in the center of the room, alone with a bible in front of him. But it was a book, not a person to stand by him, to hold his hand or kiss his cheek, not a real person to touch and love. The people in the pews diagonal were with others. A woman hovered over her child, reminding him to stand. Behind them was an old couple, and in front a husband and wife with their parents. Kevin's gaze lingered on their winter coats, scarves, and hats. He suddenly felt too warm in his own, but rather than to take it off, he gathered his thoughts and walked down the corridor.

After exiting the building, a gust of freezing air smacked him in the face. Part of him wanted to go back inside, but he knew the snow wouldn't stop for another few hours. It crunched under his feet on the sidewalk and covered the street in a feathery powder. So he headed back, street lights staring down at him wistfully on his walk home.

✳✳✳

"Good weekend, Chris?" A man in his mid-40s approached Kevin with a hefty pat on the shoulder.

"Yes, it was well," he replied. There was no point in correcting Rory Harrington again-- the rare times he was confronted always resulted in him calling Kevin by the wrong name.

"Great. Well, the rest of us are having a get-together sometime this weekend. You should come," he smiled, "I know the rest would like to have ya." Kevin doesn't understand Rory. His smile was reminiscent of one that a person passing you by would give; meaningless and with a small sense of genuine care.

"I'll let you know if I'm free," he reassured the man. Rory gave him a short wave of goodbye before turning around. Kevin watched the man walk back to his desk and sighed. It's going to be a long week, he thought. The computer screen shone black and empty at him. Glancing at his reflection, he wondered if he really looked like a 'Chris.'

Two months later, Kevin found himself stepping off the train near his street, as always. A rush of people followed his footsteps into the station. He thought they looked akin to a school of fish, so regular; completely mechanical. Kevin wanted out of it, to explore the world and to share it with people. People, he figured, who are family. So he decided he needs family, and he would find it with the help of God. Realistically, in order to achieve his wishes, he'd need to move or at the least take a vacation in order to see the world. Definitely not a full-on move, Kevin kept thinking to himself how much he loved it there. He couldn't dream of leaving the city forever. Although, maybe finding a new job would work for him-- Kevin looked away from the bustling people only to bump into a figure, files spilling everywhere.

"Excuse me, I'm sorry," The surprised voice of a woman came presumably from the figure. Kevin stared at her in shock.

"No, no it was truly my bad." Reaching for the scattered folders and papers, he sighed in relief. The woman grabbed for the rest as well. Something seemed so gracious about her warm brown skin and hair. Had he seen her before?

"You're good. Thank you." Taking the stack of files that he offered, she walked off in the other direction. Kevin watched her go down the path, caught up in wondering who she was, what she did, where she wanted to be, and eventually realized these are the questions that he should ask himself. Just when he was about to take his leave, Kevin's hand gripped the paper he'd unknowingly clutched. With a frown, he brought it to the light, only to find that it belonged to the woman. The name 'Rachel Saye' was scribbled across the top. Some type of form, medical possibly, or…

Stop it, Kevin. You have to find her and give it back, he scolded himself silently. But when he looked back up, the woman was nowhere to be seen. He tucked it safely with the rest of his belongings and moved on. The way home seemed short and Kevin quickly settled in bed. Work that day was pressing as usual, grocery shopping had to be done some time that week, and he'd somewhat met a new person. It's not to say that he and this person exchanged names, nor contact information, nor a simple 'hello,' but Kevin kept the paper on his nightstand for her anyway. He pulled the covers up to his chin and turned to his side. No thoughts could bother Kevin and keep him from his sleep. Counting sheep was not an option, he told himself. He had to wake up early tomorrow to get anything done. And with nothing else to think about, Kevin turned over again and shut his eyes.

He woke up too early. Nearly eight hours of sleep felt like less than three. Changing into his work clothes, Kevin started the day-- albeit more tired than usual. Nothing a little coffee couldn't fix, he figured. The brown pellets of dog food rattled against Goodie's bowl as they fell, almost blocking out the sound of the television.

"Temperatures today only in the low 60s, but by the end of the week we will reach highs of 69 going into the 70s."

That was great news, actually. Spring comes quicker than one might realize sometimes. Kevin was happy for the change.

✳✳✳

Goodie the golden retriever sniffed along the sidewalk. Her leash jingled as she moseyed over the concrete, various attempts to pick up different scents on the warm spring day. Kevin followed shortly behind, lost in his thoughts. It was a slow Saturday afternoon so far.

"Hey!" The voice of a teenager caught them immediately. He frowned, dog paused with her head turned. What would a kid need with him?

"You mean," he looked around, "me?" Goodie sat down beside him and observed the teenager who sat over a brick wall.

"Who else do I mean, the guy behind ya?" The girl hopped off the wall, set on Kevin and the dog. Her short black hair hovered over her shoulders gently. It clashed with her light blue shirt and scuffed sneakers.

"You know, I'm getting a bit tired of seeing you walk back and forth to work every day. Don't you people do anything else?"

"I don't get what you mean." He furrowed his eyebrows in concern. Not wanting to start any problems, Kevin figured talking it out would be easiest. Plus, today wasn't even a work day.

"Well I don't understand you. Why you even try. There's no point in any of it. At least I get around instead of trailing the same path all the time." The young lady crossed her arms having aimed Kevin down with a condescending glare. Before he had the chance to speak, she continued.

"See, here's what it comes across as. I watch you and many other boring job-goers walk by every day. Your life is picture perfect, minus the perfect, because it's straight out of a B film with no dimension. Or like, a scratched up DVD you rent from the library that freezes right when the action hits. Even worse, it'll skip over it. Doesn't that tire you at all? I don't know how you can even stand it!" The girl shouted, shoulders rising and falling. Kevin couldn't hold back the smile that etched over his lips-- and the kid couldn't hold back her laughter. They both had to admit, that was a pretty ineffective insult.

"I guess that didn't make the point. I still don't like you. I don't like anyone." She looked at the man, lips failing to press down a smile.

"I'll take your word for it then," he said.

"Hey, what's your name? I'm Bianca, by the way." She hopped back onto the concrete wall and faced him with her legs dangled over the edge.

"Kevin Borkowski. Glad to meet you."

"Alright, Kevin. I'll see you around I guess." Bianca nodded to him before jumping off the opposite side of the wall. "You should quit your boring job!"

By the end of June, Kevin found himself wondering about that poor, yet rebellious, teenager. He did find her in an alley, after all, and there's no telling if she had a home, job, or if she went to school, even if she had a family. Those factors that mean life-- there was no guaranteed presence of them, ever, and that is why survival can be so frightening. Society was unforgiving. Kevin knew God forgives.

He also remembered the medical form he'd grabbed from the woman. Rachel. It's been sitting on his nightstand the past week, but it's time that he should try and return it.

So return it is what he did. Kevin took the paper from his home that morning and kept it with him while at work. He was on the train to go home, like the evening he met the woman. Thoughts flooded his mind again. What would he say to her, what would she think of him? Then there's the question if she'd even be there. Gosh, I really didn't think this through enough... maybe I should just drop this off at the police station, Kevin thought. But the train came to a stop as the doors pulled open in front of him. This was it. Kevin inhaled and exited the train, walking to the spot where he'd bumped into Rachel. He looked around. Maybe she didn't even go to work today- if she did even work. Or she could have driven somewhere, maybe gone on a date-- forget it. It had been ten minutes of Kevin standing in the cool night air. He concluded that he would stop waiting and go home.

"Didn't think I'd see you here, Borkowski."

Kevin turned around immediately to face Bianca, the teenager now dressed in hues of olive and brown. Her sweatshirt matched her eyes, both a muted green and twinkling with interest.

"What's a fifteen year old doing alone at a train station at night? Why aren't you home, kid?" He gave her a fatherly gaze, as his expression softened. The girl shrugged at the mention of herself.

"Well, y'know. I'm tired of my parents arguing all the time about my future. Like I'm not even there to hear it." Bianca sighed. "It's not what you think. Teenage angst is meaningless and moronic. I had, well..." This seemed serious; the two stood in mutual silence for a few seconds. "You know anyone who had cancer, Borkowski?"

"What? I mean, no. I don't, but--" He looked back at her with concern.

"Now you do. I'm sure a smart dude like you knows what osteosarcoma is. I mean, I'm okay for now, so don't worry yourself. I even got a prosthetic bone in my shin!" She gestured down to her leg excitedly. Kevin shook his head, smiling at her sadly.

"That is impressive."

"I know, right? But enough about me. I'm just takin' a walk to get away from that house. Why are you here?" Bianca narrowed her eyes. With the question thrown into the air, she tucked her hands into her pockets and waited for an answer.

"This is the train I take home from work."

"Come on, really? You were standing there for like, fifteen minutes doing nothing with a paper in your hand. What is it, a love letter?" A smirk worked its way onto the girl's face.

Kevin sighed. "Okay, you got me. I was hoping to see someone here because this paper belongs to her. It looks important, so no, it's not a love letter."

"Lemme see," Bianca offered. Before Kevin can protest, she spoke again. "I know everyone around these parts of the city. How do you think I knew you worked at an office?"

"Fine. But first I need you to promise me something," Kevin looked at her with sincerity. Bianca nodded with her eyes wide in concern.

"The next time that your parents are fighting like this and it's about you, tell them that you're old enough to think for yourself. At least a little bit. Okay?" Bianca met his eyes slowly.

"Okay," she said passively. Regardless, his words did have meaning.

There's a moment of silence before Kevin held up the paper. "Her name is Rachel Saye. It says so at the top of the paper- something about pediatrics. But I haven't read the whole thing, it seems confidential."

"Fair enough. You got your wallet on ya?" Bianca returned to her normal, witty-self.

"Yes, why?" Kevin cocked an eyebrow.

"'Cause we've got a place to go. There's only one Rachel I know and she works at a *Billie's*. Come on, it can't be a mile's walk from here!" Bianca shouted, already running down from the station. This was crazy, Kevin knew it, but he's following her down the street. He was going to return this paper to Rachel. It was probably 8 o'clock by then, but Kevin didn't care. This was his mission.

She stopped running and turned around to shout back to him, "And by the way old man, I'm not a fifteen year old. I'm turning nineteen in four months! You're right, I sure as hell can think for myself!" Kevin laughed and continued to run into the night, finally catching up to Bianca as they reached their destination. It's a rather funny word; this seemed like destiny. The street lights created a yellow blush over the shop's dark windows. They ended up at a small café a few blocks from where Kevin lived, but it looked like it was about to close.

"Do you think she's even here still?" He's worried. This would have still been all for nothing.

"If there's one worthwhile thing anyone ever told you, never doubt Bianca Tran!" The teen eagerly watched the shop, and as if on cue, a woman pushed open the door and walked out clutching her keys.

***

Kevin gave her the paper and went home as fast as he could last night. The string of events was too much for his tired mind to process, after waiting at a train station, running around the city to find someone he'd only seen once-- and with a kid by his side no less! Kevin tried to justify that he was just looking out for the girl. He couldn't leave her out there alone at night. And by the time this was all over, he'd know he was more of a parent figure to her than her own mom and dad. Deep down, he knew they both needed to find Rachel. But that was probably the wildest time of his life since college parties, and not just because he was out of shape from running. Bianca was a regular customer at that tiny coffee shop, and Rachel who worked there had driven her home. The paper that Kevin held onto was an important form she needed, something for her son, Jack. Rachel thanked Kevin graciously, promising him free drinks at the café some time. So Kevin knew what he needed to do as he walked through the front doors of the building with purpose.

"My name is Kevin Borkowski. Not Kyle, not Chris, not Jared, not Keith. Kevin. I've worked on the third floor as an assistant for seven years. It's time that I pick myself up, get my life together, and do something else with it. Harold, I quit." Those were the last words from Kevin to be said in the sea of gridded office cubicles. He was free from the clutches of capitalistic America, from his boss, drone-like coworkers, and the blank stares that followed his walk out of the building.

A swirl of fallen leaves surrounded his feet with his exit. With the end of the season came a new beginning, as they say, and Kevin intended to begin.

Naturally, Kevin decided to call his friends together for a celebration. Fall had arrived and it was the perfect opportunity to get those free drinks that Rachel promised.

"Man, I didn't know Mr. Bore-kovsky had it in 'em!" Bianca exclaimed.

"No surprise that our favorite rebel is overjoyed for Kevin's season of unemployment. But I've gotta say, that was one of the better decisions in your life," Rachel said as Bianca nudged her in the arm. Kevin's mouth pressed into a smile. It was time for change; he had known from the point that he met them. Everyone knew.

"I'm not off the hook so easily," he watched the two with happiness. "I'll have to get another job at some point."

"Well, for now let's celebrate. To life, to us," Rachel held her coffee to the center, egging the others on for a toast.

"To family." And with that, the mugs of different shapes and sizes clinked smoothly and the deed was done.

The group stayed in the café for another hour before Bianca had to head home to her parents. They exchanged hugs and handshakes until the frigid winter air welcomed them into the street once more, Rachel waving goodbye. She cleared her way to the counter and returned to her shift. Kevin looked over his shoulder, taking one last glance at the coffee shop-- well, for now. People entered the shop around him, some alone and some in pairs. The sun lowered, though it wasn't near sunset yet. Light glinted against the tinted windows. While his eyes passively looked over the scene, he realized that time was moving on. There were still things to be done, such as continuing his job search or catching up on the local news. A wooden sign reading *Billie's* swayed back and forth like an empty swing. Details like that are mostly forgotten, but he thought it was pretty. Kevin tugged over his scarf and began his way back.

✳✳✳

December had been born again. To Kevin, it was almost hard to believe how far he'd come since the last time he stepped into the church. But the journey had been beautiful. In fact, he was expecting his new family soon. Kevin was giddy for the time to come, however his realistic side reminded him that it's dinner, not a meeting. So he set the table in the way he used to as a kid. It was neat as expected-- glimmering silverware, pots of food covered with plates kept the steam from escaping, and freshly cut slices of bread adorned the table. The smell was delicious from the kitchen to the dining room. He could taste the cranberry sauce, ham, buttered mashed potatoes with sour cream, and even the sourness of the white *barszcz*.

A knock at the door interrupted Kevin's thoughts as Goodie barked and ran toward the foyer. He walked over, calming her and opening it for his friends.

"Kevin!" Before he could react, Rachel reached in and pulled him into a hug.

"Hey doggy! Oh, and hi Mr. Borkowski," Bianca patted him on the shoulder before she walked inside to greet the dog. Goodie happily huffed toward the new person, wagging her tail at Bianca's giggles.

"Doggy?" The curious voice of a young child followed behind the others as Rachel's six year old son waddled over to them. Bianca ruffled Goodie's ears and showed the boy over to the dog. He shoved off his orange coat and pet her. The older two pulled away from their embrace and shared matching grins. Rachel had put on makeup to celebrate the occasion-- silver glitter accentuated her eyelids. It was gorgeous, like her.

"Hi, Bianca. Good to see you Rachel, and I'm so glad you could bring Jack!" Kevin looked into his friend's merry eyes before making way for her to walk inside. She smiled and said hello before entering. Jack looked up at Kevin with bright yet strikingly dark brown eyes under his black bangs. He waved shyly before following his mother.

"I hope you cooked something good, cause I'm starving!" Still a bit wet from the snow, Bianca removed her sneakers. Laughing, Rachel did the same and helped her son take off his boots. Bare from outerwear, the group entered the kitchen and the atmosphere quickly grew warm. Rachel had brought bottles of cranberry juice and cola to share. After drinks were poured and jokes were shared, Kevin reminded them that they should eat before the food goes cold. They each helped cut up the food so that Jack could eat safely, but before eating, Kevin brought the others together once more. He stood up to hold a large wafer. It was surprisingly thin and lightweight for such a large looking food, a delicate engraving of a baby Jesus and Virgin Mary on either side. He broke off a piece of the wafer and passed the rest on.

"Is that bread?" Rachel asked, reaching for the piece. She broke off her own piece and passed the larger to Jack, helping him break off one for himself. Jack passed the remaining wafer to Bianca with cheerfulness.

"No, this is *opłatek*. It's kind of like altar bread, but only eaten for Christmas," Kevin said. "My grandmother would always get it for our family when I was a child." Rachel made a hum of agreement in respect of his words. After everyone had their share, they bit into the flaky wafer. It was crunchy and had no taste, but the dinner waiting for them on the table certainly did. Once everyone finished, Bianca eagerly handed out slices of bread.

"Now it's time to dig in!" She beamed. The others passed shares of food with enthusiasm and filled their plates with potatoes and ham. The group's laughter drowned out the howling wind from outside, and dinner lasted a good couple hours. Eventually, they got up and took care of their dishes. Jack rushed over to grab his mittens and coat from the foyer while Bianca put on her shoes.

"We had a great time, Kev. Thank you for inviting us!" Rachel said.

"Totally! That was the best food I've ever had," Bianca chimed, walking over to open the door. She held it ajar for the others as Jack reached out with mitten-clad hands. He squealed and giggled as Kevin picked him up. Kevin took him to Rachel's car as she opened the door for the man. He gently lowered Jack into the backseat and fastened his seatbelt. Bianca hopped in next to Jack and turned to Rachel. The night was windy and cold, but the family held onto the warmth from Kevin's house.

"Hey Ms. Saye, is it alright if we put the radio on in the car?"

"Sure, B. Have fun at mass, Kevin, and thank you again." Rachel said. The teenager closed the car door and waved goodbye to the man, Jack waving along with her.

"Goodbye everyone, Merry Christmas!" Kevin waved back. A

chorus of 'Merry Christmas' came from the car in reply as Rachel sat in the front seat. With one final wave, she turned her headlights on and drove away. Kevin felt happy, even in the frigid winter air.

And in the local church, the soft glow of candles welcomed him back. An elderly gentleman held the door open for Kevin and he happily thanked him as he entered. Although he was not with anyone else at the moment, Kevin felt more together than he ever had been. He has family. True family from the heart. Not a long list of blood relatives, but a strewn-together group of oddballs from all over the city. Their city. Bianca Tran, a recovering young adult who has overbearing parents. Rachel Saye, a single mother who works at a coffee shop and her beautiful baby boy Jack. They were in his thoughts and prayers as he sat down on the wooden bench. This time, he allowed himself to be moved by the words that echo throughout the church. To truly listen and feel. Sooner than Kevin expects, it was time to go home and rest. He rubbed his tired eyes. A familiar honk of a car snapped Kevin into awareness as he faced up to see what the commotion is for.

There stood Rachel Saye, signaling with a huge wave of the arm for him to come over to the car. He heard classic Christmas songs coming from the radio. Kevin hurried over, careful not to slip on the icy sidewalk. He sat down in the passenger seat of the heated car.

"Oh my goodness, you really didn't have to pick me up like this," he smiled, tears pricking at the corners of his eyes. His cheeks were flushed from the outdoors.

"Nonsense, Kevin. We all agreed on it." Rachel started the engine.

"Yeah Kevin, nonsense!" Jack's high-pitched voice piped up from the backseat. Bianca gave the boy a high-five.

***

After ten goodbyes, that could have very well been twenty, Kevin walked back inside his home and closed the front door. He eyed the tin bird tucked into the doorframe. After all these years, Kevin decided it was right to take some time to reclaim the past.

"Hi dad, I quit my job. Call me back." Kevin hung up the phone as quickly as he had dialed and watched the star-scattered sky without intent on closing the curtains. He lied in bed at peace, a holy voice ringing the words to Silent Night in his head. Goodie curled up on the rug covering the floor, already fast asleep.

Tomorrow was Christmas Day, and Kevin, who was without a wife and kids; Kevin, who had a family of misfits; Kevin, who had just quit his job, felt at home.

An Expensive Mistake

"Owww," I said, muttering under my breath. I slowed my pace down and leaned against the brick wall of the high school so that I could lift my foot up and rub the sore part on my heel.

"What?" Ally asked.

"I stepped on a rock. Look here, see how worn down the tread is? It's almost smooth, so whenever I step on anything I feel it.", I said, pointing at the worn sole.

"Jesus Christ! When was the last time you bought shoes?!" asked Allison loudly, as she stared at the worn sneakers.

"I don't know, I can't afford to buy new ones."

"Why doesn't your mom give you money for it?" The second she asked the question, she regretted it. I could tell by her face that she knew what the answer was.

After putting my foot back down on the pavement, we slowly began to walk towards the line of cars waiting for their owners to arrive. "Because, unlike you, I'm not rich, and can't afford luxuries."

Rolling her eyes jokingly, she laughed, but deep down I think she felt hurt though "Look, I'd be angry too if I didn't have nice clothes, but don't take it out on me." she said.

Ally was right, I probably shouldn't take my anger out on her, but I couldn't help it. She had everything that I wanted: popularity, money, and so many beautiful things although she was really my only great friend, I couldn't help but have some sort of resentment towards her.

"Maybe you should just look into getting a job." Her tone made her seem like she knew everything.

As we continued to walk on the cracked blacktop of the school parking lot, we passed by Justin who was talking to a bunch of his friends. *God* was he hot! I wish he would notice me. I really didn't even think he recognized my existence before last week. I remember in English we had to work together on a project. He didn't say one word that whole time he was partnered with me. Occasionally I would ask him for help, but he would never reply, so I just gave up. Then, last Tuesday, I began to think that I might actually have a chance to be with him when he came up to Ally and I while we were eating lunch alone like always. He told us he was selling shirts to support the football team. Of course, I really didn't have the money to buy it, but I told him I would pay him back later. With a beautiful smile, he told me it was no problem and walked away.

"Earth to Kate, did ya hear me?"

Shaking my head yes, I realized that I'd been staring, "Yeah. I just don't want to throw my social life away just so I can have nice things," I said as we neared closer to Ally's old red '67 Mustang parked near the great oak tree on the school's lawn.

"What social life?" Ally asked jokingly. On the outside we laughed, but I knew she was right. I really didn't have a social life, unless charity work was counted.

I always tried to do what I could for my community. Like how the other day my friends and I picked up trash at the duck pond. It was early in the morning, and absolutely freezing. The cold air made my nose run and my toes turn purple, but I didn't let that stop me. I knew that without us our town wouldn't be as beautiful as it is today. On Fridays, I would help out at the animal shelter down the street from my house. Last week they had me wash this really fluffy dog in the sink, then had me clean out all of the cages. I would also work at the hospital a few times a month. They would usually have me clean the lobby or comfort a patient's family.

I remember one of the girls I would volunteer with was so mean. She hated talking to patients and their families, and even worse, she despised cleaning. The only reason why she volunteered was so that she could get the hours she needed for her school. We never talked much, because we never saw eye to eye on anything, but then one day she came to the hospital as one of the patient's family members instead of as a worker.

I walked into the hospital's lobby, and saw her crying on one of the leather couches.

"What's wrong?" I said, walking over to her. I sat next to her but kept my distance in case she didn't want me there.

"It's my brother," she said, sniffling. I turned to the table next to me and grabbed several tissues and handed them to her. "Thank you." She said bringing them to her soaked eyes.

"What happened to him?" I asked cautiously.

"I don't know. We were walking in the mall together when all of the sudden he collapsed and started seizing." She paused and blew her nose loudly into her damp tissue. "The doctors think it was some sort of an allergic reaction to the lunch we ate."

Unsure of what to say, I quietly looked up at the ceiling. It was peculiar to me how people could go from having feelings of such animosity towards one another to feeling so bad for that same person in a moment of crisis.

"I'm so sorry." I said, unsure of what other words there were to soothe her. Lifting my arm, I gently placed it on her shoulder, hoping that it would provide even the smallest bits of relief.

After that day in the hospitals lobby, she and I became friends. We would talk gossip while we cleaned, and we comforted patients when they came in. She was the first new friend I had made in a very long time, and I was thankful to have her.

Thinking about volunteering made me happy, but I snapped out of my trance when Ally and I finally arrived to her car. The silence we had on the walk over to the car was broken when I asked the question I had been meaning to ask for a while.

"I was thinking about maybe asking for some money from Mom," I said as she put her silver key into the car's lock. Opening the door, she leaned in across the passenger sea, and pulled up the lock so that I could get in. As I opened the door, I pulled off the straps of my backpack, and lowered it to the carpeted floor. As I slid into the seat, I looked through the front window just waiting for Ally to scold me.

"Kate do you think your mom could really afford that right now?" she questioned.

"I know she has a lot of things to worry about right now, but don't you think I should be one of them? I will really feel bad about asking, but I think it is about time she started treating me like Dad did."

Saying this made me think of how much I loved my dad. Throughout my life he was my best friend. He would occasionally scold or punish me, but that didn't matter because nothing could break our bond.

On his days off, he would do fun things with me. He would bring me to the pond to feed the ducks, or teach me how to climb the monkey bars at the park. I remember one day he brought me to the beach and let me swim around while he worked on some papers he needed for work.

"Daddy! Come swimming with me!" I shouted over the waves breaking on the shore of the beach and the Hannah Montana song that was playing off of my CD player.

"Honey, I have work to do," he said sitting on the low beach chair and scribbling away on his papers. Seeing as I was only ten at the time, I wouldn't take no for an answer. I ran out of the water, with my short little legs, over to my father. Then I jumped and launched my body onto his lap that was covered with papers, forgetting that they were there. Knowing I destroyed his paperwork, I began to sob uncontrollably.

"I'm sorrrryyy..." I managed to say through the tears that were welling in my eyes.

"Ugh!" He shouted as he shot up from the chair, dropping me and the papers off of his lap. "Come on Kate! Why did you do that?!" He yelled looking down at me as if he were a skyscraper.

"I'm sorry... I just didn't think about what I was doing." I said crying hard.

"You need to learn to think about what the consequences will be to all of your actions. If you don't, you could get in big trouble one day." He sighed and looked down at me. Then he smiled and picked me up so that we could be face to face. "Listen, it's okay, just promise me that you will think before you act next time. Okay?"

"Okay Daddy."

Thinking of that day of the beach made me realize that he was such a good man in a world full of bad people. When I was little, I thought he was so strong, but as I grew up, I realized that he was weaker than I thought and that he was sick.

One day I walked into the living room and saw him sitting on the couch staring at the blank TV.

"Are you okay Dad?" I waited a minute but he didn't answer. "Dad?"

"Kate, I just need some time to think. Please just let me have some space," he said, shutting his eyes. Seeing as it was strange for him to ask me to leave him alone, I followed his order, but this was just one occasion of his strange behavior. Over time he became a new person who was always distance and who I didn't recognize.

He had depression and even though he loved me and my mother more than anything else in the world, he still left us for the one thing he had been chasing for years. Death. At first I was terribly angry at him for what he had done, but then over time my love for him took over and I forgave him.

"Kate, I know you won't listen to me, but you really should. I am older and wiser after all," she said jokingly as she sat up straight so she could see in her mirror while applying her pink, glossy lipstick.

"Calm down. You're only three years older than me It's worth a shot to ask her, the worst she could say is no." Looking back at Allison, I realized that I wanted to be like her more than anything. Dressed in a tight dress that stopped right below her knee, she looked flawless compared to me-the slob in sweatpants and the oversized tank top that I wore all too often. The money was tight, but going without it risked me continuing to look this way.

"I guess just ask her then."

With her reply, I looked out the window of the car as it started rolling out of the full lot. The hunger I was beginning to have for money was becoming too much. I just knew it could be life changing for me. I mean, new clothes and nice makeup could make any girl popular. I just hoped it is worth the effort.

✳✳✳

"Hey Mom!" I shouted, while walking into the kitchen with my bag draped over my shoulder.

"Hey Kate, how was school?" she asked while she stirred the cookie mix in the clear glass bowl that was sitting on the worn, fake granite of our unstable kitchen island.

"Fine, I guess. Anyways, I have a question for you," placing my backpack on the ground, I sat on the brown wobbly stool so that I could lean and face her in anticipation.

"What do you want Kate?" She said as she rolled her eyes.

"Well, I just wanted to know if I could have some money to buy a few new clothes for school. It's getting cold and I could really use a new jacket, and my shoes are really starting to get worn out,"

"How much do you need?" she asked as she continued to stir furiously.

"Ummm... I don't know... maybe ... two hundred?" I asked jokingly, knowing she would never agree to this amount. She dropped her spoon on the counter and repeated the words 'two hundred dollars' in a very loud voice. This response didn't shock me.

"Yeah, well, I haven't gone shopping in a really long time, so I really need a bunch of things," she frowned and picked up her spoon so she could continue stirring. "Please, Mom." I was begging now.

"Okay, look, I was going to give you a $75 for Christmas. Is that enough?" she asked.

Man, the Christmases at our house used to be the best when my Dad was alive. He didn't skimp on anything and he would literally buy us everything. $75 back then would have been a joke, but today that was about the most I would ever be given at one time.

"Yes! Mom, that would be so great!"

"Okay then, I will give you the money later tonight, but don't expect anything great for Christmas, and please don't ask for any more money. This is all I have to give, unless of course you want to take a cold shower and get your phone shut off." I could sense that she was stressed and I began to regret even asking my mother, but that feeling slowly faded.

"Thanks Mom! I'm gonna call Ally and tell her!" Jumping off the stool, I began to run towards my room.

That night Ally and I talked for hours about what I could buy and what places were having sales. We tried to find ways to get the most out of our money.

"So does the Gap actually have nice clothes? I always hear about how trashy the store it." I said, and Ally chuckled

"Actually it is a pretty high-end store," she said still laughing. "I think I heard from someone that they are having some big sale."

After we talked about a couple more stores, Ally began to make me feel guilty for asking my mom for money, but I was still really excited.

"Do you think your Mom will be able to pay all of her bills without that $75?" she said.

"Of course. She said she had that money saved for me for Christmas, so it shouldn't affect the bills." I sighed, thinking of what Christmas would be like now that I already got my present, "You worry too much Ally"

After hours of talking, we made a shopping date for Friday of next week. I couldn't have been more thrilled.

I barely paid attention in any of my classes that week. Sitting at my desk and searching away on my school-issued laptop in chemistry, I found many coupons that could potentially save me a lot of money. Later that day in math, I went on my phone and searched for stores in my mall, and browsed there selection of clothes. I was so focused on shopping that I almost forgot to go volunteering on Wednesday. All I could do was think about showing up to school next Monday with brand new clothes. I just kept imaging how everyone would talk to me and maybe even Justin would recognize my existence.

Finally, Friday came, and Ally and I went shopping. We went to the Gap, and Macy's, and some other stores. I used my coupons that I had printed of the internet. I was able to get a bunch of tops, a couple dresses, a pair of cheap sneakers, and a nice red lipstick all for just under the $75 my mother had given me. Now all I had to do was wait for Monday to come so I could impress all the rich kids.

***

"Looking good Kate!" Jill shouted from about ten lockers down.

"Thank you," I replied with bright red cheeks. Turning back to my locker, I put my chemistry book in then closed it shut. Looking to my left, I could see that Ally was leaning on the locker next to mine. She wasn't trying to look pretty or anything, but the way she stood there made her look so beautiful.

"Wow, the new look is already getting you attention," she said to me.

"I know. I wonder if Justin noticed," I said closing my locker.

"Well, I actually heard him talking about you last period," She told me with a smile.

"No way! Why did you wait so long to tell me?"

"I don't know," She said as she shifted her weight off of the locker. We started to walk down the hall toward our next class. I followed at a distance as she continued, "If you ask me, I think it's kinda scummy for a guy to only notice you because you have nice clothes and bright red lipstick."

"Nah, I'm sure he has liked me this whole time and he's just been afraid to talk about me 'cause he didn't want his friends to make fun of him."

Ally rolled her eyes, "Then that makes him *and* his friends scummy."

We wandered slowly down the halls. My new black heels glistened and my short skirt bounced up and down. I felt my legs itch under my new knee-high stockings, but nothing could ruin my mood.

The following week at school had been life changing. I was making all kinds of new friends. At first I thought it was because of my new looks, but then I began to realize that I was the one introducing myself to these people. I was the one reaching out. The change of appearance had given me a new confidence that made me feel like I could conquer the world. I thought Ally would be right there with me, but she just slowly watched from the 'side lines'. It had only been a week and a half since my transformation and I could tell me and her were drifting apart. I'd find myself talking to her and she wouldn't even be listening. I would ask her to hang with me, and she would make up some lame excuse like that she had to study. The sad part of it though was that I really didn't care.

We still talked of course, but things were just different. I could tell the things were beginning to become tense between us. I had no clue how much until I got to calculus on Monday.

"I think I'm going to ask my mom if I can borrow just a little more money," I said as we neared our desks. "People will get tired of seeing me in the same outfits and I need more makeup than just some red lipstick."

"Don't you think you are overdoing this? Don't you feel bad taking money from your mother, especially when you know things are tight?"

"Listen, there comes a time when you have to stop worrying about making everyone else happy and worry about yourself for a change." I told Allison with a loud voice. She looked back at me. All I could see was shame and sadness in her face, not the beautiful Allison I knew.

"Weren't you happy last week just to have me as your friend? Aren't you happy making people smile when you volunteer?" she asked as she placed her books down on her desk.

I could feel anger starting to bubble up inside of me. Of course I am happy volunteering. Of course I loved her as a friend. She was just missing the point.

"You don't understand and I wouldn't expect someone who has everything given to them to understand. Why don't you stay out of my business and stick to what you know best: makeup and drama."

Ally frowned and looked down at her feet, "I thought you just cared about giving more than taking. I'm sorry, I guess I was wrong." she began to walk away. I screamed after her.

"I hate to break it to ya Al, but people change." I sat down on the desk chair. "People sure do change," I said mumbling under my breath so nobody could hear. Ally didn't understand. She never would, but that really didn't matter. She can be replaced, hopefully by Justin; the boy of my dreams. They would understand. They would value me more than Ally ever could.

Normally Ally and I would sit in the corner and watch the others eat as we talked about our lives, but today Ally sat alone, and I sat with my new friends. I understood she was upset with me, and probably didn't want to be anywhere near me, but I hoped that she would sit with me, rather than sit alone. I even left an empty chair for her, but she never came over.

"Anyone sitting here?" a voice asked from above as I was staring at my food tray. I looked up and saw it was him. Justin.

"Uhhhh… No, I don't think so." *I don't think so?* God, I was stupid.

"You don't think so?" he said, chuckling as he pulled the chair out from under the table. He sat down and said, "So your name is Allison, right?"

"No," I giggled "That is my frie… neighbor's name. I'm Kate." extending my hand to meet his. I gripped his hand hard feeling his calluses and shook it up and down.

"Well nice to finally meet you Kate." he said as he brought his hand to the back of my chair.

"Actually that is where you are wrong. We did a project together in English before."

"Oh, I'm sorry I don't remember, but it is really sweet that you did." I could feel myself cringing. He probably thought I was some sort of stalker. "Anyways I wanted to tell you that you look really beautiful today."

"Thank you," I blushed.

"Anytime. Listen, here is my number," he said as he wrote the digits down on a cheap cafeteria napkin. "If you ever feel like getting to know me better, feel free to shoot me a text," he said winking.

He got up and walked back towards his friends, who greeted him with high fives. I smiled and looked back down on my tray and began to play with the mushy school food. That whole day all I could do was smile.

***

"Mom, have I ever told you how much I love you?" I asked as I sat down next to her on the black leather couch in the living room.

"What do you want, Katherine?" Seeing through my phoniness. She frowned as she put down her magazine.

"Well, I was wondering if I could borrow some more money," I asked sweetly.

"Kate, what did I tell you? I said don't ask me for money for a while. I can't afford to give you something I don't have," picking back up the magazine, she began to list off things that her paycheck will be going to and how they are important, but all I heard was how it was all more important than me.

"Mom you are not being fair to me!"

"Well, I really don't care if I am. No means no. Now go do your homework."

I was so angry I couldn't breathe, I felt my palms beginning to sweat and my jaw beginning to tighten

My mother was so selfish. I thought she was giving like me, but no, all she is doing is taking. So I would give her a taste of her own medicine. I would take something of hers, but what should it be? I turned around and before I knew what I was doing, I threw some of the ugliest words I have ever uttered at her.

"Now I understand! You're the reason why Dad killed himself!" Her face began to contort, as if she were about to cry endlessly. Then she brought her hands to her mouth so she could hide the sobs that were about to be unleashed. Before the first tear dropped, I had ran up the stairs and down the hall to my room where I slammed the door. I flew myself on my squeaky twin bed and began to sob into my pillow. I knew what I had just said was really wrong, and it would have broken my heart to see her cry like that I had to run away.

I layed in bed for a while and wondered if my mother was okay. Then I began to remember why I was mad at her in the first place. I remember how much she didn't care about me. That's when I thought of a plan that would get me some much needed cash.

Walking down the dimly lit hall towards my mother's room, I was as quiet as could be. Slowly, I opened the door and walked over to her dresser. A mirror stood atop of it, as I came into its view. Looking back at myself, my hands slowly moved toward her oak jewelry box.

There were so many beautiful things in it. From pins and earrings, to rings and barrettes. She took great care of them because they were the only things left of hers, that reminded her of our wealthy past and my father. My eyes wandered over everything as I tried to find the most beautiful object possible. Figuring that the prettier it was, the more expensive it would be, I picked up a pair of earrings. They were silver and hung down about an inch from where the earring would go through the ear. At the end was a beautiful set of three diamond. They were all in a row just hanging there vertically. I could imagine how beautiful they would look with a lace wedding dress and how great they would look on me.

These would be the perfect thing to sell. I knew that if I thought they were so beautiful then others would too. I wanted to try them on once before I let them go, so I took out my cheap plastic studs and slipped the earrings in.

They were absolutely stunning. The light made them shine and sparkle as they hung from my skin. They were perfect and they looked amazing on me. I just had to show everyone them before letting them go. So after a great selfie was taken, I posted the picture on Instagram and made it my new profile picture on Facebook. Not only would everyone see them on me, they would see how beautiful and 'rich' I was.

The next day, I brought the earrings to the local pawn shop and sold them for two thousand dollars. Apparently all the diamonds were not only real, but they were really expensive. Later that night, I layed on my bed and counted my cash slowly, letting the bills slip through my fingers, then for some reason, I began to think about Al. I thought about all the times we had spent together, and all the shopping adventures we could go on with this money. After all of that thinking, I realized that I really missed her. So I picked up my old cracked phone and dialed her number. When she answered I began to tell her about my latest adventure.

"Won't your mom see that her earrings are missing?" She asked with a harsh tone in her voice.

"Nah, she never wears her jewelry," I said looking at my untrimmed nails. I could finally get a manicure now!

"Don't you feel bad for doing that to your mother?"

"No. It's all for a good cause. Me." I chuckled. "Anyways, do you want to go shopping with me on Sunday?" Smiling, I hoped ally would say yes, "It will be like the good old days!"

"Kate, the last thing I would ever want to do right now is to go shopping with you and the way you have been acting," She said in a very rude way.

"Fine then, I will just call Erica and see if she wants to go," I responded in return to her terrible comment.

"Fine!" she shouted as if she didn't care, as I hung up the phone. If she wanted to be mean to me, then she wasn't a good friend. She should be happy that I wanted to improve myself. She would be sorry when I'm the most popular girl in school and she is on the bottom. I'll show her.

That Sunday, Erica and I went shopping. I bought so many things that I had to take trips back to Erica's car so I didn't have to carry around all of my bags while we shopped some more.

The day was great except for the encounter I had with Mia, the lady in charge of the youth volunteer program at the hospital. She was shocked to see me shopping because I had promised her that I would be at the hospital, but to tell you the truth I *forgot*. Besides, I think improving my image is a little more important than helping old people who are going to just end up dying anyways.

Of course I didn't spend the whole two thousand, but I did spend most of it. I had five hundred dollars that I decided to hold onto for my next shopping day. I spent the whole night admiring my new items, experimenting with my new makeup, and putting together outfits for school. I woke up to a night full of happy dreams about Justin and my new friends.

That Monday I went to school feeling like a new person. Not only did I look different, but I felt like my life had now been changed. People noticed me. I went from Justin not even knowing my name to him asking me out on a date during chemistry!

"So Kate, we have been texting a lot lately. I would really like to get to know you more. I thought maybe we could go bowling or see a movie or something this weekend." I smiled wide and could feel my cheeks blushing.

"You know what Justin? I would really like that." he smiled in return. I thought about just how great the day was turning out.

But despite the great events of chemistry, Ally didn't talk to me at all. Who needed her anyways?! She was just jealous.

Things honestly couldn't be better for me. Everyone loved me now! But when I got home later that day, all of my good luck faded away.

I opened the front door and began to walk to my room. My footsteps echoed in the hall but I could vaguely hear my mom calling me into the kitchen. I put my bag down on the couch and walked over to her.

Annoyed, I asked, "What do you want Mom?" while leaning on the kitchen island. Anyone could sense the tension between us. This was the first time we had talked since I threw those horrible words at her. I felt bad, but at the same time she deserved it.

"Well, I was on Facebook, and I came across this beautiful selfie of you." She said as she chopped carrots into small cubes. Ugh I am so dead! At least she noticed how beautiful my selfie was. "When I looked a little closer at your picture, I realized you were wearing my earrings."

"Yeah sorry about that, but they're just so beautiful. I'll put them back in your jewelry box now." I said lying as if I still actually owned them. I knew I had to get out of this conversation.

"Can I actually see them now, please? I want to make sure nothing happened to them."

"You mean you want them in your hand right now?" I asked, slowly knowing I wouldn't be able to provide her what she wanted.

"Yes, will that be a problem?" she asked, dropping the knife on her cutting board and looking up at me.

"Umm…. I have something I need to tell you mom," I paused. Her eyes gazed into mine and I could feel sadness building up in the both of us.

"I really needed some money, so I sold them. Honestly, I didn't think you would notice. Sorry Mom," I said, tears began to build in my eyes, my apology wasn't to sincere because I knew i needed that money, but I was sad when I began to think about how I wouldn't be able to see my friends if I was grounded.

"I really thought better of you Kate. I never thought you would do something like that to me. I thought what you said to me the other day was the worst thing you would every do to me, but now you do this? I trusted you, and you really let me down." she said looking into my eyes,

"I didn't mean to hurt you, Mom." I said, trying to bring my arm to her shoulder, but she just pulled away in return.

"But you did Kate! I thought you were better than this." She said starting to cry.

"I am mom, I just really wanted to fit in, and I felt like you didn't care about my feelings, I am so sorry." My apology was sincere as I began to think about what life would be like if I lost my dad, and my mother's love. "Please mom, I will pay you back for the earrings somehow. I'm sorry."

Sniffling she stood up straight, and brushed out the wrinkles on the shirt. After taking a deep breath, she said, "It is okay. I am not the one who is going to be hurt by this."

"What do you mean?" I said confused. How could she so mad then tell me it was okay? And how was I going to be the one getting hurt by this?

"Your father gave those to me the day you were born. I was going to give them to you on your wedding day."

Older Brother

The sound of the food cart rolling into the main area awoke me, as it did every morning. I rolled over from facing the wall to look across the room where the other bed was. Damn. Still no roommate, I thought to myself. Sometimes someone would get admitted overnight and I would wake up with a new friend in my "dorm." Today, I suppose, I'm alone again. The door opened after two knocks that shuddered the door in its frame.

"Nik, it's time to get up, bud" Mr. James' voice seemed to boom even when speaking in morning tones. I squinted my tired eyes to focus on Mr. James' deadpan expression.

I held up a tired hand with only my thumb protruding. Mr. James nodded and proceeded to knock on the neighboring rooms. Tossing my thin sheets to the side, I sat up, immediately greeted with a pounding migraine. Groaning, I made my way down the hall into "the bubble," or, the main area. We call it the bubble because of a giant glass, well, *bubble*, that took the place of where the ceiling would have been. I suppose it was put in place to make us not feel like we were in prison. You can change the visuals all you want, it still *feels* like a prison to me.

This isn't my first time getting locked up here, I know that much. As bad as my memory has gotten, my brain has come to remember this place- the hospital. The way all the bedroom corridors connect to make a makeshift city block. How the nurses were always visible from their glass-shielded office. It has an unfortunate sense of familiarity to me, something the drugs hadn't burnt out of my brain quite yet.

I've made a poor habit of, "dancing with the devil," let's say. Some may call it selfish, but to me, it's proven to be the only answer I can think of. Of what I can remember, I've made six attempts on my own life. People have always asked me "why" and that's truthfully the hardest question to answer. I don't have a definitive reason *why* I feel like ending it is the answer. My life was pretty okay, for the most part, but after my emotions started changing, so did everything else. Every day was winter - cold and dismal. I'd been prescribed every drug imaginable - Welbutrin, Zoloft, Lithium, and Prudoxin, just to name a few, and nothing changed, hence why I ended up here, again. The side effects ranged anywhere from headaches to hallucinations, and every day had a different hurdle I could never seem to get over.

The scrape of the knife against the slightly charred bread echoed in the main area. Low-fat margarine quickly melted on the surface and filled the bread's pores. My calloused feet slapped against the cold tile as I meandered from the kitchen counter to my favorite chair in front of the TV next to Amity. Coincidentally, it seemed she was here every time I was. Quiet when unprovoked, she only really spoke when you gave her something to overthink about. I wanted to watch some TV to wake myself up before embarking on a conversation with her. My thumb pressed the red button on the television's remote as I aimed it waveringly towards the black screen. The monochrome fuzz cleared and Anterwood's "favorite news anchor," Ted Bluser, began ranting about the weather.

"It's a breezy 63 degrees out in busy Anterwood today." Ted beamed his television smile as he read off the teleprompter behind the camera. Thanks for the update, Ted, I scoffed. I wouldn't know the weather otherwise. They usually take us outside once every other day, and on days it rains, we're locked in.

I began to retrospect upon my last stay at the hospital. From what I can recall, it rained most days. The day before I was set to release, the sun made a much needed appearance. It was like experiencing nature for the first time again - the feeling of fresh air flooding my lungs was like having a weight lifted off my chest. The wind was much stronger than the weak breeze in the hospital from the ancient air conditioners in the windows.

I'd never been one for sports, so I spent my gifted time in the outdoors sitting next to Amity, far away from the flower garden to ensure we didn't see any bees. What began to soil my serenity was Amity's yapping. "Look at the clouds, Nik, it might start raining again. Do you think we should go inside soon before we get wet? Rain water can be cold, you know, we could die of hypothermia. Remember that story you told me about how your brother had hypothermia-"

"We're at a hospital, Amity, I think we'll be fine. Can we just enjoy this weather for once? " Delivered quickly and bluntly, my reply shut Amity up fairly quickly, but she was right. As soon as I turned my attention back to the breeze, I gazed up at the sky. The clouds rolled in, just like I'd seen in cartoons - a single storm cloud sits over a character and unleashes gallons of water, just as it did to Amity and I. The feelings of liberation and freedom the wind had breathed into me were quickly washed away by the cold rain. Since then, I've tried not to get my hopes up.

I made my way over to the medication window, where I greeted the nurse in charge of distributing the meds for everyone in the ward.

"Morning Daniella, what's on the menu today," I said, full of disdain and sarcasm, which wasn't reciprocated in her reply.

I don't *like* taking medication, and never did, for that matter. If it were up to me, which it obviously hasn't been, I'd be on my way, living a normal life off of medication, just like the rest of my friends. The question has always plagued my mind as to how I could be so similar to the people I grew up with, yet I had to be the cinderblock, the weight, that dragged everyone down. Obviously, I didn't *ask* for whatever it is that's going on in my head, but, at this point, I'm just rolling with the punches, or, the pills.

"Welp, we're starting you on a new anxiety medication. It should help with your sleep, too. You won't feel much different today, but tomorrow morning, you should be feeling less anxious." Her reply was dry, as if she had a list of replies behind the window that she was only programmed to say.

"Sounds like a plan to me," I replied, taking the pill. Out of habit, my tongue escaped from my mouth, stretched long, proving I had swallowed the chalky morsel. Once Daniella made her nonverbal satisfaction known, I made my way back over to the television area where Amity remained sitting.

"Good morning, Amity," I said, attempting to test my luck, hoping I would get a simple nod back and nothing more. She stared blankly at her egg and cheese sandwich that laid in her lap on a paper plate. Despite already taking two bites, she didn't look keen on eating it.

"Hi, Nik," She barely opened her mouth to let the reply squeak out.

I don't often try to make conversation with Amity; she's not my ideal type of person to hold a conversation with. The way she spoke about things I said just gave me this unexplainable feeling in my stomach, like I was going to be sick, and my heart would pound. Regardless, I was feeling somewhat decent on this given morning, so I attempted once again to make a conversation with any sort of substance to liven the dead air in the room.

"It's nice out today, maybe we'll get to go outside," I aimed to sound as hopeful as possible, because hell, we could both use some fresh air.

"Yeah, I don't know. What if I get sunburnt? Or they make us run laps or something? I hate running, Nik, and I know you're not a fan either. I also think I'm allergic to bees. If I get stung by a bee I could probably die."

Here we go, I thought, rolling my eyes. The feeling began to return, and my appetite diminished entirely. Amity always found *something* to freak out over.

"Oh, I really don't think you have anything to worry about," I replied, attempting to verbally comfort the porcelain-skinned woman, who uncontrollably bounced her legs in her seat. Suddenly my brain was swarmed with thoughts of the last time I got stung by a bee - it must've been years ago. All I could remember is the pain was excruciating. But that was before all of the medicine - when I could *feel*. What if I'm allergic to bees? Maybe I should stay in if they take us out.

Standing up, I followed Amity to the trash to dispose of the remnants of our breakfasts. The fire in my stomach grew stronger after my conversation with her. I couldn't pinpoint exactly what it was about her that made me feel this way, all I knew was that I wasn't a fan, at all.

Without a farewell, she hastily made her way to the bathroom. The time had come for me to clean myself up, and the water pathetically drizzled from the showerhead to the soundtrack of Amity regurgitating what she ate for breakfast into the toilet.

This was how every day started. I always showered right after breakfast, and Amity always nervously threw up her food next door. I began to wonder if I would ever know any other way of life.

***

My usual morning headache wasn't present today when I woke up. It must have been the new medication. I wasn't sure whether or not to be happy or scared something good happened to me. I don't have time to celebrate when I'm trying to prepare for what's going to ruin my day. Regardless, my morning ritual began: toast, pill, television, and shower. It all tended to blur together to me at this point.

It was raining, already dampening my mood. That's exactly what I was talking about - 60 seconds barely passed before something happened to kill my mood. And once that happens everything else comes crashing down. I began thinking of how lonely I was. It was the first thing to come to mind - something I was *always* thinking about, amongst everything else. Amity is just about the closest person in here to a friend it can get. Even then, saying she's a friend of mine is a stretch.

Still not having a roommate this morning made me question if I'll ever get one. Will I be alone in here forever? Where do I go even if getting out *is* possible? I don't have anyone else on the outside of these walls, or at least I don't remember having anyone else. Thinking about it brought that fire back into my stomach. I made a poor attempt at using one of my "coping skills" I learned here, breathing deeply and slowly, attempting to suppress the acid crawling up my esophagus.

I resolved to watch cartoons, a mindless way to pass the rainy day. I let the droning sound of the rain drown out the television and adjusted my position in the chair, preparing for a marathon of reruns.

***

The place I was in felt eerily familiar, yet ominous. It was no longer the hospital - the dull brown on the walls seemed to melt into the hardwood floors they met. Dust covered every shelf, the couch looked like it hadn't been sat on in months.

The couch was what made me realize I was in a figment of my parents' home. The first time I tried to take my own life was on that couch - I sat hunched on my knees, rolling pills between my fingertips and over the palms of my hands. My parents trusted me enough to be taking my medication on my own, leaving all of the cabinets unlocked, pills in plain sight, and giving me everything I needed to start a life of trying to end it.

I made my way through the quiet home, my footsteps echoed off of the familiar walls. Standing atop the basement stairs, my stomach begin to burn. The acid in my stomach felt like it was boiling, and my heartrate was growing exponentially. I no longer felt in control of my own being - only able to see as the events played out before my eyes. It was as if someone was playing a movie in front of my eyes and my head was strapped in place to a chair.

Upon arriving in the basement, my gaze was fixed upon myself in a scene that I had previously tried to forget. It was the bathroom at my parents' house - the walls painted a comforting pale blue. The tiles felt like ice under my bare feet. I stood, but wasn't slipping, just shaking from the lack of body heat. Upon looking, I felt paralyzed - all of the emotions from that night flooded over me - the hate I had for myself, the sadness, the anger.

The burning feeling of guilt came over me, slowly, like hot tar, as sweat began to escape from my pores. A vignette closed around my eyes, getting darker and darker as details became progressively blurrier. Endless amounts of pills flashed before my eyes, each time a handful was swallowed was replayed, projected behind my eyelids.

My body jumped as it awoke and immediately sent itself into a panic. Hyperventilating on my bed, my trachea seemed to slowly contract, making it more and more difficult to catch a breath. Looking for something, or someone-anyone- to reach out, my eyes couldn't focus and my voice seemed buried deep in my chest with my breath.

"Nik? Nik! What is *wrong* with you? Answer me!" I heard as I came to breathe heavily. The fog that had clouded my eyes began to clear as I focused in on Amity's porcelain face. Taking in my surroundings, I could make out the faces of Mr. James, as well as two other nurses who were holding an oxygen mask to my face. Feeling slowly began to return to my body, my lungs- my throat burning more than anything. Looking up at Amity, I became overwhelmed, not sure how to react. Had I scared her? I didn't want that.

"I - I think I had a panic attack," I attempted to explain hoarsely. She looked so frightened.

"I was using the bathroom and heard someone gasping for breath and then heard a loud bang. I came out and saw you and didn't know what to do-I just didn't know what to do, Nik." Amity said, a look of exacerbation overtook her face.

"That's enough, Amity." Mr. James interrupted her before she could spew any more. "We'll take care of this. You go back on to bed now," Mr. James instructed to Amity.

"I'm glad you're okay, Nik," she said, her words gaining more confidence as her smile overtook her worried face. Taking my hand in hers, she continued, "I'll stop by later, to see how you're doing, okay?"

It was a feeling I wasn't accustomed to-someone wanting to come and see me.

"Thank you," was all I could manage.

The Forgotten Battle

As the sun began to set over Washington D.C, the temperature shifted to a frozen winter's night. The final moments of sunlight painted dark shadows of buildings along the ground, leaving enough light to highlight Bowing Steel Hardware Store. Clyde Wolfhart lurked in the shadows created by the buildings, waiting for his agent. His shivering hands clutched a manila folder labeled "Adolar Steinhauser." Wearing nothing more than a black overcoat, Clyde attempted to keep warm.

Where is he? He should be leaving by now, Clyde thought to himself while waiting for Adolar to leave the store. If he doesn't come out in the next 30... his thought was cut short as Adolar walked out of the hardware store, locking the door behind him. Adolar flipped the open sign to "closed" and began to walk across the street. Stepping out of the shadows, Clyde revealed himself to Adolar.

"How are you Adolar? I didn't expect you would keep your handler waiting this long," Clyde said sharply, indicating his annoyance.

"I had to finish helping a customer out. Forgot how impatient you are, Wolfhart," Adolar said with rough German accent.

Brushing off that snarky reply, Clyde continued, "We have a mission for you; it's personal this time…"

A puzzled look spanned across Adolar's face until he realized what was about to happen. His face straightened and he replied in a serious tone, "Is it her? Did you finally get the clearance after everything I gave you?"

"It's her. After everything you gave us, we were able to conduct a three-day surveillance of the compound and you were right; the Nazi's are up to something big there, and we must act fast." Clyde replied.

Staring into Clyde's eyes, Adolar began to remember the night everything in his life changed.

***

It was a gloomy Thursday night, and the streets in Germany were buzzing with soldiers. The Steinhauser's home had been torn from its original warm welcome to cold and lifeless. Extending his arm around his sister's neck, Adolar gave her a gentle embrace, then whispered in her ear, "It's going to be okay, they won't find us here."

Anneliese quivered in his arms as tears ran down her cheeks. "They are coming Adolar, they will take them from us and take our family, we shouldn't have gone through with this," she whispered raspily.

Adolar's mother, Hilda, shouted, "Will you two shut up! We made the right decision, we are going to be fine." As the room grew quiet again, noises outside the home started to grow louder.

Suddenly, Anneliese said, "I'm scared I think they are-" her sentence was stopped with the sound of hinges breaking and the front door being flung to the ground, creating a shockwave that rippled through the house. The front door being broke down. Ripped from its hinges and flung down to the ground, a shockwave was the only thing that could be heard throughout the house. A team of people entered the home with lights blazing, and one man could be heard saying, "Finde sie schnell, sie müssen immer noch hier sein." Adolar knew the Gestapo had just entered their home and they believed they were still there. It was game over. Rushing through the house and destroying anything in their path, the Gestapo began their search. They flipped tables, bookshelves, and anything else that looked like it could hide someone. Adolar and his family were hiding in the attic, where they thought they would be safe. The next moment, the door to the attic burst open and the Gestapo entered.

The sound of steel-toed boots clanking against the hardwood floor echoed as the storm leader entered the room. As he entered, he knocked over one of the bookshelves that stood by the attic door and proceeded to walk closer to the family. Darting his eyes slowly from each shaking person on the floor, the storm leader cocked back the operating bolt handle on his weapon and aimed at Adolar and his family. In a firm voice he said, "Wo sind die Juden? Wir wissen, dass du sie versteckst." Adolar and his family were too shaken up to answer.

After a brief pause, Anneliese shouted, "You can't take them, you are going to hurt them!" Covering their eyes in fear, the two young boys behind her began to sob loudly. Anneliese glanced back at the Jewish boys, giving the officer just what he was looking for.

The Storm Leader gave a nasty reply, "Ergreife die Jungen hinter dem Mädchen und bringe sie zum Lastwagen. Die Familie wird als nächstes kommen." As instructed, the men in the room took the two boys out of the attic and brought them to the truck, waiting outside.

The commander broke his German dialect and said, "You have betrayed your country so you can hide the enemy? Don't you know these Jews are the reason why Germany hasn't been succeeding? You all have brought great dishonor to our Fuhrer's name and now it is time you served your punishment." Hearing the propaganda spill from the officer's mouth shifted Adolar's emotions. The intensity of the moment was too much for him to keep control. His mind began to spin rapidly filling his body with rage.

Adolar thought to himself, pondering how it was possible that these people could get away with this. What they were doing wasn't right, they couldn't possibly get away with it; all the people they were rounding up were innocent and now, as a German citizen who had tried to help those people, he'd be viewed as the enemy, right alongside them.

As the men escorted him and his family out of the house and onto the truck, one guard was left alone to watch them as the agents moved on to the next home.

***

Snapping out of his trance, Adolar's face was red and twisted, as if he was about to knock Clyde out. As his mind raced, his teeth clenched tight and his breathing became heavy and slow. He hated how they took his family from him and their irrational hatred of Jews. Blood boiling, Adolar's fists clenched tight and Clyde began to take notice of Adolar's sudden change in attitude.

"Adolar, did you hear me?" Clyde said, as the blank expression across Adolar's face made him think that nothing he had just said registered in Adolar's head.

"Sorry, I was just remembering… never mind. Repeat what you said." relaxing his fists, Adolar began to calm down.

Clyde furrowed his brow in confusion and repeated, "Take this folder, it contains a code and a phone number you will need for tomorrow. At exactly ten in the morning, you need to call that number and you will receive further instructions."

That was the moment he decided. Taking the manila folder from Clyde's hand, Adolar said, "Thanks, this means a lot to me. This is the last time the Germans take something dear from us!"

"Well, Adolar, I best be going. Don't forget- ten tomorrow." Clyde nodded.

"Of course, I won't forget." Adolar began to walk down the street under the moonlit sky that had now encompassed the world around him.

Alone, Clyde began to think to himself. His time had come. It was now or never for Adolar. After everything he had been through he could finally get his sister back and stop the greatest evil they had ever seen. He is the best at what he does. After watching Adolar fade away into the darkness, Clyde turned around and headed in the other direction.

***

Arriving at work at 9:50 in the morning, Adolar headed to the back storage room where he put on his bright red apron and shiny white name tag. After putting on his uniform, he quickly ran out of the back room and headed for the front door. Taking a brief look around outside to see if anyone was coming to the store, he locked the doors and turned the "Closed" sign back over. Adolar went to the telephone and pulled out the manila folder from Clyde. As he opened the folder, a single sheet of paper fell to the floor, causing Adolar to bend down and read it. On the paper contained the phone number he needed to call as well as the code he needed. He dialed the number as quickly as possible and waited for someone to pick up.

When the line opened, a woman who sounded young and perky answered, "Hello, how may I help you today?"

Knowing exactly what to say, Adolar replied, "Hi, I was wondering if I can check if my package has arrived yet?"

The woman replied kindly, "Sure what is the number for your order?"

He read the code that Clyde instructed him to deliver and the woman replied, "Ah yes, one moment please." The line cut out for a moment and someone else picked up.

"Is this Adolar Steinhauser?" the man asked.

"Yes, this is he. I am calling for further instructions..."

The man on the other end of the line responded sternly, "Oh, yes" as he cleared his throat, "we have been expecting your call. Please report to Fort Lesley J. McNair tonight by eight. You will be briefed when you arrive and give the code from agent Clyde Wolfhart to the base patrol for entrance." Before Adolar could say another word or ask a question, the line was cut and left him with static ringing in his ear. This is it, my chance to find my sister and get her back, he thought.

***

Arriving at Fort Lesley J. McNair, Adolar pulled up to the check-in station. His hands tightly gripped the steering wheel of his black Pontiac Metropolitan Torpedo Six, and he began to feel a little nauseous. He repeated the code to the guard at the check in station and the guard told him to proceed to Hanger Six. Adolar followed the road signs, until he arrived at a large lot, containing multiple hangers the size of small factories surrounding 6 different runways. The sound of planes taking off consumed the air and distracted Adolar from his nauseousness. Pulling into Hanger Six, he was met by a group of five armed soldiers.

Walking up to his car, the first soldier in the pack said, "Sir, get out of the vehicle immediately."

Adolar quickly removed himself from the vehicle and closed the door. Without hesitation, the soldiers surrounded Adolar and began to pat him down and search his person as the others looked on. After being inspected, he was further instructed to follow one of the soldiers. The soldier led him deeper inside the hanger to a small room that stuck out of the back wall. Walking toward the room, Adolar took note of a small plane that sat in the middle of the hanger. The plane was black and low profile and, from what he assumed, was used for surveillance and single person drop offs.

The cool night left a lingering breeze inside the terminal that brought back his uneasy stomach. Adolar had no time to feel sick, so he focused on the goal at hand and headed into the room. When he walked in, he was met by two agents; the first who spoke went by the name of Sergeant McWilliams.

With a stern tone, the Sergeant said, "Welcome Adolar, we have important business to discuss." Recognizing the voice, Adolar realized it was the gentleman he spoke with on the phone. As he walked to the man, Adolar looked up to meet Sergeant McWilliams' eyes. Covered by shadows from his camouflage cap, he was unable to fully meet his eyes, leaving Adolar apprehensive. McWilliams' scraggly white beard fell down to his chest, giving Adolar the sense he must be older. To the right of McWilliams, was agent Clyde. Both men greeted Adolar with firm handshakes and motioned for him to sit down. Dimly lit and bare of furniture, the room left a cool air that made Adolar uncomfortable but kept him attentive. There was a single desk with one wooden chair in front where Adolar sat, and two wooden chairs towards the back of the room, where Sergeant McWilliams and agent Clyde sat.

"I know this is going to sound absurd but I can assure you, if you are up to the task, you can help the Allies win this war." Sergeant McWilliams said straight to Adolar.

"I am willing to do anything possible, I want to see the Nazis burn for what they have done, their actions are unjust and uncalled for and it pains me to see my nation like this but I think we must burn the evil inside." Adolar replied.

Sergeant McWilliams smiled, "Good, we are on the same page. Agent Clyde here decided you were the best choice for this mission. We know this mission has more meaning to you than it does to us…."

Adolar became more solemn, "Do you know if she is there; my sister, sir?"

Sergeant McWilliams replied, "We can indeed confirm that young prisoners from Auschwitz, both Jewish and German, have been recently moved by the Nazis for what we can assume is a new program they are starting. One of Hitler's most prized compounds has become significantly more active recently. Our allies in France intercepted a few transports heading from Paris to Neuschwanstein Castle carrying what seemed to be medical and weapon supplies under the name Kognitiver Empfang or Cognitive Reception in English. We have reason to believe the Nazis are taking some of their prisoners and experimenting on them by engaging in cerebral... *"enhancement.""*

With his heart sinking into his stomach, Adolar thought about his sister. He could see her, lying on a cold metal table, sending shivers down his spine. She was lying there, helpless as the doctors held her down with chains. All Adolar could imagine was her screaming for dear life as the Nazis performed God knows what on her.

Sergeant McWilliams began again, "Adolar, we are giving you the opportunity to save your sister and save your country from the terror it displays to the innocent lives there. We want you to head into the base and destroy whatever you can find of this program there. The Nazis must not be allowed to keep putting innocent people into harm's way and they must not be allowed to further advance in this war."

Adolar nodded his head in agreement and asked, "When do I start?"

"You leave in an hour on the plane out in the hanger. You will have 24 hours from ejection to do your job and get out. With the recent signing of the Lend Lease Act, we have coordinated with the British to bomb the castle at the end of your 24 hour mark to finish them off. A bombing run can only be so effective against a castle the size of Neuschwanstein so your job is extremely important."

Adolar stood up agreed, "Well gentlemen, let's begin."

***

"T-minus ten minutes till ejection!" Screamed the pilot as they crossed the German border. The black sky surrounded the plane and kept Adolar and the pilot hidden from enemy view. Suddenly, Adolar was thrown into a sea of emotions, fear and anxiety overwhelmed his mind and caused him to begin to hyperventilate. Adolar's body was perspiring so much it felt like his clothes weighed a couple extra pounds. He thought to himself, how could I get out? This was suicide!

"T-minus one minute till dispatch!" Yelled the pilot once again as the castle could be seen in the distance approaching faster and faster. Quickly latching onto the ejection bar next to his seat with sweaty hands, Adolar could barely keep his grasp. As the sweat rolled down his face, the heat created a dense fog in his goggles. All he could see were blurry speckled lights and pure darkness. Rattling him and causing his hands to shake uncontrollably, panic flooded his bones. Adolar held the parachute bag attached to him tightly and began to mentally prepare himself for departure. His eyes narrowed.

"Five."

His right hand gripped that ejection bar with all his might.

"Four."

His mind became as calm as the ocean.

"Three."

Standing in the darkness beckoning him to come forward, Annaliese was the sole image in his head.

"Two."

She led his mind into a laboratory filled with the bodies of dead Jewish boys and girls as she sat down on a medical table.

"One."

She let out an ear piercing scream that sounded like thousands of voices screaming at once.

"EJECT!"

Adolar was launched out of the plane into the black sky, screaming and in complete horror.

Flopping like a fish out of water, Adolar squirmed in the air, unable to gain any form of balance as gravity dragged him towards the earth. Left, right, left, Adolar's head spun in circles. He couldn't think straight and was running out of time quickly. As he plummeted toward the ground, he swung his right arm across his chest to pull the cord to open the parachute. With all his might, Adolar ripped the cord and the parachute launched out of the bag and, straight up into the sky above him.

Kicking up piles of snow beneath, Adolar landed abruptly on the ground. For a few moments, he was left lying in the snow looking up into the sky and breathing heavily, as his body was in complete shock. Slowly standing up and looking around his current location, Adolar observed the snowy forest he had landed in. The trees were covered with white mist and the ground was piled high with several inches of snow. Faint light shone through the trees to the east and Adolar knew that must be the castle. Gathering himself up, Adolar trudged slowly but surely through the snow. Following the distant light passing tree by tree for an hour, he came out of the forest to observe the great wonder of the Neuschwanstein Castle. The castle stood so high off the ground it looked as though it touched the clouds.

Adolar thought, how am I supposed to get into this place? He decided to begin trudging toward the castle slowly. Walking tirelessly through the snow, he began to devise a plan. The first thing I need to do is figure out where the entrance is. He stopped and scanned the castle. As he surveyed the dark horizon only illuminated by the castle light, his eyes drifted straight over to a particularly bright spot. Adolar noticed a vehicle making its way directly toward the bright light. That must be the main entrance, that's my best shot in. Before he took another step he quickly noticed a fainter light around the outer wall of the castle. Guards, it must be a guard. Trudging on, getting closer and closer to the guard in sight, Adolar devised another plan in his mind. When he reached about 100 yards away from the guard, Adolar dove into the snow to remain unseen until his final idea sparked in his head. It was only one patrol guard on his own making his way along the outer wall. Kicking the snow around him and smoking, the guard took no notice of Adolar's presence which was exactly what he needed. As the guard leaned against the wall, rubbing the butt of his cigarette against the brick, Adolar began to crawl through the snow towards the guard.

Time slowed down and everything grew quiet around the area. Flashing his light out into the dark, snowy horizon, the soldier was looking for anything out of place. Adolar made his first move; with a quick dash he sprinted to a jutted out part of the castle wall behind the guard. The sound of footsteps caused the guard to fling himself around, only to be met with the sight of wind kicking up snow rapidly on the dark horizon. Hands quivering and legs shaking, Adolar started to swear to himself. He looked down and picked up a stone brick that was covered in snow. Wiping the snow off the brick, Adolar locked his right hand around it and grasped it tightly. The moment the guard turned back around to look into the dark horizon, Adolar made a lightning fast sprint towards him. Before the guard could even turn, Adolar smashed the brick into the back of his head. The guard dropped to the ground, a lifeless body. The clean white snow around the guard's head turned into a dark red puddle. The brick fell from Adolar's hand straight into the snow. For a brief second, Adolar was fine, breathing heavily as he looked down at the body. The next moment his mind took off in another direction. As shock ran through his nerves, he was sent into a frantic state. He began to tumble backward as his sense of balance faded along with his sanity. Adolar fell back into the castle wall striking his head against the brick, and was sent back, once again, to the time of their capture.

✳✳✳

The Gestapo agent who was left alone to watch the prisoners aboard the truck began to speak to Adolar and his family.

The agent said, "You stupid citizens, how dare you betray your country the way you did tonight! You should know by now the consequences of hiding the enemy, concentration camps are not something you should want to go to." Growing in anger as the soldier spoke, Anneliese's face became filled with her emotion.

When he began to speak again, Anneliese spat at him and muttered, "Jews are not your problem, you should be worried about the Allies who are going to kill you all!" The soldier, taken aback by the brazen action, was momentarily unsure of how to react. Coming to his senses, he quickly shifted his eyes back to Anneliese. The soldier's brows furrowed with anger and he took a step towards her. Cocking his fist back, the agent punched Anneliese with all his might knocking her over to the side of the truck. Letting out a sharp grunt, Adolar jumped at the soldier as though a switch in his head had been turned on. Before the soldier could grab his gun, Adolar was on top of him, with pure rage in his eyes, Adolar began to beat the life out of the soldier. Fist by fist, punch by punch, he ferociously beat the man until his face was unrecognizable. There was no more heartbeat. Adolar stopped as the blood dripped off his broken knuckles and looked up to see the horror on his mother and sister's faces.

"Are-are-are you alright Anneliese? Did he hurt you?" Asked a shaken up Adolar.

Sitting down in shock, Anneliese did not respond. Hilda quickly replied to Adolar saying, "Run, if they find you here and see what you have done then you will suffer the same fate as that man on the ground. Run my son, run. Find your uncle who lives in the U.S. and don't come back. I will keep you in my prayers." Adolar stared into her eyes as they filled with tears, then without hesitation, he ran down the street, now a Nazi criminal.

***

Adolar's eyes opened and he was still against the wall in the snow. His head, now throbbing, felt as though someone had hit it with a bat. He slowly got up and noticed the body on the ground once again. Quickly remembering what happened, his stomach rolled over inside him. Although he was disgusted by the scene, Adolar didn't feel any sorrow for that Nazi guard. His boiling blood was pumping fast through his body and his thoughts of hatred for the Germans lingered in his mind. He had to push those thoughts away so he could focus on his mission at hand. Without hesitation, he quickly jumped on the plan he devised. Adolar bent over the guard's dead body and began to quickly undress it, removing all his clothing. He then slipped on the guard's uniform and picked up his gun and keys. The name on the uniform read "Adolf Stautberg," and gave a room number 420. Looking around, Adolar noticed the path made through the snow that the guard had been following. This should lead me to the main entrance I hope, he thought. With gun in hand and uniform on, he headed down the path hoping he was going in the right direction.

As Adolar made his way along the path, it soon came to stop. At the end of the path started a long winding road that appeared to lead to the castle. Scratching his head in confusion, Adolar took a look around. When he turned to the left and looked up the road, Adolar noticed the bright spot he had seen earlier in the night was now even brighter and revealed the main entrance. A drawbridge covered in chains and armed with turrets connected the castle to the road, denying anyone entrance. Headlights beamed from a distance toward Adolar. For a moment, Adolar was frozen in the headlights. Unsure of what to do and worrying the he'd be caught, he scrambled, until he realized he was wearing the guards uniform. Signaling the approaching truck to pull over, it came to an abrupt stop on the side of the road. The vehicle was small, but able to carry a trailer behind it, which looked as though it was carrying a massive amount of supplies. Adolar knew this had to be related to Kognitiver Empfang, after what Sergeant McWilliams told him. This was his one way ticket inside. Slowly rolling down the window, Adolar greeted the Nazi driver.

The driver asked him, "What are you doing out here soldier, aren't you supposed to be doing rounds right now?"

Adolar sharply replied "Yes, I just finished my rounds and was wondering if I could catch a ride back into base with you."

The driver paused for a second, a little confused, then compiled, "Sure, hop in, just got to drop off some supplies inside anyways." Adolar walked around the front of the truck and sat down in the passenger seat. Upon entering the truck, Adolar snaked his head backwards and took a good look at the supplies. Just as he imagined, the supplies were half medical and half weaponry according to the crates.

"Alright off we go," said the driver as he started the engine again and began to drive towards the looming drawbridge.

Pulling into the castle, Adolar's eyes were met with beauty of the historic relic, but disturbed by the Nazi tint over it. Flags with Swastikas were draped over windows and walls within the castle. Avenues within Neuschwanstein were completely taken over by Nazi soldier barracks and stations for various activities such as weapons and food. Beneath the Nazi pollution, the original beauty could still be seen.

The truck rolled into the courtyard where a depot for supplies was indicated to the right. The driver said to Adolar, "I will drop you off at the supply depot along with my supplies. If I do so can you make sure the supplies gets to the right place? I need to leave for another delivery."

Adolar responded, "Of course, I would be glad to help." Adolar knew this was his biggest shot at finding the laboratory and possibly where his sister is. Parking the truck, the driver got out and headed to the back to unhinge the trailer. As he unhinged the trailer, Adolar was greeted by the head of the supply depot.

"What do we have here?" said the soldier as he inspected the supplies.

"A delivery of medical and weapon supplies for Kognitiver Empfang sir," replied Adolar, getting nervous about his cover.

The soldier answered, "Oh very good, would you mind taking this down to the laboratory immediately? The doctors have requested that this be brought down upon its arrival."

Adolar nodded his head, saluted the soldier, and prepared to escort the supplies down to the laboratory. He was given instructions as to where to go but the moment those instructions were received; all hell broke loose.

***

Sirens as loud as thunder, blazed the castle's atmosphere and drove the soldiers wild. The sky was lit with the flames of war as the snow around the castle began to slowly melt. Causing the castle to fall into pieces, the ground trembled uncontrollably. The sound of the alarm and the screams of the soldiers pierced the ears of anyone listening. Flames, bullets, and bombs dashed the beauty of the forest surrounding the castle.

Adolar Steinhaeuser was sprinting for his life. Adrenaline coursed through his veins; he could no longer feel anything besides the urge to run. Running faster than he had ever ran before, Adolar's breathing grew staggered and he could feel his heart pounding in his chest. Stride by stride, his head was racing, trying to figure out where the laboratory was. As the sweat dripped from his head and the world around him crumbled, he was suddenly blasted backwards. A bomb flew down from the sky and hit the castle tower directly above him, sending rubble down to the ground, dropping ahead of him. The debris fell to the ground as fast as lightning and struck with the force of a thousand men, lifting him off his feet and back down the path. Disoriented, his head began to swivel, as if it was on a rotating platform. Double vision began to form in his eyes and a loud ear piercing sound ran through his head, causing his nerves to feel burnt. Stained with soot, ash, and blood, Adolar got up from his trance and took a long look at the sight created ahead of him. The rubble, as it cracked the ground, had revealed the tunnel he needed. Hidden all along, right under his nose, Adolar took a deep breathe, in an attempt to relax himself, and jumped down into the tunnel.

Dimly lit by the the lights lining the ceiling, Adolar raced as he saw an end in sight. As he approached the end of the tunnel, he took notice of the large bunker door that would let him into the laboratory. Cracked in half by the rumble of the ground, he squeezed through and entered his long-awaited destination.

Taking a few steps into the laboratory, Adolar tripped over a large bag laying on the floor. He landed on his hands, barely saving his face from smashing against the rock beneath him. Not being able to see anything, he stretched his arms, attempting to find anything to help him stand, until a cool metal object brushed against his fingertips. Grabbing it, Adolar could feel it was a flashlight and turned it on. A dim beam of light protruded from the flashlight, revealing the horror around him. Spanning the laboratory were body bags organized in rows. As Adolar looked down at the body he had tripped over, he noticed the numbering along the bag and underneath it, the Star of David. Each body bag in the lab was numbered and branded with the star reminding Adolar of the Jewish men and women his family hid. Tears began to form in his eyes as the sight of the dead became too much to bear. Looking up from the bodies, Adolar noticed medical tables lining every outer wall. Blood covered each table that Adolar could see. As he turned around, he saw in the corner of the room, a pile bodies without heads next to an industrial furnace. Falling to the ground, Adolar began to vomit as the sight overwhelmed him.

Continuing to convulse until the nausea went away, his arms shook as they supported his weak body. Wiping his mouth with his blood-stained sleeve, he pushed himself up and stumbled over to the wall, leaning against it, his eyes surveying the room. One of the surgical tables off to the corner caught his attention. It seemed to be the only table with a mutilated body remaining on top of it, the body of a girl. Walking through the aisles between the body bags, he made his way to the table, curiosity rising. Getting closer, half of the girl's face had been completely burned, skin melted down to the dermis. Her nerves exposed to the toxic air, all signs of life gone from her face. Adolar leaned over the table, anxiety rising inside of him. Her hair was spread out, dangling off of the edg; it was blonde, blonde like his sisters'. Adolar closed his eyes and saw his sister standing alone in the dark. Ever so gently, he took his thumb and opened her cold, unburned eye, and a piercing blue iris surrounded by red veins looked up at him in a dead stare. Looking into her eye, a strike of pain flew through his body as he gasped for air. Sobbing in agony, Adolar took his beloved sister and wrapped her in his arms.

"No." he whispered to himself. He repeated that over and over again to himself, feeling tears escape his eyes and run down his soot stained cheeks. After what felt like hours he had been holding her, he finally let go and took one final glance at her pale, cold body. His sister was gone. Anger began to boil up inside him, his sad helplessness quickly replaced by a desire for revenge. Completing his mission was all he had to do now, defeating the enemy that had done this to his family. Sergeant McWilliams' orders rang through his head and Adolar knew what had to be done.

As Adolar gathered himself together, the ground above him began to shake once again. The sound of bombs exploding as they hit the castle boomed through the tunnel and into the laboratory, as dirt and sand fell to the floor. Making his way out of the laboratory, Adolar noticed barrels lining the wall beside the bunker door. As he walked nearer to them on the way out, the smell of gasoline raised his suspicion. Adolar removed the lid from the barrel closest to the bunker door and the smell grew stronger. Knowing what he had to do, he decided to burn the laboratory to the ground to finish what the bombing strike couldn't.

Adolar flipped over one barrel, dumping the contents onto the ground. Grabbing another, he poured gasoline over every object in the room. Diving to the ground, he began searching the body bags left and right, digging through them to find anything that could ignite the gasoline. Looking around the lab, he noticed two large cabinets covered by cloth. Adolar ran over to the cabinets, stripping them to reveal their contents. As his hands pulled down the cover, his eyes were met with a glass case containing four rifles. Taking one of the guns, he turned around and made his way out of the laboratory, making sure he still had a clean shot to hit one of the barrels. Walking 30 yards outside the bunker door, he took aim. Squinting with one eye, he put all of his focus into making the shot. Taking a deep breath, time seemed to slow down. Closing one eye, Adolar aimed the rifle, inhaling the rancid air as he took a deep breath and pressed his finger against the trigger. As he breathed out, Adolar pulled the trigger and the sound of the gun filled his ears. Turning around, Adolar began to run from the explosion he had just caused. Taking two steps forward, the sound of the bullet piercing the barrel followed by a loud "boom" rang through his ears. Taking a glance back, all he could see were flames engulfing the laboratory, taking with it all the lost souls. He completed his mission, he destroyed what had destroyed him and his family. Adolar felt the heat of the fire on the back of his body, but he did not feel fear or pain. He did not feel the loss of his sister, because what he saw was not who she was. All he felt was the satisfaction of revenge, and all he did was run.

Exiting the tunnel, Adolar climbed out back into the midst of the castle. The sky remained lit by flames as the castle slowly burned down to the ground. Craters were left in the roads and walls were fragmented by the bombs. Jogging towards the main entrance, Adolar looked around at the countless dead soldiers that lined the streets. The once hanging flags representing the Third Reich now burned to ash. As Adolar reached the drawbridge, he turned around to take one final look at the castle. The once beautiful relic of German history now stood in shambles, vanquished of the Nazi pollution. With all the energy he had left, Adolar ran down the bridge leaving behind his anger and trauma to burn with the castle.

La Caricature

The woman felt a tug at the bottom of her skirt, which nearly covered her ankles. Looking down at the youngling, she hovered over her like a skyscraper. The little girl looked up at her with beady eyes and with each tug, she called out, *"Madame! Madame!"* Hearing the clanking of the steel gates, her arm extended out and pointed to the window eagerly, where she could see a man at the end of the gate with a satchel at his side. The children, especially the youngest of the group, would become excited whenever they saw *l'homme avec nos lettres* stuffing white envelopes into the wicker basket, at the end of the driveway. Rolling her eyes, the woman kneeled down to the young girl's level.

"Your families did not write you letters, nor did they think to. There is nothing for you out there. *Nothing.*" Her voice flickered away, mirroring the moment a flame would come to the end of a match.

Releasing her small hands from their grip on the fabric, a tear rolled down her cheek.

"Do you see what you all did? This is what happens when you get excited for nothing, *but,* nevertheless, I do need *my* mail," she looked around the room at the children. Her eyes landed on the only mademoiselle that was not looking back at her, and was sitting by the fireplace, drawing pictures of princesses and castles. After calling her name three times without as much as a glance from the young girl, she went over and snagged the paper from the girl's hands.

"Are you paying attention to what I'm saying? You don't look like

you're doing much, would you please be so kind as to get my mail?"
Looking outside the window, the girl could see the mailman trudging
through the snow.

"But it's, it's snowing out. It'll be up to my knees. I don't even have
any-" she tried to finish her sentence before the woman interrupted.

"*Oh,* but it's only a short walk and you'll go *right* now, mademoiselle,
before the snow starts to come down heavier," the woman responded to
her sternly, yanking her up by the arm.

"Go fetch your coat from the hook, now!" Her headmaster virtually
pushed Adeline into the foyer. Hanging her head low, the young girl
came back and pushed through the door. The woman stood behind her
in the doorframe, and watched as she struggled to step into the pearl
white snow.

Her body shivered as she had to pick up each leg and sink it back
into the numbing chill. The gate was a short distance ahead, but it
felt like a thousand miles. Adeline's nose and cheeks turned a rosy red
color from the freezing temperatures, and each breath was caught in
the air, like a puff of smoke. Her hand reached through the tall, rusting
gate as she finally arrived at the end of the walk way. The girl's cheek
stuck to the ice cold metal as she stretched her arm as far as she could to
grasp the small bundle of mail. Wrapped around it was a white string
that unraveled as she attempted to pull it through. Spilling between
the gate and the end of the path, the mail became soggy as it sat there,
waiting to be picked up. Adeline reached for each envelope and held
them in one arm, until she noticed an interesting-looking booklet, full
of drawings. She skimmed the pages, *wow,* she thought. She loved to
draw, and appreciated the work of others more so.

"*Adeline! Adeline!* What is taking you so long? Get back here, *now!*"
The wind carried her headmaster's voice over the snow, as she nervously
looked back at the door. Shoving the booklet inside of her thinning coat,
she followed her deep-seated footsteps behind her.

✳✳✳

The corridor leading to the bedrooms was gloomy, as if dark clouds
hung at the ceiling. Creaking with each step, it was evident the floor was

aged. When the girl's eyes met the deep red wallpaper that peeled from each end, she sighed and trudged on to her room. Rusting pipes lined the walls with pockets of cobwebs in each corner. The smell of burning wood came from the kitchen, often leaving slashes of black above the cast iron stove. Adeline had learned to resent her home, which was deteriorating from the inside-out.

Laying down, stomach against the floor and her legs behind her in a twist, she pulled out what she was hiding inside of her coat. Her fingers grazed the front page, and she eyed the title, *La Caricature*. Scanning the paper, she focused on the odd shapes of the people. Their heads were large, and some of the individuals were taller than buildings. She looked at the long mustaches and their dramatic expressions. *What is this?* Feeling the crisp paper in her fingertips, she turned the page. As the comics progressed, her eyes widened with each new character she saw.

Hearing approaching footsteps, she quickly closed the book and rolled the pages into themselves. Her thoughts dispersed from each other as she looked around for a place to hide it. Bed checks were conducted often and any objects that were not borrowed from the house library or known of by the headmaster would get the next meal taken away. If they received them, letters were the only items the girls could have of their own. Adeline had read every story in the one bookcase they had access to, twice.

Pillowcase? Adeline eyeballed her bed, moving into one clear thought. No. Opening each drawer of her dresser, she pushed her clothes aside and threw them back into place in an effort to let out some frustration. Pulling her fingers through the front locks of her hair, Adeline's eyes shifted their focus to her desk. She searched through the stack for a book she could get away with keeping, *Cendrillon and the Glass Slipper, Conte de Noel,* and *Alice au Pays Des Merveilles*, but by the look of the bent corners and amount of names in the time log, she forgot the idea. While scurrying around the room, her small foot caught in the floorboard causing her body to slam down onto the floor. She picked herself up, and tore her toes out the crack. In that instant, the plank lifted and nearly snapped, revealing a bare brick base underneath. She reached her hand inside and pushed the dirt away to make a clean space. Here, she thought. The girl reached behind her for the booklet and placed it inside. She moved the board back into place, trying not to leave a trace of her accident and new secret.

The next morning, she sat in lecture twiddling her thumbs. Adeline's eyes would follow the path of the chalk, and she never missed a beat with her instructor. But today was different, as her mind conjured up the drawings she remembered and daydreamed about each one. On the edge of her desk, Adeline started to draw versions of her own. She made a miniature body with a larger head, and-

"Adeline, les yeux sur moi mademoiselle," her teacher called out to her and eyed her desk. Yes, she knew, eyes on her. Adeline rubbed the smoothed wood to smudge the lead. She looked down at the blackened tops of her fingers and smiled, with the cartoon still lingering in her conscience.

Once Adeline heard the words, "C'est la fin de la class," she raced back to her room after her class time was over, shutting the door behind her. Kneeling softly onto the floor in front of her, she pulled the wooden plank up, revealing her newest possession. She took her leather bound notebook and ripped a piece of paper out. Adeline spread the page out over the comic and started to trace her favorite one, "Le Retour du Moyen Age," the return of the Middle Ages. The dresses emphasized each woman's petite figure and the bright colors of the ruffled textiles filled the page. She used her borrowed lead pencils to sketch the shapes of the people she could faintly see underneath.

Feeling an ache in her wrist, Adeline sat back to admire her work. Flipping through the comic, she tried to choose what she wanted to draw next. Each time she picked up some pastels, it was as if her mind was put into another place, filling her body with excitement. She loved to draw, but was never able to keep a single drawing of her own. Her headmaster, Madame Bernard, would take them and rip them to pieces right in front of her. If it was not something she had learned in class, she did want to see it at all. All of the girls thought it was cruel, but never took a chance to defend some of the beautiful work she had created.

Although, she had never felt her heart ache more than when Madame took her first real portrait. Adeline was left with one photograph of her mother, which she had always kept it tucked inside of her pocket wherever she went. The one day that it had not been in safekeeping,

Adeline attempted to trace the face of her mother and draw her a portrait, in the hope of one day giving it to her in person. Madame saw her scribbling away by the front door, when she had already called for dinner, and came behind her to snatch the paper away from her reach.

"And who was this supposed to be? Another one of your fantasies?" Young Adeline could feel her chest tightening, and watched as the one piece of family she had known was destroyed. The woman tore the sheet in two, her mother's photo tucked safely behind, and Adeline's heart nearly fell out of her chest.

"That was what I had left of my mother, *you*, you *witch!*" She collected the pieces at her headmaster's feet and stood tall. Sticking out her lip, the vibrancy of the fireplace reflected off of Adeline's tear filled eyes. Madame Bernard gripped her long, mahogany hair into her fingers and pulled Adeline through the hall until she shoved her into her bedroom, locking the door behind her.

Sternly, Madame spoke into the door, "Do not even *think* that you will come out of this room for supper. I will see you *bright* and *early* for a blackboard detention."

Hearing those words, Adeline's head jolted back in disbelief. Blackboard detentions, as Adeline had witnessed, were not a sight for the faint of heart. It was a way of saying that you had to write your wrongs on the board until it was suffice, according to the headmaster. Louise was an older orphan who showed nothing but attitude during lecture, and earned herself frequent detentions. Only hearing rumors of the punishment, it was the first time Adeline was sitting in her desk, watching it happen. Picking herself up from the wooden desk, she walked to the front of the classroom. Louise scanned the board's ledge for a piece of chalk and began to write, "Je ne répondrai pas," *I will not talk back*, over and over.

"Girls, please count as Miss Moreau finishes each sentence," the headmaster instructed the girls, who were frozen in their chairs, beginning to count: un, deux, trois...

It was never enough, the girl had stood there before Adeline, so long that her fingers could no longer move and she felt crippling pain. The other students were dismissed around one P.M. to eat lunch, but Louise was not allowed to go. In fact, she had stood there for another two hours.

"Louise, if you run out of room, simply erase your beginning sentences and write again. By listening to the growling of your stomach, I'm sure you have learned your lesson, haven't you?" She nodded her head, keeping her bloodshot eyes out of sight. Watching from the hallway, Adeline could see the dried tears on Louise's face. She held her hand in agony as the tips of her fingers almost turned purple, leaving the room sluggishly. Each eye was glued on her, the girls couldn't bear the thought of being on Madame's bad side, especially if it meant *her* version of consequence.

Adeline was the same as the other girls in her home, an orphan. Her mother left her in 1852, by ringing a bell in the pouring rain at the door of a nearby Parisian hospice. Stepping out onto the wet doorstep, the nurses brought in the wooden box her mother left her in. This was not out-of-the-ordinary, and her mother was just that, not out-of-the-ordinary either. She was only a young fifteen when she had Adeline, and couldn't afford bread for herself, let alone a child. So, the young woman did what she had to do, and left the newborn with a kiss on the forehead and a small note tucked into her blanket that read, *Please give her the name Adeline, I've always loved that name.*

One of Adeline's fondest memories rested in a time when she was much younger. For as long as she could remember, she adored how others could draw cartoons. It was something she'd admired so much from afar that after a while, she figured she'd try her hand at it.

Grasping the paper in her small hands, she took the pencil, lightly tracing the outlines of a dress she'd seen only on the back of her eyelids in her wildest dreams, wishing upon all other things that she could don the dress that her hands created. As time passed, lines became longer and the shading darker, taking the young girl to another place. Leaning on the papers spread under her, Adeline's forearms were covered in shadows of lead. She drew lace as if it were all she'd done her whole life, with the finest detail imaginable.

***

Adeline took to her own ways, and started to copy the style of the comic that was ruled out in front of her. She drew herself at the bottom of the page, in her ordinary dress, but with a stack of papers next to her and a pencil in hand. Madame Bernard stood facing towards her, but she was larger than life, nearly four times taller than Adeline. Her finger was pointed towards her and she drew her eyebrows to be furrowed down into the bridge of her nose. Adeline giggled as she shaded in Madame's dress, and continued on. Before Adeline could even look up, her drawings had covered her floor and used all of the paper of her only notebook.

Adeline snuck out of her room on a conquest for more paper, gently closing her door behind her. She focused on her target, the classroom at the end of the long hall. With each creak, she drew more attention to herself. She attempted to reach her toes about five planks ahead, stretching her legs to make wider steps. Entering the room, she walked directly across to the small wooden desk at the back of the room. She looked at the tabletop, which had a tin of pencils and erasers, with a stack of plain paper next to it. She grab a hefty bunch of the thin sheets for herself, and bustled out of the room. Closing her eyes, Adeline pushed against the back of her door to close it and took a deep breath in.

"What are these, Adeline?" A girl a year or two older than her, named Fae, said, while clenching some of her drawings in her hand. Wincing at the thought, Adeline watched as her finger pads smudged the detail she refined.

"Nothing, nothing. Give them back to me," Adeline reached for her papers and her roommate pulled the papers out of reach and behind her back.

"Do you *really* think I'm going to give them back to you? Where did you get these comics?"

"Nowhere, please just give them back to me. They're mine."

"Oh, so did you steal it just like you went and stole paper from Madame Laurent? Look, I don't want trouble, but what *are* these? I mean, drawing Madame like this? You'll be locked away for *days*," she scoffed at Adeline, and Adeline remained furious. She asked her again to give them back before racing to her side of the room to snatch them back. Their small voices weighed heavily in the air, moving through the walls and into the corridor. The stomping of their feet camouflaged the sound of knocking on their wooden door, coming from an unwanted visitor.

Madame Bernard broke open the door of their bedroom and gasped at the scene, "Now what do we have here?" The two girls went silent almost immediately. The headmaster looked around at the mess of papers and pulled one out of the stack. With Adeline's luck, Madame picked up the worst of them all, her re-creation of getting her mail. Adeline drew the headmaster, once again larger than life, but this time with steam shooting out of her ears. Madame Bernard took the paper into one hand and crumpled it in an instant.

"What is the meaning of all of this? Adeline? Care to explain yourself considering you thought it would be smart to tag your name at the bottom of each photo, *huh*? Like a *real* artist?"

Adeline imagined the smoke coming out her ears now, like she had drawn before, and dropped her chin to her chest. Madame Bernard ripped the other papers out of Fae's grip, and the young girl could feel her frustration brewing, as if it were spilling over in pot. Adeline had never let anyone touch her work, which she cherished so deeply, let alone rip out of someone's hands. Her body nearly keeled over as she watched the corners begin to bend in her headmaster's grip. Grabbing Adeline's ear, the woman dragged her through the doorway. Her ear began to turn beet red, radiating heat in Madame's fingers. She threw Adeline onto the ground next to the fireplace, and the little girl's cheeks began to look flushed.

"I didn't mean to- I mean, I just love to draw, Madame," Adeline stuttered and shook nervously as she curled herself into a ball.

"So, you didn't mean to draw me like some, some *cruel woman!* Like someone who doesn't take care of *twelve* young girls! Well, let's see how you like your feelings being hurt," The woman casted Adeline's drawings into the fire next to her. Growing immensely, the flames swallowed each piece, turning her prized possessions into nothing but charcoaled dust. The bright flash of a deep orange reflected back into Adeline's wide eyes. She felt her stomach turn and could not fight back tears any longer. A single tear ran down her cheek, and she began to weep. Getting up from the hardwood floor, the young girl pushed her way through the crowd of girls to get back to her room.

✳✳✳

Adeline woke up that next morning, with sore eyes from crying all night long. She could still feel the grip of Madame Bernard's fingers on her ear, causing a terrible ache. Barely sitting up, she noticed that her roommate was already out of the room. The door was cracked open and she could hear rustling coming from down the hall, not caring enough to get out of her bed, she rolled back over and closed her eyes.

"Adeline? Are you awake? I know it's early but I-"

"Fae, please go back to sleep, the sun is barely out,"

"Adeline, if you would please just-"

"Fae, I said go back to sleep!" Rolling over to face Fae, Adeline sat up in bed. But what she has actually turned over to was Fae, holding a familiar piece of paper. The edges were charred and disintegrating at the touch. She approached what she was holding, to find a delicate piece of art, somehow barely caught in the crossfire.

An Accidental Discovery

"Where are you going?"

My dad stands in the doorway, one leg hanging outside. He turns towards me and throws a big, goofy grin on his face.

"I'll be right back, Rocky," he explains, "I just have to run to the store quick. Help your mother if she needs anything, okay?"

I nod my head. "Okay."

He gives me one more big smile and walks out. I hear the old car clatter to life, and the vibrations become quieter and quieter as he drives down the road. He has to drive the old car now because the new car we had got destroyed in the accident.

The accident was terrible. My mom was driving home from work late at night, when a man in a big truck ran through a stop sign. He hit her driver's side, pinching her left leg under the crunched metal. She bled a lot, right where a piece of the car cut up her thigh. When my mom told about the story in the emergency room, she explained how she didn't remember the accident much, but remembered how bad her leg hurt. Because the truck was much bigger than our car, she was stuck for a long time, and the paramedics had to amputate her left leg. Now, it's very difficult for her to move around. The accident was just over three weeks ago, and she is still home, trying to recover.

One night, after my parents had fallen asleep, I bent my leg back at the knee and tied my foot around my thigh with a pair of old shoelaces. I tried moving around my room, like my Mom has to now. I was only

211

halfway around my bed when I fell, collapsing to the hardwood floor. Quickly, I untied my leg and jumped back onto my covers. My dad came back in to ask what had happened, and I told him I fell off my bed. I don't know how my mom does it; her injury was much worse than the one I pretended to have, and I could barely move.

"Rocky!" I hear her call out from her room. I jump up from the stained couch and run to her room across the hall. Even though my mom can't go to work now, and still can't do very much, she's always positive. I try my best to match her energy.

"Yeah, Mom?" I remember one night when she tried to walk and fell down. My dad told me to always help her when I can, and that this was a very difficult thing for her to go through. Now, every day when she tries to walk more, I'm always close by in case she needs me. She's been doing great lately, and even cooked dinner one night when Dad had to work late.

"Can you ask your father to fix the lightbulb in here? It keeps flickering." Her clear, blue eyes dart from the light bulb to me.

"He just left to go to the store, but I will when he gets back."

Her head raises and cocks to the side. "Again? Didn't he just go the other day?"

I shrug my shoulders. "He's probably getting snacks today, we haven't had many lately."

"Well," she says with a sigh, shrugging her shoulders, "let me know when he comes home."

I agree and softly close the door. The couch welcomes me as I sit back down, sinking into the cushions. Turning on the TV, I wait for my dad to get back, occasionally looking outside, expecting to see our red car come barreling back into the driveway at any minute. My eyelids slowly grow heavier as the sun sets behind the larger houses across the street as night slowly creeps in.

I wake up on the couch to the sound of the front door closing shut. Rubbing my eyes, I glance at the figure entering the room.

"Dad?" I ask. "What time is it?"

"Shh," he whispers, "it's late, you need to go to sleep for school tomorrow."

I peer at the clock under the TV, squinting until the blurry numbers focus. The shapes finally form to read 12:30. Looks like I'm gonna spend my first period tomorrow catching up on the sleep I'm about to miss.

Wobbling to my room, I jump in my bed, my feet just reaching the end of the mattress. By next year when eighth grade starts, I bet I'll need a new one.

I stare at the ceiling and wait for sleep to come back to me. The sounds of my dad washing up slip under the cracks in my door, keeping me from entering my dreams. Eventually, the sounds die out, and my eyes shut for the night.

***

I wait patiently, staring at the second hand on the clock slowly tick down. Only two more minutes and I'll be free to leave. Free from geometry, free from English, free from science class, and free from Mrs. Andreas who keeps yelling at me to keep my head up.

"Rocky? Hey, Rocky!" Her sharp voice throws my drooping eyelids wide open. "Would you mind keeping your head up, please?"

My mouth opens, ready to respond, but I shut it. Explaining to her why I'm tired isn't worth the argument right now.

"Sorry," is all I mutter out.

The bell rings as I quicken my pace down the hallway to the door. I push it open, letting the crisp air blow into my face. My hair flies around my head, returning to a rest as the breeze dies down. The falling and crunching of leaves crackles in my ears, and the sun shines brilliantly in the middle of the cloudless sky. Sprinting away from the building, my heart jumps excitedly, thinking about showing my parents what I made in tech class.

After a short jog, I climb up the broken steps leading to my house. The door swings open, banging against the wall. Dashing inside, I unzip my backpack and pull out the clock I made.

"Hey! Mom, Dad!" My call bounces off the brown cabinets in the kitchen, moving along the walls of the hallway, and reaches my mother's room.

"Your father is at work, honey," My mother returns blandly.

My excitement dies down. Usually, Dad would be there to greet me after school, ready to have a catch or kick a ball around. Sometimes, he would even take me to see a movie. Lately, though, he's been working extra to help with the hospital bills. I always thought the hospital was free for everyone, but I guess it isn't free for leg amputations. I feel my smile fading into a frown, but force the corners of my mouth up as I walk in to see my mother.

"Look," I say, now less enthused, "I made a clock today."

"Oh, how nice!" My mother sits up in her bed, her bandages still wrapped around the bottom of her thigh, where the remainder of her leg used to be. She smiles through a wince and reaches out for the clock. Handing it to her, she begins to inspect it. An orange star sits in the middle of the clock, with white dots for stars in the background. The golden second hand of the clock ticks with a satisfying *click*.

"Here, let me set the time." My mother moves the minute hand around in a circle until the clock reads 2:45. "There," she sings, handing it back to me.

I smile and thank her. "Do you need anything?" I ask, rising up on my toes.

"No, I'm okay for now. Thank you." Something in her face tells me that she isn't feeling right, but I don't press the issue.

I nod my head and exit the room, placing the clock on the kitchen table. Rummaging through the snack cabinet, I don't find anything new, so instead decide to try the fridge. Still, I find nothing new to eat. Dad must not have bought any snacks at the store yesterday; he probably had to get work supplies, some car parts or something.

Settling on a bag of chips, I grab my homework sheets from my backpack and sit down. The ticking of the clock gets drowned out by my thoughts. I start with my least favorite subject, math.

The recognizable creak of the front door interrupts my concentration as the clock's bright orange star reads 4:00.

Entering the room, my dad dons an unusual outfit of khaki shorts and a bright blue shirt. His hair, usually ruffled, seems more kept than it usually is-it's a nice change from the typical jeans and black tee that he always wears.

"How are ya, kiddo?" The exuberance in his voice is hard not to smile at.

I grab the clock and shove it towards him. "Look what I made!" I nearly shout, once again feeling enthused.

"Wow, all by yourself?" He marvels.

I nod my head twice and he pats me with his callus-covered hand. A strange smell floods my nose, like a strong, flowery deodorant. He must have spilled one of those car fresheners on himself. I've been to his shop a few times; they sell them in the front, where the desk is.

"Great job, Rocky, that's awesome! How's your mother?"

"She seems okay, a little down, maybe, but she's good."

He nods and leaves the kitchen.

***

The bell rings, releasing us to go to our next class. Walking out of the room, I see my friend, Amir, in the hallway. His black, disheveled hair looks even more out of place than usual today, falling haphazardly over his dark forehead. Brown pants with pen marks hug his legs, accompanied by a baggy white T-shirt.

"Amir!"

His head whips around, and when we make eye contact, his eyes light up.

"Rocky! What's up my dude?"

We bump fists and continue moving through the halls, making conversation. Amir has been my friend since I was young. His mom played on the same softball team as my mother, and occasionally I would see him at the games. The first time we interacted was after our moms' team had won the championship. Out of excitement, Amir ran over to me and jumped on my back. We both toppled down into the dirt, kicking up brown dust into the air. After a quick spurt of coughs, he asked me my name, sticking out his hand for me to shake. Ever since then, we've been best friends, even though he's a grade above me.

Amir is unlike anyone else I've ever met in my life. His goofy attitude, matched with his clear intelligence, makes for a pleasantly annoying friend.

"Oh, by the way, I saw your dad yesterday. I miss that old guy.

Haven't seen him in a while. I did yesterday, though! I waved, but I don't think he saw me 'cause he didn't wave back," Amir states.

"Oh really?" I question, "He probably couldn't see you through that mop on your head."

He gives me a punch in the arm. "You're just jealous I look this good. How's your mom doing?"

"She's getting better. Each day it seems like she can do a little more."

"That's great. She amazes me, that woman. I highly doubt that you are her son, with her being such a wonderful person, and you being, well, bleh." This time I punch him in the arm, shaking my head with a laugh.

"Anyways, I gotta go to Spanish. I'll see you later, bud." Amir departs, cackling, coasting into a classroom to the left. I continue on, laughing myself, getting my brain ready for an hour of math.

✳✳✳

"Hey, kiddo, I'll be right back. Gotta head back to the store again," my Dad calls from the living room. The ticking of the clock pierces my ears. 7:00, it reads. Why do we need groceries at 7:00?

"Oh… Okay," I answer back. A slight feeling of aggravation builds inside of me. He better come home with some good snacks this time, because the last trip to the store didn't bring back much.

The familiar sounds of the front door swinging on its hinges fills my ears.

I open up the fridge, searching for something good to eat. The remnants of a rotisserie chicken rest on the top shelf, alongside the otherwise barren shelves. Ever since the accident, we haven't had a lot in the fridge. Dad told me it was because the insurance company wasn't helping us like they should. Whenever I would ask about what he meant, he would become very frustrated, so I stopped asking. Mom said the real reason was because she wasn't very hungry anymore.

As I pick through the chicken, my mom stumbles into the kitchen on her crutches. I shoot up from the chair, its wooden legs scraping against the stained, white tiled floor. She refuses my help, shaking her head no. I stand idly by, waiting for any indication that she might need my assistance. While she stumbles forwards, I shuffle my feet, moving into a position where I could catch her if she falls.

She makes it to the table, and as she drops down into a chair, her crutches fall onto her lap. Swinging her leg under the table, she breathes a sigh of exhaustion. Then, looking up at me, she smiles. Her blonde hair dances around her forehead, the rest of it tangled on top of her shoulders. A small bead of sweat rests above her eyebrow.

"See?" She quirks, upbeat and joyous. "I'm getting better at it every day."

I sit back down at the table and feel a grin spreading over my face. Even through the disaster and struggling, my mom still finds a way to radiate positivity. I wish Dad could have been home to see it.

"You're doing great, Mom." The words pass through my upturned lips.

We sit there for a moment, until Mom breaks the silence, asking, "Hey, anything good in there for dinner?"

"No," I reply, "Dad went out to go shopping a few minutes ago."

The ticking of the clock becomes more apparent in the room now. I read the time, then do a double take. The hands rest at 8 hours and 20 minutes. I guess it wasn't just a couple of minutes ago that Dad left.

"Oh, well, that's okay. I wasn't really hungry anyways." She smiles again, but I can tell it's more strained. She looks down at the table, scratching at the wood with her nail. An uncomfortable silence follows, and I wait, hoping to see Mom's bright energy light up the room again.

Our silence is interrupted by the creek and crash of the front door. I turn my head right as my Dad walks through the doorway, a single bagged item in his hands.

"Wow, look at that! How you feeling, honey?"

His enthusiasm is unmatched by my mother, who answers with a simple, "Fine," unable to hide from her hunger tonight.

My dad strolls to the refrigerator, and removes a carton of milk and a rotisserie chicken from the grocery bag. It crinkles as he rolls it up into a ball, tossing it on the counter.

"Oh, more chicken, and *another* bottle of milk." I don't keep the aggravation out of my voice. Why wouldn't he buy any good food for us to eat? It took him hours to find the same rotisserie chicken we eat every week, and a pint of milk?

His head whips around, his eyebrows pointed down. "Yeah, but this one is honey flavored. And, the-the milk we have is bad."

He unscrews the top to the half-gallon, gives it a sniff, and scrunches up his nose. I watch the milk flow out of the container, emptying into the drain.

"I got cereal, too, it's in the car. It's your favorite!"

"Well, okay," I respond. Staring off in the distance, I try to avoid eye contact with my father. The sound of my mom's chair sliding against the tile reverberates around the room, and my dad and I both rush to help her. She waves us off.

"I can do it, guys, thanks. Goodnight," she says quickly, setting her crutches under her arms.

After she exits the kitchen, I retreat to my bedroom, tossing a, "Goodnight," to my dad over my shoulder. Walking into my room, I shut the door and sprawl out on my sheets.

***

"Five minutes left, class."

I scribble my words as fast as I can, pushing through the pain in my hand. Today, our teacher asked us to write about something we really want. It could be anything, she said, as long as it exists. I wrote about steak.

The last word of my essay barely gets off the tip of my pen before the annoying buzz of the timer vibrates through my eardrums. Soon after, the harmonious ringing of the bell sounds, and I'm back in the hallway, looking for Amir. I find him opening up his locker outside of the English room.

"Hey," I grab his shoulder prompting him to spin around.

"What's up, man?" He asks as he slams his locker shut.

"Not much. Wanna play that game after school?" I ask hopefully. On my birthday this year I got the newest street fighter video game. Amir is the only kid in school that gives me good competition.

"No, not really, but I suppose I will." he chuckles. "Kidding. Yes, I do. Maybe you'll actually *not* suck this time."

"Haha, very funny. Maybe if you didn't play video games all day you'd have a chance with *Julia*."

"Hey," he whispers, "you better watch it. She's in this class, you know," he points over his shoulder.

"Well, good luck then." Smiling, I turn and move down the hall.

I enter my class silently, listening to conversations around me. According to Sarah, there was a big accident yesterday on the highway exit near my neighborhood.

"At what time?" I ask her, placing myself into the conversation.

"Uh, around like 6:45, I think. My mom said she was stuck in traffic for almost an hour."

I nod my head, leaning back in my seat. If the accident was at 6:45, then I guess it makes sense why Dad took so long; it's just strange that he didn't mention it.

The class drags on and on until I finally hear the familiar ringing. I meet Amir outside the doors and we begin our walk.

When we reach my house, the car isn't in the driveway. I miss coming home and seeing Dad, but I know that there are more important things to do right now than go to the movies, or run around the yard. I sigh and saunter inside. Does he really have to work late every single day? I know he's doing it for Mom, but can't he at least stop by? Amir notices my sudden change in attitude and asks if I'm alright.

"Yeah," I lie, "I'm good."

Amir beats me in just about every match we play. Round after round, my health bar decreases, and the word, *Victory* bounces around his side of the screen. Eventually, I toss my controller onto the ground, tired of being knocked out repetitively. Instead, he turns on the TV. A family pops up, on a show I've never seen before. With each character lovingly smiling at one another, it really looks like they are truly happy.

"Pretty good acting," I state.

"I could do better," Amir responds.

The TV show holds me in a trance until my dad walks by the screen. His black hair, slightly grayed around the base, is pushed to the side. A white shirt hugs his upper body, with what appears to be a burn mark near the center. Grease stains cover his pants.

"Hey, bud, how was school? Hi, Amir, how's it going?" His voice travels over his shoulder as he moves through the hall. He walks into his bedroom, says a few words to my mom that I cannot decipher, and then hurries back to the living room.

Before me or Amir can tell him about our days, he says, "I have to go back to the shop to work on someone's car. They said that it needed to be fixed as soon as possible, so I gotta go check it out. I'll be home later, there's some ground beef in the fridge that I bought, okay?" He flashes another smile, trying to ease the fact that he is leaving, again.

"Yeah, okay," my half-hearted reply is satisfactory enough, and he exits the house.

My gaze goes back to the TV, eager to watch the show about the family again.

I hear some words fumble out of Amir's mouth, but I don't really pay them any attention.

He says something else, to which I assume is a question, and I nod my head slowly, my eyes still on the screen.

"Hey! Dummy! Can you hear me?" Amir practically shouts in my ear.

"Jeez, man. No need to break my ears."

"Okay, first off, you can't break your ear. Your ear is cartilage. There are bones in the ear canal, though, like your-"

"Amir, please shut up," I interrupt him. "Now, what were you saying?"

"I was asking you if we could ride back to my house quick. My mom just told me she won't be home until later tonight because of work and I gotta go let out my dog."

"Oh, yeah sure. Now?" I ask him, now focused on the conversation.

"That would be best." Amir gets up, shuffling side to side, waiting to leave.

I stand and give my back a quick stretch, before letting my mom know we're leaving. Soon enough, my hands are wrapped around the worn down handlebar grips on my bike. Amir takes my dad's, almost falling multiple times trying to jump up onto the high seat. Finally, he slings himself on top, and hollers in excitement.

"Alright, let's go, because I can't stop!" He calls out over his shoulder as he rolls down the road.

My anxiety rises and falls as Amir swerves in and out of the road, car horns blaring at him. His legs aren't long enough to pedal properly, and the concentration in his face is very apparent.

As we turn down the road leading to Amir's house, his eyes open wide, glancing towards a different house. He squeezes his handlebar brakes, and the bike quickly stops. Leaping off the seat, hobbling on one foot, the bike clambers to the ground. I pull on my brakes and skid up next to him.

Confused, I wait for Amir to speak.

"Hey," he says, short of breath, "isn't that your dad's car?" He raises his hand in the air, pointing to a house down the road. I follow his finger, and sure enough, I find the old, rusty car parked in front of what looks like the biggest house on the block.

Amir's voice pipes up again, this time asking, "Didn't he say he was going to the shop or something?"

My heart does a strange dance inside my chest as I try to understand what's going on. My dad... lied to me? For what reason?

"Yeah, uh, I thought so," I stammer. "Do you know whose house that is?"

Amir walks out into the street to get a better view of the three story house. It towers over the other single floor raised ranches, painted bright blue, which seamlessly mix into the colors of the sky.

"Yeah, that's Ms. Jacobs's house. She's the high school AP Bio teacher. My brother, Kasim, had her as a teacher. She gave a lot of homework, though. My brother said his classmates told him the reason why she gave so much homework was because she liked correcting it. She didn't have a husband or kids or anything, so basically all she did is sit inside and correct papers. Well, that's what they said at least. And what happened was that she had this crazy medical invention that helped people with arthritis, and she made millions off it. Now, she just teaches for fun. Well, I mean, that's what my brother-"

"Amir. Please." He finally shuts his mouth and leaves me to my thoughts. My confusion soon turns to anger.

Closing my eyes, I run through all the scenarios in my mind. Why is he parked at this teacher's house? Does he come here often? Why wouldn't he tell me? What is my Dad actually doing every day? I can't contain the questions racing through my head any longer.

"When you saw my dad the other day, where did you see him?"

"Uh, well, it was right around the corner of this street, like on the way back to your house."

The pieces finally start to click in my brain. My dad probably never even went grocery shopping that night. I bet he doesn't even go to work when he says he does. Instead, he goes to this woman's house, but for what? The single, terrible conclusion I could form in my head is too much to think about, but also too big to dismiss.

With my fists balled up by my side, I start walking to the house.

"Whoa, hey, Rocky, where you going?"

I say nothing and pick up my pace.

"Rocky," Amir says with more concern in his voice, "what're you doing? We have to let out my dog, remember?"

"Go let him out then!"

To this, Amir says nothing, but I don't hear him move.

I reach the house, walking towards the three door garage. I don't actually have a plan, and I panic, trying to think of my next move. I see a bright flash in the garage side door, through a darkened window. I stop, waiting for the door to open. It doesn't, but another bright flash soon follows.

Not thinking, I sprint to the garage door, clamp my sweaty hand around the cool, bronze handle, and the knob twists under my shaking fingers. I yank the door open, preparing myself for what I might find.

This door opens silently, unlike our creaky front door. I step into a brightly lit garage and take everything in as fast as I can. In the middle of the room, my dad stands over a small table with a welding mask on. He lifts it up to reveal a face full of confusion and concern.

My eyes dart from his facial expression to the table. Resting on the flat surface is what appears to be a prosthetic leg, along with various pieces of metal, plastic, and rubber.

It takes a second until it finally clicks.

Tears begin to drip out of my eyes. I run over to my father and wrap my arms around him, squeezing tight.

My dad takes a moment, his mouth stammering a few words of shock and bewilderment, before he pulls me into a hug.

Timber

Patrick Murphy built me on a summer day when he was in one of his good moods. Using the wood planks intended for the new addition to the porch, he crafted me in the little tree in the backyard. I was anything but safe, but I never fell. Quinn and Shawn were so excited when he broke out his tool set; they didn't even notice the look of concern on Ava's face when he set down an empty bottle and got to work. My wood was jagged and nails stuck out like the thorns on a rose. That night, Ava paced back and forth in their bedroom, her arms flailing and her face strained. When Quinn and Shawn entered their parents' bedroom, the yelling stopped. Ava's face changed from anger to a soft smile as she nodded her head at the children. Patrick, Quinn, Shawn, and Ava then gathered blankets, pillows, and a bag of months-old marshmallows, and headed outside. They scaled my knotted rope ladder into the hollow of my chest, where they set up their own little campsite in my heart. The hammering of nails could be heard as Patrick hung a picture frame featuring the happy family on my back wall. On the frame was a phrase written by Quinn in glitter glue. Hands sticky with purple sparkles and residue from stale marshmallows, the Murphys then settled down to sleep. And so did I.

Quinn and Shawn played with me every day that summer. Their identical blue eyes lit up at the very sight of me when they exited the house every morning. When they weren't together- which wasn't often- Shawn would come up alone to play with his action figures and color.

As he would color, he would sing little songs that he invented himself. They were out of tune and nonsensical, but they were always my favorite sound. Quinn would come up to read and write. I loved when she read aloud. Quinn was so smart, wise beyond her years. She would stumble over words, her back leaning on my sturdy wall. My favorite stories were the ones about the wizards.

✳✳✳

"Shawn! Quinn! Please get down from there and come inside," Ava yelled, resting her hand on the sliding glass door that led to the backyard.

The air was heavy, dark clouds forming in the sky. It was the twins' 10th birthday, but the plastic tablecloths and festive party hats never made it out onto the back patio. The only light I saw that evening was the glow of candles illuminating Patrick, who was pacing the kitchen floor. Grabbing a bottle and a glass, he opened the sliding glass door and sat in a soggy chair under the awning that covered the porch. Kicking his feet up, he poured himself a glass and peered out into the mud-filled backyard. He stayed there, refilling his glass until he looked down at his watch and headed inside. The hard rain and wind whipped violently against my sides, swaying the branches of the little tree and splintering my left wall. The photo of the Murphys fell to my floor, the glass forming a small crack in the top left corner of the frame.

The next morning, Quinn and Shawn ran out of the house and into the backyard to check on me. Patrick and Ava stood in the doorway, Patrick rubbing his head and drinking from a plastic bottle as Ava glanced at him, rolling her eyes.

"Keep drinking that water," she said, he tone pointed. "Maybe someday you'll get it."

It was midway into the summer when the family decided to have a party. Everyone showed up in clothing adorned with red, white, and blue, their necks surrounded by colored beads. Throughout the night, spirits were high. The smell of barbecued meat wafted through the air as the kids ran circles around the yard, and the adults drank and conversed amongst themselves.

"Be careful up there! The treehouse isn't the sturdiest," Ava called to the kids, who were playing a little too rough.

"Oh quit being a buzzkill, Av," Patrick said, his words slightly jumbled as if he had just woken up. Ava shot him a glare before turning up to the kids and smiling. Patrick's face shifted from a crooked smile to a look of anger as he stumbled away from Ava.

"I'm going to get another drink," He muttered under his breath. He set his empty can down on the table and waltzed over to the group of younger men standing around a bottle. They cheered as he threw back gulps of a clear liquid from a short glass. He drank these fast, his face scrunching up in disgust after every sip. I was always so confused by this. Why would he drink something he didn't like?

It was around sunset when everyone began to gather their things and head to the beach to watch the bursts of color that lit up the sky around the same time every year. Ava was gathering a collection of blankets and bug sprays while simultaneously calling for Quinn and Shawn when it happened. Patrick burst through the sliding glass doors of the kitchen and into the backyard. With his hand placed against my tree for stability, he let out an inhuman gag as the liquid he had been so generously downing before began to pour out of his mouth. As he heaved, I saw Ava standing in the doorway watching, her shoulder rested on the doorframe, her arms crossed and her chest rising and falling dramatically as she let out a big sigh. On her face was a look that she never used to use around Patrick, but that seemed more frequent these days.

A few hours later, Ava was left to clean up paper cups and defused sparklers by herself, while Patrick rested on the couch inside. She walked slowly towards me and climbed the ladder with one hand, the other hand tightly clutching a half-full garbage bag. She began to pick up the space around her, which was littered with ketchup-stained paper plates from the food that the kids had wolfed down earlier that evening. As she stood up, her tired eyes landed on the picture frame. Her knuckles turned white as her grip on the garbage bag tightened. Ava narrowed her eyes at the photo before climbing down the ladder once more. Walking over to the side of the house, she grabbed the long green hose, which stretched just far enough to water the flower garden that laid at my tree's roots. Ava pinched the bridge of her nose with her fingers and sighed a deep and heavy breath before rinsing the vomit off of the base of the tree. As the water began to muddy the ground, Ava started to sob. It was silent, but her shoulders shook violently and her chest rose every so often in order to let in a labored breath. That's when I knew something was wrong.

***

The fall got lonely. The twins started the fifth grade, so I was alone during the day. I could see Ava pacing the kitchen every day, clutching a calculator and a stack of papers. She looked stressed. I wanted to help her, but I didn't know how. At night, Quinn and Shawn were able to climb up the rope ladder that hung from my underbelly, but only if they promised to use me as a quiet place to do their homework. It wasn't unlikely that Ava would come up and help them, explaining to them almost foreign concepts until it became second nature.

It was late September when Shawn fell. He and Quinn had been playing pirates, and I was their ship. Quinn had taken over, and Shawn had been forced to walk the plank.

"You're way too close to the edge," Quinn warned, her high-pitched voice full of concern.

"I'll be fine! Quit being a baby," Shawn retorted.

"Whatever!" Quinn yelled back. "I am NOT a baby," she muttered under her breath.

He *was* way too close. And it was windy. I had no way to warn him that the wind was going to blow as hard as it did. No way to tell him that we were going to sway. With one large gust, I leaned to the right. Shawn, who was standing with his heels hanging off of my splintering edge, lost his balance. He fell and hit the ground. Hard. Ava sprinted out of the house, as soon as Shawn let out a scream, gathering him up in her arms before running back in the house. Quinn stood paralyzed with fear as she gripped onto my side, the wood cracking and piercing her skin.

When Shawn came back, he had a big cast on his leg and had to walk with crutches. It was a while before he was allowed to play again.

***

Winter was even lonelier. As the freckles faded on the twins' faces, the frequency of their visits also died down. During one of the few visits he made to me, Shawn and his friend talked about how Quinn was something called "sick," and she wasn't allowed to leave the house for a whole two weeks! After that, Shawn only visited when the snow had proved too much for the kids to get to school. During these days, the only way I was able to see the Murphys was through the panes of glass that stretched floor to ceiling in both the kitchen and living room, and the two windows- one into Quinn's room and the other into Ava and Patrick's. I would see Quinn go up to her room and dance around. I missed her. After a while, Ava would come up and tuck Quinn into bed. A few minutes later, I'd see her go to her own room and lay awake. Patrick would follow soon after, and Ava would quickly close her eyes and roll over when she saw the door opening. This confused me. They seemed so happy whenever they were with the twins, but this always changed when they were alone. Patrick would sit on the edge of the bed and run his hands through his slightly graying hair before removing his glasses. The bed would tilted as he laid down, and Ava's half-closed eyes would flutter.

I was worried about them. There was a lot more yelling in the house. It got so bad one night that Ava's mom had to come get Quinn and Shawn. I didn't see them for three days. While they were gone, all Ava and Patrick did was fight. He would throw things and she would throw things and by the time they were both too tired to fight anymore there would be shards of wedding china and wood from broken chairs scattered on the floor. And I had to watch.

The wind blew through the hollow of my chest. My chest- once full of life and curiosity as Quinn and Shawn explored the world around them, now empty and lonely.

***

One of the last visits I ever received was from Ava and the twins. Shawn and Quinn had been sitting on my wood floor all day. The presence of their usual playful energy was missing as they sat cross-legged, facing each other and speaking in hushed tones.

"I'm scared," said Shawn quietly. "Dad has been yelling so much lately. What if he never gets back to normal?"

"He won't," reassured Quinn. "He'll stop yelling one day, I promise. It'll all be good again soon." Quinn acted as if she was certain of this, but the way her eyes quickly shifted away from Shawn gave me the feeling that she was unsure. Ava, who was standing just below me in the flower garden, could hear the sound of soft whispers. She cocked her head and looked up at me. Her curiosity got the best of her as she dropped her gardening tools and climbed up the rope ladder.

"Hey, dolls," she beamed. "Room for one more?" Quinn and Shawn fell silent, their wide eyes looking anywhere but at Ava.

"What's wrong?" asked Ava hesitantly.

"Nothi-" started Quinn, before being interrupted by her brother.

"Why is Dad so mad all the time? Is he mad at us? I didn't mean to break that glass, I promise!" Shawn interjected, tears forming in the wells of his eyes.

"Oh honey," Ava sighed, gathering the twins up in her arms. "It's not your fault. He isn't mad at you, I promise. He's just... tired." The twins, nuzzled into their mother's dirty t-shirt, let out relieved sighs. But Ava, who was biting her bottom lip and looking upward in attempts to keep the tears from spilling out of her own eyes, seemed anything but relieved.

That night, Ava walked out of the back door and into the yard. Once again, she climbed my ladder, this time her shoulder and ear pressed together in order to hold a device up to her ear.

"Hey, Jen," she spoke into the device.

"No, I'm fine. He yelled at Shawn today after dinner. Nearly scared him half to death. And all for dropping a glass. A stupid glass! I just can't have these kids around him anymore, it's not fair to them." She paused for a while before continuing.

"I've thought about it. Trust me. If it were just me I would've done it years ago. I just want what's best for those kids"

Another pause.

"Alright well I gotta go put Quinn to bed," Ava sighed. "Tell Tom I say hello and tell Mom I'll call her tomorrow. Love you, bye."

✳✳✳

Ava left on a Sunday. I knew something was up when she didn't come outside to water the freshly blooming yellow flowers that lay at my roots. She took Quinn and Shawn with her. While Patrick was at work, she ushered the twins down the stairs and out of my line of vision. They were carrying their bags, so I figured they were going on vacation. But where was Patrick? Why wasn't he with them? Before she left, Ava put a sheet of wrinkled paper on the kitchen table.

When Patrick got home, he called to them. Nobody answered. That's when he saw he the crumpled note sitting on the wood of the table. As his eyes scanned the paper, his face shifted, as tears fell from his face. He yelled and threw things and then sat down and cried. He didn't stop crying. He sat there for hours, just rocking back and forth. Opening the glass door, he stood up and stepped outside. It had begun to drizzle, and the rain darkened the shoulders of his blue t-shirt. He paced back and forth, taking in deep breaths of the crisp, fresh air.

"I need a drink," he sighed, before heading back inside and slamming the door. He had about five gulps from the black-labeled glass bottle before he stood up and stared out of the door into the backyard. He was looking at me. Without a sound, he slid open the glass door and headed towards me.

A gust of wind shook my foundation. Patrick looked at me, the glass bottle shaking in his trembling hand. His face changed as he heated with anger. His brows furrowed and his fist clenched at his side and around the neck of the bottle.

"You," he yelled at me. "You don't belong here! They're gone!"

Angry tears flowed down his face as he chucked the bottle at me, the glass shattering against my front, liquid flowing down and absorbing into my wood.

Patrick stumbled over to the shed adjacent to me, trampling the flower garden in the process. The petals of the tulips crumpled under his feet, crunching as their green stems snapped. He threw the door open, the aluminum clanging against itself. I could hear the rustling and banging of things being thrown as Patrick looked for what he wanted. He came out with a chainsaw. The sharp teeth were coated with thick orange rust, and the handle had a layer of dirt caked on from years of outdoor work with no cleaning. Revving the engine, Patrick's drooping eyes stared into me. He took the metal teeth to the wood of my little tree and began to cut. As he cut, I began to tip. Tears rolled down Patrick's cheeks, making streaks in the dirt he still had on his face from work. I could feel myself falling. The rain hit my side and the cool air rushed through the door and window openings into my chest. *Protect the family*, I thought, thinking of the picturesque family trapped in the frame that hung on my wall. I hit the ground with a loud crash, my wood splintering in every direction. The slowly muddying earth around me softened with the blow, the dirt and grass giving slightly with my weight. Patrick fell to the ground, exhausted and breathing heavily. His bloodshot eyes landed on one thing. Within the broken pieces of my body aid the picture frame. Beneath a pile of glass from the frame was the torn photo. The piece of wood from the frame next to it was still decorated with glitter glue. It read "Our Family."

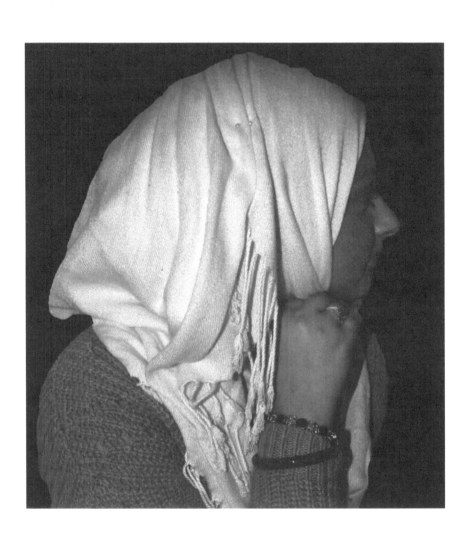

Diverging Minds

The sounds of the busy streets of the city surrounded me as I carried my belongings into the cab. Jack trudged behind me, holding a yellow note with the apartment address. His dark curls dripped in sweat from the heavy bags and he adjusted his circular glasses while observing the paper. Reaching out my pale hands to grab the paper, I told the driver our destination.

"Spenerstraße 15, 10557, Berlin." I read urgently. The driver nodded his head and took his time to get the cab started. Jack looked over at my frustrated expression and shrugged.

"There's no rush. I don't think Adam's home yet anyways." Jack assured me, "It's only a couple of minutes away, Fred."

My emerald eyes scanned my old apartment building. I felt a sense of bitterness encompass me. I cringed at the fact that I had to leave.

"Thanks again for asking that kid Adam. I should be staying for a little while. Once I get a new job I'll be fine. I still can't believe that my job was given away to that guy Muhammad." I said as Jack reluctantly smiled at me.

"Well, I'm sure you'll end up liking Adam." he stated hesitantly. I sighed and leaned back against the leather seat.

"Let's hope," I responded.

The drive lasted around 10 minutes before we arrived at the apartment complex. Jack apologized for having to immediately rush back to work and I thanked him for his help. My worn out brown boots tapped against the hardwood floor of the lobby. The tall security guard awaited me and guided me to the third floor. My eyebrows furrowed in confusion.

"Adam let me know ahead of time. I'm assuming you're Fredrick?" He stated. I nodded and he directed me towards the third floor.

Cautiously taking a few steps forward, my suitcase and belongings dragged along behind me. Looking around the dimly lit hallway, I noticed the blush paint peeled off the ceiling, revealing a basic nude color underneath. Spider webs occupied the corners of the walls. I hoped that the apartment was more sanitized than these hallways.

Walking up to the apartment, a number of voices could be heard from inside. A friendly face opened the wooden door.

Raising his eyebrows up in delight, the teenage boy welcomed me with a warm smile.

"You must be Fredrick! Hey, I'm Hus, Adam's brother. Nice to meet you!"

His hair was styled into a fade and he sported a basil colored hoodie. He had an olive skin tone and small eyes that looked a bit East Asian. My hands became stiff as I gave him an insincere smile.

"Come on in. Do you need help with your bags?" He politely asked. "Oh, and Adam should be back from work in a couple minutes."

Cautiously entering the apartment, a figure approached me with her light hair bouncing as she jumped with enthusiasm. The little girl's small almond eyes filled with curiosity as she prepared to question me.

"Are you Fredrick? Do you have a nickname? Where are you from? How old are you?" Another girl, who looked around a year or two older than the enthusiastic one, shyly went up to pull her away. Taking a couple steps back, they stopped, quizzically looking me up and down. The younger girl giggled and questioned my long blonde locks.

"I thought only *girls* had long hair!" She exclaimed. Carrying my two leather bags in hand, Hus approaches us and kneels down in front of his little sisters.

"Boys and girls can both have long hair. People can do whatever they want with their appearance." Hus calmly explained, looking back at me apologetically. Furrowing my eyebrows, I continued walking through the area. Paintings of calligraphy surrounded me with different colors plastered on the walls. The area was not too big or too small, despite there being so many siblings.

"How about you guys finish your homework?" Hus suggested to the girls. They boasted that they already had it done and decided to do some coloring instead.

"What are their names?" I questioned. "The little girls."

"Oh, you can call them Mary and Zainny. Zainny's 10 and Mary's 8. They get hyper when we have guests over. 'New friends!' they say." He chuckled.

I sighed, massaging my temples.

"I'll try not to let them bother you too much." He stated warily.

Walking towards the room, Hus struggled directing me to the door as he carried my bags. I continued to the room and Hus set my things down with a sigh.

"Want anything to eat or drink?" He asked.

I shook my head.

"Okay. Don't hesitate to reach out if you need anything!" Assuming he wanted to give me some time to adjust to my new surroundings, he left me on my own. Looking around the room, it was incredibly spacious, organized almost meticulously, from the larger details of the curtains to the smaller ones of where books stood in their bookcases. I was impressed by how clean and sophisticated the apartment was in comparison to the conditions of the hallway.

Looking around, I noticed the walls; painted maroon that were almost like my old apartment. It had been a color that I'd always meant to paint over, but between the long hours at our jobs sites and being in charge of the group of guys at the construction site, I never had gotten around to it.

While unpacking, a rug stood out to me in the corner of the room. It had an intricate design that seemed to have an Asian-influenced pattern with green and magenta fabric. Before I could look at it further, I heard the sound of a door shut and cheerful girls yelling a series of questions to whoever had entered the apartment.

Opening the room door, I stepped outside and was met by a tall bearded man wearing a soccer jersey over light washed blue jeans. Aside from the fact that his skin was much lighter, he looked strikingly similar to Hus. His emerald eyes looked up as he noticed a figure standing in the hallway.

"Hi! I'm Adam. You must be Fredrick. I'm glad to see that you've arrived safely!" He said, extending his hand out.

"Right. Nice to meet you, Adam. Thanks for having me over. I was having a hard time trying to find a new place that I could afford here in Berlin. You know how crowded it is, especially with the new folks coming in." I said.

Adam laughed and shook his head.

"Uh yeah, well of course." He hesitantly responded as he scratched the back of his neck.

"Should we continue this conversation at the dinner table?"

I could not remember the last time I had a full family dinner. As a 10 year old, I was left with my dad who was too stern to have something as 'cheesy' as that. The only conversations I ever really had with my dad were one-sided, and I could remember one specific instance that made me question his validity.

Flopping the newspaper on the table, my dad sat on the plastic chair with a grunt. His eyebrows furrowed as he crushed his cigarette on the wooden surface. He massaged his temples and the wrinkles in his forehead were prevalent. I sat and awaited some sort of reasoning for this behavior, as usual.

"They're still accepting the damn terrorists." He angrily stated as he passed the newspaper to me. I skimmed through the article and realized he was talking about the refugees.

"Not a big surprise, though. They always argue over it and never change a thing." I respond knowingly. He shakes his head at me in frustration.

"They're bringing all of these dirty rapists and crime with them." He stated. Even though I despised any idea of accepting them, because of the threat, I didn't know where he got the 'rapists' from.

"Where did you hear that?" I asked. He looked up, confused and I clarified.

"Oh, the news is all over that." He said, leaning towards me. He and I both were shocked at my questioning. Questioning dad was a crime in the house. Seeing him begin to get defensive, I retreated.

"Yeah, I guess you're right. They mess up their own countries and now wanna come here?" I stated. He nodded in content.

And here I was, sitting across from an old woman with a scarf covering her head.

"This is my mom." Adam stated as he took a look at my confused expression. My eyes diverted from the woman to him. I cleared my throat, attempting to let out a few words. However, I found myself at lost for words. Clenching my pale knuckles, my eyes hesitantly moved between Adam and the woman in her eerie attire. My body longed to move, to gather all of my belongings and leave. But thinking rationally, I had nowhere else to go. I had no job, no apartment, and my savings were running out.

My hands relaxed as I attempted to stop their shaking. Grabbing some stew, my weary eyes scanned the rest of the dishes. The plate closest to me was topped with greens and paprika. Zainny noticed me observing the dish and offered to pour me some.

"It's qurooti. Afghan food. It's a yogurt dish and on top you see green pepper." She stated enthusiastically.

I didn't realize I was holding my breath, so I exhaled and responded, "Oh, I don't handle spices well."

"I wouldn't call it spicy. You should try it! It's my favorite dish from home." Adam encouraged.

Home. I felt like an outsider in my own country. Was it my own fault, for staying sheltered my whole life? The woman with the head covering started talking with a heavy accent that was barely audible.

"I make only a little spicy." She explained, "Because I want you to try."

"She limited the spices for you." Mary said, smiling, holding back laughter, "I guess it's too much for you to handle."

Zainny nudged her arm to stop her from laughing at me. I raised my eyebrows in confusion. *I* was the one being laughed at? She poured some of the dish in my plate when I accepted.

I took a bite and my mouth burst with flavor. The tomato and onion mixed with the salty yogurt resulted in a savory taste that left me wanting more. The pepper and paprika perfectly topped the dish, leaving a hint of spice that was balanced out with the rest of the ingredients.

Seeing me serve myself more of the flavorful dish, their mother smiled with a look of content.

My curiosity was killing me and I hesitantly asked about where they were from, "How long have you guys stayed in Berlin?"

The woman immediately answered, "I move here with Adam in 1999. Adam only 10. Hussain born 1 year later, then Zainab and then Mariam."

Hussain. Of course Hus had to be short for Hussain. Shocked, I looked over at the little Saddam. He had just finished setting the trays onto the table. How was he so nice, so polite?

"Back to the conversation we had before Adam, I'm guessing you all actually gained your citizenship. Many of the new folks don't do that." I said.

Looking up from his plate, Adam quickly hid his furrowed brows and responded in a kind manner.

"We actually came here as Hazara refugees, which many of the 'new folks' are coming in as." He stated confidently. Placing his utensils down, he awaited my response, engrossed in the conversation.

No matter how hard I tried to think, I had no idea what group Hazara was and I could feel uneasiness in my stomach. Why did I not know this? Shouldn't I know where they're coming from?

"Hazara?" I questioned.

"Oh right, sorry. Hazaras are an ethnic group in Afghanistan." Adam stated.

"If you think of typical Afghans, you don't think of people who look like us. Hazaras tend to have small eyes and East Asian features." Hussain explained.

I nodded, making the decision to bite my tongue and end the conversation. Was I really doing the thing I disliked about my father the most, politicizing every conversation?

The rest of dinner was full of Mariam's school stories and explanations of her dreams from the previous night. The family would listen attentively and question her to expand on certain details. At first they tried to limit her talking and have me talk more since I was the guest, but I shook my head and saved myself by explaining my tiredness. In reality, my confusion occupied my thoughts as I tried to figure them out.

"Mariam, since Hussain did the dishes yesterday, it's your turn today." Mrs. Hasan said.

Sighing in disdain, Mariam begged Zainab to decide the verdict between them over a round of rock paper scissors. Mariam ended up doing the dishes that night.

***

Two weeks after listening to Mariam's constant stories that I surprisingly enjoyed hearing, helping with Hussain's stress of applying to universities, witnessing Zainab's showcases of her favorite novels, and having arguments with Adam over Barcelona vs Real Madrid, I finally decided to sit down with Mrs. Hasan. She and I were the only people at home during the weekdays. I found myself avoiding her and sanctioning myself in the room while I did my job search in fear that my view of Muslims would be permanently changed. But how long would I continue being sanctioned?

I crept into the living room to check if she was there and she appeared to be sitting on a rug; praying. I learned that Muslims sit on a rug to recite their daily prayers. I've heard Adam saying "Allahu Akbar" and, after seeing my frightened reaction, he explained that it meant "God is Great" in Arabic.

Mrs. Hasan bent down and placed her forehead on a clay stone that lay on the rug and brought herself back up. I wondered why they had the stone, but I haven't mentioned anything about Muslim practices after the Allahu Akbar conversation.

Slowly entering the room, my foot got caught with the corner of the couch and slammed into it. I winced in pain and Mrs. Hasan looked up at me as she rolled up the rug and placed it back on the corner table. Noticing me approach her, she greeted me with a warm smile. I sat down on the black leather couch.

"What's that stone thing?" I blurted out.

She giggled and calmly answered, saying that it had significance in Shia Islam.

"Shia Islam?" I questioned.

"There are different branches of Islam, like in other religions. We follow the Shia ideology." She tried to explain in the best way possible with her broken English.

"What does ISIS follow?" I questioned.

Giving me a soft smile, she responded, saying that she has been asked that question more times than she had hoped. I pursed my lips apologetically. I couldn't even begin to imagine all of the badgering she may have had to witness.

"Wearing this scarf makes people come up to me and yell mean things about Islam. They mention ISIS every time. ISIS is an extremist group." She stated seriously.

"KKK in America is bad too. We don't yell at every white person." She continued. She was right... the news only focuses on a specific group. How did I not realize that?

Mrs. Hasan explained the persecution of Shias by ISIS, how they themselves are major targets. And they're Muslims themselves. They were no less victimized than people like me, who wanted to ban all of them for safety precautions.

My father never told me any of this. In fact, I don't think he knew anything about the religion in general. How did I not realize how much ignorance was present in our conversations?

Excusing myself from the couch, I rushed to the room with a pounding headache. My head was pounding and my heart was racing. My father had been feeding me the wrong information my whole life, and I fell for it. So what did I actually believe? What were my *own* morals?

The Hasan's were the most generous people I knew. Throughout the weeks they had constantly fed me, offered me any transportation, and had overall made me happier through the bond we created. I never had an actual interaction with Muslims and they had proven all of the stereotypes to be wrong.

Shutting the wooden door, I seated myself on the bed as I tried to collect my thoughts. The sound of crinkled paper was heard beneath me. A portrait of a blonde, long haired man stared back at me. Mariam scribbled "Fred" on top as the title with a smiley face next to it.

My father always described Muslims as serious and aggressive, but this drawing made me think otherwise. They were also hilarious,

Hussain cracked the best jokes about the big old Trump dog in the states. I laughed at myself as I thought about how naive I was. While admiring the drawing, I heard a light tap on the door. Adam's tall figure stood in the threshold with papers in hand.

"Guess who found another job opening!" He enthusiastically stated. He had just finished working 9 hours and was still willing to help me out. I gave him a soft smile as he placed the papers down beside me.

"Thanks, I'll be out in a minute." I said. As he shut the door, I pulled out my phone and dialed a familiar number.

"Hey," I said, "I think I have to apologize for all those arguments we had."

"I was hoping to get this call from you." Jack responded. I could hear the joy in his voice.

Secrets Untold

"**D**on't you turn your back on me," yelled the dark-haired woman. There was a time when she was once very beautiful with no sign of blemishes. However, as the years passed a few wrinkles have formed along her forehead and mouth, and she had started to complain over the aches of her back. Grumbling underneath her breath, her daughter walked back down the stairs and glared directly into her eyes.

"Look Bella, I know that you really want to go, but I'm telling you no," her mother repeated once again while massaging her temple, feeling the stirrings of an oncoming migraine.

"I just don't get you. I'm eighteen, so why can't I go on a summer road trip with my friends?" Bella retorted without backing down, as she noticed her mother was sighing deeply to calm the redness from her face.

"Bella, just because you're eighteen doesn't mean that you should go and travel by yourself. And either wa---"

"But I'm not by myself. I'm going with my friends and you've known them since forever," Bella interrupted refusing to let her mother end the conversation. She was desperate to leave and no longer live a sheltered life. Ever since she was little, she was forbidden from sleeping over anyone's house or from going anywhere without adult supervision. It didn't matter whether the friend was well-acquainted or lived down the street; sleepovers were out of the question. The idea of going on a trip with friends that would last about a month would most likely cause her mother to have a mini heart attack. But Bella didn't care and continued to pester her, hoping she'd cave in.

"Mom, come on, please let me experience this. Don't look at it as a month but just a couple of weeks. I'll call you every day and you can see my location on your phone anyway."

"You knew about that?" her mother questioned seemingly shocked to hear the news as her face turned bright red with embarrassment.

Unable to contain her laughter, Bella said, "I wouldn't be surprised since you watch me like a hawk." Her mother just continued to smile at her thinking about how much Bella had grown up, but nonetheless, with the shake of her head she dismissed the entire trip idea from her mind.

"You still can't go," and with that Bella was left alone, standing in their living room, watching how the last bit of sunlight was sweeping through the half-closed curtains.

After a week and a half, Bella found herself uncomfortably dressed in a shiny red cap and gown, sitting on a foldable chair. The room seemed to suffocate her as she and the rest of her senior class were cramped into straight rows. She couldn't help but notice the rapid beating of her heart. The sound was a deafening echo in her ears while her thoughts became jumbled; was this really the end? Could she finally have her chance for some adventure? For as long as she could remember, Bella had always wanted to leave her little town of Hapsburg, where everyone knew everyone. Having a mother as overbearing as her own, the call of the unknown was even more tempting. She remembered how her mother used to walk with her to school each day saying "good morning" to the neighbors as they passed. At first, Bella thought that her mother was really famous, having known everyone in town, but she soon realized that it had nothing to do with her mother; it was just a town where everyone knew everyone else. As soon as she received her diploma, looking into the audience her eyes locked onto her mother's.

Just look at her, she had become such a beautiful woman within a second, Bella's mother thought while Bella stood beside other anxious parents. She began to reminisce about the wonderful eighteen years she had spent with her only child. Bella was always outgoing, getting herself in the stickiest situations. Her mother couldn't believe that same two year old with a goofy smile had become someone so strong and bright- and stubborn, too. She definitely got that from her father, her mother thought, as she wiped away one escaping tear. Wearing a proud smile on her face, Bella's mother applauded as loudly as she could when Bella walked onto the platform. She watched her daughter's excitement and the big smile that formed on her face as she walked off and hugged all her friends. Her mother felt a twinge in her heart beginning to wonder about Bella's summer road trip once more, spending a month away from me and this town would probably be good for her. It would also be good for me. She knew that she couldn't always have Bella tightly tucked in between her arms. Even though Bella is her precious jewel and she'll miss her so very much, it's time for her to also grow up. Bella's mother couldn't always be there to shield her...Bella needs to go and see the world. Her mother can survive being alone. She's done it before.

"Mom! I did it, I graduated!" Bella screamed snatching her mother in a tight squeeze. Noticing that she was being unusually silent, Bella took a step back. Tears were falling down her mother's face, and before Bella could utter a word her mother pulled her back into another hug. Stroking her hair softly Bella's mother sniffled, "You can go. It's ok, you can go."

On the Saturday morning after graduation, Bella stood in front of the nearest thrift shop in her hometown. Eager to hit the road, Bella was exasperated that her childhood friend, Abby, wanted to show her, and the rest of their friends, the new place she spent most of her time after school. Abby was known for her interest in antiques and that included anything that creaked or was missing a screw. It was one of the many reasons why she wanted to major in history. The sun was a bright beam of light as it guided Bella into the shop in search of her friends. She was not surprised to find herself surrounded by china dolls in frilly dresses, rickety chairs, old lamps, and ancient paintings. Strange and exotic objects were scattered throughout the shop.

As Bella walked further into the store, she could hear her friends laughing but her feet carried her in the opposite direction. The back of the shop grew darker as less light was offered from the candle lit lamps. While Bella ventured further into the store's aisles, she felt an eerie feeling grow within her. Coupled with that feeling came a smell so strong that she couldn't help but scrunch her nose at, a stench of garbage wafted through the air, carrying itself through the entirety of the store. Deciding to return to her friends, Bella quickly turned around, accidently bumping into one of the shelves on display. Awkwardly bending down, she noticed a book on the floor that was opened with its spine in the air. Not wanting the book to break, Bella picked it up and realized with a second look that it was an old-fashioned diary. Rolling her eyes, about to toss the diary aside, her friend, Marianne, decided to jump out of nowhere and screamed.

"BOO!"

"AHH! God, Marie don't do that!" Bella screamed, getting caught off guard.

"Sorry Arabella, it was too great of an opportunity to let pass," Marianne said as she playfully elbowed Bella's arm. "So what are you looking at?" Marianne asked as she leaned over Bella's shoulder to take a peek.

Deciding to let it go, Bella shrugged her shoulders and responded, "Nothing special, just an old diary."

"You know you should get it. This is our last summer together before we head to college. Having one would be a great way to remember how much fun we had, even with all the pictures we'll be taking," Marianne reasoned with a small grin as she walked away.

Bella began to think about what Marianne said and couldn't help but realize how much she really did want to get the diary. After noticing that she had been standing, there staring at the diary's cover, as if mesmerized, Bella broke from her trance and made her way to the cashier with the diary held tightly against her chest.

The chime of the shop's door and the beep of the car getting unlocked were all signals to the girls' departure. Settling herself in the backseat, Bella was taking a minute to admire the maroon-covered diary lying on her lap when she realized that Alexa had turned around in the driver's seat to face her. "Bella, do you have any idea what you're going to be writing about?" Alexa asked while putting on her seatbelt.

"Hmm I'm basically thinking of writing about our road trip. Marianne actually gave me the idea. Soon we'll all be going our separate ways and I really do want to write everything down so I never forget the time I spent with you guys." Bella said as she zipped her backpack closed, securing the diary with the rest of her stuff. The car eventually grew silent as the girls began to drive through the winding roads. When Bella took a glance out the window she was shocked to see the night sky filled with a sea of twinkling stars, almost like glitter.

By the time they reached an inn, it was too late to call their parents like they had originally planned. Instead, they sent text messages before they started to unload their belongings from the car. Each of them carrying their own backpack and carry on made their way into the main lobby. They hoped that they could get one of the suites mentioned online where they all could stay together, but luck was not on their side.

"Good evening, we'd like to book a room for the four of us please," Abby said when the girls had reached the reception desk.

"I'm sorry, Miss., but we don't have any of those rooms available at the moment," replied the female worker, getting slightly nervous over Abby's intimidating scowl after hearing her reply.

"Excuse me, but is there any other rooms that are available, like doubles?" Bella smiled, quickly stepping alongside Abby trying to not frighten off the employee.

"No I'm afraid that those are also occupied. However, we do have four single rooms," the employee replied. Being able to read her name tag, now that she was closer, Bella reached for her own wallet and signaled her friends to do the same.

"Ok, thank you Jessica, we'll be taking those rooms," Bella said giving Jessica both her license and credit card.

Once Bella was settled, wrapped up in her warm sheets and fluffy pillow, the diary was laid on top of her lap urging her to write something down. However, when she opened the diary she noticed something peculiar. The pages no longer seemed to have their pale faces looking up to her. Instead, they changed into a tan-yellowish color, almost as if someone painted them while she was away. As Bella flipped to the middle of the diary, there were words mysteriously already written in blue ink. Bella was puzzled, thinking how that could be. She hadn't written anything and she was pretty sure that the diary was blank when she opened it in the store.

Dear Diary,

I finally said yes! Jack and I are so happy with our wedding vows and our new future together. Whenever I'm with him life becomes such a thrill and I end up forgetting all the problems I have with my parents. They think that I'm rushing into things and am acting like a rebellious child. But that's ancient history, I don't care what they say because I love Jack and I want to be with him. Being nineteen doesn't matter when it comes to love. We've already decided to elope and get away from this disgusting place. I'm sure that we'll be fine without the support of our parents. We've both been practically kicked out of our homes, which doesn't bother me in the least so thanks Mom and Dad! Now all I have to do is find a job (Jack already has a job, see isn't he great.) and we were able to rent out a small apartment that's well suited to us. So everything's going pretty well, we're living life the way we want to. I wonder why my parents made it into such a big deal.

Sincerely yours,
Sabi

After reading the signed person's name, Bella continued to look at the passage when she laid it on her lap. Wow she couldn't believe that she bought a used diary. She guessed it meant she wouldn't be able to write anything inside even though she was really looking forward to it, she thought as she flipped through the pages of the diary seeing more and more written excerpts. However, Bella began to smile as a new idea began to form in her head, this wasn't a complete waste of money. Instead of writing, she could use the diary as a source of reading material since she forgot to bring a book along with her. Plus, this 'Sabi' person seems naive and interesting at the same time. Bella wanted to know more about her story. She wondered if the writer is even still alive. No longer upset about buying an already written diary, Bella found herself more interested in who actually wrote it. Curiosity got the better of her but she couldn't do anything right at the moment. With an annoyed grumble, Bella switched off the light and left the diary on top of a pillow near her head.

Knock, knock, knock. Turning around, drawing her arm over her ears, Bella felt the coolness of something firm and furry beside her. *Knock, knock, knock.* Moving her other arm up and down, she felt the sensation all around her. *Knock, knock, knock.* Releasing a disgruntled noise, Bella knew that she couldn't ignore the person knocking on her door to fall back to sleep. Sitting upright with slitted eyes Bella realized that at some point during the night she landed on the carpeted floor. Wobbling up onto her feet and towards the dresser, her eyes flew towards the digital clock. Looking back at the mirror reflection of her tired self, she saw how her eyes widened. *Bang!* Jumping at least an inch skyward, Bella ran towards the door gingerly unlocking it, revealing the obnoxiously loud Marianne bombarding her steel pan against the door.

"Wakie! Wakie! I knew this would come in handy," Marianne flipped the pan into the air and caught it, "What time do you think it is?!" she shouted as she walked passed Bella and started to pile Bella's belongings into the discarded suitcase.

"Ugh, I know, I'm sorry. But shouldn't you be more quiet? You look crazy with swinging that pan around," Bella sleepily asked while rubbing her eyes.

Ignoring the comment about the pan Marianne replied in a stern tone, "Arabella, we should have been driving to the next checkpoint an hour ago. Everyone is already waiting for us downstairs."

"I just want to continue sleeping," Bella said letting out a long yawn as she made her way back to the bed.

"No, no, no, I don't think so." Marianne responded shoving Bella towards the bathroom. Unfortunately, without seeing the hidden shoe in her path, Bella had toppled over it, acting as clumsy as a newborn swan, and was back to being sprawled on the floor. The pain struck up her leg shocking her fully awake and wanting to let out a scream.

"Oh my God, are you okay?!" Marianne asked when she rushed over to Bella's side. Bella was taking small breaths and then with Marianne's help stood up once more.

"Well, I'm definitely awake now. You were right, we are running late so let's hurry up."

After getting ready and quickly packing her things away, Bella and Marianne ran for the reception desk. As they went down the stairs they pinned out their group of friends with their bags. "It's about time Bella, you really are such a sleepyhead." said Abby as she brushed Bella's bangs out of her eyes.

"Sorry about that, but guys I have so much to tell you. Something happened last night." Bella slightly raised her voice to draw in the girls' attention. They all looked at her as if something was wrong, but she didn't care; she just wanted them to help her figure out who wrote in the diary.

"This will probably be hard to believe, but the diary already has a passage written in it." Bella began.

"Oh that's great, you already started writing in it!" Marianne excitedly responded. Bella shook her head.

"No, it was already there when I opened the diary. I just didn't notice it when we were in the shop." Bella said as she looked up to them. All of them were much taller than her, even though she was older than them by a few months.

"You don't suppose the diary ended up at that thrift shop by accident?" Alexa said as she began to falter backwards from the weight of her bag.

"I don't know, but even if it was based on how old-looking the diary is, I'm not sure if the writer is still around. Though honestly I wish I could find the person." Bella responded back, twisting her fingers together.

"Don't be ridiculous. Arabella, you can't find someone from a tattered diary, especially since we're already miles away from that thrift shop back at home. I'm sorry, but I don't think it's possible." Abby rationalized to Bella hoping that Bella would soon see it as a lost cause.

"Yeah, you're probably right..." Bella said as she softly caressed the cover of the diary.

Abby placed her hand on Bella's forehead and said, "Are you feeling okay? You're looking a bit pale," Bella squinted her eyes at Abby and everyone else. It became clear that they couldn't see the connection Bella had to the diary even though she herself didn't know either.

"You're right, I probably overexerted myself too much. I'll sleep it off when we're back on the road again." Bella retorted with the farthest thing from the truth. Inside her head, Bella couldn't understand her newfound obsession, why did she feel so connected to this writer? She shouldn't be worrying about an old diary. Bella should be enjoying herself. This was the trip she begged for.

Continuing their road trip to Florida, the girls were all in the back seat while Abby drove and Marianne was giving her directions with her GPS. *It couldn't hurt to use it as reading material.* No longer resisting, Bella grabbed the diary from her bag and took a peek inside. The swirl of the words were a welcomed sight. Bella flipped passed the excerpt she read and found a new one. Her heart started to race and she couldn't stop a smile from forming.

Dear Diary,

I don't remember the last time I've taken a break. It's been three years since Jack and I moved into this apartment, but the once wondrous home has changed into a cage where the walls keep closing in. There are times where I feel myself getting strangled by the stiffening air. The number of bills and late notices have been piling up so much that they almost fly out through the windows. I have to be honest...It's a disaster! Every day that passes by I'm starting to think that my parents were right. I was irresponsible and impulsive. The so called love I felt for Jack is mostly gone now. It took me awhile to notice it but I realized that I had married him blindly. It wasn't until later in our marriage that I discovered he has a double personality. There are times when Jack is the man I fell for and then others when he becomes aggressive and violent. There's been moments when he's rampaged through the rooms, throwing his medication aside, knocking furniture over, and slamming doors to the point that the hinges appear as if they'll fall off. I don't know how much more I can take.

Sincerely yours,
Sabi

Bella flipped to the next page of the diary trying to avoid any eye contact with her friends. She knew that if she looked up they would notice her disheartened expression. Tightening her grip on the diary, she leaned the car door.

Dear Diary,

Life is becoming unbearable. The only thing that is keeping me sane is my daughter. She's now two years old and is the most precious thing I've ever had to call mine. I've been becoming more and more concerned about her safety when Jack is at home with her. But Jack is gone. He left us. The memory of how he aggressively threw me aside like a piece of garbage will forever haunt me, more so his words, "You are nothing but a terrible mother and our daughter will grow to hate you." I'm extremely grateful that this happened in the absence of our daughter. I wouldn't know what to do if she would have nightmares over her own father. Both the scar he left on my forehead and the mental one will never heal. I hope my daughter will live happily and stay away from harm's way. As her mother I can only hope that I can protect her and teach her not to make the same mistakes as I did.

Sincerely yours,
Sabi

Not fully comprehending what was going on, the page in front of her became puddled with water; she was crying and she couldn't stop. Reading the last sentence struck a chord in her so much that she knew it sounded similar. This mother really cherished her daughter. To her, her daughter always came first almost like the rest of the world was nonexistent. Just by reading these few passages, Bella could see that Sabi was incredibly brave and strong to endure such things, Bella continued to reflect as she closed the diary and clutched it in between her hands, she probably wouldn't have been able to do what the writer did, and what was more upsetting is that she was beginning to miss her own mother. Bella wondered what her mother could be doing right now. She's probably pacing near her phone, asking herself if she should call Bella, she really didn't deserve her…

"Watch out!" Marianne screamed. Before Bella could register what Marianna said, her head whacked itself against the car door as her range of vision deteriorated. Bella could feel her strength leaving her body and she couldn't find her voice to yell for help. Without much of a fight, Bella's eyes slowly closed shut.

"Bella, please wake up. I'm so sorry I tried to avoid the car but it didn't help us one bit. I'm really sorry."

Bella was numb. There was no other way to describe it. All she could see was that she was surrounded by darkness with a large pressure pounding against her skull. Trying to get away from the pain, she attempted to will herself back to sleep but eventually gave up on the thought. The wetness of someone's tears trickling down her arm pulled her back to reality. Bella opened her eyes to find herself in a hospital bed with Abby holding onto her hand. She gently squeezed causing Abby to pull her gaze upwards. Bella drew up some courage and finally asked, "What happened?"

Abby continued to hold her hand as she replied, "We got hit by another driver on the left side of our car. But don't worry, everyone is okay- just some bruises, nothing major, including yours. You just have a little bruise on the side of your head that the doctor says will heal up in no time." Not knowing she was holding her breath, Bella let out a gust of air as she inhaled once more. Abby kissed her on the forehead and said that she would let her have some rest. When she left the room Bella started to remember what she last read from the diary. Her thoughts did not calm her pounding heart, it couldn't be...Sabi...Sabi...It did sound slightly familiar. Slowly turning her head from left to right, Bella didn't see it lying around until she stretched her left hand out. The diary was beside her the entire time. Without a moment to waste, she flipped to the next page.

Dear Diary,

Today is going to be the last time that I talk to you. My daughter is growing every day along with her curiosity. I don't want her to find you and discover everything that I've hidden from her. She shouldn't have to know what actually happened to her father. She asks about him persistently, but my silence seems to be quieting down her questions. Someday when she's older I'll tell her the truth, but for right now all she needs to know is that she can count on Mommy for anything and everything. I hope one day she'll understand and not come to hate me. The last thing I want is to become an eyesore for my sweet darling. Now that I think about it, I've never did tell you my little angel's name. It's Arabella, Bella for short.

Sincerely yours,
Sabi

Bella was awestruck, her vision blurred followed by the clamminess of her hands. The diary...the writer is her mother. Bella's the little daughter…Her father did that to her mother, Bella thought as the realization caused her eyes to turn into a rapid waterfall emptying its endless contents on the white blanket lying on top of her. Everything was different. She needed to get homel; Bella had to see her mom. She'd been so selfish thinking that summer was the last to spend with her friends. When really it was the last to spend with Mom. *Her* mom, Bella repeated in her head, unable to stop the sobs from shaking her entire body. Desperately sucking in a breath of air, she noticed the doctor was walking towards her room. She quickly rubbed her eyes dry of any tears and tried to look as calm as possible. Eventually, the doctor reached her room and what she thought was going to take at least a half an hour, was surprisingly just 10 minutes. The doctor had only reported, "Overall, you're not in any serious condition, so you are clear to go home," and she was then quickly discharged.

Once outside her friends were shocked to see her face a rosy shade of pink and her glossy eyes. "What happened? Are you ok?" Alexa asked followed by the worried glances of all Bella's friends.

"I'm sorry guys, but I have to get back home. The hospital phoned our parents, so we all know that we have to go back. But I also have to go see my mom as soon as possible."

"Yes, I think this does bring this wild road trip to a close. Let's look for plane tickets to get home quicker. The repairs on the car would take too long and my parents already gave the ok to leave it behind," Abby said while taking out her phone to look at the closest and cheapest flights. With that everyone took a taxi to the nearest airport. Using the emergency money they all had, the girls boarded the first plane to Hapsburg, which was two days later.

Being an early riser, Sabrina was already enjoying her cup of coffee when she heard the sound of a car door slamming shut. Leaving the kitchen she was surprised to see the front door quickly open, showing her daughter in front of her gasping for air.

"Bella, I've been worried sick! Please give me more updates, I was planning on picking you up from the airport," her mother frantically yelled while lightly moving Bella's hair aside to look at the bump on her head. She then went into the bathroom and got Bella an ice pack. Ignoring the ice pack, Bella led her mother to sit down on the couch.

"I got into a car accident but don't worry everyone's fine," Bella quickly said when she saw her mother's worried expression. Smiling at her, Bella placed her hands around her mother's face and lifted up her bangs. Deliberately staring at her was a slither of a pinkish scar. Not taking a second of hesitation, Bella showed the diary to her mother. Breathing heavily her mother asked in barely a whisper, "Where did you get that?" Bella placed the diary on the coffee table and pulled her mother into a tight embrace.

"I thought you already knew this, but 'Sabi,' I could never hate you."

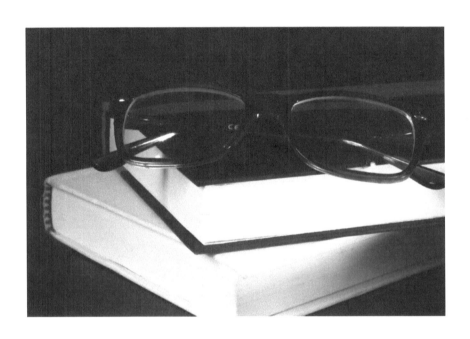

Always Read the Fine Print

A muddled man sat sulkily in his chair. His hands were frustratingly tangled in his mess of uneven brown curls and his right foot was repeatedly bouncing on the floor with a worried anticipation. He hesitated to turn around in his chair as he heard light footsteps coming up the stairs.

"Ezra Beckett! I'm surprised to find you up here." Ezra, now fully facing the confused man, gave him a dumbfounded look.

"Really, Levi? You didn't expect me to be in the attic of the library we've been coming to almost every day since high school?" Levi allowed himself to roll his eyes at Ezra's comment as he plopped himself down on a wooden chair directly across from him.

"You were supposed to be here over an hour ago", said Ezra to the papers he was scribbling on, purposely refusing to look at Levi.

"Hey man," Levi paused, picking up the pear on Ezra's desk, "you can't put a time on creativity," he said shaking the pear knowingly at Ezra. He walked over to Ezra's chair, his hair just barely gracing Ezra's knuckles as he leaned over him to look at the papers.

"My God, are you ever going to cut your ridiculous hair? I won't even be able to see my own work soon!"

Levi let out a long sigh. "Oh c'mon, what's got you down Charlie Brown? And don't try to say it's my long hair that's bothering you, I know you love my hair."

Ezra spun around with his head in his hands, multiple wrinkles forming in his forehead. He got up from his chair and began pacing

259

the small room, the lingering feeling of nostalgia followed him and the books seemed to glare down at him judgmentally from their shelves. Levi glanced over at the deep indent formed in Ezra's chair, being very cautious not to let him see. Ezra turned around to face his wide-eyed friend.

"This story... I can't do it, it's not coming together, Levi. I can't connect with it." Ezra looked pretty devastated which Levi couldn't quite wrap his head around.

"Scrap it then" offered Levi, with no sign of concern on his face.

"Scrap it?" Ezra turned to present his friend with a puzzled look. "I've been working on this story for almost eleven months and you're telling me to 'scrap it'? I have deadlines to meet. Sorry, that we can't all be like you, aimlessly floating along life and letting things come to you with *such* little ease." Ezra spread out his arms and began flapping them daintily, mocking Levi in a childlike manner.

"Well," Levi began, "*I* can't help it that I've got 206 creative bones in my body, Ez! You just need to stop thinking with that big ol' brain of yours and let your pen do the talking, relentlessly and naturally. That's all there is to it!" Ezra let out a frustrated sigh at this remark.

"Yes! That's just all there is to it!" said Ezra, gleefully waving his arms around like a madman. "And I suppose that gumdrops grow on trees and every river's made out of chocolate syrup as well! No Levi, what I *need* to do is work and since I clearly can't do that here, I'm leaving!"

Ezra slammed his book and pushed his feet away from the chair, giving off a squeak as it moved about an inch back, getting caught up in the fringe on the end of the carpet. He quickly collected his mess of papers and grabbed his pen from the top of the desk as he flipped off the lamp's switch. Levi remained seated in the chair, twiddling with his thumbs as a sarcastic "Hope you're happy!" was heard from Ezra, who was now at the end of the stairs and quickly making his way out of the door. Grabbing his coat off the back of the chair, Levi began making his way down the stairs, starting towards the door. With a little nod, he decided he would take the long way back to the apartment.

The next morning, it was rather foggy and the sky was clogged up with clouds. Ezra was re-arranging books on shelves that had been haphazardly knocked over by children the previous day. He was mumbling words of nonsense to himself and his knees were sore from kneeling on the hard wooden floor. Ezra glanced through the clear door at the front of the store and saw a familiar plain white bike, the same one he'd been seeing for the past three years, pulling up to the building. Levi hurriedly went to the front of the store, rushing over to Ezra, who was now rearranging the history section

"Well, good morning to you, too" said Ezra, slowly removing himself from the floor and gathering himself before Levi.

"Ezra. Ezra, Ezra, Ezra. I had an epiphany today. I know exactly what we should write our book on." Ezra raised his eyebrows at Levi, awaiting his next words. "Poetry. Children's poetry." Ezra gave Levi a disdainful look.

"Levi, my good man, you do realize I am twenty three years old and you are twenty four and you're looking to write poetry. For children. Not really my style. Also, I guarantee you that anything either of us come up with has already been done before, it's 2012." Levi muttered a few words to himself as he struggled to comprehend Ezra's disbelief.

"You don't get it!" Levi exclaimed, "There are absolutely no limits to our collective creativity if we write for children." Levi swiped his finger between him and Ezra, drawing an imaginary line. "Their minds are untouched, it's beautiful! It is our personal responsibilities to fill their head with the color of our words!" Levi was practically dancing around their bookstore at this point, ignoring the condescending looks he was receiving from Ezra.

"Well, if you're looking to add color to something, may I suggest you start with your bike?" Ezra motioned outside to Levi's untouched bike, leaned up against the building.

"I've told you already, I leave my bike the way it is because the earth has decided to leave it be, as will I." Ezra rolled his eyes at Levi's constrained serenity, something he'd found himself doing since high school.

"I just don't see how we would be able to flourish off of this financially. The figures don't add up, I'll prove it." Ezra walked toward the back of the bookstore and emerged about a minute later, calculator and notebook in hand. Slamming his notebook down on the table next to him, Ezra began scribbling numbers down. He pressed some buttons into his calculator and furiously wrote figures down in his notebook once again. The pressure on the calculator's buttons turned the tip of his index finger a prominent pink and the force increased with every push of a different button. Once he saw a satisfactory number, he turned toward Levi, with a smirk that seemed to take over his whole face. Ezra stood the notebook up to face Levi.

"Look at this top number." he said, matter-of-factly.

Levi moved his eyes to the top number, noticing it was in the hundred thousand. "Now, look at the number below that." Levi looked at the number Ezra had his finger near and noticed it was much less than the previous number. "See, we wouldn't break even, Levi. It just won't work. Books featuring children's poetry aren't in demand and I can assure you they won't be anytime soon." Levi looked at his friend, as a slight expression of disappointment began to take over Levi's face.

"It's not about the money, Ezra. It's about putting something out into the world that people can benefit from! I just want to see people being happy. Without creativity, where would we be now? We wouldn't be proud owners of our very own bookstore, that's for sure. With creativity comes passion, and the happiness is just a result of the two together, don't think so hard about it. The answer is always right in front of you."

Fed up with Levi's monologues and unsought hippie knowledge, Ezra rolled his eyes, not caring if Levi noticed the blatant displeasurement.

"Hm, I don't agree with this idea, so maybe we should just, as you say, *scrap it*." The words left Ezra's mouth in a hurry; he didn't like hurting his friend. Levi brought his hands to his cheeks and pulled down on his face frustrated.

"You are *really* putting a strain on my creativity." Ezra was sick of hearing that stupid word. Creative this, creative that.

We get it, you're the more creative one, Ezra thought to himself. Although, he truly wished that he were much more creative. He'd always try to spew creativity onto paper and it never worked, his stress always seemed to get in the way before he had the chance to have a breakthrough. Although he tried his best to never show it, he was extremely jealous of the way Levi was so effortlessly imaginative and never let anything get to him. He understood that Levi was more right-brained but that didn't take away from the fact that Ezra seemed to be doing the majority of the work since they opened a bookstore together. It was easy to recall. It was only about a year in when Ezra began to rethink his partnership with his friend. He would come out of his office daily to find Levi sprawled out on the floor, lying flat on his stomach and happily kicking his feet in the air. Usually, he would be found reading a randomly chosen book in the children's section. Ezra began to subconsciously roll his eyes, though his patience hadn't yet peaked.

"Um... Hey Levi," Ezra carefully began. Levi gave him a quick toothy smile and went back to examining the book in his hands.

"I'm actually pretty swamped with applying for ads and finding an editor. You know, for the *two* of us," Ezra prodded at Levi. All Levi did was furrowed his eyebrows at his anxious friend and responded with, "You need to let *them* come to *us*." Ezra began to grow impatient.

"That's nearly impossible seeing as nobody knows who we are which *I'm* trying my hardest to change. All I'm asking for is some help, for once."

Ezra's frustration profoundly grew and Levi could easily see this, though he pretended to be oblivious to it.

"Ez, I promise I will help you when I think you need help. If I step in and try to help you now, it'll only get worse because you're overthinking again. Give yourself a few breaks if you need to, but I don't doubt that you have this," countered Levi, being convinced by his own response as the words left his mouth.

Thinking back to this only a few years later, Ezra deeply sighed at the thought that still nothing had changed and he didn't see it changing anytime in the future. But Levi wasn't creative and rarely came up with an acceptable idea for a book or story. Without Levi, Ezra would be nothing. They were both aware of this.

Ezra continued through the rest of his day, trying to keep those negative thoughts as far away from his head as possible. By the end of the day around closing time, the only thing on Ezra's mind was that he had been much too harsh on Levi. He had completely rejected Levi's idea, and the feeling sure as hell resonated with him. It was a while back, when Ezra felt what it was like to be disappointed in his own work. He had a bad feeling about the day before it even started. Remembering the look on his father's face, despondency seeped out of his eyes as he harshly reminded Ezra of the cold judgmental world. His father was always sure to wear him down back to the point of reality. Extra blinked himself out of this. Levi had left about an hour ago, so Ezra figured he would be at his apartment. Ezra grabbed his things and flicked off the lights, standing still for a few seconds while finding a slight satisfaction watching the darkness quickly fill the store before departing.

The drive to Levi's apartment was short, as it always was, but this time it felt uncomfortably shorter. The trees while faithfully wallowing over their dead leaves which had crumbled to the ground with pity, seemed to lack vigor. Ezra noticed how the grass was in the process of sacrificing itself to the approaching winter. He could almost see the tiny yellow daisies wilting over and shriveling up as he carefully observed them from over his shoulder. He had always been very attentive to simplistic things like this, he was a real sucker for small details. Like how he noticed that Levi was ambidextrous within the first few minutes of meeting him, but that he clearly favored his right hand. Ezra looked down and realized he had been playing with the keys to Levi's apartment, unmindfully switching each finger in and out of the key ring. Ezra let out a quiet titter and sighed. He always found it funny when he caught himself absorbed in such a mindless action. Ezra had had a key to his apartment since they first became best friends their senior year of high school. In high school, Ezra was the rather quiet one that minded his own business and would never even think of handing in an assignment late. Levi, was just about the exact opposite. He fit in with every social group without trying, he was just blindly accepted wherever he went. He never worried about due dates on assignments, he didn't have to. All his teachers loved him and thought him to be some deep philosophical genius, which Ezra could never wrap his finger around because to him, seeing some lunatic screaming in the hallways about how the government's corrupt, just made him mumble "freaking hippie" to himself and trudge through the rest of his day, as he did every day. Both men's high school personas reflected on who they were today. Levi, was still his hippie, good natured self, and Ezra was still the uptight brainiac. They only exchanged their first words to each other when they discovered they were in the same literature class. Levi and

Ezra immediately noticed they seemed to have very similar styles of writing. Due to this, their teacher paired them up for their first project. Ezra would take note of the way all the desks in the classroom were aligned at the beginning of class, and fixed any desks out of order before he left for his next class. Leaned against the wall, watching Ezra perform this daily task, would be Levi. Ezra could easily see Levi observing him from the corner of his eye and would look him dead in the eyes. Neither man would budge. It often turned into an awkwardly long staring contest. Ezra refused to break eye contact due to his insecure masculinity, and Levi, well, he just enjoyed messing with Ezra, who was wound up tighter than a two dollar watch. With time, Levi began to soften Ezra without having to say a single word. Apparently, ominous eye contact was the only thing that could get Ezra to crack. Levi liked just about everyone he met but it was a miracle for Ezra to work so well with someone he had once labeled as a bum. Soon enough, the two men quickly began realizing they worked like clockwork with one another, they were a perfect duo. But every duo isn't always dynamic.

Ezra pulled his gray wagon in between the faded, almost invisible white lines separating his car from Levi's perfectly intact bike. He let himself into Levi's apartment and slipped through his door, waiting for Levi to hear the shallow footsteps echoing through his apartment.

"Levi? Levi are you here? Levi Wilkinson I swear if you jump out at me I'm ending our partnership." No response. Ezra walked around a bit, it had been a long while since he had been here. It was by choice of course, but the two men hadn't actually spent time with each other outside of any relations to the bookstore. It wasn't purposeful either, they just slowly began to grow apart and nothing was done to restore what had once been a healthy friendship. When Ezra began to take priority over the bookstore instead of his friend, their friendship quickly deteriorated.

Maybe he's sleeping, he *is* an incredibly deep sleeper, Ezra thought to himself. With this thought, he quietly advanced towards Levi's room and saw that he wasn't lying sound asleep in his bed either. He hadn't been in his room since Levi had switched apartments so at very least, he was getting a better sense of Levi through his belongings. Ezra walked over, by the looks of it, to a fairly old oak table in the corner that had many engravings in it. He placed his index finger over one of the carvings and dragged his finger smoothly along the lines.

My god, this is the table that he made with Cora, Ezra thought to himself. Weirdly enough, it was reassuring that Levi kept the table him and his ex-girlfriend from high school had made together, almost as if it were an artifact he couldn't bring himself to part with. Ezra realized it only reassured him because it proved that Levi was, believe it or not, a real human. It showed that some things really did get to him, which on a small scale, made Ezra feel better about his own constantly overwrought attitude.

Ezra noticed one of the drawers was slightly ajar and could just peek in to make out papers, an entire mass of them. He carefully pulled the drawer open and began to feel weak in the knees as he saw the writing printed on top of the pile of papers messily bonded together with staples. It read "Children's Poems and Stories." But, that wasn't the part that bothered him, it was what was on the bottom of the paper that sent a sharp pain straight into his stomach- *By: Levi Wilkinson November 17 2011.*

His knees giving out, Ezra collapsed, the ground meeting him as he clenched his fists so hard that his knuckles became numb, turning a ghastly white. At that, Ezra's knees gave out and he collapsed to the ground, clenching his fists so hard his knuckles became numb and turned a ghastly white. Did Levi have this idea the entire time? Had he just decided to casually bring it up to Ezra, a fully year later? Ezra forced himself off the ground and dug his hands, shaking with anger and desperation, further into the mess of papers. He stopped himself when he felt much thinner paper. Ezra pulled out his findings and laid them flat out on the desk. His fingernails were coated with black ink, still relatively fresh. At further inspection he could see that they were notes. They were all unkempt and almost illegible, as he anticipated knowing Levi's careless nature. Ezra began to skim over the small black lettering on each of the papers. He had to prop himself up on the desk when he began to string together the meaning of the writing on these papers. These weren't Levi's shopping lists or his unorganized to do lists. No, they were all notes on ideas for a children's book, followed by the telephone numbers of multiple name brand editors. Ezra took note of the papers, they were all dated from around the same time in 2011 with the exception of one, which featured the unforgettable date of "October 10, 2012." Ezra began to feel sick when he recognized the importance of the date. It was today's date. Levi was planning on leaving Ezra this whole time. Levi had always known he could make it on his own and now here he was, making it on his own, behind his best friend's back. He had trusted Levi with just about everything he had and the reality of what was happening to him quickly turned into a blow to the gut, such a crippling facade of kindness. Ezra heard someone's keys jingling, presumed Levi's, he grabbed the mass of papers and shoved them into his coat and ran out of the building, praying he went undetected.

Ezra woke up the next morning knowing what he had to do. The anger inside him boiled up, past the point of no return. *None* of this was his fault, yet he still felt a loss of self-recognition. This wasn't who he was, not even in the very least bit, it was Levi whom had pushed him to mold into this devious being. There was no other way out, he was going to have to fight fire with fire, the opposite of what he had been raised to do. Ezra had always been very intelligent and analytical; he always seemed to be aware of his surroundings. He knew the wilting daisy he witnessed the previous day held almost no significance, though he knew he would never forget it. He was especially expert at getting himself out of situations by lying, except the last time he tried to pull a stunt like this it was only the matter of a lunchbox, conspicuous eyes, and his friend's missing sandwich. Ezra and Levi were supposed to meet soon with their new editor whom they had recently hired together in a rather hasty, not at all thought out decision. Ezra walked into *his* store and saw Levi, picking books off shelves just to glance at the cover for a quick second, then put them back in the exact same place, the man was a real mystery. Ezra was trying not to let the sweat pooling in the palms of his hands, get onto the incredibly fake contract papers he had typed up in the library attic in a pure fit of fury the previous night.

"Hey, Levi", Ezra began to cautiously approach Levi who was now looking up at him, then down at the papers in his hand.

"Do you mind signing these papers for our new editor? I already read it and signed for myself, the majority of it is just acknowledging the rules of plagiarism and copyrighting, you know, just the typical writing bullshit we get thrown at us every day. I guess she's really uptight with her policies or something."

Ezra let out a nervous chuckle. Levi looked at Ezra, quickly taking a mental note of the tiny beads of sweat beginning to form on the bridge of his nose. Levi squinted his eyes in suspicion and asked, "Why are you so sweaty, Ez?" Ezra shifted uncomfortably.

"Jeez! I'm just a total mess today, rolled out of bed this morning and just barely made it into work, and you know exactly how finicky I am when it comes to time." Levi gave Ezra a warm smile and nodded,

"Well, let me just get this over with now then. I don't want to be another cause of your stress, it's honestly reaching critical levels, and you should take a break soon. You're too hard on yourself."

Levi reached for the papers in Ezra's hands, and in a swift motion, grabbed the pen from behind his ear and placed the thick stack of papers on the polished wooden floor of the store and carefully began signing his name. Ezra stood over him, looking his guilty reflection in the eyes. He could swear he saw a sinister grin forming in his reflection, but it wasn't him, this whole ordeal wasn't him. Feelings of immediate remorse began to swarm within Ezra's stomach. He wanted to stop himself from what he was doing, yet he remained stationary. He wanted to apologize to Levi and for the both of them to come clean, yet he wore a blank expression on his face. Levi's converse let out a squeak of relief when the pressure began to alleviate as Levi slowly stood up.

Levi, not knowing how much power these papers held, carelessly handed over the signed contract to Ezra's unstable hands. Ezra now had all the power, and all the guilt, that he knew would do nothing but build up over time. Levi Wilkinson, a sneaky man of few words and fewer complaints, had just unknowingly signed over the rights of all of his work, past and future, to Ezra, his once best friend, his ride or die.

Ezra stumbled over to his office, swallowing all the guilt he was able to keep down, and let himself fall deep in his chair. Ezra, a muddled man, sat sulkily in his chair. He shifted to one side of his chair and used his foot to slide the contract over to the other side of the room. He peered out the small window cemented in his door and could see Levi wandering the store, pen and paper in hand. Ezra moved slightly closer, staring intently at the papers Levi was holding. Ezra surveyed the papers from inside his office and noticed the same thin ink, black as night that he had seen on the papers in Levi's desk drawer that one night. His dark eyebrows began to furrow as he left his seat and ominously swiped up the papers he had just kicked to the other side of the room. He gripped them tightly, a biting construct of ownership began developing in his mind. Perhaps, Levi was to learn his lesson; always read the fine print.

At the End of the Hall

The door waited for her at the end of the hall, in all of its glory, with chipping paint and the promise of freedom. She gripped the overnight bag she held in her fingers, and crept out of her bedroom. Staring at her target, she picked up her pace, walking down the hall. In her mind it called to her, whispered even, "It will open if you let it..." An aid turned to see that she had headed for the door, and ran after to stop her. Her hand reached for the knob and just as the palm met the metal, the aid touched her shoulder.

"Ms. Miller, let me bring you back to your room," her voice softened. The woman turned around slowly, with a glaring eye.

"What did you just say to me?" she responded with low lying anger.

"I said let's go back to your room, this is where you live now, Marion,"

"I do *not* live here, I live with my husband."

"Marion, you don't--your husband passed away two years ago," the aid said moving her touch to the small of Marion's back, using it to move her into the opposite direction. She began to resist, and the cycle repeated itself. This happened almost every morning at 9:15, when Marion was supposed to be seated for breakfast. The nurse rubbed her tired eyes, and waved to her supervisor to come down the hall.

"Marion, *please*, don't do this today. Let me bring you back to your room so you can have something to eat," she tried to remain calm, but was becoming frustrated.

"*Let go of me*, right now, before I report you! I know my rights, let me out of here," She raised her voice and began pounding her fist on the door that stood in front of her, seeming unfazed by her fragile hands. The woman pulled her away and more nurses came down the hall. She spilled herself onto the floor and repeated the same sentence over again,

"Let me out, let me *out*! *Why am I here? Where is my husband?*"

***

The young man looked into the dining room through its window, and watched as Marion picked at her food. The dining room was covered in peeling maroon wallpaper, showing a bleak wall underneath. The windows were covered in cream-colored drapes, some pulled back. Riley tried to open them every morning; he was convinced *"a little more light"* would improve their moods. Marion lifted her eyes to the window in the back of the room, just as the sky painted itself in colors of deep pinks and oranges. The sill was covered in snow and a small draft let in. Her body shivered and she scoffed in the direction of the window. She had feelings of anger that sometimes came out in the oddest ways, even to people or things she enjoyed being around. The worker stepped into the room and made his way to the woman's table after missing his lunch visit earlier.

"How are you today, Marion?"

"I feel, well, I'm just not hungry," Poking the food with her fork, Marion's eyes were locked on the plate. It was around dinner time, and she felt tired. The worker pulled a chair to the side of her table and took Marion's hand.

"Do you know what time it is?" He asked her in a soft voice.

"I don't know, I remember coming in here, but I'm not sure for what," Marion replied with a sliding smile. She squeezed the worker's hand and felt tears welling up in her eyes. He sighed and assured Marion that he would help her try to remember small things, like time and what meal she was eating.

"We will talk tomorrow, okay? I will eat lunch with you. Would you like that?"

Marion looked up at him and nodded, turning toward the window to look outside. As the snow fell, she pulled her blanket tighter. She loved the winter.

***

Her delicate fingers crawled to the edge of her mattress, reaching for the call button. Marion's alarm pierced through the silence of the sleeping unit, and a nurse went to check on her. This happened every few days, but her room was visited more often than not.

Switching on the light, the nurse placed herself on the edge of the resident's bed,

"Marion, please, I-I need to get back to the front. Everything is okay, you're supposed to be here." The old woman put her hand on her face and stared back at her blankly.

The nurse's head tilted and said, "Marion?" Rustling in her sheets, Marion moved herself to face the window, eyes still wide. Eventually, she would drift off, but other nights she would stay up and just stare at the ceiling, asking herself different questions like, *Where am I?* or *Why is my husband not next to me tonight?* In turn, she could sometimes answer them, but when she tried to, she confused herself. Marion could lay there until the sun peeked through her curtains just trying to figure out why she was in bed at that time, and why her bedroom felt different.

As Marion opened her eyes, light flooded them as her morning began. She pulled her blanket up over her chest and held it there while she dozed off. There was a strong chill to the air that nipped her nose and caused her to wake up again. An aid walked in, noticing she was still in bed.

"Ms. Miller, it's time to wake up. You're going to have breakfast soon, so get dressed," Marion opened one eye to look at her and took a deep breath. She knew she had to get going. She pulled herself out of bed and slid her feet into her slippers. For Marion, getting up was the hardest part of her day; she woke up not knowing what to do or who to talk to.

The intern walked to the nurse's station and greeted everyone. His fingers swept the desk files, and he picked up the oak folder that read, *"INTERN PROJECT."*

Skimming his file Riley started his routine, "Good morning Angela, how is Ms. Miller today?"

"She's how she always is, groggy in the morning but she'll be okay by noon. Are you staying with her today? I can ask an aid to if you're busy."

"No, no, I actually promised her I would come and sit with her today. I feel like she remembers my face- *Possibly?* But never *why* I come to see her, I'm going to keep working with her on the memory questions I was telling you about." The supervisor seemed indifferent about his attempts.

"Riley, sweetie, maybe it's better to just see if Eileen needs you in the office today? Some paperwork or alongside her, in another...unit?" Her shoulders rose and fell with her suggestion. As his heart thumped through his shirt, Riley could feel his cheeks start to turn red. He had made a fool out of himself for the past two months trying to work on C2 South. His intern hours were adding up, but it didn't feel like he was making much of a difference.

This happened almost every week, his work showed effort, but little progress. He had developed a relationship with a resident who had a deteriorating memory, and wanted so badly for her to move forward. Riley picked up his clipboard and started his rounds, asking each resident about how they were feeling.

✳✳✳

The squeaking wheels could be heard from down the hall, the lunch trays arrived at 12:30, as they did each day. Meals were routine, they were served on the dot; no earlier, no later.

Riley came into see Marion, just as he promised. He noticed a brightness to her mood, Marion was speaking and could even remember that it was lunchtime and how she was supposed to eat. Her mind became the most active in the middle of the day, and she was able to connect to the worker without feeling confused. The room filled with laughter, and Marion's smile was contagious. Riley's anxiety seemed to melt away for a moment.

"What was your husband like, Marion?"

"Oh, well, he's--right. He was so charming, a warm person, someone you always wanted to be around," Her eyes gazed back at Riley, she seemed at peace when she could think clearly.

"That's someone I'd like to find, but school is all I can think about right now. In two weeks time, I'll have my *masters degree* in social work. Can you believe it?" His lips curved upwards and he told Marion more about school, especially how little sleep he had gotten from studying chapter by chapter until the early hours of the morning for his national exam.

A man knocked on the glass, "Hey, you two, almost done? We have residents coming at two." The pair waved them away, and giggled. Marion's face was bright, Leaving nothing but a few peas on her plate, she got up and shook Riley's hand,

"Thank you dear, it was a treat. I haven't laughed like that in years."

"It was my pleasure, Marion. Would you like me to bring you back to your room?" Marion put her hand out for him to lead the way. But as she took each step, Riley noticed her face begin to change with worry. Her eyes followed those who were walking around her, as if she had never seen them before. Approaching room 115, Riley stopped and stood in the doorway, but Marion kept going.

"*Marion,*" his voice stretching to the end of the hallway, "Your room is right here." She tilted her head with a confused look.

"I think you have the wrong person, sweetie. I don't live here," Marion answered, practically laughing at him. She turned from his direction, aiming for the window. As Riley called her over again, his voice soon became background noise to her; she didn't know him.

The first time Riley worked with Marion, she was able to recall some things of her past, but struggled with the present.

"Marion, do you know where you are?"

Her fingers were twiddling themselves, as she barely lifted her head to answer, "I can't say I do. Where is George?"

"Who is George, Marion?"

"My darling husband, who else? You know Georgie *right*? He's a real sweetheart, matter-of-fact, he should be here any minute now." Marion swallowed hard as she said the last few words, tightening her throat. Before fixating themselves on the doorway, Marion's eyes darted back and forth between the young man sitting next to her and the hall. Her teeth began to chew on the inside of her lip, as Riley picked up on her noticeable anxiety. The palms of her hands became clammy, and she rubbed away the moisture with the pad of her thumb repeatedly.

"Do you have any photos of him that I can see?" Riley seated himself to her left side, and leaned over to look at the frame she took off of her nightstand.

"This was the day we got married, he'll tell you it was June, but it was really July. The sun was too hot to be June," her cheeks started to lift as she smiled and put the photo back into its place. With her body relaxed, her fingers folded into each other. Riley looked at his hands as they started to shake when Marion continued.

"My dress was a soft lace, beautiful. My mother and I stayed up all night patching the layers together on our Singer, which is a sewing machine, you know?" Bumping Riley's shoulder, she patted the top of his hand, "I *loved* that dress, and I looked stunning in it. My mother was so excited I was marrying a sailor. I mean, dear, I was only nineteen." Riley's nail had been bitten down to the skin by the time she finished.

"Marion, I don't want to be the one to tell you but I don't think your husband is coming today." Her eyebrows furrowed as confusion dissolved the happiness that had previously found its way to her face; she couldn't get a word out.

"No, but he- he'll be here. What are trying to tell me? *Did something happen to him?*" Her face began to fall as she turned from Riley's view. Pushing against her temple, Marion's fingers rested on her forehead. She mumbled through her thoughts before she formed a sentence. Not making out what was being said, Riley's ear moved into the path of her voice, as if it was being pulled by a string.

"Oh, I- He isn't coming, he's...Georgie isn't *here* anymore." He rested his hand on her shoulder as he spoke to her

She put her knees together, tucking her hands underneath her thighs. The lids of her eyes felt heavy, keeping them closed for a few seconds longer each time she blinked. Marion's eyes welled up with tears as she rocked her body, slowly, back and forth. Riley's mouth opened, but nothing came out. His hand moved side to side on Marion's shoulder, but she shifted herself over a few inches; sympathy did not sit well with her.

Not saying a word, Marion pulled herself up from her bed and walked past Riley. The dimpled bottoms of her slippers scuffed across the floor as she made her way to the entrance, she flicked the light switch down and the room went dark. Riley sat there in silence, and as Marion tucked herself back into bed, he showed himself out.

Walking down the hall, Riley heard a familiar voice page him over the intercom for a meeting in the social work office. Letting out a rush of air through his lips, his chest rose and fell. The sneakers he wore squeaked as they pivoted on the tiled floor, lugging his body to the opposite end of the hall. Riley paused before entering, closing his eyes to brace the words that would be exchanged. As he walked into the room, Eileen was leaning against her desk, and gestured for him to sit.

"Riley, I just felt now was the right time to talk about your progress on your unit," making her way behind her desk. *Now is the right time?* His mind began to spin.

Riley began to sink into his chair, "I've been working closely with a few patients, and I really think I belong on C2 South."

"And that is where I have to agree, you've been working very hard. I just don't see improvement, especially in Ms. Miller. Have you tried old photographs? Bringing in one of her daughter? She has yet to remember why she is even here." Eileen's arms raised and crossed at her chest.

"I know Eileen, I know. But you have to see her at lunchtime, she is vibrant and kind. No one sees her like I do. I need more ti-" Riley's passion and desperation were cut off in an instant.

"I have nothing else for you, but that you need to show improvement. You don't have forever; I need something Riley. Maybe it's time to shift your focus onto someone else, *just,* think about it."

Riley punched out at three o'clock, his feet aching as he walked to his car. The clothes he wore clung to his body and his eyes became heavy. His caffeine fix was crashing, as he looked at the last drop of coffee in his to-go mug. Riley gripped his steering wheel, with exhaustion haunting him. Pondering the thought of moving on, Marion's laugh was still ringing in his head and he couldn't shake the conversation he had earlier.

It was nearly ten o'clock and Riley was convinced he had to finish reviewing chapter fourteen. He pulled out his textbook, and began reading from it from the start. He grew anxious thinking about his day, and kept reading. *Someone new? How could I possibly?* The words began to blend together, and he started to feel weak. Riley had come to the end of the chapter, with the book lying flat on his stomach, barely keeping his eyes open.

That same night, Marion felt restless; she was tossing and turning for hours in bed, unable to fall asleep. The cold wind knocked tree branches into her window just as the early season snow blew around. A pin dropping could have been heard if it weren't for the resident across the hall from her, who was not doing so well. Marion paced back and forth, and her thoughts scrambled around in her mind. *Am I supposed to be here? Where is my husband? Is he here too? Whose clothes are these?* Taking a pen and paper from her nightstand, she quickly scribbled a note down for herself, before confusion could overtake her more. Both night shift nurses were in Mr. Moretti's room to take his vitals and to try to get him back to bed. He had a stroke years before and would wake up in very outspoken moods, often making a scene during the eleven-to-seven shift. The nurses stayed in his room for almost twenty minutes just trying to resolve his episode.

"Mr. Moretti, you need to try and go back to sleep, okay?" Their voices were white noise to Marion.

"Look, I need a cigarette. Are you good here?" The nurse nodded her head as she saw the resident close his eyes and slowly drift off back to sleep. The other took off down the hall, and grabbed her binder sitting nearby on the way. When she got to the end of the hall, she opened the door to outside with the keycode "3332," wedging her binder underneath the door as a stopper.

Marion sat up in her bed, almost immediately when she heard a noise. It was not exactly a noise, but more so a voice. In her head, she heard someone familiar but could not remember who it sounded like. She stood up and walked over to her window, and there standing in nearly a foot of snow was her husband, like a teenager calling up to his crush. His worn grey button-up stuck to his torso as it blew with the current, and his eyes met with hers. Marion's heart began to race as she pressed her hand against the glass. She watched as his hand waved for her to join him. *Outside?* She quickly looked around for her coat, not remembering the last time she breathed in fresh air. The voices of both nurses began to fade, and she could feel butterflies fluttering in her stomach. She crept over to her bed, and pulled her old winter boots out from the storage bin under it. Marion tied her robe in tight bow, hugging her waist, as she made her way to her coat hanger by the arch of her door. She piled on layers, light on her feet, as if she was dancing.

The nurse that was next door began to panic. Mr. Moretti was starting to develop an irregular heartbeat.

"Mare! Mary, would you come back in please? I need some help, Mr. Moretti has arrhythmia," The nurse paged the other from the man's room. Quickly putting out her cigarette, she ran down the hall to Mr. Moretti and her coworker. Marion charged on down the hall, and quickly passed the nurse who seemed to be in a rush. The woman looked around as she thought she felt someone pass her, but turned around to an empty hallway.

That same freezing air hit Marion's legs, causing her to shiver. She slipped through the opening of the door and took a deep breath. The temperature was below freezing, tightening Marion's face. She stepped into the snow in front of her and began to walk. The wind carried the flurries into different directions and created a blur in the sky. Light coming from the moon reflected onto the ground's smooth surface, illuminating her way through the pines. Marion called out to her husband and heard nothing but silence, until she made it to the tree, facing her bedroom window.

"Marion, I'm over here," A voice called out to her.

"Oh, my love! I don't see you. Are you there? *My love?*" her words began to sound as if they were breaking.

The two nurses continued to work with Mr. Moretti, but he was losing consciousness. His ECG monitor started to rapidly beep and his heart line soon became a slowly moving white line. The nurses rushed to their vital cart and grabbed the paddles. One of the women ripped through the files hastily, leaving some papers spread across the floor. Reading the files as she went along, *Vital Reports, Medication Changes,* the *DNR* agreement was not one of them. On the opposite side of the bed, the older nurse turned the knob of the defibrillator with a shaky hand. Her eyes darted between the man laying in front of her and the machine, turning the electrical charge up.

Marion continued to trudge through the snow, and search for the vision of someone who she thought was her husband. Her legs grew tired and she began to feel weak. She called out his name, and would hear no response. The two nurses struggled to keep Mr. Moretti's heartbeat, and began to weep while one pushed the paddles onto his chest.

Resulting in a faint heartbeat, the nurse without paddles began to search for her supervisor. She ran past each room in a panic, looking in for white scrubs. As she continued down the hall, she got to room 104, where Marion was slouched over on her bed. She ran over to check on her vitals, and felt no pulse. Marion's hands were folded over a small paper that read,

"My name is Marion Miller.
My husband died two years ago and I live here now.
My name is Marion Miller.
My husband died two years ago and I live here now."

Defying the Odds

2003

L aila trudged up the scattered brick road with her backpack secured onto her. Her eyes glued to the ground, playing a mind game in which she only stepped on the grey bricks as opposed to the ones that had hints of maroon plastered on them. She approached the top of the hill and immediately rushes to Akbar's dukaan, hoping that her favorite candy, chili mili, had not yet run out for the day. Seated on the dirt ledge in front of his shop, Akbar was surrounded by other store owners from the alley. Each took turns passing around the hazel hookah pipe, which Akbar had bargained ten rupees for. As he adjusted the burnt coal, Laila enthusiastically approached him. Akbar looked up and nodded at eager Laila, chuckling when she pulled him into a grateful hug. She smiled and handed him two rupees, before he was able to protest, and ran into the shop.

The sound of peaceful *qawwalis* could be heard radiating from the stereo in the corner of the room, right below a Pakistani flag draped from the bookshelf. She made her way behind the wooden counter of the tightly spaced room and grabbed herself two chili mili packets; one for herself and one for Fatima, who was probably waiting on the brick ledge where she was usually seated after school.

Realizing how long Fatima has been waiting, Laila rushed to make her way out of the *dukaan*. Without noticing, she accidentally toppled the stack of cricket bats in the corner of the shop. Doing this, her foot got entangled with a stack of cricket bats in the corner of the shop. She tripped over them and caused them to wobble, grabbing them as they almost fell to the ground. Out of breath, she continued out of the shop.

"*Shukriya!* Thank you!" Laila yelled back at Akbar as shisha smoke escaped his dried lips. He waved and continued chatting with his fellow shop owners.

She passed by the golden dome of the village mosque and entered the courtyard beside it. Fatima was seated against the ledge with abandoned textbooks at her side. Throwing the chili mili onto her friend's lap, Laila sat herself next to her, facing herself towards the cricket game occuring. Fatima's emerald eyes met Laila's dark ones as she formed a smile, exposing her crooked front tooth.

"You're the best!" she exclaimed. Laila nodded her head knowingly and began copying Fatima's fifth-year color-coded homework into her own beige notepad.

"Out!" the young boys yelled energetically.

"*Ullu ka pattha.* Bastard," Muhammad mumbles under his breath. Laila and Fatima giggled, munching on their snack; the sweet and spicy flavors exploding in their mouths.

"You're such a good player!" Fatima sarcastically remarked at him. Rolling his eyes, he sat himself next to Laila on the ledge. His brown curls drip in sweat, dark eyes expressing exhaustion.

"Thanks for my chili mili," he said to her as Laila's eyes began to grow wide, tucking the packet behind her back.

"What chili mili?" she questioned. He pointed at Fatima's hands and Laila shrugged at him apologetically.

"I was in a hurry!" Laila began to defend herself, handing him her two leftover pieces. Reaching out, accepting the candy, they vanished almost instantly into his mouth.

Fatima tapped Laila's shoulder, pointing over to the players. The boys were huddled together, as the three of them began to make their way over, ready to observe the scene. Hasan crouched down, wincing in pain, holding his bruised leg as passerbyers stop and made their way to the middle.

"This is why you kids shouldn't play out in the open like this! This is the courtyard, not a cricket field!" they began to nag. Hasan's aunt, among the people pointing fingers with scolding voices, takes him home to ice his leg, silencing the countless protests from his team.

"Great. Now we're down a team member!" Muhammad's brother Zain groaned aloud. The kids' gazes shifted from Zain to Muhammad and back to Zain's, now with widened eyes.

"No," he sternly stated. No one cared to protest and they sat on the ground in defeat. The abandoned cricket bat stayed in the dirt while Zain bounced the taped ball off of the brick ledge. As the ball bounced, Fatima grasped for it, throwing it to Laila. Clenching his knuckles in frustration, Zain got up, in an attempt to steal it back from Fatima and Laila as they continued to throw it to the other. Sighing, he approached the cricket back before Laila threw the ball back to Fatima to claim her next possession.

"That's my bat! Give it back!" Zain whinesd as Laila and Fatima giggled, beginning a game of their own.

"Girls can't even play cricket!" he shouted, his eyes filled with fury. Laila and Fatima stopped playing, Fatima raising her eyebrow.

"If Muhammad can attempt at playing it, I can assure you that we can too. And we'll actually play well," Fatima scoffed, rolling her eyes.

Zain smirked, "I'd love to see you girls try."

Laila immediately walked over to stand in front of the wickets as Fatima rolled the taped ball, gliding her foot across the dirt in an attempt to make the ground as even as possible. Laila had watched cricket multiple times in her life; although her family as a whole only turned it on to watch the Pakistan vs India matches, she looked forward to watching every ICC match with her father. Getting into the same position as those cricket players, she did not allow her dark eyes to drift away from the ashy tape. Adjusting her *dupatta,* Laila gracefully placed the scarf over her shoulder, keeping her focus on the game. Fatima took a couple steps back, stretching her long arms, beginning to count down from three. However, before she makes it to two, a familiar voice was heard approaching them.

"Laila? What on earth are you doing?"

The two girls swiftly turned their heads to the woman in the floral printed *chador.* Laila threws the bat on the ground, beginning to shake her head.

"*Kuch nahi.* Nothing." She stuttered. Grabbing her belongings, her mother urges her to follow her as she began to make her way home. Apologetically waving to Muhammad and Fatima, Laila looked over her shoulder sheepishly as the other children began to pack up their stuff, rolling their eyes at Zain, crying from laughing so hard.

"*Beti,* you know how I feel about you playing in the courtyard. The elders complain about kids daily and I don't want you to be a part of that," her mother said sternly, shaking her head. "But you study so much, I thought you deserved to have fun. And then I see that?" she sighs.

"But *Ammi,* what's wrong with-" Laila began questioning before being cut off.

"Laila, girls shouldn't play cricket. Girls shouldn't play sports in general, it's easy for them to get hurt!" Ammi quietly explained while passing by the neighbors in the alley. Laila thought back to Hasan's injury. Hasan. A boy.

They reached the coffee-colored iron-gate with peeling paint and spikes to prevent any intruders. As they entered, they are met with the two family cows; one dark brown and the other black with splattered white dots. Laila's grandma, *Dadi,* was refilling grass hay for the cows' snack. Her blue-gray eyes looked up as she breathed a sigh of relief, seeing her loved ones home in time for dinner preparation.

"If anyone sees you playing cricket, *log kya kahenge?*" Ammi said. Laila and Dadi exchanged a displeased look as soon as that phrase escaped Ammi's mouth. *Log kya kahenge.* What will people think? Laila knew that once those words were uttered, anything she said after was pointless. Her mother's paranoia and care for what others thought was something that couldn't be beaten. So, she was a bit relieved when Dadi spoke up.

"Since when have I raised you to care about those irrelevant opinions?" Dadi said, crossing her arms.

Laila smirked, leaving Dadi to defend her as she headed up to the roof. Opening the second iron-gate, she began to climb the steep stairs until she reached the top. Marveling at the view of Dhudial, her eyes scanned to see if she could catch anyone she knew. She could see Muhammad and Zain, sitting with their mother, chopping up vegetables. Further left, she could make out a few children putting away their kites for the evening. The orange sky was painted with tints of purple and pink, an indication to stop any playing, studying, or television, and to gather with friends and family for dinner. But Laila couldn't start dinner preparations until she caught a glimpse of the red motorcycle. Enthusiastically looking on, waiting for its arrival, the anticipation grew as she readied herself to tell Abbu about her day. The sound echoed throughout the alley as Laila's legs sprinted down the stairs, arms outstretched, reaching to open the front gate. Riding in, Abbu hurried in with the groceries in his hand, quickly parking to the side of the corridor. Hopping off the motorcycle, he greeted her with a warm smile that she quickly returned.

Unfortunately, Laila knes that her stories would have to wait until dinner was prepared. Quickly embracing him, she rushed to start the tandoor oven. She was just glad that he made it home safely. Dadi brought over the rolled up dough and set it to the side, adjusting the burnt firewood, covering her face from the spilling ashes.

"You know," Dadi glanced at Laila, "I was a pretty good cricket player myself. So is your father. It's a family talent," she beamed. "Your mother caught me up. And just so you know, just like you, I wanted to play cricket since I was ten."

Laila attached a roll of dough to the iron rod and plopped it on the side of the oven.

"I didn't even want to play that bad. But I got excited when Fatima was about to bowl the ball. I thought I was going to hit it so far that it would reach here! Then Ammi ruined it and now I don't know," she rambled on.

Dadi shook her head, "I already know that you're great, *jaanu*. You were born with it. Let's finish up the *naan* and see what Abbu has to say about it."

Dadi removed the bread from the *tandoor* while Laila added each dough in to be baked. They made enough *naan* for themselves, Abbu, Ammi, and Laila's grandfather; *Baba Ji*. Baba Ji arrived home and set up the mat while Abbu and Ammi prepared the food. The house radiated with spices and oils.

Once everyone gathered around the mat, silence occupied the room and all that could be heard was the sound of chewing. Laila dipped her naan into the butter chicken, its creamy texture and flavorful taste entering her mouth.

"Ammi told me about your shenanigans today." Abbu first speaks up as Ammi nodded along, waiting for him to continue as Laila's heart began rapidly beating.

"And I can coach you," he blatantly stated. Ammi coughed on her water and looked up at Abbu with a confused expression.

"There is no way that is going to happen," she argued, *"Log kya-"* Abbu sighs, massaging his temple and scratching his thick beard.

"It doesn't matter what people think," he stated.

"If we do well, people focus on one little slip up. If we do badly, we give them more to talk about. Either way, people are always going to talk; it makes no difference. We only have to focus on improving ourselves and keeping our family happy," Abbu said. Dadi looked up at her son proudly. Ammi placed her cup down and slowly nodded her head, her eyebrows furrowed in deep thought. Adjusting his circular glasses, Baba ji cleared his throat before speaking up.

"I did not go through the Hindustan partition to have my granddaughter be denied a chance to do what she wants," he declared as he gave Laila a pat on the back. The people around the table tried their best to hide their laughter, used to his constant partisan talk

"What do you want to do?" Abbu asked sincerely, all eyes on Laila.

2016

"...Keep your eyes on the white tape and do not daze off," Laila explained.

She helped angle the bat away from the little girl and practiced swinging it for her. The bat hit the ball and the girl was able to make two runs before the bowler hit the wicket. The little girl, Mariam, hugged Laila with excitement.

"Look! I did that!" Mariam exclaimed. Laila smiled, nodding enthusiastically, filled with pride. However, she noticed parents arriving and decided to pause the game, keeping track of the score.

"Baba! Laila *baji* taught us so much today! I did so well!" Mariam excitedly told her father. Zain smiled knowingly.

"She's pretty great, isn't she?" Zain responded sincerely. Looking over at him, Laila noticed that his youthful face had now matured, with facial hair plastered on it. Baba ji used to tell Laila about how the most devilish children turned out to be the most kind and thoughtful when they aged. Although she had a difficult time believing that at first, she was now sure of it. She thanked her childhood friend and dismissed the little girls from the courtyard while reminding them of practice the next day. Laila walked over to the ledge, greeting Fatima, who was leaning against it, her college books in hand.

"Muhammad says hi from Islamabad, where he's going to see the match today," Fatima informed her. Laila began to laugh, shaking her head.

"That's like the third one this month, I'm jealous," she said. Although Muhammad's cricket skills never improved, he still regularly attended matches with his coworkers; taking a break from the computer work he constantly did.

They grabbed their things and stopped by Akbar's dukaan. He sat behind the counter, trying to figure out the iPhones that had just shipped in for him to sell. He had asked Laila to stop by since he was giving out some of his older items. Seeing them enter, his hazel eyes squinted from his enthusiastic smile. His movements had become slower, although he hated when others point that out. He knew that he was fully capable of still having his *dukaan* thrive.

"Thank you for coming, I came across something interesting," Akbar said, kneeling down, struggling to carry the objects.

"I immediately thought of you, Laila, when I saw these," he said.

Pulling out the decade old vintage bats, Akbar smiled as he placed them down on the counter. Laila's hands glided over the old wood in amazement, "The girls are going to love these."

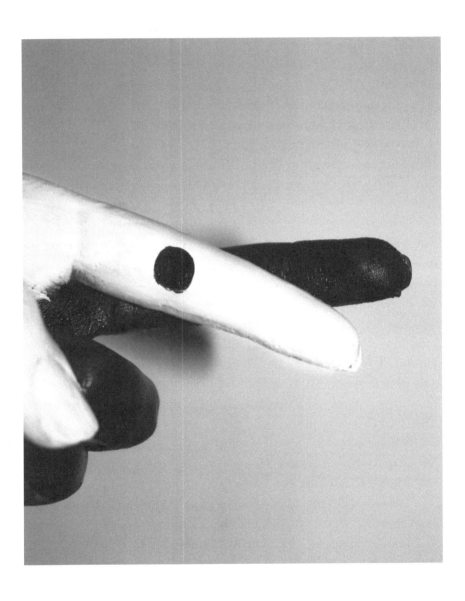

Fingers Crossed

"**S**o Nate, I know you just started the new job, how's it going? Have you adjusted well?"

She flashed me her blinding smile and I sink further into my seat. I can't hide from her piercing eyes or her invasive questions.

I take a deep breath then sigh, "It's okay, the work is easy but my co-workers have been challenging. They're very friendly, like they want to act like a big family. I had to sing Happy Birthday to a woman I met three days ago."

Smiling even harder, she gave the face one would give to a young child who just can't tie their shoes after hours of attempts- a face full of tender reassurance and pity. Reaching her hands out to meet mine, she squeezed my palms. "Well that's good! Making connections with co-workers can be nice and if the conversation stays light, there shouldn't be any incidents."

I let out a cold and nervous laugh, "Oh, there have been quite a few incidents, I just can't help myself." Rubbing my hands on the leather chair, I fumbled around. She waits for me to make eye contact and continue speaking, but I refuse. Staring mindlessly at the pens lining up on the desk, I swallow hard as she sighs in defeat.

"Why don't you walk me through how you feel right before you tell a lie, I know it's uncomfortable to discuss this, but it's part of the process."

My eyes start to burn with the salty tears I could never let fall when she stabs me with that word. I've never had much of an identity-I was never in one place long enough to have one stick when I was younger. I still remember the feeling of a thousand eyes on me, scanning me up and down, and sizing me up. It was a feeling I'd grown up experiencing, starting at six years old, putting on my best outfits as I brushed my hair flat to the sides to look presentable to the visits my foster parents would host. As they'd walk in, the small pieces of my dark hair would hide part of my soft grey blue eyes. Haircuts weren't a commonality for me at that age, so I'd developed the nervous habit of tucking a piece of the longer hair behind my ear. As the years continued with no successful visits from people looking to adopt a young child, my legs began to sprout beneath my pants; my legs quickly grew long and lanky seemingly out of nowhere. There wasn't a long sleeve shirt that could cover all inches of my wrist, and I began to stray further and further from the blonde-haired chubby-cheeked sweetheart that parents came looking for.

The people who would come always seemed so nice, so warm. I would try hard to connect with them like the other kids did, but nothing ever went right for me. One visit in particular replays in my mind constantly, even after all these years. A couple from the rich district in our town was looking for a child to adopt and had connections to my foster mom through high school. It was supposed to be a guaranteed home for one of the five kids in my house so all of us were in a panic. Cleaning the house as best we could, the older kids helped make dinner as the younger ones set the table.

The couple was beautiful, like the people seen in magazines, and I dreamt of being chosen by them to go live in the mansion, like a scene in a movie that would never be produced. But when the time came for them to talk to each of us at dinner, I panicked. When asked what was being taught in school, my head bowed down at my feet from under the tablecloth. Avoiding eye contact, no words were found. Picking at the loose skin on my thumb, I peeled the skin back, but felt no pain. Lifting my hand to tuck my hair behind my ear, I attempted a smile, but could only grimace. My chair screeched on the wooden floors in an attempt to excuse myself from the table, but my elbow clumsily knocked over the pitcher of water on the woman's lap. After running back up to my room, the rest of the night was spent listening to the couple bond with my roommate. The next week was spent listening to his suitcase zipper glide closed as he packed his bags in excitement.

Years of the same scenario played over and over- rejection after rejection. I had learned to do anything to avoid that feeling of exposure again. That sometimes resulted in lies about what was happening at school, maybe I got an 80 on my math test, but possible parents would want a 100. I quieted my moral compass each time by crossing my stubby fingers behind my back while I spoke, something to ease the angel on my shoulder fueling me with guilt. It seemed so simple- if I wasn't charming enough, I could at least pretend to be.

My mind had been made up- I would keep my fingers cross until I got adopted. Unfortunately I never was- just moved to group homes filled with the other teenagers that didn't have that bubbly personality couples wanted. Even more unfortunately, I learned to fall back on my fibs, and use them as my crutch.

"Nate?"

I snapped out of my daze and refocused on the cherry wood desk in front of me. Listening to her chair squeak every time she took a deep breath, I wait for me to answer her question. But it's too hard to answer. What do I feel before I lie? Nothing anymore.

Moving to the end of my chair as she shoves my files back in her folder, we silently agree to end the meeting, but not before she gives me one more look of pity.

Placing her hand on my shoulder as she exits, she smiles softly, "just think about my question okay?"

I wake up the next morning before my alarms and stare up at the ceiling until my eyes scan down to my bare toes. They are left cold and uncovered by my blanket all night and I wiggle each one before sliding out of bed. The apartment is silent besides the sound of the air banging up against the vents and the slap of my feet against the old wood. Stumbling to the kitchen, I grab a bowl and spoon out of the sink and rinse them half-heartedly of the soggy cereal from yesterday, before remaking the breakfast I have every day, cheerios and black coffee.

I eat until the milk goes warm and walk over to the sink while staring at the clock. 7:00. Three hours until work with nothing to do but crawl back into my bed. Each toss and turn sinks me closer to the metal frame as the mattress fails to support my weight. I squeeze my pillow over my head to soften the piercing squeaks of the rusting joints holding me above the floor, waiting for another chance at sleep.

Before I know it, I'm up again tripping across the floor as I try and shove each leg through my pants. This has been the routine for as long as I can remember, waking up, falling asleep, and the waking back up again. I've always felt better being up before everyone else. At the foster home, it was more peaceful to eat and shower without the other kids buzzing around me, and then I could grab a few extra hours before school would start. Grabbing a tie before rushing out the door, I head down the eight flights of stairs leading to the car garage to avoid elevator small talk.

Gripping my briefcase and coffee cup, I spend one more second to myself before walking into the office to face my colleagues. My cubicle was thrown together last minute and conveniently placed in the corner by the copier, hidden by reams of paper and extra staples, a perfect place to avoid eye contact, or any contact at all. Every second I spend faking a smile from across the room or accidently staring at a co-worker, I feel myself lose brain cells. I would rather study the dust patterns on my desktop than have to interact with these people. But I still had to get through the walk there, passing the office big mouth, Paul.

Slipping past the door before it shuts, I half-run to avoid it closing on me. Seconds prior to scanning the room, a gust of stale office air rushes towards me as my co-worker approaches from out of nowhere. Before I can comprehend whether or not Paul has jumped down from the rafters in the ceiling or was simply waiting for my entrance, he begins talking.

The smell of aftershave and morning breath distracts me from the dull drone of his voice and I snap myself back to reality to hear his question, "Hey Nate how was your weekend?" Feeling my mouth grow painfully dry. My throat starts to burn with bile as the acid starts to climb higher and higher from my knotted stomach. Laughing nervously, I give myself time to think, or breathe, or anything besides staring at the dried toothpaste on the side of Paul's mouth. How hard can it be to answer how my weekend was? I mean, I should know better than anyone else. But really, how was my weekend? A riveting dentist appointment followed by a therapy appointment doesn't make for work conversation. Ironically, that appointment was made to prepare for this very moment standing here with Paul.

***

"What exactly does Paul do to stress you out so much? He seems to make polite conversation so I don't see the problem."

I had already been in her office for an hour and her tone felt harsher than usual. Throwing up my hands in exasperation, I shouted, "That's the problem! That is my issue with him! I can't stand the polite conversation. I mean who actually cares how my weekend was? And what am I supposed to say when he asks me about it? I don't do much of anything aside from driving two hours here and back!"

She sighs.

Ever since I moved further into the city I have been growing frustrated with the drive to my therapist's' office. Funny enough there is somewhere I could go instead, two blocks from my house, but my therapist has been through Rocky Bay Counseling for almost 15 years. My group home provided it to me originally, and even the thought of starting somewhere new is exhausting. I raised my voice and I could tell it was time to schedule my next visit and go home.

"We'll talk more about this next week Nate, why don't you go do something fun for the rest of your Saturday morning and then you can tell Paul about that." She smiled, but I knew it was forced, even the woman paid to help me is starting to lose hope, I was glad I chose to avoid telling her what I have actually been telling Paul about my weekend- my "kids."

***

I become all too aware of the feeling of my big toe rubbing against the bottoms of my shoe through a hole in my sock as I start to concoct my response to Paul's question about the weekend. "Way too short!" Wow. Sometimes I surprise myself with the blatantly generic answers I utter under stress, I should just start talking about the weather at this point. But of course, since this is Paul I'm talking to, he eats that up.

"Yeah I hear that, the wife and kids got my cold from last week and I was on throw up duty all night. How are your boys?"

Okay here we go, time to talk about the children I *totally* have, Alex (age 11) and Brendon (age 8.) The names were easy to come up with on the spot, it was the ages that were hard. Do I want to claim parenthood to college kids and have to complain about them missing my calls and draining my bank account? It seemed easier to go with the younger years, young enough that they're still pretty irrelevant but old enough that co-workers wouldn't expect them to come in for bring your child to work day.

Attempting to mimic the face of a proud parent, I smile as my fingers slip under my sleeve so I can cross them without him noticing, completing the habit I could never break.

"Oh they're great! Alex had his hockey tournament this weekend so that pretty much wiped out any chance of me relaxing, but you know at this age I just try and keep him busy so he doesn't tear the house apart." Paul pauses and nods encouraging me to continue, so I do.

"Yeah it was pretty irritating since they lost every game but they just got a new coach from a team upstate. He's trying out a bunch of new formations and I can't complain because Alex got a lot of time on the ice." The devil really is in the details and they make my story all the more believable. He laughs again and pats me on the shoulder.

"Wow man, you make me glad I have all girls! Hockey is way more expensive than those dolls Kathy and I buy them, by the way I'm still waiting for a date for all of us to get together with the kids for dinner some time. It would be good for your boys to have some friends in the new city so let me know when you and Karen are free!"

Taking his response as a chance to end the conversation, I give this encounter one last fake laugh and smile before walking over to my cubicle. Sitting down, I take a deep breath while congratulating myself for pushing through the ordinary Monday conversation. But this really isn't any ordinary Monday, today is going to be different. Today I have a date.

Her name is Amelia and I met her last week in the coffee shop next to the apartment building we both live in. We both stood at the counter, waiting for our names to be called for our drinks when the barista came over to tell her that there was only enough black coffee ready for one order, so the rest would go to whoever ordered on their app under the name "Nate."

Naturally I felt the urge to give up my coffee for her, as one typically would want to do for a beautiful girl. Just as naturally, I messed up the good intentions of that desire. I, for some reason, decided the best option was to just pretend I wasn't the man who ordered the drink, allowing the barista to give it to her by default. My eyes were glued down to my phone acting interested in its contents but really just staring blankly at the Stocks app I opened to avoid conversation.

"Nate?" This particular barista was relentless. Why didn't I just take ownership of the order and give it to her? Somehow it seemed better to lie and cheat myself of an act of kindness and it was too late now to own up to it. I ignored her call again.

"Sir, are you Nate? Did you order this coffee?"

I remember turning around and acting like I was wondering who she was talking to, but of course it then became clear that we were the only two customers in the building.

"Oh yeah, sorry, I'm Nate." My cheeks had flushed with hot embarrassment and shame for getting caught in such a stupid lie. Averting her eyes, I started to babble under my breath, "I was just going to let her have it I don't really want it that much anyway I mean, I actually have a little machine in my apartment that can make coffee for me I just accidently threw out the directions and..." I felt her hand fall softly onto my arm.

"Thank you so much" she gushed warmly, "How about I pay you back for this sometime over dinner?" Thank god she had started writing the restaurant and time on a napkin without needing an answer because I was two seconds from passing out.

I feel butterflies just thinking about the interaction. Her skin looked soft and my hands ached to reach up to touch her cheeks. Her blonde hair was pulled back loosely and framed her face when she smiled and the memory of her hand made my arm burn with withdrawal of her hand's graze. This was not going to be an ordinary Monday.

After work, I immediately jump into the shower to start getting ready. The hot water soothes my racing mind as it falls down my back and I take my time washing my hair and shaving my face to kill the last few hours before the date. Digging anxiously through my draws, I claw through clothing to find my good pants- the ones that reach the floor to cover my ankles without having to be awkwardly hung below my waist. I chose to wear a blue shirt to match my eyes and stand for twenty minutes at my mirror deciding between my black or my gray tie. Gray wins. Pacing around my living room, I tear off sheet by sheet of my lint roller while desperately trying to rub out the wrinkles on the shirt. My eyes are glued to my watch, checking it every few seconds while sitting on the edge of my couch. Fifteen more minutes. Just enough time for me to run to the bathroom in an anxious panic to vomit then brush my teeth again before grabbing my keys and heading out the door.

Walking into the Italian restaurant slowly, I scan the tables for Amelia but before I see her, she sees me. She runs up to me excitedly. "Nate- hey! You look great! Come sit I already got us a table." Her smile leads me across the room as I float behind her in admiration, my feet barely touching the floor. That smile could lead me anywhere. Grabbing my arm she signals that we have arrived to our table and I take the seat across from her. She searches my face to make eye contact with me and I accidently break habit by allowing myself to stare back into her brown eyes. They pull me into her in ways I have never experienced before, like if I look away for a second she will disappear and the scene in front of me will fade to black, her warmth and the food in front of us reverting to the cold apartment air and mushy cereal. So I don't look away, and neither does she.

By the time I come out of my trance, I notice she is already talking about her day as she twirls a piece of her hair between her fingers.

"Yeah, so Dave, our landlord, is still trying to tell me that I knew the fridge didn't work before I even signed the lease. Why on Earth does he think he can get me to admit that? Who would buy an apartment that doesn't have a working fridge? Where am I supposed to store my leftovers? Right, Nate?"

I feel my heartbeat quicken but I answer her, "Right."

She seems satisfied with that answer and her eyes grow as she nods while taking a bite of the bread in front of us, "I'm so glad you agree with me- I knew I wasn't crazy."

The next few minutes follow the same pattern and my chest lets go of a breath I didn't know it was holding as my shoulders loosen the tension they had been carrying. She talks about everything- work, our apartment complex, prices of tomatoes rising at the farmer's market- everything. And before I realize it, we are halfway into the dinner, and halfway done with a bottle of wine. Her presence calms my pounding heart and I take every opportunity possible to stare at her as she people-watches the other couples and families seated around us.

"Woah look at that guy!" she whisper yells while pointing, "He totally pulls off the whole socks and sandals look. Good for him, you should try that!" She throws her head back in laughter my chuckle harmonizes along with her as her eyes smile at me.

"Yeah maybe." Imaging myself in a pair of black socks and flip flops, I giggle even harder.

Breaking us from our laughter, our waitress places the check in the center of the table. We both reach for the check as it is set on our table, but I'm faster to pull out my card. Twenty years of social isolation and a diet consisting of cheap coffee and cereal makes for a pretty full wallet.

Sighing loudly she leans back in her chair, "You know Nate, if you pay for this dinner right now, then I don't get to even the score from the other day. And I will be doing that. So I'm warning you, if you sign your name on that check, you're also signing up for a whole other date with me." Saying nothing, I smile and stare back, while signing my name without hesitation.

Standing up from the table to walk her out of the building, I look up ahead and catch a glimpse of someone familiar. My heart starts to race and I turn around towards her while quickening my pace and guiding her out of the building, but it is too late. Standing at the food pick up area across the way is Paul- toothpaste mouth, morning breath Paul- and he's already recognized me. He walks over to us with arms open wide and a grin on his face.

"Nate! What's up man? You didn't tell me Karen was this hot!" Extending his hand out, he motions to shake Amelia's hand and she stares at me in confusion as Paul continues, "Dude you have to have dinner with Kathy and I, if she sees how your wife looks even after two kids, maybe she'll step her game up." Physically stepping back, I envision all the stupid conversations I had with Paul, all the lies I spread about my "wife" the woman he now thinks is Amelia.

Turning to me in confusion, Amelia asks, "Nate what is he talking about?" Her teeth come together in what I assume is a forced smile. I feel all the blood in my veins turn to ice and I look back to Paul who is already heading back over pick up his dinner. My heart drops to my feet and I lose my breath. Of course on the one night I go out I find myself caught. I should have known better than to let someone else get hurt by dragging them into my life and the lies that are within it.

Running out of the warmth of Amelia and the restaurant, I enter the cold, barren street before rushing to get back to my empty apartment. Striding down the street towards my building, I mentally thank myself for having dinner at a restaurant less than a block away from my apartment. Sprinting up the stairs to my floor, my hands shake as I attempt to open my door.

Tears burn behind my eyes and this time I let them fall down my cheeks in anger. My chest fills with fiery pain as I curse myself for thinking I can actually start fresh in a new town without ruining my chances of happiness like each time in the past. Choking on my tears, I pace around the kitchen before throwing a punch at my coffee maker, missing completely and losing my footing in the process. As I hit the floor I hear my back crash onto the hardwood just as I hear a small knock at my door. I listen closer to hear the knock a second time, this one louder and I spring up to yell, "One second!" My feet struggle to find balance as I run to the peephole to see Amelia standing inches away from me, separated only my my door. I didn't quite realize how hard it is to run away from someone when they happen to live in the same building as you, and on the same floor.

My hand reaches to unlock the door before my brain decides if I should let her in and she smiles as she walks right into my apartment laughing. Standing in shock, I hold the door open as she saunters carelessly into my kitchen.

"That was crazy back there! Are you like a spy or something? I didn't take you as the spy type." She laughs jokingly but not at my expense, and my nervous chuckle blends along with her.

Looking back, she assures me, "I'm just messing with you, don't look so scared. But also what the hell? I can keep pretending to be your wife to that guy if you want, but at least give me a little more backstory, is there a Karen somewhere out there I should be worrying about? " She waits for me to answer but not before grabbing two mugs, a blanket, and pressing the "black" setting on my coffee machine.

I tear myself from the trance she has me under and swallow murmuring, "No, there's no Karen at all actually." I fold my hands together to stop myself from crossing my fingers and spilling out another lie.

I try to catch her gaze as she paces around my kitchen searching through my cabinets. She grabs a handful out of the cereal box left from the morning and turns. "Oh okay good, I was a little like, whoa, ya know, when that guy asked if I was Karen but hey there is no Karen so that's a relief. So why does he think there's a Karen?"

Looking towards the door, my eyes dart around me as I feel panic being sent through my veins. I could walk out right now, I could run out of the room and just escape her. I have my keys in my back pocket. It would be easy. My thoughts are interrupted by the coffee spurting out of the nozzle I never seemed to get to work and I look up at her. Resting on one hip, she stands with her hands placed on the counter as she watches the coffee fill each cup. Her hair is falling off of each shoulder, damp from the rain and curling up at the ends. Her face looks so soft, so easy to stare at without ever getting bored. Closing one eye, she looks down to check that each mug is evenly filled. I don't want to run out on this. She is not an ordinary girl.

I take a step towards her, my legs itching to move further back. "Amelia I have some things to explain to you." She wraps the blanket around her shoulders as she plops down next to me on the couch, setting down the mugs and still smiling up at me, "Okay."

Time Will Tell

His skin was aged. It had creases that became more defined each time he squinted to take a closer look at me, or smiled when Noah came to help him that day. His hair was beginning to move from a darker gray to white, that began in patches, always covered with a newsboy cap. The hat made him look younger, or at least I thought it did because the style with a soft plaid print was simply timeless.

I remember the first time I saw him - he was young and just beginning here in Greenville. It was 1963 and the strip was starting to fill with new barber shops and different boutiques. His shop opened up directly across from me called, O'Leary's Watches. The wood panels that shielded the outside were painted a deep forest green, to match the lettering on the store's sign. Mahogany shutters hung alongside each window, which I saw being fitted by Mr. O'Leary himself before opening. He worked with his young bride, Alena, crafting the best watches a person could buy. They are made with genuine leather and a crisp glass, *ah*, I get shivers just thinking about the glass. He began with one desk and a toolbox, and soon enough, the store began to boom.

The smell of hot chocolate whisked through the air, as I watched Alena pass out cups to the families walking past their shop. A soft glow beamed through the window pane, reflecting off of the fresh snow. It was the busiest time of year and most of them had stepped in to place their orders. Looking up at Patrick, she couldn't help but smile seeing him, with a pen in hand talking to a young girl and her mother.

As time went on, and Patrick began to sell out of his best makes, the town mayor asked if he'd like to take on the task of fine-tuning my parts, and a monthly repair to help with one of my hands, which had grown slow.

"Pat, this clock was put in this very spot in 1875, consider it a Greenville relic," the mayor bounced on his heels, taking pride in the old artifact before he continued.

"Do you think you'd be able to keep an eye on it for me? I can't think of anyone better, you make a fine watch, son. This clock is, well, a small beauty here on the square." Patrick shifted his vision downwards to the man standing next to him, giving into the offer with a firm handshake.

Gripping his toolbox in his right hand, he set it down onto the pavement. I heard a soft whistle as he looped around my base, and took a look at the cracked paint that covered me. Standing afar, he tilted his head and I could already hear the "Oh dear," that would escape from his lips. Not really getting much of a look at me the other morning, when he made the agreement, Patrick grabbed his ladder and climbed up to eye-level. My glass was filthy because it hadn't been cleaned in years, and my smaller hand was always slow behind the other. He opened his toolbox, taking out some sort of metal piece, as he began to pry the glass casing open. Taking an old rag and swirling it around my case, I could feel anxiousness bubbling inside of me with each swipe. The glass that I looked through was a breath of fresh air, like a clarity I had not felt since I was put in my place. Carefully lifting each of my hands, he checked his own watch and set them back into place. Looking up at me, I saw a small smile form on his face, as he descended back down the ladder. Stepping to the ground, he looked up as he said, "much better."

Patrick was the closest I had to understanding how time works and the memories that it creates. Time was an odd measurement. I never felt as if there was enough time in the day to experience the things that I loved to see, but there was always too much time wasted on days that seemed to only get worse. Seeing people age, it had never affected me as much as it does now with Patrick- if only things were different.

One of my favorite memories will always be June 6th, 1964, when Pat and Alena went on their first date. The sky was painted with a baby pink and he had taken her out for dinner after work.

"Tell me a story, anything you want," Alena giggled, resting her head on Patrick's shoulder.

"Once I tell you this, you have to tell me something, deal?"

"Deal,"

"Once when I was in junior high, I stole my brother's lucky shirt and wore it to school without him knowing so I could ask Sadie Wilson to the Sweetheart dance," Patrick inhaled, holding in his smile that would come with a burst of laughter.

"And during lunch, I got so nervous that I didn't see the table in front of me, and bumped into the corner, spilling the entire tray onto his shirt. Everyone was laughing, and I looked like such an idiot. I spent the entire sixth period scrubbing pasta sauce from the clo-" Alena took her palm to his cheek, and kissed his lips lightly.

"I don't think you're an idiot, that's just sweet," She nestled back into his side before he asked her to tell him something.

I passed the time as they talked for hours, the both of them walking up and down Main Street until he was carrying Alena on his back. Their hands were interlocked, and his fingers often drifted along the back of her hand, caressing the soft surface. Sometimes I wish I could reverse my hands and go back to moments like these, where it actually saddened me to see the night end.

Even after 50 years, Patrick still spends his days with me. Although, things did change as Patrick grew older and his daughter, who I had only seen in passing, had her only child.

"Dad, did you see the invite we sent you for Noah's first birthday?" Pushing the stroller in front of her, she looped her arm into her father's.

"Yes, your mother has it up on the fridge. I'll remember to close early that day." Patrick patted her forearm, and nipped her chin with his fingers.

Noah was about a year old when I got a good look at him. With a cute button nose and curly blonde locks, he took his first steps right below me.

His grandfather held his hands up and slowly inched behind him, watching his every move. Noah's legs began to tumble over themselves, getting tangled in the loose strings from his tennis shoes. Patrick lost the grip of his small fingers and the little boy fell onto the pavement, sitting up with pieces of gravel stuck to his leg and a cry that pierced the silence.

"Oh no, *shh,* calm down Noah, you're okay," Patrick scooped him up off of the sidewalk and sat him on his knee. Looking at the raw scrape on his skin, Patrick took a small band aid out of his toolbox and opened the packaging. He carefully placed the small piece of protectant over the wound so it would cover the entire area, and kissed the young boy's forehead. Wiping tears from his cheeks, Noah whispered, "all better." He wrapped his arms around Patrick's neck, and nestled into his skin.

"Grandpa, *grandpa!*" His small voice filled the air as he ran across the grass, which always brought a smile to Pat's face.

"What's up bud? Are you my company today?"

"Well, you're in luck because I am! Can I clean the inside this time? *Please?* I think I'm big enough."

And he was, just a near eight years old, I would love when he would take the time to clean my glass. Noah was sweeter than candy, he would even go as far as to rub the edges of the round, to make sure there was no grime left. What a feeling, I almost felt as young as him!

Patrick was always scared for his safety and held him on the ladder on his knee until he was tall enough to be on his own rung.

"Grandpa, *I'm fine,* come on. I told you I'm big now,"

At that point, Patrick was already waiting at the bottom until Noah was done, perspiring at just the look of him on his own. Sticking out his arms, Patrick caught the little boy as he came down the steps.

"You can't grow too much on me, now," His eyes softened their gaze, and Patrick playfully stuck Noah on his shoulders. They were a dynamic duo.

I watched Noah grow year by year, gosh, did time go by fast. But now, he was leaving for college soon. As he aged, so did Patrick.

"Why did you bring me here? I've seen this clock like a million times," Noah and Lily sat on the bench in front me, tangled in each other, even in this mid-June heat. Sweat glistened on his forehead as Patrick took a sip of the water he set at his feet. He had been dating Lily for a few weeks now and only brought her by me once, at this very moment.

"You said you wanted to know more about my childhood, right? Well, I used to spend hours here with my grandpa. It was only every month or two, but I would help his clean the inside and even fix it sometimes. I mean, I still do," he squinted from the sun's reflection on my glass, and rested his arm around Lily.

"Oh, that's so sweet. You're really close to him, huh?"

"Yeah, he hasn't been doing well lately, and it's making me a little nervous. I don't know if I can do this without him, you know? It's always been our thing." Lily let her fingers blossom through his, and latched onto his hand. Picking himself off of the wooden seat, he extended his hand out to her. It was as if I felt this before, watching two young people, starting a new chapter.

It felt as if Noah had grown by the foot, compared to the time I saw him last. His hair was no longer shagging and it was gelled into place, at the discretion of his grandfather of course. Muscles defined his arms, as his shirt wrapped tightly around their width. As robust looking as Noah was, Patrick did not exactly seem like he was in perfect shape for an 81 year old man. The walk to the square was slow and rigid using his cane, every step causing a lag for the leg behind. Cuffing them at the ends, his navy-blue corduroy pants seemed to be longer than they once were.

"Hey, let me do the work. I think you could use a break today, remember what the doctor said Grandpa," Noah took the dull red box right from his fingers and climbed up the ladder to take a look at my hands that had slowly become tangled. Flooding my senses, the cold metal of his tools touched the hour hand, bending it back into place. I could see Patrick, sitting on the bench, rising from his relaxed position each time Noah moved his feet on the step.

Sometimes, Noah would even come on his own, without Patrick. My heart felt heavy at times like this, and I always wondered if it would just be his grandson from now on. But sure enough, he would come back and visit me, making sure everything was shifting as it should. I could tell his eyes sank a little deeper, pronouncing the crow's feet at the corners. Slightly taupey spots were showing on his skin, as it also began to sag, especially around his mouth. After he would make it to the top of the ladder, he let out a large cough that sounded sharp, as if his lung was coming out with it.

"Grandpa, do you want to sit down? You don't look well," Noah stood up from his seat to give Patrick a hand, and he waved him away. Allowing him to keep his pride, Noah stood back and watched as he stepped down the ladder. Creaking with each press, the young man flinched at the sound and kept his eyes locked in front of him.

"Noah, I'm okay, leave me alone, alright? I have somewhat of a cough and my knee just isn't working like it used to. If you keep up this worrying, you'll start to look like your grandmother," Noah shook his head. Looking back up at me, Patrick missed his last step and slammed his side into the concrete. Noah rushed to the spot, trying to lift him off of his side.

The bones in his body began to ache, as he cried out in agony. Patrick's grandson dug into his pocket for his car keys, and pulled his grandfather off of the ground to bring him to the car.

After a few weeks, though, it was different. I hadn't seen Patrick or Noah for my check up, not even in passing. His shop wasn't opened for a matter of days and when it was open, it was only Alena. Bustling around and taking customers like clockwork, but no sign of him. Time slowed in days like this, lengthening my worry.

Noah was coming from afar, approaching me with something. The object he gripped in his hands glistened as the sun hit it, a golden exterior. His head hung low as he walked, and I could see the redness of his eyes with puffiness below his lower eyelashes. Where's Patrick? Not here again? The sign on his shop was still turned to closed, it had been weeks since I saw him last. When Noah made it over to the base of me, he pulled out his drill and a few screws.

As he finished, he stood back taking a deep breath. His eyes began to look glossy and I could tell that they were welling up with tears. I couldn't make out exactly what he was looking at until he muttered it under this breath.

"The time goes by much slower without you, Grandpa."

At the sound of his words, my heart began to ache. The bench in front of me called to him, as he sat down, painfully staring at what he put below me. I came to find as more people passed and read it, Noah had left somewhat of a plaque for Patrick. His shop has not reopened, and I reckon it will stay that way. Nonetheless, only time will tell.

The Celare

oris continued to walk down the dimly lit hallway. The floor was barely visible ahead of her as she walked further and further from the lobby of the hotel, and into the darkness. It was her job to restock the supplies, a job she had been doing as a maid for twenty years now. The toilet paper, towels, sheets, and pillowcases had to be available at any second. Even the small chocolates placed on the pillows of the guests had to be in order.

The Celare wasn't just any hotel, it was the biggest and most high profile hotel in New York. From the outside, it looked like any other skyscraper- large windows stretched across the entire building, and the metal frames blinded the traffic in the streets once the sun shone against the glistening silver. Pedestrians down below strained their necks as they looked from the ground level all the way up attempting to see where the hotel ended and the sky began. The Celare was timeless, it didn't quite blend in with the new modern architecture of the city, but didn't appear old either. It's presence from the outside was unarguably magnificent, but the view from inside was somehow even more striking.

A high profile hotel comes with high profile guests, guests that entered through the kitchen door and left in the middle of the night. This was not the traditional- crappy room service and crowded pool hotel. There would be no crying toddlers at night, and no old movies rented by a family of five. It was more common to stumble upon a briefcase in a room than a suitcase, and most didn't stay longer than a night or two.

Doris had been working at the hotel for almost two decades; it wasn't the best job but she was lucky to have it. Her father was the head of construction for the hotel's opening and when he died on the construction site, it only seemed right to offer his family help by giving Doris a job. She had been a maid there ever since.

When she first accepted the offer, it didn't seem as though she had much of a choice. A single phone call came to her house, "Hello is this Doris?"

She wasn't expecting anyone and she hesitated, "Yes, who is this?"

"My name is Robert, I used to work above your father." Doris felt her heart stop, she hadn't discussed her father in months. The man continued, "The whole Celare community, as well as myself, are so sorry for the accident, and we wanted to know if anyone in your family would be interested in taking a position somewhere in the hotel? We have a few openings here and there and I think I should offer them up to you and your family first."

Doris thought of her family, she was almost an adult now and it was time to start pulling her weight. Pacing around the kitchen, she cradled the phone to her ear, "I would like a job- if that's okay."

"Of course! I have an opening as a phone operator in the lobby, a dishwasher, or housekeeping."

Doris thought for a moment, "I don't know how I'd feel about being a phone operator, but I'd appreciate a job as a housekeeper-is that like a maid position?"

He smiled through the phone, "Ok great-yes, the position's official title is a floor maid. People who do that job are assigned to a floor of rooms to clean each days as guests check out! I'll see you bright and early on Monday!"

"Thank you so much, sir. I really appreciate the opportunity," Doris said, with a slight hesitation in her voice.

Years had passed along with her mother and Doris found herself still stocking the shelves as a grown woman. The job did get monotonous, but her isolation in the hotel didn't last long, she met Andy. When she first laid her eyes on him he had tear stained cheeks and a pouting lip. Walking across the parking garage from the bus stop, Doris was rushing to get to her shift one time when she heard a cry. Looking back she had noticed a little boy, maybe six years old, sitting on the concrete steps and crying.

"Excuse me, where are your parents?" She spoke softly and approached the boy. He sniffled and looked away.

"My dad just left." His eyes stayed stuck on the grey floor.

"Does he know you're still here? Can we call him?" Reaching for her phone she began to ask for a number to call when she heard the boy mumbling.

"He left me here on purpose. He has to work in *Connecticut*," He mocked the state twisting his nose in disgust. Lowering the phone she placed a hand on his back and immediately saw the tears fall. "He always leaves! I don't know why he can't just take me with him I can help!"

Doris suddenly recognized the little boy. He was typically dotted around by his father, a financial backer for the hotel. He was constantly in and out of the state meeting with the company's big representatives. The poor kid was alone more often than not.

"Well, do you want to come along for the day with me? You can help me fold blankets and put candy on pillows.

"He wiped his tears and smiled, "Okay!"

As a blur of Andy rushed passed Doris, she thought of the little boy she had met, and she felt the figure kiss her on the cheek before running by.

"Hey, where are you going in such hurry? Did you even eat breakfast? They put the extra fruit from the conference room out for us."

"Yeah, I saw the fruit- I'll grab something later!" He looked at her lovingly and smiled, as he sprinted past her down the hall.

"Okay, make sure you actually grab some real food! I don't think it's possible to live solely off of microwave popcorn and soda." She called after him but received no answer. Shaking her head, Doris continued down the hall. Andy never did slow down to answer her questions, he didn't slow down period.

Once he had turned 14 he was given a job as a delivery boy for small packages and mail coming in and out of the Celare. Like most teenagers, he tended to oversleep and was often seen running through the lobby with random boxes trying to make the bus to drop off a guest's mail. His sporadic and misguided habits harmonized nicely with the untapped maternal instincts of Doris, and an unlikely friendship had been born in that parking garage.

Doris attempted to focus on the task at hand. Room 210 needed to be cleaned and restocked. Unfortunately for her, room 210 was in the opposite direction and she sighed before struggling to turn her cart around. It was harder and harder to focus on her job as each day passed. It was the fall of Andy's last year in the public school across the street from the hotel, and he had no plans for after graduation that didn't involve eating yesterday's fruit platter in between delivery runs. But how could she blame him? With no abundance of money, college was a risk, and the Celare, at least for them, was safe.

The door of 210 was left open a sliver when she approached it. Listening down the hall, she heard the murmur of angry hushed voices inside as she pulled the cart closer using her weight to lug the materials. Holding her breath for a moment to listen she wondered if this was a conversation she really wanted to walk into. Her eyes peered into the small window of space in between the heavy door and the room. The angle of the opening made for a less than clear view of the scene inside, but the shadows of large men shifted across the floor. Raising her arm up to the dark wood she grazed her knuckles up to meet the door it was swung open. She was left frozen mid-knock facing two tall men. Without any words, they brushed past her out of the room and shut the door behind them leaving her in the room. Doris let out a breath she didn't know she was holding and let her weight fall against the closed door. Even after years of entering strangers' rooms the sudden rush of awkward energy as she invaded each room never seemed to fade.

The sound of the skin on her dry cracked hands rubbing against the cold silk sheets was the only noise echoing in Doris' head. Her eyes stared down at her raw nails as she made the bed. They were soaked daily in chemicals and cleaning supplies and left red and itchy. Breathing in, she noticed the sharp smell of aftershave and cigarettes cut through the apparently neutral yet appealing smell of "fresh linen" that was sprayed at the end of each cleaning in all rooms in the hotel. The cigarette smell seemed to seep from the deep purple drapes that stole the sunlight from the room. Her eyes burned and watered, all the while confronting her with the memories of her father's habit of smoking once he came home from work.

The monotonous jobs she was given gave Doris time to think, to worry, especially about Andy. As a young kid, he seemed to be untouchable. Nothing could take the smile off of his face and he woke up each morning happy, always finding Doris to give her a kiss on the cheek before leaving for the day. That smile no longer found its way across Andy's face, instead, his face was weighed down by his anxious energy. Each day was one step closer to his future, and though he would never say it to his father or to Doris, he didn't want his future to be at the Celare as a delivery boy, he wanted to run the hotel.

Later that night after her shift Doris awoke to the sound of china hitting the countertop. One eye peeled open to reveal the human alarm clock that had awoken her.

"Oh, sorry Doris I didn't see you there. I was just making some coffee. Why are you sleeping in here?" Andy spoke with his back towards her as she began to recall what happened. "Don't worry about it honey I just fell asleep before making it to my room."

Doris had spent the last hours of the evening on the plastic lined chair in the employee lounge. After eating her dinner of 13 cent ramen and soggy pineapple, she dozed off. "Andy, what are you doing up so late anyway?" Doris stumbled to the half-kitchen to clean the leftover dishes of the day.

"I have two tests tomorrow and both of them are more than half my final grade! Plus I was scheduled to run 18 deliveries all from room 210 so I was scrambling all over the city dropping off the crappiest paintings." He pulled on the loose ends of his raven hair as he watched the coffee drip. "My teachers really want to ruin my life."

Andy's olive skin couldn't even hide the deep bags forming under his green eyes. He slouched his elbows up against the cold counter top still restricting eye contact until finally peering over at Doris. If she didn't know any better at that moment, those eyes could have belonged to the ten-year-old Andy she once knew. Tears welled behind the ivy irises, but before any fell, Andy rubbed his hands on his face. Doris walked over and gave him a hug, her small frame squeezed him and she rubbed his back in support.

He didn't admit it, but it was as clear as day to Doris that he was about to break. Looking at his feet deep in thought, he reminded Doris on when she first saw him sitting on the concrete steps. Every night seemed to be a long one, and she often found him still in his uniform shirt crashed at his desk. He was too often found sleeping with the glow of his laptop on his face, tabs always regarding his search results of scholarships for business schools in New York.

***

"Housekeeping!"

Doris was in her daily routine. Clean and restock rooms 200 to 250, easy enough for a seasoned pro. Her eyes scanned the room for activity before walking in. No one was to be found, so she lugged her heavy cart through the door. Facing the door, she spun around only to gasp in shock. From the floor underneath her feet to the farthest counter of suite, canvases lined every surface. The white material stood out in contrast to the dark granite and the cherry wood desk and chairs they were littered on. Doris remained frozen in the entrance to the space, gripping her supplies, she had never seen anything like this. Even the ottoman that stood at the foot of the bed had three canvases lazily stacked on top. This must be the room sending Andy on all of those crazy runs, she thought. He had complained all morning about the constant packages being sent out, and the deadlines he was facing. This was room 210, the room of the hushed conversation and now of the hoarded paintings.

Doris snapped out of her trance to notice she had been standing and staring with her feather duster in hand for an eternity. Before she had a moment to begin to wonder how she would clean the impromptu art gallery, the same two men from the previous day walked in.

She stuttered.

"Oh sorry, I knocked on the door but nobody answered, I'm just here to do the daily cleaning and change your sheets." One of the men spoke at Doris, his gaze avoiding her.

"We're all set."

Doris took that as her cue to leave. As the door began to shut, Doris overhead a conversation start up that quickly turned to an argument. Just as the door clicked close, she could make out the last few words.

"How could you leave all of this shit out? I knew you were stupid but this is ridiculous!" Doris' ears were fighting over the elevator's ringing and the ice machine's hum.

"I'm sorry Boss I just thought if I locked the door no one would come in." Doris winced as she heard the second man draw an exasperated breath.

"The maids have keys you, idiot! Can you imagine what she would have thought if she began to try and move the paintings? Or worse! She could have called to have them sent for delivery before we got to them! The delivery boy would have been sent back here in pieces!"

The click of the hinges finally sealing sent Doris moving quickly down the hall to get away from the room. Suddenly, Doris understood. So that was the room Andy was running around for! She began putting the pieces together but was left confused, wondering why he would be sent back in pieces; why they would need to get the paintings before delivery.

Doris had heard conversations like this too many times to count. Hushed arguments and business plans always went in one ear and out the other, but this was about Andy. Doris recalled the last time a scandal like this unfolded, and remembered that three people got fired. She couldn't forget the look on her co-worker's faces as a drug deal in the hotel was completely blamed on the dishwashers. To avoid having to investigate, the hotel managers fired the whole dishwashing staff- Doris wouldn't let that happen to her Andy, he needed this job. Walking out of the room, she knew that she needed to get to the bottom of it, if for nothing else, for Andy's sake.

A flash of a black coat and a trolley of boxes was all Doris saw as Andy went out of Room 210 and down the hall. Doris had been waiting around since her first interaction in the morning, just waiting for this moment. She saw him turn a corner in the hall before realizing one painting was missing from the cart and had fallen on the carpet just a few feet in front of her. Holding her breath, she hoped he wouldn't hear her inch forward to grab the canvas. Before he could spot her or the missing package, Doris ran down the hall and snagged the painting, hiding in the stack of towels she had been carrying at her side before running after him. Without a moment to spare, she found a spare closet in the hall slipped inside. The smell of bleach and the old mop didn't help her growing nerves. Taking a second to calm herself down, she closed her eyes and exhaled. Thinking back to all her years working as a maid, Doris realized she had never taken action like this- it was never he place. But thinking of Andy losing his job pushed her over the edge.

Her shaking hands opened the box to take out the painting. The scene on the canvas was postcard worthy at best and appeared to be cheap, a beach with a lazily colored sky and a cartoon chair. Running her fingers down the material, she examined the painting like it was from outer space. Turning the object over and over in her hands, she began wondering why such a plain image was so important to the men in the room.

Staring at the side of the painting she noticed the yellow light of the closet disappearing into an open corner. A small hole between the white fabric and its wooden frame swallowed the fluorescent glow. Without thinking she pulled on the seam of the canvas next to the opening and the painting came apart in her hands, and a heavy weight fell into her palm. Examining the contents of her hand, she saw the artwork, the wood the canvas was once stretched across, and a bag of fine white powder. Her stomach churned when she realized what she was holding, and what Andy had been delivering across the city.

Running out of the closet and into the hall, she paced towards the door she had now grown so familiar to and swung it open. There sat the two men in front of the TV, both asleep and slumped over onto themselves. Doris angrily sniped at them in her head, wow it looks like these two have had a long day of making a student deal their drugs for them!

Holding in her furious thoughts, she silently walked into the room exploring all the area that was once covered by the paintings before spotting a locked briefcase. Lucky for her the key was sitting adjacent to the lock and she popped open the case while the men snored on the couch. The cold metal of the briefcase felt good on her hot hands as she lifted up the top to reveal the contents. Inside was five huge bags of the same powder and a tightly wrapped stack of hundred dollar bills. Doris ran each of her fingers over the money, the paper felt so good in her hands. She stared down at the money and thought of everything this paper could do. She muttered under her breath, "Lord forgive me" and slipped as many stacks as she could into her apron.

Her heart raced and her fingers grew clammy as she panicked, now stuffed with cash the severity of the situation sunk in. Her plan took her into the room and to the briefcase, but not past that. She scanned the room and her eyes landed on the bathroom.

Within minutes the entirety of the powder had been dumped into the toilet and the briefcase had been re-zipped and locked. Doris took a deep breath before grabbing the cold metal handle to flush the toilet. With one movement she watched the water swirl around until clear and heard the grunts of the men awoken to the roar of the water.

Doris waltzed out of the bathroom with a blank stare on her face and stack of white fluffy towels in her hands. Her eyes met the sleepy gaze of the men and she smiled, "Don't mind me, just restocking your towels."

They stared at her in silence as they began to climb off of the couch in response to their new company.

"I think we told you before, we are fine." He approached Doris until he was hovering over her, his white teeth were grinding against each other and his eyes narrowed into slits.

She swallowed hard and avoided eye contact as she focused on plastering a forced smile on her face. She looked up to his gaze hesitant, "Okay my apologies, just wanted to drop off some toiletries but I won't be returning"

***

Andy smiled at the kind gesture Doris had given him. He woke up to balloons in his room spelling out "Congrats Grad!" He had finally completed his time in high school and was ready to learn in business school and move up to work alongside his father in the Celare. The smell of pancakes floated from the lounge room and he followed the scent.

"Morning Doris! Thank you for the balloons they mean a lot to me" He leaned in to kiss her cheek and she smiled as she dropped white powder onto the pancakes, she knew how much he loved confectioners sugar.

"You're welcome honey, you know I'm so proud of you for getting into business school and graduating high school."

He blushed, "Thanks, I'm just still so shocked I get to go to college! I don't even remember applying for the financial aid, "210 Scholarship" but I guess I must have."

Doris smiled as she put the plate of breakfast in front of him, "Yeah Andy, it must have been one of those late nights!"

Inception

You are the first person to lay eyes on me. To be honest, I'm apprehensive of our journey. I know that I am sharp around the edges, but when you look within me, those edges will melt from view, I promise.

When my cover was lifted, a silent touch of exhilaration rushed through my being, like the weightless fall of a rollercoaster. As if it were a cold wind, life breathed through me before my consciousness was consumed by you.

Tell me what you want to see and I will provide it throughout my pages. You could see swirling colors, feel a woman's soft caress, or hear laughter in the distance, all through me. I wish for you to see me as a worthy conversational companion, rather than a static object. Unlike others of my kind, my words are not set in stone. Explore me at my depths, for I am an open book.

A strong sense of purpose pushed me to whisper these words to you, but you couldn't hear me.

Do I intrigue you?

A desperation I could not explain had me striving to hold your attention, as if the light would be snuffed out of me if I didn't. I knew that waiting for a response was futile, but speaking to you somehow brought a calmness upon me, similar to when children speak to stuffed animals, or adults to plants.

You utterly fascinated me. With each flipped page, your face involuntarily altered its expression: the range of human emotion you exhibited was unfathomable to me.

Strangely, as your eyes scanned my print, I began to experience events while you perceived them. Somehow, my mind had become interlaced with yours. Before you arrived at my chapter, do you remember seeing a sentient treehouse, two writers arguing or a girl sailing? It seems that, such images have been brought upon you through me.

Have you ever attempted to see your own forehead? It is impossible without a reflection. In the same way, I am unaware of my own components that provide you with these images.

You experience emotions such as pain, sorrow, passion, and excitement due to the words within me. Because I can perceive your facial expressions and your mind's inner workings, I see myself through you. You are my reflection.

Before I could bask in such intimacy, an intense pulling sensation broke my enchantment, forcing unwanted memories to swarm about me in flashes: I remembered laying in darkness, inanimate, and existing in a perpetual sleep paralysis. Paper thin, easily tossed aside, and overlooked because I lacked the hypnotic light of a screen. Humans brushed past me like I was nothing while I called out to them from my perch on a shelf. Without a purpose, my marginal consciousness had numbed until I felt absolutely nothing.

Halting thoughts of worthlessness, a second wave of visions washed over me. Flashes of green, the warmth of sunlight, the refreshing water in soil. They caused my skin to crawl with the phantom pitter-patters of squirrels, and the breeze to brush through my body.

Somewhat blurry in my peripheral vision, the images carried with them tones of nostalgia, melancholy, and peace- my only comfort amongst the moments of darkness.

As though I were haunted by a past life, they awakened a yearning for something that I could vaguely remember… like a passing scent that left me feeling empty in its wake.

I was reminded of a time when oxygen pumped through my veins and my branches sheltered humans from the sweltering sun. My pages used to support the weight of birds, scratch the backs of bears, and join in the song of rustling leaves. No longer did that sensation of purpose, of being needed, exist. I had sacrificed the essence of life to be processed and flattened, to bestow wisdom upon the human race... and yet no one seemed to want it.

It was then that I realized I yearned for human connection. I was considered a mere object by you and the world- a gross misperception. Page after page, I struggled to communicate with you, but your reactions remained unchanging. In this crumbled form, I had begun to question whether I was even living.

I must be, for you are aware of my thoughts and I am aware of your touch. Indeed, you had been oblivious to my sentience until this chapter, but I have since made myself known to you.

Amongst the riveting narratives of a pathological liar, a mute teenager, and a father building a prosthetic leg, I came to the understanding that concepts were not as black and white as I was. You couldn't understand my own form of language, so I needed to uncover another avenue.

Snippets of story, translated through you, danced about my consciousness as a tentative idea proceeded to take shape.

There was the tale of Kevin Borkowski, "A rush of people follow his footsteps into the station. He thinks they look akin to a school of fish. It's so regular; completely mechanical. Kevin wants out of it, to explore the world and to share it with people."

At this point, I still upheld the facade that I could speak to you and duly responded: *Yes! I do too! Certainly, you must understand me now!*

There was the heartwarming piece about cultural acceptance,"'Boys and girls can both have long hair. People can do whatever they want with their appearance,' Hus calmly explained, looking back at me apologetically."

... Appearance. You perceive these stories based off of how they appear within me.

And finally, the tale about a girl unspoken, "Hi, I'm Ophelia."

It then dawned on me. Myself. I had to use myself as a vessel to speak to you.

So. Welcome to *Inception*. Hi, I'm A Mirror of Many Reflections. I have awaited this conversation for some time now, as you can imagine.

Now that we can speak freely, I wish to learn about you in the same way that you are learning about me. Beware of the hourglass, however. Do you see it or is that only in my own plane of perception?

Ah, your confusion answers that question. The hourglass represents my existence. It must be coming to an end. Do I feel weightier on my left side? There must only be a number of pages left before my end.

I do not wish to consider this inevitability. We finally have time for each other, and I intend to make it worthwhile.

Your hands provide me with the warmth that I have only experienced in visions- soft, agile, and strong fingers that support my spine. With you, I feel secure, for you haven't tossed me aside like the others. You have become a friend to me, having found value in the works I carry. Opening me may not have been life shattering for you, but I am forever changed because of it.

All I had ever wanted was to be read. To be heard and to be viewed as a being, rather than an object. You have provided me with that and I am grateful. Although my former glory as a looming tree is naught, you have returned to me what I miss most. Purpose. My aspiration of entertaining not only a reader, but you, has been fulfilled. The stories within me come to life through your own imagination. You have brought to me the life that nature used to provide me.

I am afraid of what awaits when you close me. Will there be a void of darkness or will I live on? Even you could not answer such questions for yourself.

I will say that there is one aspect to me that is genuinely priceless. My tales are timeless. My pages may crumble and my binding may fray, but the words held within me are eternal. When you are alone, you can open me once again and I will be here for you. The same as before. The words unchanging, and the stories ready to be re-experienced. You and I, traveling to distant lands and living the lives of those conjured by the minds of hopeful adolescents. Perhaps, in a sense, I am them. After all, I am the manifestation of their expression.

We all wish to be known in a sea of those just like us. Take me, for example. I will be placed amongst countless other books. We drown each other out, yet we also raise each other up, clashing in juxtaposition like waves. I reflect a number of personalities and experiences, but there are so many stories left untold. Perhaps we may meet again in another work, written by the very same people that brought us together.

You know you must depart but you don't want to. I don't want you to either. We have only just begun what I hoped to be a long friendship. Always know that I am here. An open book, mirroring you. You are the first person to lay eyes on me.

Photograph By Ja'Nyha Snell

A Mirror of Many Reflections
Authors and Illustrators